The Savant

Allen Hively

Dedication

To everyone who has loved, lost, and found love again.

To emily,
Team mate &
Friend!
Hope you enjoy!

Al

Chapter 1
Kelly

I met Peter Allen Shaw on my twelfth birthday. He was tall with long curly brown hair and had a smile to die for. Until that day boys just weren't very interesting to me and even though it may have been a childish crush. There was something about him that stirred my interest. What made that awkward. Peter was my sister's boyfriend and for the first time in my life. I experienced envy. Being sixteen—Amy could date and I couldn't. Life seemed especially unfair at twelve. I was too young to do adult stuff, and too old to do kid stuff.

Peter wasn't just an ordinary handsome boy, he was a musical savant. I didn't know until later what that meant but being a savvy young lady with awesome computer skills. I found my answer on the internet. I learned that most savants were autistic and unable to take care of themselves. Those who were lucky enough to have strong families would live at home their entire lives. The less fortunate ended up in assisted living facilities. Most of them struggled with social anxiety making it difficult to maintain a close bond with anyone. Peter was one in a million. He could function socially and had a great family.

It seemed like my big day always hit during the week. So when I realized it would be on a Saturday this year. I was very excited. I guess my birthday party was typical for a girl my age. The boys stood on one side of the room talking about boy stuff and the girls stuck to the other side— pretending to not notice them. I had no clue what the boys talked about but my girlfriends giggled and gossiped about the boys, the cute new music teacher at school and clothes. I pretended to listen but my attention stayed on Amy and Peter. They sat on the bench of our old Steinway grand piano, holding hands, smiling, and talking in quiet tones. Smitten with curiosity, I had a sudden interest to know what people in love said to each other. Even at the tender age of twelve, it was easy to recognize what love looked like. Their eyes danced over each other with a sweet and innocent affection, much like characters I'd read about in a love story, late at night, with a flashlight under my covers...

Abigail Stevens, our mother, was a self-made woman. It wasn't a surprise when she didn't show up for my birthday party—she was always working. Abigail put herself through law school, which I considered an amazing achievement, but according to her, it only meant she had to work harder and longer than anyone else... So, it was rare for her to be home, even on special occasions. I guess you could say Amy ended up being my full-time sister and fill-in mom.

I don't remember much about my father. If not for the abundance of photos throughout the house, it would be hard to recall what he looked like. He died in a motorcycle wreck when I was five. The funeral is really the only thing I remember about him. I guess that's because everyone cried all day, ate, then continued to cry. I had never seen so much food in our house, and considering the occasion, I hoped to never see it again. I don't get how food is supposed to keep you from being sad.

After the funeral, it was just us girls—until Peter showed up. From that moment on my sister/best friend didn't have much time for me. She spent most of her free time with Peter somewhere else. Of course, I understood... Sort of—after all I *was* twelve going on sixteen. Amy and I were very close despite our age difference. When we did talk she went on and on about his phenomenal talent in music.

Anyway, back to my party... Once we'd consumed the cake and ice cream and I had opened the token gifts. My little soirée began to lose its cohesion fast. If something interesting didn't happen soon, my party would be over and I'd be entertaining myself. So—I did what any pain-in-the-ass little sister would do and solicited the aid of my big sister's boyfriend.

As I walked toward her, we made eye contact—Amy's eyes rolled in contempt. She knew I was going to ask Peter to play something before I could make the short trek from the kitchen to the adjoining living room. Before I could get the request out of my mouth, Amy pantomimed zipping her lips closed and throwing away the key—her signal for me to run along and shut up. Then it happened... Peter must have felt the imaginary darts flying between Amy and me. In that brief moment, he looked up and smiled... at me. I'll never forget the happy look on his face but it was his eyes that locked me up. They were a deep blue color—like the sky in October. I looked into his eyes and tried to speak but nothing came out.

Oh my God! I thought.

My big moment had arrived, and I had gone mute. Never in my life had I been tongue-tied. If anything I talked too much. The destruction of my personal coolness was like watching a bad silent movie. My jaws jacked up and down like an automaton but Peter had no subtitles to understand me. I wanted to crawl into a cave until I was really old... like thirty or something... and then he spoke to me.

"Hey, Kelly, what's up?" he asked. His eyes sparkled with kindness but that didn't help.

Automaton... Yep—the jaws even failed me and then I imagined how stupid I looked just standing there. I started worrying that my affliction might be permanent and that I wouldn't be able to talk again. I struggled to catch my breath and figure out what to say. Instead he saved me from my temporary panic attack.

"Would you mind if I played a song for your birthday? I wrote it last night just for you."

Oh my God! I thought.

Now my mouth shut tighter than a clamshell. The lip-smacking stopped but I still couldn't talk. I did manage to nod my head like one of those stupid toys people put in the back deck of their cars. There I stood, a speechless bobble-head, making an awesome first impression. I guess he understood my yes as my head bounced around in excitement.

"Cool..." He said. "Sorry I haven't worked out the words yet, but it's your song." He smiled mischievously, then turned to the keyboard and started to play.

For the very first time in my life, I was jealous of my sister twice in one day. The song started and Amy put her arm around him and laid her head on his shoulder... as he played *my* song! It sounded so familiar though... Kind of similar to that crappy classical music my grandmother liked. But I didn't even think about complaining—it was *my* song after all. It danced around many styles and eventually made its way to a classic rock sound. I was a nut for the older rock-and-roll stuff, something Amy and I had in common. But then it hit me... It was like a grade-school recital that had gone bad. Peter was playing *Happy Birthday to you*. My heart sank. There I stood, in the middle of the family room, in front of my closest friends, with a deer-in-the-headlights look, swooning like a schoolgirl. Of course, several years later I realized... duh... I was a schoolgirl, but it still took me a long time to forgive Peter. My song indeed—oh how cool... the twerp! I didn't realize, or appreciate, until much later, the talent it took to blend three different genres of music into a simple little tune.

Later that night, Amy came to my bedroom. She knocked on the door and poked her head in. I threw my favorite stuffed monkey at her, but instantly regretted it... It wasn't really Mr. Jangles fault! Amy walked in anyway, uninvited, picked up Mr. Jangles, and sat him on my bed.

"Kelly, I understand how your feelings got hurt, but Peter really did put quite a bit of thought into your birthday song. I know you have a crush on him, and if you weren't my sister, I would have to smash you into little pieces."

That made me smile. I loved that even when I was completely mad, Amy could always help me get over it. Her empathetic smile faded into the serious look she had when she wanted me to do something for her.

"I need a huge favor... But it has to be a secret, between you and me" she said.

Every time my sister prefaced a favor involving a secret, it meant she wanted to do something without our mother's knowledge. Even though Mom was gone a lot, she had an uncanny ability to show up when we least expected it. On those rare occasions that one of us broke the house rules, we covered for each other, of course when we were caught, we both suffered the punishment. Usually Amy just wanted to stay out a little later than Mom's mandatory 11:00 curfew. Not this time.

"Mom got home just a little bit ago and told me she is leaving again on Friday morning, and won't be back until Monday. I convinced her we didn't need anyone to stay over and that we would be fine. It's the perfect opportunity for Peter and I to drive up to Chicago."

"Chicago?!" I shouted loud enough to wake the dead.

"Shush! Mom will hear you. Yes ... Chicago," she said quietly. "I convinced Peter that he needs to go to a music studio and record some of his stuff."

"Isn't that, like, expensive?" I asked, really proud of my adult-like observation.

"It runs about fifty dollars an hour. I've already booked six hours for Saturday," she said.

"That's three hundred dollars. How are you going to come up with that kind of money? Wait a minute. Why don't you just go to Dallas? It's an hour away. Chicago will take like forever to drive there."

Amy just rolled her eyes—like she always did when she had a plan and no interest in my voice of reason.

"Because, little sister, to make it big in music, it's either Chicago or Los Angeles, and there's not enough time to drive to California. I googled it and it's only going to take about fourteen hours. Peter and I pooled our money. We have over five hundred dollars between us. It will be more than enough to make the trip."

"Fourteen hours!" The shock and awe of my sister's plans became seriously clear. "Amy... that means you'll have to spend the night... in a motel... with a boy. Have you lost your mind?"

Amy immediately bowed up like a petulant little princess. "First of all, we are planning to leave Friday evening and drive straight through. And if we're too tired to drive all the way home, then sure, we'll spend the night somewhere. Good grief Kelly, it's no big deal. It would just be to sleep. It's not like we're going to, well, you know... do it or anything."

"I think I'm going to be sick." I rolled over to the other side of the bed to hide my smiling face and pretended to throw up with what I thought was an extraordinarily well done dramatic production.

"Kelly... would you stop? I'm trying to have a serious conversation, and you're acting like a kid."

"Uh... I am a kid," I said.

"You only act like a kid when it's a convenient distraction that steers the conversation in another direction. Now... tell me the real reason you are dishing out grief instead of being supportive," Amy said.

I could never figure out how my sister knew my thoughts before I even knew I had an opinion. It took me a while to sort out the answer. Amy made it even harder for me to concentrate as she stood there with her arms crossed, tapping a foot, just like Mom did. And then I realized what really scared me. I sat up in my bed, and even though I knew there was no reason for it, tears welled up and started their way down my cheeks. Embarrassed, I tried to mop them up with the sleeves of my pajamas, but it was too late to cover up my emotions. Amy sat down on the edge of my bed and took my hands in hers.

"What's the matter, sis?"

"Well, we both know Peter is really good, and when he gets a recording contract, then everyone else is going to know how good he is, and then he'll become famous, and since you're his girlfriend, you'll be famous too and I'll never see you again."

Of course, I blubbered and sobbed through the whole discourse, so it took like forever to spit it out. My most vivid memory of that night was Amy's sweet attitude and what she said.

"Oh, Kelly... being famous is what you make of it. If a person wants to have time for their family, then they will make time no matter how popular or busy they might become. You're my family, and I love you."

She smiled, and it made me feel better. At least I quit crying. Mission accomplished there. We hugged, and Amy went off to bed. I tried to go to sleep, but in my heart, I knew that a big change was coming to our lives—and my mom was already too busy for me. How would I deal with my sister being gone all the time as well?

Friday came quicker than usual and I remember thinking how ironic that was. I should have been really excited. My mom and sister would both be gone for the weekend. I went through the motions and invited a couple of my best friends over but they were more excited about the prospect of no supervision than I was. Mom left around noon, clueless of the deceit and debauchery about to encase the Stevens home. Peter showed up about an hour later in his old Toyota Corolla. He banged on the door and let himself in. Even he acted somewhat awkward. Amy came downstairs with just the backpack that she took with her everywhere. She gave me a hug and proceeded to do the maternal thing, instructing me on how late I could stay up and what types of foods were in the fridge. When she finished, I turned it all around and pretty much told her what to do and when to do it. We showed each other our cell phones at the same time and giggled. I guess knowing that we were just a phone call away made us both feel a little better. Then in what seemed like seconds, they disappeared down the road, bound for Chicago.

Chapter 2
Peter

We drove for over thirty minutes—with neither of us saying a word. The awkward quiet made me more than a little uncomfortable. Social stress is unbearable for me. More times than not, I will regress into what I call my "hermit mode." It's very difficult for me to act like an ordinary person because I am not what most people would call normal, in any sense of the word. The only time in my life I've ever felt relaxed in a social environment around people in general, was with Amy. Since communal wellbeing has always been alien to me, it made our occasional awkward times even more uncomfortable. She was the first girl, or person for that matter, that I felt a connection with. So times like these felt difficult because I never knew what to say or do. To make it even more confusing, Amy told me on more than one occasion that sometimes a woman doesn't want a solution. Women are so complicated, and I'm smart ... really smart. To me, if there is a problem, it only makes sense to just fix it. And the problem is solved—simple.

The only thing I shared in common with every other sixteen-year-old was my age. Some would say what I have is a gift, but for most of my life, it seemed more like a curse. I just wanted to be a normal kid who could fit in and do the stupid stuff that every other teenager did; but life plays out differently for everyone, which for me meant being a musical genius with the social skills of a slug. I learned early on that since I was socially inept. It would be best to remain silent and quietly slide into hermit mode. The problem with putting your head in the sand and hoping a situation will pass you by. Is that more often than not, it's just a matter of time before it comes back and bites you on the butt. This analogy came from Amy, and she was the closest thing to a social expert I have ever known.

We were driving north on Highway 75 and were almost to Sherman, Texas when I decided to break the ice. As luck would have it, there are those times when you may not be able to fix something, but a smart guy will listen. It's not a comment from the memoirs of a genius. That's verbatim from Amy's unpublished, soon-to-be best-seller, *The Moron's Manual to Understanding Woman*. I pulled over to the shoulder and stopped. I had been dating Amy for nearly seven months, and we had never gone this long without conversation—although most of the time, I just listened while Amy did most of the talking. That was okay. I loved to hear her voice. Even when she got mad, her tone remained constant and sincere, with an almost melodic nature about it. So, to me, silence meant something had to be wrong. I put the car in neutral, turned sideways in my seat, and looked at her in silence and waited.

Amy was a beautiful girl in more ways than just outward appearance. She was the first non-family person that I could really talk to who actually cared about what I had to say. I have no idea what she saw in me, because nearly every guy in school would have jumped at the chance to date her. She was petite; if she had pointed ears, I would have coined her appearance as that of an elfin princess. In a single word I would describe her as "aristocratic." I suppose it was the way she carried herself, never without a kind word for those who, in my mind, didn't deserve it. She always seemed to know what to say and when to say it. With that thought in mind, I finally summoned up the courage to ask the million-dollar question.

"What's wrong, Amy?" I said, smiling with all of the warmth and affection that I felt for her.

She looked up at me with what appeared to be a forced smile and used her right hand to pull her long blonde hair to the side so I could see her face.

"Nothing's wrong, Peter... not really. I guess I'm feeling a little guilty about lying to Mom and leaving Kelly alone for the weekend."

"As much as I want you to come with me, you don't have to. The last thing I want is for you to get in trouble. Not to mention, if your mom finds out, she might never let me see you again, and that would be horrible."

I meant that part because I had never been stricken by any girl until I met Amy, and I knew to lose her would be devastating.

"Peter, you are without a doubt the smartest human being I will ever meet, but if you make this trip alone, you will run home the first time somebody is mean to you. You would not be doing this if I hadn't coaxed you into it, and I definitely want to share this moment with you. I just wasn't counting on the whole guilt-trip thing getting me down." She paused for a moment, I suppose to collect her thoughts, and then continued. "Peter, I love you... and it's been clear to me ever since we met that you are an extraordinary person and will be famous someday. There is no way I could miss the day that starts it all off. I want to be important in your life and for us to be family. You must know one thing about me though. I need to know that no matter how famous or rich you become, you'll never forget what's really important."

It took me a full ten seconds to realize that she had stopped speaking and was waiting for me to respond. So I answered to the only thing I heard: "You love me?"

She responded with a smile that I'm sure could stop wars. "Yes, Peter... I love you, but what about the other stuff?"

I have an eidetic memory and could have recited the entire conversation word for word. Focusing on the significant part of the conversation that she was interested in took me a few seconds.

"Amy, I will always love you no matter what. We don't have to do this. In fact, we can turn around and go home right now. We'll finish high school and maybe get married. I can go to work for my dad installing carpet. I pretty much already know how."

I would have continued on with the longest collection of words I had ever spoken at one time, except in songs, but she put a finger on my lips.

"Peter. Thank you, but there is no way someone like you would ever be happy in a regular job. Love means caring about what makes each of us complete, and that includes being happy with yourself. The question is. Will family always be the most important thing in your life? People can love each other without making each other a priority. For example, my mother loves Kelly and me, but we're not the center of her world. Work is the most important thing in her life."

"There is nothing in this world that will ever be more important to me than you," I said.

She smiled that smile again, and I felt like the luckiest guy in the world.

"See how easy that was? Now there's one other thing you should do," she said with a serious look.

I felt dumbfounded. All of the tutoring I had received on the ways of women, according to Amy, had gone out the window. She beamed that smile, kissed me, and laughed.

"Drive!' she said. "We'll never get to Chicago sitting here."

The smile never left her face as she talked all the way to Chicago from there.

/////

The rest of the drive went by without any problems. Amy was a good navigator, and we passed the night away talking about being rich and famous and what worthy things we could do with both. The subjects of family, love, and marriage did not come up again, which was okay by me because, honestly, that seemed like some scary stuff. I did know that when we were both old enough for marriage, Amy would be the one. She always served as the lightning rod that absorbed my social inhibitions and my inability to deal with some people. Like sarcasm, for instance: I understand the definition, but why not just say what you mean? More often than not, the whole concept confused me. I never knew for sure if it was mockery, cynicism, or just a way for some people to feel superior. That was one of the great things about Amy and I felt confident that she would always speak her mind.

We made it to Chicago around three in the morning. An hour later we were parked in front of the music studio. It definitely didn't look like a very nice part of town, and looking back, we were really lucky that someone didn't rob us—or worse. We snuggled up and fell asleep.

Early the next morning I heard a persistent tapping that coincided with a very pleasant dream. I was in this beautiful meadow, lying in the grass talking to Amy. The scene was picturesque, like one of those animated Disney films where all the little animals were friendly and hanging out with each other. Life was good, uncomplicated, and the colors were fabulous. But this woodpecker just would not stop pecking on the tree above us. What began as an irritation became really annoying—and I woke up.

It turned out to be a policeman tapping on the window. He looked to be an older man with a round face that matched his body. He peered into the car with a noticeable amount of apprehension—trying to decide if we were dangerous, I guess. He tapped on the window again and indicated for me to roll down my window. It's interesting to me that being polite is an uncommon skill for kids my age. Aside from being smart, having respect for others had always come easy for me. The skill came from my upbringing—and from knowing firsthand how painful the disregard of someone's feelings could be. Something my dad always said stuck with me, *you never get a second chance to make a good first impression.*

I rolled my window down and nodded. "Good morning, Sergeant O'Malley." I'd read the name on his uniform, but I suppose it came out as though I knew him.

He frowned, not sure exactly what to say, then answered, "Do I know you, son?"

"No sir. I'm Peter... Peter Shaw. I guess we fell asleep. I have an appointment at the studio at noon. We drove in from Texas last night and didn't have any place to stay."

He finally smiled a little bit, no doubt taken aback by my respectful attitude.

"Well, Peter, you couldn't have chosen a worse place to take a nap. This is a really rough part of town. I'm guessing that's your girlfriend," he said, looking past me as Amy began to stir.

Amy sat up and tuned into the situation. Like me, she had been raised with the right kind of manners. "Good morning, Officer," she said with a smile.

Now he was smiling fully and said, "Looks like manners are a way of life in Texas. I can't tell you how refreshing that is. You two are probably hungry. Tell you what, there's a diner about a mile down the road. The food's pretty good and not too pricey. Why don't you head down there for some breakfast? It's a little after nine, so you have plenty of time before your appointment." Then his serious look came back and he said, "Don't disappoint me by being here again in the morning, or I'll have to run you in for vagrancy." He winked and took off down the street, twirling his baton.

Realizing that we were starving, we decided to take Sergeant O'Malley's advice and headed off to the diner. It was an old railroad dining car and looked really cool. The wheels had been taken off to lower the car to street level and the entry took you through a revolving door. A lady named Claire waited on us. She gave us a peculiar look when we sat down. I guessed we must have looked out of place. For some reason, we got preferential treatment, which was great... because she didn't seem very nice to anyone else.

After a large Chicago-style breakfast, we sat back and took in the sights and sounds for a while, talking about how different it was from McKinney, Texas. All of a sudden Amy had a quizzical look on her face. "What are you going to play?" she asked. "Have you thought about it?"

There I sat a musical savant, a supposed genius, and the subject of what to play had never come to mind. "No," I said. "Do you think that will matter? I can play pretty much anything."

Amy rolled her eyes and looked at me as though I were a dork, even though she knew nothing could be further from the truth. Even so that look made me feel a little foolish.

"Peter, playing other people's songs will only prove you are a great musician. You're not auditioning to play in a band. You have to show them you're an original artist."

"Okay. How much time do we have before the appointment?"

Amy checked the time on her cell phone, then said, "It's just after ten thirty, so about an hour and a half. Why?"

I just grinned at her; I knew that she knew what I was thinking.

"Oh, Peter, you can't be serious! I know that look. You're thinking you can write a song in less than two hours. You're good, but that's just crazy."

"I have a tune in my head. I just have to work out the words. Do you have a pen?"

Amy fumbled around and produced a pen from her backpack. She handed it over to me while continuing to rummage through the contents. Finally she looked up at me, frustrated, and said, "Crap... I can't find any paper."

I motioned to Claire to get her attention. When she came to our table, I asked, "Do you have a couple of sheets of paper we could use?"

Claire's run on being nice to us had apparently run its course, because she just sighed and shook her head.

"Look, honey," she said, "it's a diner, not Office Depot." She stopped for a moment, then dug into her apron and pulled out a handful of napkins. "Best I can do, sweetie."

Amy and I looked at each other and laughed out loud. I suppose we realized at the same instance the irony of starting my musical career out of a stack of napkins. Amy started to stand up, muttering something to the effect that somebody there had to have some real paper, but I stopped her.

"It's okay, really," I said. "I assure you it's not the first time I have done it this way."

Amy sat back down and stared at me for a few seconds, probably trying to think of something positive to say. She was clearly still struggling with the whole napkin thing, but she managed to keep it to herself. For the next half hour or so I blocked out everything around me; the people talking, the kitchen noises, and Claire coming by every few minutes to ask if we needed anything else. I'm sure she hoped we would just leave, but Amy kept asking her for more coffee so we had an excuse to stay and occupy the booth. Thirty-three minutes later, give or take, I started to show Amy the lyrics but then snatched the napkins back. Her startled expression made me realize that I had been somewhat grabby.

"Sorry," I said. "I forgot to write down the title."

I wrote down the two-word title and passed the napkins back for her to read.

Chapter 3
Amy

Peter scribbled the words for a song that he had less than ninety minutes to write. I did my best to not disturb him and sipped on the bitter concoction the diner passed off as coffee. The taste was more akin to motor oil, but the cream and sugar helped—and the refills were free, not to mention they kept the café Nazi at bay. Claire, our waitress, seemed nice enough, but I didn't like the way she looked at us. She had a condescending smile that never seemed to leave her face. I realized as the minutes ticked by that it was her game face and everyone got the same look. Still, in that moment, I felt glad that Peter could be oblivious to some of the not so finer nuances of people. He took everyone at face value, and although he had a grasp of the concept of sarcasm, I don't think he understood it. What he lacked in perception ironically ended up being a gift that shielded his sensitive and somewhat fragile personality. He was the proverbial nice guy, and in view of what I would call common social aspects of typical humanity, he was too nice for his own good. That innocent sincerity is what I loved about him the most.

I considered Peter the most beautiful human being I have ever met. In my mind, if we had more people like him in the world; it would be a much nicer place to live. I'm convinced that he's clueless of his good looks, and I have every intention of keeping him in the dark as long as I can. Most boys my age have one thing on their minds, getting busy or at least engaging in some sort of groping, every chance they get. Don't get me wrong, I'm not a prude and I do understand desire. Boys are not the only ones in our species who have urges given to us by a million years of evolution. Most boys just have a harder time restraining themselves than girls. After all, we have to carry the product of their desires for nine months. I'm not opposed to having babies, and someday I want a family of my own, but I will have plenty of time for that later... much later.

If I had to identify the one thing I like about Peter the most, I suppose it's the fact that he listens to me. Not only does he care about my feelings, he cares about what I think, which is something foreign to me. He likes to just sit and talk, although usually I talk and he sits and listens. When he plays music, it's a pleasure to be the one who listens. There has never been any doubt in my mind that Peter has a very special gift and that he will go far with it. It's funny, because for Peter, music is like putting on and taking off a shirt. It's so easy for him that he doesn't view his ability as exceptional. As talented as Peter is, he would have never pursued a professional musical career without my gentle prodding. More than anything, he just wanted to be a normal kid. But Peter would never be considered normal, not by any stretch of the imagination. Somehow he does manage to fit in—in a wallflower sort of way. His brilliant intellect runs so much faster than anyone else's. It makes him painfully different. In his mind, Peter thinks something is wrong with him, and is socially intimidated by most kids our age. Most adults are intimidated by his intelligence, so they treat him differently as well. It's a catch-22, and no matter what he does, it's like trying to get a square peg into a round hole. It's a shame that teenagers and adults aren't all that different when it comes to making fun of someone different. When Peter doesn't buy into their torture, they shun him as a nerd and an outcast. His fabulous mind more often than not—is an albatross around his neck that creates a huge social handicap. I guess I'm weird in my own right. Because not only do I understand him better than anyone, I consider him my best friend.

My dad died when I was nine. I remember him being sweet to me, and I know he loved me. He was an airline pilot, and when he wasn't working he was riding his motorcycle, the latter being his undoing. I miss him still, and sometimes lay in bed at night and wonder what life would be like if he were still alive. It's a common trait not to appreciate the simple things in life until they are gone. Many times I've wondered what it would be like to have Mom at home and not working so hard to support us. As it is, Kelly and I hardly ever see her, at least for any quality family time. My mom, being the analytical person that she is, never has anything nice to say about anyone. I suppose her negative outlook on people in general has made me all the more determined to see the other side of human nature. About all she ever had to say about Peter is that he could play the piano really well but that he was certainly an odd fellow.

I suppose I was daydreaming, because I didn't notice Peter trying to get my attention until he touched my hand.

"Okay, it's done," he said.

I looked at the time. It had been around thirty minutes. "You're done already?" I asked.

"Yeah, do you want to read it?"

"Well of course I want to read it."

He started to hand me the napkins, and then snatched them back to write the title down. I turned the napkins around to read the scribble but for some reason stopped and looked up. Peter's piercing blue eyes—a color of blue that I recall my sister describing as October-sky blue—looked as happy as I had ever seen them, gleaming with a twinkle I couldn't begin to describe. I'll never forget the moment I read my song for the first time:

"Amy's Song"

If you want me, I know you do
All you have to say is, I love you
Life without you just won't do
If you won't love me
I know I'm through
Love me

The time has come, for no good-byes
What I need to see, is in your eyes
Give me your heart; it's safe with me
Come to my arms, stay with me
Hold me

Now love's not fair, you know it's true
My love for you can't go unused
Come with me now, before it's too late
Don't wait too long, don't hesitate
Kiss me

It's all been said, you have to admit
There's nothing left to do but say I do
Life together will be so grand
Loving you is easy
Marry me

    Well, I did what most girls would do. I started crying, and of course Peter thought he had done something wrong.
    "What's wrong?" he asked.
    How can anyone so smart be so dumb at the same time? I thought.

"Nothing's wrong," I blubbered while desperately looking for a napkin that didn't have anything written on it.

About that time, Claire showed up table-side. She gave Peter a huge frown before she looked at me.

"What's wrong, sweetie?" she asked.

As if duty-bound to do so, she looked down at the napkins with my song on them and just snatched them up and started reading. I couldn't believe it. Before I could grab the napkins scrawled with, in my opinion at the time, my most valuable possession ever, Claire started getting weepy too. In one panic-stricken moment, I thought she might use my song to dry the tears from her face. In the course one or two minutes, the other three waitresses showed up, and the napkins got passed to each and every one of them while I sat their dumbfounded. Moments later, pandemonium ensued at the diner. All the servers were crying, and I think every woman in the place was thinking about it. After that, all the servers in turn hugged Peter's neck and went back to work.

Claire took possession of the napkins and returned them to me. "You better hang on to this one, honey," she said.

Then she gave Peter a big wink and hugged my neck before going back to work. As I watched her leave, I realized that every person in the place was looking at me. The diner's staff thought they had shared my wedding proposal. I looked back at Peter and realized he was mortified by what had just taken place.

"What was that all about?" he asked.

"That... was a group of women enjoying a happy moment together."

"So why is everyone crying if they're all happy?"

I managed to get myself together enough that I could answer him but still drew a blank. Instead of a good answer, I posed a question in its place: "Don't tell me that you've never seen a woman cry from happiness before?"

"Sure I have. But I've never seen a whole restaurant cry about being happy… over the words to a song."

He had no clue as to what just happened. So I smiled and told him, "Peter, they were crying because they thought you just proposed to me."

Then I just sat back and enjoyed watching as the mystery unfolded on his face.

"Uh… Amy, it's just lyrics to a song dedicated to you," he said, squirming from discomfort.

I'm not mean-natured by any stretch of the imagination, but for some reason, I just couldn't help myself and decided to let it play out and have a little fun with Peter. I managed to pout, somehow without laughing, added a couple of sniffles, and then said. "You mean… You mean… it's not a proposal? And now you're telling me that you don't want to marry me? Oh, Peter… how could you?"

His reaction came immediately and made me regret my little joke. I knew by the expression on his face that he had bought into my façade. It was just the type of humor he did not understand and there I was toying with the feelings of the guy I loved. I could feel the tears welling up again, but I regrouped my thoughts and focused on how to repair the damage from my poorly chosen attempt at humor. Where sarcasm was dust in the wind, bluntness was a format that made perfect sense to him.

"Peter… I was just playing with you. I'm sorry. I know you don't get the humor, but you have to agree that most people would read these words and think it's a poetic wedding proposal."

That distant look of withdrawal started to reverse, and luckily for both of us, his mental regression stopped. I have no idea where he goes when it happens, but I have seen it before. The fact that I caused it, made me feel even worse. The last time I remember witnessing a similar episode when one of the kids at school decided to make fun of Peter. It is one of those things that happen to kids in high school all the time, and for most of us, it is only matter of bruised feelings. But in Peter's case, it pushed him into what he called his "hermit hole." The aftermath of that incident resulted in him not being seen for three days. It took me another month to pry out of him why it affected him so, and even then, he didn't have a definitive answer.

"I'm sorry, Amy." He smiled, trying to be sincere in an apology that was without a doubt not his to make.

"No... It's not your fault, and there's not anything you should be sorry about," I said.

He shook his head in disagreement. "Yes... It is somewhat my fault. It's simple levity on your part and I took it wrong. I know you would never hurt me on purpose. It's just... well... it's hard to explain. Sometimes my brain tries to shut down—like a switch turned off."

"Peter, we've had this conversation before. You don't have to explain yourself."

I knew that, in the end, it would be a hopeless endeavor. As brilliant as he was, he didn't know why it happened, and therefore there was no way he could explain it. I fidgeted with my cell phone and noticed the time. It took a few seconds for the digital display to register, and then it hit me.

"Peter, look at the time. Your appointment is in fifteen minutes. We need to go."

Peter hurried up to the cash register to pay our bill, but Claire waved him off with a smile.

"This one is on me. Good luck, you two." She gave me a big wink, confident that her diner had shared a memorable moment that I'm sure she planned to share with most of Chicago.

Ten minutes later, we parked in the same spot that we had vacated a couple of hours earlier. I looked around for a sign hoping to confirm that we were in the right place. We stood there gawking like a couple of kids, which we were, at the old three-story redbrick building. It was ugly, run down, and I remember hoping that we had made a mistake on the address. Peter got his guitar out of the trunk, took my hand, and almost dragged me to the front door. He seemed unconcerned by the gloomy exterior, but I could tell his apprehension seemed as elevated as mine. He was quiet—not uncommon for Peter, but he also seemed aloof, not typical behavior toward me. The door had been painted white at some point in time. Now it appeared unkempt and the finish was cracked and peeling. Peter gave the doorknob a sharp twist and pushed—but nothing happened. He gave it another try, putting his shoulder into the effort the second time. The door swung open in an exaggerated slowness, creaking loudly from the weight on its old rusty hinges. If it had been at night rather than broad daylight, I would not have gone in. The place felt spooky and reminded me of the haunted houses you see in the horror flicks. I love to watch scary movies but it's different when you're wrapped up in a pillow watching the carnage between the cracks of your fingers. My hands were shaking so much that Peter noticed and gave me a reassuring smile; even so I could tell he looked a little scared as well. Just as we stepped through the doorway, a shadowy figure lurched into view.

"Hey, what are you kids doing in here?"

The man staggered toward us, but when we cowered back away from him, he stumbled and fell on the floor in a heap. A pungent smell of alcohol mixed with sweat and body odor wafted around us. I had to put my hand over my mouth for fear of throwing up.

Peter ushered me past the homeless man to the elevator that stood in the center of the lobby and looked as though it hadn't been used in years. I felt relieved to see the handwritten sign on the folding metal gate that read *Out of Order*. We found the stairs, and next to them hung a small poster-board sign that said *W. C. Studios—Third Floor*. A sudden feeling of doom washed over me as I contemplated my poor choice of music studios. The website had given me the impression of a successful company, although I realized at that moment the site hadn't shown any pictures of the office building, just a couple of shots of the sound room and another of the mixing board. I groaned a sigh just loud enough for Peter to notice. He stopped to look at me.

"What's wrong?" he asked.

"Nothing," I said, doing my best to look positive.

I gave him my best smile. He put his hands on my shoulders and searched my eyes with a serious intensity.

"Something is wrong, Amy. Tell me."

"It's just … Well, the website made me believe this place was nicer. I'm worried I picked the wrong studio for you."

He smiled and squeezed my shoulders with reassuring affection. "Don't worry about it. We'll scope the place out. If it doesn't feel right, we'll leave… fair enough?"

"Sure … sounds good," I said, trying to be brave and act like the adult I was pretending to be.

As we continued to the third floor, every step creaked and groaned, echoing into the quiet emptiness. I suppose Peter's words made me feel a bit better, because the rest of the way. I kept up rather than allowing myself to be towed up the stairs. Just a few steps down the third-floor hallway, we saw an old-fashioned half-oak and half-frosted glass door with *W. C. Studios* stenciled in bold black letters. Under that in smaller print, it said, *By Appointment Only*. Peter tried the door and found it locked. His confidence had been unwavering until then, and I could see a fleeting look of indecisiveness in his eyes. I took the initiative and banged on the glass with a lot more bravado than I had intended. We waited for a few moments, and just as I was about to knock again, I heard heavy footsteps. The door swung open unceremoniously to a giant of a man. He wore shorts and a flowered Hawaiian shirt that looked so wrinkled I figured he had been using it to sleep in. The man's hair was messy and from its looks, had not seen a brush in some time. He had a black beard and tangled bushy eyebrows that almost concealed the reddish hue encircling his dark brown eyes. Peter and I stood side by side in the doorway, and together we weren't as wide as the man. He looked past us as if looking for someone else, scratched his beard, and then looked at us with what seemed to be idle curiosity.

"Look, whatever you guys are selling, I'm not interested," he said, then sighed and started to close the door.

Panicked, I just blurted out, "We're not selling anything we're buying! We made an appointment for six hours of studio time."

He blinked a couple of times, apparently trying to make sense of what I just said.

"You're Peter Shaw?" he asked with obvious disappointment. "You guys booked six hours of my time. Do you know how much money that is?"

"I'm ... I'm Peter's manager, and yes, it comes to three hundred dollars. We brought cash, as agreed. I hope you're worth it," I said with as much arrogance as I could muster.

Peter's mouth sagged open, and he just stood there, speechless.

"Cash is good," the man said. "I'm Antonio Giordano, proprietor of W. C. Studios. Come on in. Your time starts in five minutes." He turned and led the way in while continuing to talk. "Most clients get here early so they can get unpacked, but it looks like you're the whole band. Oh, you can call me Tony. I can guess this is Peter, but what's your name?" he asked me, looking over his shoulder.

"I'm Amy. Sorry we're running so close on time, but we drove up from Texas last night."

"Up from Texas huh? That's a long drive. Why did you come all the way up here? There are plenty of studios in the Dallas area."

His comment made me realize that perhaps we had not needed to travel all the way to Chicago for Peter to get noticed. I decided that the intelligent recourse would be to play on his ego. After all… all men have one; some are bigger than others, but they all like to feel good about themselves. So I went with my intuition.

"We decided on Chicago for its musical diversity—and your customers had good things to say about your company."

Tony stopped at a big padded door. He pushed it open, turned to me with what appeared to be a smile; it was hard to tell through his shaggy beard and said. "Thanks, Amy. I hope I'm worth your long drive," he let out a deep throaty chuckle as he led the way to the control room.

I started to apologize for my crack about hoping he would be worth the money but held my tongue. The control room was small and cluttered. I saw piles of folders and assorted electronic gizmos everywhere. The tables, chairs, and the floor itself all looked to be stacked so deep that I wondered how he could find anything, much less actually work in there. I noticed a huge window above what I decided had to be the mixing board, and on the other side sat the studio. Tony began rearranging his piles to uncover the control panel. Peter, who had not spoken a word since we'd met Tony, walked over and peered through the glass. I joined him, then took his hand and gave it a good squeeze for reassurance. For the next few moments, we just stared and contemplated what would happen next.

I noticed from the lack of paper shuffling that Tony had finished his task. I turned and looked at him; he was watching us with a curious expression.

What are you looking at? I thought to myself.

He just smiled and shook his head. "First time in a music studio?" he asked.

"Yes... it is," I said.

I felt too embarrassed to admit that neither Peter nor I had any clue what to do next, so I waited for him to tell us. He managed a tired smile then laughed quietly to himself, just loud enough to hear. I knew my face was turning red from the slight burning sensation as my cheeks flushed. Tony gave me a cordial wink. The gesture calmed my nerves, and somehow I knew everything would be okay. That little display of kindness gave me hope that Tony was a good guy.

"Okay, Peter... I'm pretty close to being ready, so feel free to go on into the studio and get set up."

Peter looked nervous, he glanced at me for reassurance, but all I had to give was a smile. He opened the heavy padded door to the studio and went inside. Leaving the door standing open, he set down his acoustical guitar case and started milling around the array of instruments. In the center stood a big Steinway grand piano, almost identical to the one we had at home. To the right of the piano sat a drum set that took up most of that side of the room. The other side was lined with an assortment of electric guitars. Next to them stood an assortment of saxophones, trumpets, clarinets, and a flute.

Peter was in his own personal Candy Land. He methodically walked around the room and touched every instrument, treating each one of them with a gentleness and affection that few could understand. Then I saw Tony motion toward the open door.

"Amy ... would you shut the door please?"

"Oh, sure," I said.

As I pulled the soundproof door shut, Tony flipped on a microphone at his console.

"Okay, Peter, we're burning up your time here, so you might want to unpack your guitar and we'll get started."

Peter peered through the glass at us, and I could tell he was talking, but I couldn't hear him. Tony sighed, and this time, I could tell he was a little bit annoyed.

"Peter you need to turn on one of the microphones for us to hear you."

He acknowledged Tony with an awkward smile and fumbled with a switch on the mike nearest the piano.

"Uh ... Tony, would it be okay to play the Steinway instead?"

The big guy didn't say anything at first. As I watched him, I noticed that he had the peculiar ability to raise one eyebrow—a quizzical expression that he conveyed to me with a glance. I nodded yes without a sound.

"Sure, Peter. I didn't know you played anything other than the guitar. So you play the piano as well?" Tony asked.

Peter looked up from the ivory keyboard with a distant look on his face that he gets when thinking about several things at once. Peter's brain is as close to a computer as biologically possible and was a thing of beauty—but also a curse. He had a photographic memory for the language of music, numbers, and words. His curse was the most human characteristic of his remarkable mind; like the rest of us, he could only talk about one thought at a time. Peter's outward appearance caused a common reaction for those who didn't know him. They would label his blank stare as being slow rather than realizing his brilliance. So in the course of a ten-second lag, heaven only knows what was spinning in Peter's mind. I could see him focus just before he replied, "Yes."

Tony clicked the mike off and gave me a perplexed look. "Man of few words."

"Peter is very smart ... sometimes too smart. Try to be a little more specific with your questions," I said, not wanting to embellish the facts just yet.

"Okay ..." Tony said. He turned the audio feed into the sound room back on. "Peter, which instruments do you play?"

"All of them," Peter replied, as though the expertise involved was commonplace.

Tony clicked the mike back off, and for a moment, his jolly eyes almost glared at me. "Are you kids jacking with me?" he asked.

I suspected we would come to this junction sooner or later, so I had prepared myself, but I'd also hoped the conversation would come later.

"Peter is a musical savant," I said, realizing too late, that I had blurted out five words that were not a part of my well-rehearsed speech. Fortunately it seemed effective, though, and Tony must have been smarter than he looked.

"He's a musical savant? Come on, he's way too normal. A socially functional savant is like one in a—"

"Million... yes, I know," I said, finishing his sentence. "Now, Tony, I would love to fill you in on your time, but three hundred bucks is a lot of money to us. I'll bet you a pizza of your choice you're going to be very impressed."

"I can eat quite a bit of pizza... he said smiling. Okay, Amy, it's a bet,"

35

He held out his huge hand, which engulfed mine, and all I could see was my wrist sticking out as we sealed the deal. I prayed that Tony would indeed be impressed since the pizza money I'd just gambled was our gas money home. If I ended up being wrong and lost the wager, we would be walking at least part of the way back to Texas.

Tony turned his mike on and, without further ado, said, "Okay, Peter, play me something."

Peter pulled out the napkins that he had written my song on an hour earlier and began spreading them out across the top of the grand piano.

"Uh … Peter, what are you doing?" Tony asked.

"It's a song I wrote this morning," Peter said, grinning.

"Peter, would you mind starting off with something that is not an original tune?" Tony asked. "You know…something to warm up on?"

I could hear the tension coming back into Tony's voice and was about to intervene, but their exchange went too fast.

"What would you like for me to play?" Peter asked, ever so politely.

"I don't care, Peter; play one," Tony said, sliding near the threshold of being completely frustrated.

Peter's smile never left him, and he missed Tony's slip of sarcasm. Without as much as a second thought, he took Tony literally and started playing the song titled "One" by the old rock-and-roll band, Three Dog Night. Peter had barely made it through the second verse before tears started welling up in my eyes. I considered it the perfect song for Peter because it was what I imagined life to be like for him … lonely. At that moment, I felt inadequate and wondered how I could ever fill the empty void in Peter's world. The emotion he put into the words and the ad-libbed melody was unbelievable. Neither

Peter nor I had a clue that it was Tony's favorite classic rock tune.

I heard a loud thump as Tony's shoes hit the floor. He had been reclined in his chair and had his feet propped up on a corner of the mixing board. I missed most of the cursing that came out as a whisper under his breath. His frantic efforts to power up the control board were quite amusing. The debacle perpetuated when he realized he had forgotten to put a CD in to record the session.

"Tony!" I said, louder than necessary.

He looked up briefly from his self-degrading whispered tirade.

"It's okay... he'll play it again," I said.

He took a deep breath to get control of himself and, with amazing candor, asked, "What kind of pizza do you like?"

"Vegetarian," I said with a giggle.

Tony didn't miss recording anything else after that. His mood changed from disenchanted nonchalance to animated professional courtesy. In less than fifteen minutes, Peter's status went from being a nondescript teenager to a respected musician. Tony tested Peter's ability's on a broad range of styles from rock and roll to blues and some modern jazz. He even asked him to play some classical tunes, which I didn't even know Peter could play.

After about forty-five minutes, Tony turned to me and said, "Why don't you go tell Peter to take a break? There are some sodas and water in the fridge behind you. I'm going to call a couple of friends to see if they will come over and play with Peter."

"Okay," I said with a smile.

There was no doubt in my mind we had passed the test. By the time I brought Peter back into the control room and found the soft drinks, Tony was busy making his first phone call. It didn't take long to figure out that these studio musicians were all asleep even though it was midday. I didn't mean to eavesdrop, but it was a small room.

"Jimmy," Tony said on the phone, "I don't give a rat's behind if you played until 3:00 a.m. Do you remember a month ago when I loaned you five hundred bucks to pay rent? You told me that whenever I needed you... Yes, this is payback time. Great, thanks, man ... and, Jimmy, you're in for a pleasant surprise. When...? I needed you ten minutes ago... Yes, hurry!"

Tony hung up and started dialing another number. The four phone calls all went the same, and I began to think that everyone in Chicago owed Tony money. One of the guys was a sound technician who worked part time for W. C. Studios and was already on his way. After hanging up from the last phone call, Tony leaned back in the rolling office chair and laced his sausage-sized fingers behind his head. He was a really big guy. I only knew the chair was there because I'd seen him sit in it. If he shaved, I imagined that he would look like Jabba the Hut from the *Star Wars* movies. That notion, though, was linked to his deep voice more than his size—and he was much better looking than Jabba. Tony just stared at us for a like a long time. I think he was seeing us for the first time. Tony repositioned himself with an expression that appeared to be between a grimace and a smile. He hunched over. Put his elbows on both knees, and plopped his big hairy face into his palms and became serious.

"First off, I want to apologize to you both. I've been doing this for nearly fifteen years, and after a while, you get cynical. I have a lot of friends who are good musicians that have worked hard to make it big in the business. The better ones work a studio gig once in a while or play in a club band. If they're lucky, they do both. Peter, you have more talent than anyone I've ever met. Something tells me that, you've never played in a band, and you have no idea where this roller coaster ride is going to take you."

He paused for effect, but Peter and I had absolutely no idea what he was trying to get at. He sat up and put a hand out to Peter.

"My friends call me Big Tony."

Peter shook hands with the big man. "It is my pleasure to meet you, Big Tony."

Tony repeated the introductions with me just like we had not met until that very moment.

"Look, you guys... I know you don't know me, but I'm going to give you some advice—and please stop me if you don't want to hear it."

He paused long enough for me to say, "Yes... please tell us."

Even though I still didn't know what he felt so compelled to share, I did know enough to listen.

"The music industry is tough," Tony said. "Most people spend their whole career just trying to make it. It's draining and comes with many disappointments. The top ten percent actually make a good living because they work hard and sacrifice. Then you have the cream of the crop, the top one percent that may have a chance at becoming a superstar. I'm talking Mozart, Beethoven, Hendrix, and Morrison. Peter... I think you may be one of those guys."

I recognized Peter's talent shortly after we met, but hearing it from Big Tony validated my opinion—and it felt good. For the first time in my life, I felt like an adult. I suppose the glaze of self-worth was more evident than I had imagined, because a moment later, Big Tony snapped his fingers and startled me back to real time.

"This is important … for both of you," Tony said. "I'm going to give you a short version of how life may change for you. When the boys get here, we'll practice a bit, and then cut a couple of regular tunes. Then if you all gel, we can try to mix a couple of originals if you want to. If this session goes like I think it will, you will start hearing from recording studios in two or three weeks. It can be a vicious business. Before you sign anything, get yourself an agent who knows what he's doing. They will manage your career and interests and take a percentage of what you make. If you choose wisely, it is money well spent. If you go big, it can happen fast. In less than a year, your music may be on radio stations all over the country. You'll put a band together, cut a CD, and the concert tours begin. Then comes the hard part: the money, fame, paparazzi, and suddenly you have no private life whatsoever. You won't be able to go to the movies, the prom, or even a simple date to have pizza with a couple of friends without someone wanting a picture, an autograph, or a handout. I know you are both probably thinking that I'm being negative and raining on your parade, but this is all stuff for you to think about. The money can be staggering—more than you can even imagine. You will want for nothing … houses, boats, cars, incredible vacations for you and your families. After a while, you may get bored with your new amazing life… that's when other temptations will become more attractive, like parties, alcohol, drugs, and all the new friends that come with it."

Chapter 4
Peter

I kept glancing at Amy while Big Tony went on about a fictitious career that I could not even imagine. When he finished, he scanned me, then Amy, with a piercing stare. It was an uncomfortable moment since I knew Big Tony expected one of us to say something. I didn't have a clue what that was, so when in doubt, start with good manners.

"Thanks, uh ... Big Tony for the advice, but isn't what you're saying mostly conjecture at this point?"

"Yeah, Peter, it is, and if I'm wrong, I'll apologize. I've been around this business long enough to know that once this train starts rolling it's really hard to stop it. So before we start, you need to decide if you really want it."

After that comment, Amy looked at me, and I could see that she had an assortment of mixed emotions. She was still smiling, but clearly something was bothering her, and it didn't take a savant to realize it. Amy read my reaction to her distress before I even knew I had one. She reached out, took my hand, and gave it a squeeze, along with a cute little wink that she often used to make me feel like everything was okay. Without missing a beat, she stepped into the conversation.

"Actually, Peter and I talked at great length about what it might be like to become rich and famous, but hearing it from someone else, like it could really happen, is unsettling and exciting all at the same time." She paused for a moment and continued. "We're just a couple of kids who are doing our best to act like we know what we're doing, but we're clueless. It's Peter's career and will ultimately be his decision. Even so, I know he trusts my opinion."

Amy continued. "I'm a good judge of character, and although we have just met, I feel ..." she paused and looked at me, conveying a silent conversation with her eyes as if she was seeking permission. I could read her thoughts, and we were on the same page. I smiled and acquiesced with a slight nod for her to continue. "We both feel that you would be a good manager for Peter.

"Tony sat up a little taller for a moment but his gaze scanned the floor for what felt like a long time. I began to wonder what could be so intriguing and almost succumbed to joining his survey of the floor when his head popped up.

"You see what I mean?" Tony said. "You two are willing to offer me a piece of your future, and you have no clue who or what I am. I could be a serial killer—or worse, if there is such a thing, for all you know."

I felt I needed to step in at that point, although I didn't know what I should say. I stood up and looked Big Tony in the eyes.

"You are correct," I said. "We don't know you. But I do know Amy, and I trust her opinion. Besides that, I'm underage and can't sign a contract without a parent, so you'll have to get by my dad. He doesn't miss much. Big Tony, you're one of the few people I've ever met that took me for face value and didn't treat me like a freak of nature. That has not happened a lot in my life."

Unexpectedly, Tony started laughing. It was a deep rolling laugh that went on for two minutes at least! That may not seem like a long time, but try laughing for two minutes straight—it's hard to do. Try to not to smile or laugh when you're with someone who is that amused. It's impossible to not to laugh with them. We all laughed to the point of tears.
To this day, I am not sure what Big Tony thought was so funny.

"So Tony, is that a Yes?" I asked. And then the laughter started all over again.

We were saved from "death by laughing" when the door to the sound room opened abruptly and Big Tony's part-time sound guy entered. I know all too well what it's like to walk into a room and feel awkward. In my case, I would have presumed the joke involved me, because all too often it did. That painful recollection made me somber and I had to shake the feeling off. Tony somehow managed to introduce Tommy, who by my guess was not much older than I was. We all shook hands, and then Big Tony told him what he wanted set up. Tommy headed to the studio to get started and left us to our conversation.

Tony gathered his thoughts with care and finally answered me. "Yes, Peter, if I pass your father's scrutiny, then I'll be happy to work with you. I'll send you home with a contract. There's a lot of legal jargon in it, but essentially, the bottom line is I get 15 percent of everything you make. It's a standard contract, and the percentage is industry standards. Now, in good faith, I'm not going to charge you anything today unless you decide to sign another agent. If you do, I'll understand and I will bill you for the original three hundred dollars that we agreed on. Are we in agreement so far?"

"Yeah, sure ... that's more than fair," I said, relieved to know we would leave Chicago with more than just gas money to get home.

"Okay, good," Tony said. "Now, it was my call to bring in some studio musicians so you could cut a decent demo. I'm doing that on good faith as well. Since it was my call, I can't in good conscience charge you for their time regardless of whether you sign with me or not."

Tony paused, long enough for me to get a word in. "Tony you have my word that I will pay the three hundred dollars, if I sign with someone else." I said.

"You're a good man, Peter. I want to be sure we are on the same page here, and the last thing either of us needs right now is for you to be worried about money. Now… the guys are going to be showing up very soon. Being a great musician doesn't carry as much clout as being a great musician with new unique work. So if you guys can record two or three original songs it will give me a better shot at selling your stuff."

I glanced at Amy, realizing she had told me the same thing just a few hours earlier. She put her hands on her hips and gave me that knowing look that said "I told you so." In that brief moment, I flashed a smile back at her in acknowledgment. Tony missed my temporary lack of attention, continuing on with his advice and instructions.

"I know you said you wrote a song this morning—and how you did that, I haven't a clue—but sit down here at the desk by the fridge and see if you can come up with another one. I'm going to help Tommy."

As I sat down, I watched Big Tony slip through the doorway into the studio. It's not an exaggeration that I couldn't see any daylight on either side as he passed through. Smiling, I looked back toward Amy, who startled me because of her proximity. She sat down in my lap giggling, then threw her arms around me and kissed me.

"It's happening just like we thought it would," she said.

"Like you said it would," I said.

The awkward feeling of her being in my space passed and was replaced by a warm and tingly sensation. All those hours traveling in the car and sleeping in it together didn't prepare me for the closeness of her womanly scent. It created a sensation that I understood, and my body's physical response would soon be embarrassing me.

"I don't think I'll be able to write a song with you sitting here."

I coaxed her to stand up, knowing that the evidence of my arousal would soon be noticeable. That awkward thought increased a flush of heat that tinted my neck and face with a glowing shade of red. I felt embarrassed and looked away. She stood very close and directed my face toward hers, and to my relief, she was blushing as brightly as I knew I must have been.

She looked at me with that wonderful smile, kissed me on the cheek and said, "I love you, Peter Shaw. I am so happy for you."

In an unusual moment of social awareness on my part, I said what I meant, and it came across as intended. "I'm happy for us, Amy ... and I love you more every day."

Even though I am supposed to be so smart, it's rare that I say what I mean, especially when my feelings are involved. But that day was the best day of my life, and my choice of words granted me yet another kiss that assured me it had been an excellent response.

"Okay, time to quit daydreaming," Amy said. "You need to get to work. I've heard you play some tunes at my house that I know were original. Do you have any lyrics worked out?"

Her hands went back to her hips, and Amy was clearly back to business. For me, though, the thought of her lips on mine lingered, and my mind floated in a foggy haze for one moment too long.

"Peter ..."

"Uh ... songs ... sure ... well of course. I want to play the one I wrote for you this morning," I said.

"Right and that leaves two more."

She walked over to Tony's office printer and slid a stack of paper out of the machine, rummaged through his stuff until she found a pencil, and brought everything to me.

"Get busy, mister," she said with the authority of a drill sergeant, then added a little wink and smile that made me more than willing to comply.

Although to most people it looked like writing lyrics was easy for me, in my mind I struggled with it more than music. Music flowed out of me so easy that it amazed even me. Words came harder and required all of my attention and concentration to write.

Fortunately I had been working out the words to one of my tunes, so about an hour later, I had my second song. I knew there wasn't enough time to write the sheet music, so I labeled the words with the chord changes and hoped Tony's musicians could play by ear.

"Well, that's two," I said.

I grabbed my backpack and looked through it until I came across a folded-up piece of paper. It was a poem that Amy had written and given to me. "And here is the third one," I said. Amy had exercised great patience and had remained wordless while I worked. Now curious, she got up and came across the room. Her eyes popped wide when she realized it was a poem she'd written.

"You can't use that! It's not good enough," she said, grabbing it out of my hand.

Reaching again into my backpack, I found the worn manila folder that I kept song ideas in, and I handed it to her. She opened it and realized that I had already written the music to her words.

"When did you do this?" she asked.

"I started it right after you gave it to me. Your words inspired the music but I won't play it unless it's okay with you."

"But, Peter, it's not good enough. It's nothing like the stuff you do."

"Yes it is. Your words are beautiful. Amy... please let me play it. I promise if you don't like it, we won't put it in the demo."

"You really think my poem is good?" she asked, a hint of tears welling up in her eyes, now sparkling with pride.

"Yes, I do."

Our conversation was curtailed by loud voices outside the control room. Suddenly, the door flung open and our temporary sanctuary of solitude was breached. Three seedy-looking guys sauntered in, all of them participating in a heated argument with language you would hear at a construction site. Two of them appeared to be in their mid-thirties. The taller of the three looked older, his long straight hair pulled back in a ponytail more gray than black. Even though I found myself hoping to be wrong, I knew they had to be the studio musicians we were waiting for. Amy's face glowed red from embarrassment as they carried on with a plethora of colorful metaphors. I was working up the courage and the words to quell the flow of obscenities when the sound-room door flew open and Big Tony's loud baritone voice detonated in the room like a bomb going off.

"Shut your filthy yaps!" Tony scowled... and a silence enveloped the room. Then in a subdued, even tone, he looked at the tall guy. "Jimmy... I know you don't talk like that in front of your daughter. I think you owe Amy an apology."

I don't know if it had something to do with Big Tony's size or if it was respect. Without missing a beat, Jimmy walked straight over to Amy and knelt down on one knee.

"Amy, my name is Jimmy Giordano, and I am very sorry. I didn't realize there was a lady was present. Please accept my apologies."

I'm not sure if Amy or I was more shocked. I had never heard a more eloquent request for forgiveness. Amy stared at him for a short moment and then, with the air of a queen, said, "Thank you, Jimmy. Are you related to the big guy?" She indicated Tony with a slight inclination of her head.

"He's my younger brother and sometimes is not so gentle when reminding me of how we were raised." Jimmy stood, took a step toward Big Tony, and gave him an affectionate hug.

Tony relinquished his brother's affection and scowled at the other two guys who were quietly studying the floor. He chuckled and finished the introductions by pointing them out with a chubby forefinger. "The bald one is Vince and one of the best drummers in the business. And that," he said, pointing to the short, portly one of the three, "is my cousin Frank, an outstanding bass guitarist. He's been doing studio gigs for me for over ten years. Guys, this is Peter and his girlfriend Amy. They are up from Texas to cut a demo."

Tony apparently picked up on their guarded behavior. "Jimmy...Peter here is the first person to come through the front door and really knock my socks off. You can thank me later."

He smiled and slapped Jimmy on the back just hard enough that his brother had to take a step forward to absorb the blow. "Okay, you guys know the drill. Time is money, so get set up. Peter is new to this, so help him out all you can."

The trio shuffled into the sound room, and Tony looked at Amy, then me, just long enough to consider his next words. "That's another example of what's in store for you guys. Don't take this the wrong way, but the reality is you're young and unseasoned. That's not a bad thing, though; hold onto your innocence as long as you can. What happened just now is a tiny example of the world you're stepping into. Are you sure you want to continue down this path?" Tony asked while looking straight at me.

I knew that I had a deer-in-the-headlights look on my face, but somehow I managed to nod and answer, "Yeah, I'm ready."

Amy gave me a smile and a quick peck on the cheek. "Break a leg," she said.

"I'll do my best," I replied and then headed to the sound room.

My legs felt as if they weighed an extra hundred pounds apiece. The heavy soundproof door shut behind me, and the click of the latch startled me, as though it were a cell door.

Jimmy looked up and noticed my nervousness. "So, Peter, here's the deal. I know you're nervous. If you weren't, there would be something wrong with you. I remember my first time in a studio. My hands were so sweaty I couldn't play anything. Best thing to do is just pretend you're at home or wherever you play for fun—and relax."

I couldn't have known then that Jimmy would become a lifelong friend. But his kind words were just what I needed.

I gave him an awkward smile and replied, "Thanks, I appreciate you all coming down and helping me out." I passed out copies of the songs while apologizing for my lack of preparation. "I'm sorry, guys. I only have sheet music written for one of the three songs that Tony wants us to play. I wrote the chord changes down over the lyrics for the other two. I'm not used to playing with anyone, but I'll do my best."

"You must have something really special going for you, Peter. I've never heard Tony give out a compliment like the

ALLEN HIVELY

one he gave you. Just relax and do your thing and we'll try to keep up," Jimmy said.

For the first time ever, I felt a sense of belonging and felt comfortable, considering the circumstances. I walked around the big Steinway grand piano, sat down, and lightly touched the keys. A piano has eighty-eight keys, and I had an intimate relationship with each and every one of them. I glanced up and realized that the musicians were all looking at me, attentive and ready to play. Words could never explain the curious sensation I felt from the instant connection and sense of belonging. Even though I still felt nervous—nothing in my life had ever felt so right.

"I'm going to start off and let you guys get a feel for the song. Since I am the rookie, please tell me if I screw up."

I started playing the melody that I had written to accompany Amy's poem, and about halfway through the song, I became aware that they were picking up my lead. I was surprised by how well we synced up by the end of the tune. Jimmy gave me an endearing smile that told me he too, was surprised.

"Shall we give it a go with the words?" he asked.

I nodded a smile back and started from the top:

> "I've been wondering lately
> When do the good times come?
> I'd like to believe in the future
> To know something good will come
> It's hard to be happy about tomorrow
> If I'm worried about today
> How will I know when something better comes
> Will it will make me smile
>
> "Life could end in darkness

THE SAVANT

With no time to the find truth
War seems easy
Why is peace so hard?

"Don't wait till night to see the light
You can see the future
In the eyes of our children
Teach them to smile
And they'll know serenity
Then the night will be day

"Let's take a trip together
Bring your friends and family too
Since time keeps on moving
I'm sure it will last forever
We can make a difference
One day at a time
But we're driving the train
And life is just a smile

"If we are born from love
How can we love to hate?
Hate seems easy
Why is love so hard?

"Don't wait till night to see the light
You can see the future
In the eyes of our children
Teach them to smile
And they'll know serenity
Then the night will be as day"

We played the song five more times before Big Tony was happy, and then he let us take a short break. The pizza had come during our session and was already cold, but no one cared. We managed to scarf down four large pizzas, which according to Tony were Chicago's best.

Amy was ecstatic about her poem. "Peter, I am so happy you talked me into letting you use my poem. I really never thought of it as lyrics. Your music made it beautiful."

I smiled at her compliment but had a different view. "I think it was the words that made the song beautiful."

"I guess we will have to agree to disagree on that," she said, smiling back. Her eyes wandered over a clock on the wall. It was 8:00 "Oh my gosh! Where did the day go? And we're not done yet." She hadn't said it all that loud, but Tony must have heard her because, as if on cue, he rousted everyone up and back to work.

Five minutes later, I was sitting at the piano in the sound room again. The love song I wrote for Amy in the diner had a complex melody. I didn't have sheet music for the guys, and it took a lot of tries for us to get up to speed. The time just slipped by, and I had no concept of its passage. Music puts me in a different world and I am happiest when I'm there. When Tony gave us an exaggerated thumbs-up, I knew it was a wrap. I noticed Amy pointing at her watch. My eyes scanned for a clock in the sound room, and I saw it right in front of me—2:15 in the morning.

"Crap," I said under my breath.

I got up from the piano and hurried to the control room. Tony was so excited that it took me another five minutes just to get a word in.

In desperation, I yelled, "Tony!" All the chatter stopped immediately, and all eyes were on me. "Uh … Tony we have to go," I said, quietly this time.

His eyes scanned for a clock. He closed them for a moment and then nodded his head in affirmation. He understood, but I could tell he was not happy. "You guys have to be beat," Tony said. "I'm sorry. We're all night owls here and used to working all night, but you spent most of last night driving up here."

I didn't really want to tell him the rest of what I knew would be bad news, but I felt I had no choice: "Amy doesn't have permission to be on this trip. Her mother is out of town, and she's not supposed to be back until Monday morning, and but we left Amy's little sister at home alone. We have to head back to Texas."

"Ah, crap, Peter, when were you going to tell me? I can't start off your career in a day! What were you thinking?"

It was the first time Tony had raised his voice to me, and it was scary and there were no holes to crawl into. I was left no recourse but to defend myself.

"We came here with six hours scheduled, Tony. We're just a couple of kids. We didn't expect to be here any longer than that. Heck, until a few hours ago, I didn't even know if I was any good or not. I am sorry, but we don't have the time to hammer out another tune, sleep some, and then drive fourteen hours home."

"I'm sorry, Peter," Big Tony said. "This is my fault. We talked about everything except how much time it would take. I know how long it takes, but I was so caught up in the moment…. Okay, everyone, that's it for tonight."

Amy stood at my side, and I noticed tears welling up in her eyes. "What's wrong?" I asked.

"This is my fault. If I hadn't come along, you could stay and finish your demo."

"Amy, if you hadn't come with me. I wouldn't have come in the first place."

She gave me that smile that always brightens my day. Knowing I was telling the truth.

"You know," Amy said, "when this takes off, I may not be able to be with you every step of the way."

"Yeah, I know. But I'm glad you were with me on my first one."

I gave her an awkward kiss on the cheek, which was still damp from her tears. I could taste the briny flavor. I used my thumbs to dry her cheeks and then held her face close for a moment.

"I'll love you tomorrow more than I do today," I said.

She blinked back another onslaught of tears. Then her expression changed to a stern look that she gets when she's annoyed. "Did you just quote the title of another song?" she asked.

"Maybe," I replied.

Before I could make sense of her response, she pushed me away, laughing and shaking her head.

"Just because you're going to be rich and famous, doesn't mean you can win me over, time and time again, with cheesy song titles," she said.

Before I could respond, Tony interrupted us.

"Hey, I like that song title too." He said, beaming a broad smile. "Sorry to cut in, but I know time is important. I'm going to submit the two songs we did today, and I am sure we will have responses before the end of the week. Peter, I need you to get busy and write more songs, on paper, not in your head. You saw how much better it goes when the studio musicians can see on paper what you're trying to do. If things go the way I expect, I'll need you back up here in two or three weeks. With luck, you'll be flying from DFW instead of driving. There are a couple of couches in the front office that I can assure you are quite comfortable. Go get some shut-eye

54

and I'll wake you in about three hours and send you on your way."

Tony guided us to the couches; much like a mother duck leads her ducklings to water, brought us pillows and blankets, and left us to dreamland. I didn't think I would sleep, but I barely remember my head hitting the pillow. The next thing I knew, Tony woke us up and escorted us to the door with a thermos of coffee. It was 6:00 a.m. The skies were clear blue —and I was walking on clouds.

Chapter 5
Amy

The ride home to Texas was quiet. Peter seemed self-absorbed and may as well have been on another planet. I tried several times to initiate a conversation, but it appeared as though he didn't hear me. Undaunted, I persisted, knowing how overwhelmed he was with the enormity of what had happened in the last few hours. I always had a challenge in figuring out what went on in that complicated mind of his. I knew Peter well enough to know he fretted about stuff that was either out of his control or things that didn't matter. After what seemed like a zillion tries, I finally got his attention.

"I'm sorry, Amy. I know I'm not being very good company. There's more stuff going around in my brain right now than I can sort out. If I follow through with this—life is going to change in a big way. What I'm most worried about is how it will affect us."

He gave me a rueful smile that I had seen many times before. It was how he started off an apology for something that most of the time didn't need one.

"Peter, we have talked about this for over six months. Nothing is going to change between us if we make choices to prevent it."

"I know… and that's the point. Just say I make it really big and record a CD. Then imagine my songs end up on the radio. According to Big Tony, the next step is doing concerts, and that means traveling all over the country. If I'm traveling all of the time then the chances of seeing you will be infrequent. Your mom is not going to let you travel from hotel to hotel with a band. I'll be seventeen next month, and you the month after that. That means you have no say in what you can do until you're eighteen, and that is over a year away. Even then, your mom could object."

Needless to say, I felt flattered by the fact that Peter was consumed by thoughts of my potential absence while he traipsed around the country. Truth is—I had been thinking about little else since I'd convinced him to cut a demo. I was painfully aware of what my mother thought I should do with my life. She was always working and never there for the little things that were important to me. And I wouldn't call the time we did spend together "quality time." Usually, Mother gave me her dissertation of my short and long-term goals. Problem was, and I know it sounded a little corny; I wanted to marry the right guy, have some kids, and take care of my family. Of course, every time the subject went in that direction, Mother would explode, citing every reason in the universe why I had to be the dumbest girl in it. The full circle of our debate always returned to her real-life story that had started out similar to the lifestyle I wanted. When my dad died in a motorcycle accident, it changed all of our lives, especially moms, and her opinion of life had only one view.

"Amy, you have to be prepared for what life might have in store for you."

If I had a dollar for every time I heard her say that, I could have retired a rich teenager. Don't get me wrong: I do understand the point, and I have always planned to go to college, but I have no desire to plan for a career when I don't even know what I like. What I do know is, if I have kids, I don't want them to be a pseudo-family where the kids raise each other with a little help from friends, grandparents, and the neighborhood stay-at-home moms. I only brought that point up once in our many discussions. The ensuing fight lasted for weeks. Mom has never apologized for always being gone, and I'm sure she never will. She justifies it as a necessity, and somehow always made me feel wrong for wanting her around. At that point, I began taking the role as the family caretaker—and it is why Kelly and I are so close.

So even though the ride home ended up being one of quiet reflection filled with personal thoughts and dreams, in the back of my mind I had a nagging apprehension that I couldn't shake. It began to rain as we passed through Sherman, Texas. Even though Highway 75 is a four-lane road, the traffic slowed, and the last few miles to McKinney seemed to take forever.

And then we got to my street. We lived in a big old Victorian-style house in the historical part of town that had been built in 1898. It had a huge porch that wrapped around the front and down the side of the house, with a small white picket fence out front. As we pulled up, everything looked as it should be—until I saw my mother sitting on the front porch swing. She had come home early. Peter and I exchanged a knowing look. We both knew I would face a maelstrom of repercussions for our little jaunt to Chicago. We both muttered good-byes—no hugs or farewell kisses.

"I'll call you when I can, Peter. I love you."

"I love you too. Good luck with your mom."

I gave him an uneasy smile and got out of the car with my backpack in tow and then gave him a halfhearted wave good-bye. I walked up the sidewalk and opened the little picket gate and looked up the stairs into my mother's eyes. Even though she sat in an old porch swing suspended by chain, I didn't see any kind of sway or movement at all. As silly as it sounds, the first thing I thought of was. *How can she sit there and remain so still, like a statue?* Her eyes focused as they followed me up every step. I knew she was calculating judgment and sentence; there would be no trial.

"Hi Mom," I said.

I tried to be cheerful knowing full well how it would play out. My voice sounded more like a mouse squeaking under the claws of an alley cat.

"Nice of you to come home," she said in a calm and controlled manner.

I didn't hate my mother, but I did hate what life had dished out to her and what she had become as a result. Abigail Stevens was a big-time corporate attorney. She could smile while cutting your heart out and eat it in front of you as you quietly slipped away. She always came across cool and collected, and never showed emotion. I disliked the lack of emotion the most. Sometimes I wished she would just get mad and yell and scream. Instead she would just observe you, like a python considering dinner.

I noticed that she wore a black pinstripe suit buttoned up to the top, with only the collar and cuffs of her white blouse showing. Her hair this month was red and shoulder length. It was the blazing emerald-green eyes that told me she already knew everything and that any deviation from the truth would only make matters worse. Since she was still in her work clothes, I knew she had not been home long—but plenty long enough to interrogate Kelly to tears. I had no doubt she had also called Peter's mom and confirmed the whole story. For a brief moment, I thought how nice it would be to have a family like Peter's—one you could talk to and be treated like family instead of an object of inconvenience. I didn't like being dishonest with Mom, but I'd had no doubt as to her decision about a trip to Chicago if I had presented it to her. She would have given no consideration of the request, and as a result, Peter would have never gone either.

So I stood there waiting for a verdict. I knew we wouldn't have any physical confrontation, but I almost wished she would just give me a beating and be done with it.

My sentence would instead involve mental punishment—and would last a very long time. She sighed and rolled her eyes. The mock sorrow in her eyes stemmed from the overall nuisance of it all rather than an issue of right and wrong.

"Put your stuff up, wash your face and we'll have a family meeting in five minutes." She stood up and waited for me to go inside.

On the way to my room, I passed Kelly's door and knocked softly and peeked inside. Her face looked flushed from crying, as soon as she saw me, she ran up and gave me a big hug.

"I'm sorry, sis. I tried to say you were at the movies, but you know the warden. She saw right through it. Then she called Peter's mom and it was all over but the crying."

I responded her hug with affection knowing she would suffer punishment for my indiscretion as well. "I'm sorry. Looks like you have a jump start on the crying part."

She smiled, but no humor showed in it.

"We'll get through this, you and I. It's just a thing," I said, "and it will blow over before you know it."

Precisely five minutes later, Kelly and I gravitated to the living room, where our mother awaited our presence. We sat on a faded brown leather couch in the center of the room that faced a matching big chair with the ottoman pushed over to the side. Mom sat on the edge of the cushion, back straight with her hands in her lap. The only thing that gave her anger away was her posture and the lack of emotion. I called it her "court face." I knew we would be grounded, but what came next ended up being a surprise that I was totally unprepared for.

"Well, ladies, you have disappointed me at a level that I must say surprises even me. I deal with lies and deceit on a daily basis. When I come home, I consider my time here a sanctuary, a time for reflection and relaxation. The two of you enjoy a life that is envious to most. I have provided you with a fine lifestyle and the benefit of my trust. I let you do pretty much whatever you want within reason." She stood up and peered out the window, I guess for dramatic effect, and then continued. "I thought my trust was well founded. When I'm working long hours away from home, I have always felt confident as to where my girls are and what they are up to. Imagine my distress when I get home and my twelve-year-old daughter is home alone. Then I learn that my sixteen-year-old daughter is on a road trip to Chicago without permission, with no chaperone, and with an awkward young lad with aspirations to be a musician. I usually don't talk about my cases with you. But I'm going to tell you about the case I'm finishing up on now. Our office caters to the music industry, which in short means when any of the big-time performers get in trouble, I bail them out. This case concerns a well-known musician who will go unnamed, since, number one; you would know him, and two, its client confidentiality. I won't go into the sordid details, but it involves a young girl who thought she loved him very much. The short version is, when he tired of her and sent her away. She felt rejected and couldn't bear telling her family she was carrying his child. So she committed suicide. The young lady was eighteen, so there were no criminal charges… but the family pursued a civil suit that I have spent the last year fighting on his behalf. In my career, I have never felt so soiled and dejected due to my participation in a case. Now I come home and see the beginnings of something similar happening to my own daughter. Well, I can assure you, it ends now! Amy… you are forbidden to see Peter Shaw ever again. Not only that. You are not allowed to talk to him on the phone, text or email him, or write letters. If you see him in the hallway at school, you are to avoid him as if he does not exist. Am I perfectly clear on this matter?"

Her words stunned me so much that, for a moment, I couldn't say anything—and felt glad that I was already seated. Then the anger kicked in. On trembling legs, I stood up, pointed my right finger at her, and said, "You can't tell me who I will have as friends or who I will talk to. I'm sixteen years old, old enough to know the difference between good people and bad. Peter is the sweetest guy in the world. He would never do anything to hurt me."

Mother stood and took a couple of steps toward me, and for the first time, I noticed a crazed look in her green eyes that I had never seen before. Her normal courtroom mannerism had disappeared and been replaced with something akin to fanaticism.

"You will do as I say, young lady! You being sixteen means you are a minor, and for the time being, I own you. If you disobey me, I will have your sweet young Peter locked up."

I could feel the heat in my face, and although I knew deep down the conversation seemed to be deteriorating fast, I stood my ground and lashed out with the first hurtful thing that came to my mind: "So, Abigail, after leaving us alone to raise ourselves for the past five years, you have suddenly decided to be a mother. Excuse me for being a little shocked."

She slapped me so hard I saw stars. Kelly told me later the marks of all five of mom's fingers left a visible welt on my face. I stood there, stunned. Mom had never even spanked us, much less hit us. My pride had fallen into shambles, but I still managed to glare back, my face wet with tears.

"I will make you a promise, Mother. You will regret what you just did—and this day."

62

I could see the anger in her eyes had subsided, and I knew she wanted to take back the physical part of our confrontation. No apologies hung on her lips, though—only the smug satisfaction of winning our domestic dispute. I turned and started to my room.

"This conversation is not over, Amy!"

I turned back to her. "Yes, Abigail, it is, unless of course you would like to slap me around some more?"

I left without the satisfaction of seeing her mouth open and unable to find words for a response. But Kelly told me about it later. Even then, it did not make me feel any better. As far as I was concerned, my mother ceased to exist on that Sunday afternoon. We never had a civil conversation again for the rest of our lives. I went to my room and cried most of the night. The next day, I woke up to a gentle knock on my bedroom door that I recognized as Kelly's. I uncovered my head long enough to mumble, "Come in," and repositioned my pillow in a feeble effort of suffocate myself.

"Hey Amy, I made waffles just the way you like them. Why don't you come downstairs and have some breakfast?"

Sweet of her, yes—but I did not want to see Mom and had already decided to stay in my room until I died from malnutrition.

"Thanks, sis, but I'm not hungry … and I'm not going to school today."

"Mom's gone, so you don't have to worry about seeing her again for a couple of days. She's gone to Atlanta and won't be back until Wednesday."

That good news got my attention, and without any thought, I sat up and blurted out my immediate response: "Good! I am leaving this house and never coming back!"

I jumped out of bed with renewed determination and started formulating an escape plan. It didn't take long to realize Kelly made no protests, and that made me take pause to wonder why. When I looked at her, she was staring at the floor, avoiding eye contact with me and obviously crying.

"What's up, sis?" I asked.

She inhaled sharply, and I first thought her tears flowed because I was leaving her as well. I hugged my sister, and then lifted her face so she was looking at me.

"Don't worry. I'm not going to leave you. We'll go together."

Her eyes welled up even more then the sobs came. I gave her a long hug and soon she managed to sniff back the tears. She pulled me to the window and pulled back the curtains. Confused, I finally realized she wanted me to look outside. There sat a black SUV at the curb right in front of our house. Leaning against the fender was a tall thin man with dark sunglasses dressed in khaki slacks and a light blue polo shirt.

"Who the heck is that?" I asked.

"Mom left a letter on the kitchen table. His name is Fred. He's our escort … and bodyguard."

"What!" I said, looking back toward Fred. "Jailer is more like it. She can't do this!"

I started toward the door, but Kelly stopped me before I got to there.

"Amy, it's worse than you think. I think you should read Mom's letter before you do or say anything."

We walked downstairs together. I imagine we looked like two frightened children lost in a dark forest, holding hands and expecting something evil to jump out and get us. Once I realized I didn't need to be afraid of the house. I gathered up as much sixteen-year-old confidence as I could and led my little sister into the kitchen. As promised, I found a letter lying on the table. My resolve shattered as I read the letter.

Although I thought I was prepared for anything, nothing could have been further from the truth.

> *Ladies,*
>
> *It is abundantly clear that you cannot be trusted to conduct yourselves in a trustworthy manner, so I have decided to take appropriate steps. The gentleman outside is Fred, your new chaperone and bodyguard. He is quite good at what he does, so don't try any tomfoolery. If you give him a chance, he is a pretty nice guy. This is just a job for Fred, so if you don't make it hard for him, you will find him more or less invisible. This morning, I had breakfast with a friend of mine who is a Collin County judge. I filed a restraining order against Peter Shaw. As per our short discussion last night, you are forbidden to have any contact with him. I have already called his parents, and they have assured me that they will respect my wishes. Amy, I can't stress this enough: as long as you do as you're told, there will be no repercussions toward Peter. However, if you ignore me, I can and will file charges and have him put in jail. Someday you will thank me for this, although I know that will not be the case for some time to come.*
>
> *Love, Mom*

Chapter 6
Kelly

I watched my sister read and reread the short letter from our mother. Then she started crying and went back to her room. A full week and another round of threats from Mom came along before Amy went back to school. The routine around the house became life as usual, in that Mom was always gone. In addition to Fred, we had a full-time house guest Gina—our new nanny. I resented her as much as Amy did at first. Having regular meals that didn't come out of a box was awesome and Gina was nice to us. Amy tried to ignore Fred and Gina. For the first two or three weeks, I am sure she did not speak to either of them except when absolutely necessary. As time wore on, she realized they were not the enemy. Still, Amy did manage not to speak a single word to Mom.

Mother was visibly irritated at first. But as time passed, she seemed to resign herself to it being a temporary inconvenience. She appeared confident she had done the right thing and seemed oblivious to the rift she had created with Amy. My sister still talked to me. Even so there was something missing between us as well. In my heart, I knew that a beautiful part of my sister had died. I offered to be a courier for her and Peter so they could stay in touch. She took me up on the offer only once.

"There's too much at stake for Peter's career and I don't want you to get into trouble." She said. I delivered the thick envelope to one of Amy's girlfriends, who in turn gave it to another and so on. I'm sure the precautions were a bit overdone, but as requested, no reply came from Peter. My curiosity got the better of me one night and I flat out asked

Amy what she had told him in the letter. "It's none of your business." She said. I persisted, telling her that I wasn't asking to know about their personal stuff. I just wanted to know what was going on.

Finally, after several days of badgering that only a little sister could get away with, she said, "Fourteen months!"

"What in the heck does that mean?" I asked.

She just smiled. I was a bit shocked since it was the first time I had seen her smile in a month, but she wouldn't say anything more. She just said that if I really tried, I could figure it out.

/////

Two months passed since what Amy and I called the beginning of our prison term. It was the fourteenth of November—Amy's seventeenth birthday. Once again, Mother was gone on another trip, so Amy celebrated with Gina, Fred, and, of course, yours truly. Amy didn't want a party or to have any friends over, but true to form, Gina baked a beautiful chocolate cake topped with seventeen candles. Gina was a plump middle-aged widow who had four kids—two boys and two girls. Three of them were grown with kids of their own. Her youngest, a girl, was a senior in college. She clearly loved being a parent and was a natural at it. When she talked about her kids, it didn't take long to realize her pride in them. That made her easy to like. Her parents had migrated to Texas from Guatemala before she'd been born, she had lived in McKinney all of her life. Being second generation, her English sounded as good as mine. And she spoke fluent Spanish... that was pretty cool. I liked the fact she always had a smile on her face. It was a breath of fresh air, since Mom never did.

Amy blew out all of the candles in one breath, then closed her eyes tight and made her wish. Then she looked at me.

"Twelve more months," she whispered, just loud enough that I could hear.

I started to ask what she meant but then she put a hand on mine and winked. At that moment, I understood. She was counting down the months until she turned eighteen years old—and gained her freedom from our mother's tyranny. Later that night, I interrogated her until I'm sure Amy regretted slipping up and letting me into her secret.

"Kelly, you have to swear to keep this between us and tell no one—and I mean not even your best friend."

"I promise," I said. "Why do you need to be so secretive about this? I'm sure Mom knows she can't stand in your way when you're eighteen."

She looked at me as if I were an idiot.

"If Abigail has the time to design a plan, she will." She said. "Heck, Kelly, she might try to have me committed."

"Oh, come on! I know Mom can be overbearing and controlling, but she wouldn't do that."

"Well, I am not so sure and therefore see no reason to take any chances. One year from today Peter and I are going to get married."

It dropped like a bomb. The room was so quiet. All you could hear was the sprinkle of rain on the window.

"Married," was all I could get out of my mouth.

She just smiled and nodded.

It took me awhile to manage the next logical question: "Uh … isn't it, like, common to be asked?"

Amy grabbed her purse, and from her wallet, she pulled out a little piece of paper, folded up about quarter size. She unfolded it in a careful deliberate manner until it was about a six-inch square. She wouldn't let me hold it and instead just tipped it so I could read it. It just said. *Will you marry me?* No "To" or "From" … just four words.

"When did you get this?" I whispered as quietly as I could.

"It was his reply to my one and only letter that you delivered two months ago."

"How did he get it to you? All the teachers knew about the restraining order. He couldn't come within a hundred feet without someone noticing."

She smiled and flopped down on her bed, staring at the note as if it would disappear. "His friend Johnny Walters gave it to me in chemistry class."

"Johnny Walters? You mean that skinny little geeky kid? Yuck! Are you sure it's not from him?"

"I'm sure," she said. "Johnny is the only friend Peter has in school. No one else understands him. Except that is, for me."

/////

About two weeks later, Amy came running into my room screaming like a girl possessed by demons. I knew she was excited about something, but since my mind-reading skills were undeveloped and she couldn't calm down long enough to share. I finally conceded to just waiting it out. It didn't take as long as it seemed, probably a minute or two, but when you know something really exciting is happening, it seems like an eternity.

"Turn your radio on!" Amy said.

"Okay. Any particular channel, or did you just want to listen to whatever is on?" I asked, still oblivious to the meaning.

"Turn to FM 97.5! He'll be on as soon as the commercial is over."

Still clueless, I complied and turned my little Sony stereo to the channel she requested. An advertisement from a local pizza place was just finishing up, and then the announcer came back on.

"Hello, McKinney, Texas. I have a rare treat for you this afternoon. There's a new star on the horizon tonight. A seventeen-year-old musical prodigy has hit the big time, and he is a local young man. We will have an interview on the hour, but for now, sit back, close your eyes, and enjoy the new hit song from Peter Shaw."

The DJ faded out, and bigger than life, the song Peter had written for Amy came on the radio.

I sat there, speechless. Even though Amy had shared Peter's music from the demo he'd cut in Chicago, there was something different about it hearing it on the radio. It didn't sound any better. If anything, the recording my sister had played over and over again sounded much better than what came over the air through my little radio.

As I listened, I realized. *Wow, I know this guy!*

I looked at Amy, who was crying her eyes out, delirious with happiness. At that moment, I realized that Peter Shaw was not a pipe dream anymore. My sister's prophecy had proven correct, and I was witness to the beginnings of a dream come true.

The city of McKinney is a suburb just north of the Dallas/Fort Worth area. It's not a small community, but it still has a small-town feel. It is big enough that a person can enjoy anonymity if they choose to. That was not the case for Peter. In the months that followed his popularity soared. His three new releases hit the high end of the charts. All of a sudden, he became someone everyone wanted to know. At school, every guy wanted to be him, and every girl wanted to date him. The sad part about fame is it changes your popularity—but not what you are. In Peter's case, the newfound attention made life a living hell. Although everyone's interest in Peter was for the most part genuine. There were always the hangers-on just looking to ride the train of fame anyway they could. I had not been forbidden to speak to Peter, but his sudden popularity soon made him less and less visible. I was in junior high school and he was in high school which meant our paths seldom crossed before his newfound fame. It didn't matter. Because. Everyone knew something about Peter Shaw.

It wasn't long before he quit coming to school and disappeared. A rumor began to circulate that he had left for LA and was working on new material for an up-and-coming concert tour. Winter came. Amy and I talked about Peter every day. Neither of us had cell phones with Internet capability and with Fred and Gina hovering about. We didn't dare go surfing the web at home. Aside from knowing he had a CD coming out. Thanks to a friend who saw it on his website. We had no clue what Peter was doing—so we guessed. I'm sure his everyday life was more ordinary that we imagined. But we had a lot of fun speculating about his extravagant life hobnobbing with other famous people. Every discussion concluded with Amy wondering how he was coping.

Then one day, I had an epiphany at school. I got so excited about it. I could hardly contain myself. As soon as Fred dropped me off at home. I ran upstairs and burst into Amy's room. She looked up from her homework and frowned, not very pleased that I just barged in.

So I thought, *Okay, fine, I'll just sit down and contain myself,* which was hard because I was bursting at the seams to talk.

After what seemed like forever, she put down her pencil and looked up with a mixture of irritation and idle curiosity.

"Okay, twerp, what gives?"

"Twerp? Is that any way to talk to your favorite sister and best friend in the whole entire world?"

"Spare me the dramatics, Kelly; I've got a lot of homework to do."

"Okay… here goes. It came to me during English class. I have a solution that you are going to love."

I waited for her to say, *Oh cool Kelly,* but of course, nothing came out. Amy's sense of humor had become limited at best since Mom dropped the bomb last fall.

"We both know that you're not allowed any contact with Peter, right?"

"Yes. Did you just come in here to make me feel even more miserable than I already do?"

"Crud, Amy, quit wallowing in self-pity! I have a great idea." My response came across as harsh, but I felt annoyed with her negativity.

"Could you just tell me, without the theatrics?"

"Okay, sure, I have two words for you: Big Tony."

A definite frown creased my sister's face, and I felt sure she had no idea what I was getting at.

"Look Amy… you can't have contact with Peter, but Mom never said anything about having contact with Big Tony."

She put a finger over her lips to silence me and took a couple of quick steps to her door, which I had left ajar. She looked up and down the hall to make sure Gina wasn't around, closed the door and sat back down.

"I have been in touch with Big Tony since the inception of Mom's lockdown." Amy whispered the words so softly I had to lean in closer and concentrate to hear her. "I figured that out the first week after the bomb, while I was at home sulking. The first chance I had to use a public telephone. I called Big Tony. Of course he already knew the score. We agreed that it was in Peter's best interest to follow Abigail's rules. Since our home Internet history is being monitored. I created an anonymous email address and use a friend's computer from time to time to stay in touch."

I couldn't believe my ears. "Our Internet history is being monitored?"

"Yep, it's sad but true."

"How did you find out?" I asked.

"Actually, Fred told me. I thought it was an accident at first; now I'm sure he told me on purpose. On the way to school one day, he just made the comment that all activity on the Internet was monitored."

"That's it, no embellishment?"

"Nope, we were at a stop light at the time, and he turned around and winked when he said it, so I knew it was a warning."

"So you and Fred are friends now? I asked.

"Fred is just doing a job he was hired to do. When I realized that... and that he really doesn't like Abigail any more than I do. I decided he was okay."

Fred and I had not hit it off because. I had a crush on him. I felt awkward and self-conscious every time I was around him. He had dark hair; dark brown eyes, and seemed like a skyscraper towering over me at six feet two inches. Feeling safe was not an issue with him around but every time I tried to talk to him. I got tongue-tied. "I feel kind of stupid not realizing our Internet activity was being monitored. Shoot... I thought I had come up with this brilliant idea, only to find out that you're four months ahead of me."

Amy smiled like I hadn't seen in a long time. She pulled me closer and gave me a big hug.

"Sorry I didn't tell you, sis. I figured that the fewer people who knew. The less chance the warden would find out."

I pantomimed zipping my mouth shut and locking it with a key. "Your secret is safe with me. I'll not tell a soul. Now spill the beans. What's happened with Peter? Everyone I know says he just disappeared, and his website just says there's a CD coming soon. What's happening?"

I suppose I came across as overly excited about knowing the real scoop on Peter, but my persistence was rewarded. So for the next hour, Amy filled me in on where Peter was and what he was up to. Then she made me swear, cross my heart, and hope to die if I uttered a word to anyone.

Chapter 7
Peter

My life became a sudden whirlwind of popularity. Schoolmates who used to walk out of their way to avoid me, now wanted to be friends. My cell phone rang so much; I had to get a new private number. Day-to-day life became miserable, and I found myself wishing things could go back to the way they had been. I knew life would never be the same again and the difference was fueled by the way people viewed me. Most of my newfound attention came from people who wanted to brag that they were friends with a celebrity, so I had no trouble distinguishing the rabble from the sincere. When the conversation started out with "How much money are you going to make?" or "What other rock-and-roll stars have you met?" It weeded out the hangers-on and the gold diggers. I still felt just as awkward around people, and without Amy to run interference, it didn't take long for me to back away. The few real friends I had, seemed as uncomfortable with me as I was with my newfound fame, as a result, they didn't know what to talk about either. It's ironic to be living a dream many can only hope for while wishing you could just be a normal teenager. I suppose we all want what we don't have. My mom says it's just human nature to want. For me, the simple teenage life I craved would never be in my future, because I didn't fit the mold.

Via email and telephone, Big Tony soon became the big brother I had always wanted. His advice on handling my new celebrity status helped me through most of the dark moods. He had several long conversations with my parents about school and possible options to make life more tolerable. Since

I had plenty of credits, my folks agreed to let me graduate early.

About three months after Amy and I had gone to Chicago, Big Tony called, bursting with some very exciting news. He sounded more excited about it than I was. The next day, Dad and I picked him up at DFW Airport in Dad's new Hyundai Sonata. Big Tony wanted to go to a place called III Forks in Dallas. He said there was one in Chicago and that he wanted to see if the restaurant in Dallas was as good. He said it would be his treat, so we agreed. It was the first time I had ever eaten at a place where you had more than one waiter. Every time I used a pat of butter, they would bring another. No one knew me, so it had nothing to do with my blossoming career. The service came to anyone who could afford it, and everyone got treated like royalty. It bummed me out that Amy couldn't be there to share the moment.

I had no idea they made them so big, but Tony was dressed in a fitted black suit with a colorful, hand-painted silk tie with a caricature of a busty blonde girl singing into a microphone. He saw me looking at it and noticed that I was somewhat embarrassed. His resulting Jabba the Hut laughter was infectious. I noticed to my surprise that several customers seated close to us were also affected by his laugh and were smiling with no clue as to why. Big Tony directed the conversation to the business end of our meeting. His only luggage was an old leather satchel that he brought into the restaurant with him. After rummaging through the contents for what seemed to me a long time, he retrieved a brown manila envelope. He pitched it in front of me without a word. I looked at it, then at him, then my father.

"What is it?" I asked.

"Well open it and find out," Tony said, maintaining his nonchalance.

I knew it had to be something special since Tony had decided to make a special trip from Chicago just to give it to me in person. I looked at Dad again, and he mumbled something to the effect that he had no idea about the contents of the envelope either. Tony postured himself into a noble pose and clammed up, his eyes sparkling with anticipation. I opened the folder carefully and at first felt disappointed that the only thing inside was paper. I pulled the pile out, laid it on the table, and then noticed the fifty-thousand dollar check from Chicago Records stapled onto the top page. Either my mouth dropped open or I had a dumb look on my face, because Tony started laughing again. I had never seen a check that big before.

"They are paying me fifty thousand dollars for two songs?" I asked.

"The check is just a bonus for signing the enclosed contract. I'll go over the details with you and your dad after lunch. In a nutshell, I hammered out a very nice deal for you. I'm sure you know that both songs have already hit the top twenty-five. The recording company and I believe they will be in the top ten in a matter of a few weeks." He paused for a moment, took a drink of water, and continued. "Peter, if you can manage to record a CD within the next year, their estimates project your earnings could be in the millions within two years."

A loud crash, followed by the tinkling of glass across the tile floor, interrupted Tony's news in perfect timing. Dad had knocked an empty wine glass off the table.

True to his reputation as a man of few words, my father asked, "Millions ... of dollars?"

Our three waiters cleaned up the mess seconds later, and the distraction left me wondering who would pay for the crystal wine glass.

"Yes, Mr. Shaw, millions of dollars, minus my 15 percent if you decide to keep me on as Peter's manager."

The head waiter showed up about that time and asked if we were ready to order. We hadn't even looked at the menu.

"You guys like steak?" Tony asked.

Dad and I both nodded yes.

Tony looked up at the waiter. "We would like three rib-eyes, medium rare, salads, baked potatoes with all the trimmings, and a bottle of the 1998 Château Margaux, if you have it."

The waiter's eyes widened at the inclusion of the wine Tony mentioned.

"Yes, sir, an exceptional choice," the waiter said.

I had no clue that the wine cost several times more than the meal itself.

Except for the first night in Tony's recording studio, I had never seen Tony eat. He ate his entire meal plus half of my steak and dessert, and he drank most of the wine. Dad gave the wine a try but didn't really care for it and ended up ordering a beer instead. I couldn't have either since I had just turned seventeen.

After lunch, Tony scooted his chair as close as he could get to Dad, and for the next forty-five minutes, he went through the contract with Dad and explained it to him in detail. I tried to pay attention, but in all honesty, I just didn't feel very interested. I sat there daydreaming about Amy, wondering what she was doing. Even though Dad was a blue-collar worker, he had a talent for numbers and contracts.

In the end, he looked at me and said, "The short version of this contract requires that you use their recording studio for five years. Any music you write during that time is yours, but they have the exclusive right to distribute it for that period of time. Tony says your share of the royalties is a generous offer, and according to my research on the subject, he's correct. I think Tony is a good and decent man and will make you a fine manager. The big question I have is simple: is this what you really want?"

My father, as was normal for him, rattled off an entire paragraph of things that might be important to me. It took me a second to catch up to his question.

"Dad, the most important things in my life, is my family, Amy, and music."

I guess it wasn't the answer he had expected, and although I had never seen my dad cry, his eyes got a little misty.

After a noticeable pause, Dad said, "I guess that means we're in the music business, Tony."

Dad offered his hand, and they shook on it. Then we signed the contract, got a duplicate, and walked outside.

We got in the car and started off to DFW Airport. Tony seemed unusually quiet, which I already knew was an uncommon characteristic for him. He finally cleared his throat, breaking the long stretch of silence.

"It's none of my business, but it is part of my job description to point out potential problems," Tony said. "As I told you awhile back, Abigail Stevens called me and pointed out that she had placed a restraining order on you. I know you are aware of the fact that you need to stay away from Amy."

I turned in my seat so I could see Tony's face. I could tell he was uncomfortable with the subject. I knew this issue would come up; I was just wondering when.

"I understand, Tony, and I won't try to see her until she's eighteen. When that day comes, I plan to marry her."

I surprised myself by divulging that bit of information, because I had not mentioned it to anyone except Amy. I stopped and looked at Dad, wondering if the marriage announcement would produce a reaction, but if it did, he was not sharing his thoughts at the moment.

"Well, I'm glad to hear that you will stay away until then, but how do you know you want to marry her?" Tony asked. "You're young, Peter, and a lot can happen in a year."

I knew he didn't understand. Neither did my father. I just knew that Amy and I would have a lifelong connection. I knew it would be taken as adolescent love and corny, but I said it anyway: "I love her and she loves me, and as soon as she is eighteen, I will marry her, if she'll still have me. Since we are on the subject of Amy, I want all the royalties for the song that Amy wrote to go into an account for her, one that her mom can't access."

"You mean like a trust?" Tony asked.

"I suppose so. I just want her to get the money without Abigail's tentacles getting a grip on it."

Tony mulled the problem over for a moment, and then said, "I have a friend who is an attorney in the business. I would suggest you consider hiring him, unless you have someone else in mind."

"I've never needed an attorney before. If you think he's a good fit, let's hire him," I said.

At that moment, I realized I had made the first of many decisions concerning my future.

"Consider it done," Tony said. "He's a good guy; you'll like him. I have a feeling he's going to tell you to wait until Amy's eighteen and give the rights to her then. It will be much less complicated since she wouldn't have access to the money until she's of age anyway. Does Abigail know Amy wrote the lyrics to one of your songs?"

"No one knows except Amy and me … and now you and Dad."

"Good. At least for the time being, I suggest we keep it that way." Tony paused. I suppose, to consider what advice to give next. "Life is going to change for you in a big way over the next few months. Everyone you know, and even those you don't, will want to be your best friend. Some will ask you for money, endorsements, and friendship. And don't be surprised when your popularity with the girls goes crazy. It's one of the side effects of being a mainstream recording artist. Temptation is going to come at you from every direction. I know you are a good guy, but it can be somewhat overwhelming."

"I've already been getting a taste of that, but I can see through it," I said, confident that none of those things would affect me.

Tony smiled and shook his head in resignation, then said, "Just know I'm there for you."

"Thanks, Tony, and I get what you mean about temptations."

We turned into DFW Airport and pulled up to the curb at the drop-off for Tony. I got out of the car to say good-bye, and he gave me a big hug that nearly crushed my ribs.

"One last thing, Peter, you need to give some thought to band members. I can help you with that as well if you want me to."

I felt dumbfounded at the comment. "I thought the guys that cut the two songs with me at your studio would be in the band."

"Those guys would have loved to meet you ten years ago, but most of them have kids your age. Working on the road, doing concerts two or three times a week … It's time consuming and physically draining. You will be better served to find some guys a little younger. Besides, I know for a fact Jimmy's wife would divorce him if he even suggested going on tour." He stopped in mid-stream, peered down at me with a peculiar look, and continued. "Don't look so forlorn. We'll find you a good group of guys to work with."

He slapped me on the back with a thud that shook me all the way down to my feet. It was a display of affection, but Tony was like a playful bear who didn't realize his strength.

"I don't make friends easy, Tony. I liked those guys; they made me feel comfortable."

"Not to worry, Peter. Most musicians have idiosyncrasies; we'll find the right fit. Well, I had better get going. You should plan on coming back to Chicago in January. With any luck, I'll have some auditions for you to look at."

"You're going to have auditions for *me* to look at?" I asked.

Tony chuckled. "You're the star, Peter. Don't let it go to your head, but this is your show. See you in a few weeks."

He turned and disappeared into the terminal, and I just stood there with my mouth gaping open for the second time that day. The wait until January went by so slow that I didn't think it would ever come. Since any thoughts of being a normal teenager did not look hopeful, I got together with my high-school counselor and made arrangements to finish school early. I could have tested out a year sooner, but at the time, I was still living the dream of wanting to be a normal kid. I suppose since I had not been challenged at school for a very long time, it was best to move on.

/////

Chicago is cold in January. I saw snow everywhere when I landed at O'Hare Airport. I met Tony at the baggage claim, and he escorted me out to curbside where a black stretch limo was parked. I looked around and didn't see another car, but before I could ask, the limo driver jumped out, opened the rear door, and took my bag.

"Welcome to Chicago, Mr. Shaw," the driver said, as though he had known me for years.

"Thanks," I mumbled back.

When I turned my attention to Tony, he was grinning from ear to ear and motioned for me to get in. The interior was black leather and very plush, with a shaded glass between the driver and the rear of the car. Up against the driver side was a seat facing toward us with what looked like a bar in the corner.

"You could have picked me up in a regular car," I said. "This limo must have cost a fortune."

"Didn't cost you or me a dime, its compliments of Chicago Records," Tony said. Then his demeanor changed and he became serious. "We are going to their main office to meet with the president of the company. It's mostly a formality but no surprise that they want to see firsthand what they are getting. We will look over and sign the final copies of the contract, have some lunch somewhere, and chat about the direction of your career."

"Didn't we sign the contract two weeks ago?" I asked.

"Yes, we did, but those papers were to just get the ball rolling and to have your dad give me power of attorney so I could sign additional contracts on his behalf. It's basically a done deal, but we still have to do the meet-and-greet. No worries, just be yourself and answer their questions to the best of your ability."

Chicago Records occupied the top three floors of a new downtown skyscraper. Our destination was the uppermost level—the executive and financial section. The reception area looked amazing. I didn't really notice the fancy furniture or the fact that everyone there wore formal business attire. I did notice, though, that the walls featured countless photos of contemporary artists that spanned fifty years of music. The royal treatment felt unnatural, and I knew it would take me a long time to become accustomed to it. Even so, all the attention didn't suck. A beautiful young black girl named Michelle greeted us.

"Is there anything I might get you while you wait?" She said with a gaze that made me feel somewhat uncomfortable.

Her deferential smile stirred a tingle in my face. Blushing beet red, a feeling of social intimidation ensued. It made me stumble over my reply: "No … thank you."

I looked at Tony, who apparently noticed my discomfort. He gave me a wink along with one of his affectionate pats on the back that always moves me off my feet. For some reason, his mannerisms made me feel better. I figured we would have to wait for a long time to see Mr. Jennings—the president of the company—but again got a surprise when Michelle shuffled us into his office without delay.

The president and CEO of Chicago Records stood by his desk, looking out the window at the Chicago skyline as we entered. He turned to greet us with an infectious smile that gave me an irresistible urge to reciprocate. Jennings looked to be a lean, average-sized guy who was well dressed and who emanated an air of professional confidence—the kind of guy I imagined I would like to be someday. What surprised me was how much younger he looked than I expected. I had anticipated an older man in his fifties, but he was barely thirty, if that. He walked over and offered a handshake.

"Good morning," he said cordially. "I'm James Jennings. You must be Peter Shaw. I am really happy to meet you and get acquainted."

"It's nice to meet you too, Mr. Jennings," I said, hoping to not sound like a twit.

"Please call me Jim." His attention turned to Tony. He gave the big man a hug, held him at arm's length while giving him a once over. "Tony, it's good to see you again. Is that a new suit? I didn't know they made Armani's that big."

"For the right price, they will custom-make anything. And you're still too skinny. Your mother tells me you need to eat more, and I agree. Women like a portly man, more to love."

They both laughed, and it was obvious that they had known each other for a long time. Then Jim's attention turned back to me, and his manner became serious and all business. I felt uncomfortable and squirmed around the confines of my mind in anticipation.

"Gentlemen, please sit down."

We sat, and he casually leaned on the front of his desk. The informal gesture helped me relax a little.

"Well, Peter ... I'm guessing you don't know much about me or Chicago Records except for what Big Tony has told you." He paused and smiled at Tony, then continued. "I am thirty years old and have been with the company for eight years, right out of college. My father is the major stockholder and was CEO of the company. He retired last year and gave me the opportunity to take the company into the next generation of music. I use the word 'opportunity' because that is all he has ever given me. Dad always thought position and respect are earned. To be honest, when I was younger, I thought that was a bunch of crap, but I am learning the old man is right. It's a rare occasion for something of value to come without a price. I think you'll agree with me that it's not a bad thing to have an opportunity. That's what Chicago Records is giving you: an opportunity to do something great." He looked out the window, smiled, and then continued. "There are a lot of people that come through these doors hoping for fame and fortune. About 1 percent of the top 10 percent actually find it. The difference is talent, timing, and a little bit of luck. Do you have any specific questions on your mind?"

"No, not really … I don't know enough to know what to ask," I said.

That got a room full of chuckles, and I relaxed a little more. I was smart enough to understand the meaning of "opportunity" and made a mental note to never take it for granted. Mr. Jennings slid into the business side for a while and pretty much lost me. It wasn't because I didn't understand the essence of percentages and what the company expected of me. It just didn't interest me much. I suppose I had what my dad always called a deer-in-the-headlights look, and pretty soon, he stopped and once again asked me if I had any questions.

"No," I said politely.

"In that case, why don't we finish up with some lunch and I can turn you guys loose to look over some band members."

"I was wondering when we were going to get around to some lunch," Tony said. "I'm withering away."

That was funny. I figured Tony could probably live without eating for at least a month or two. I had never had an interest in fancy food but had resigned myself to the certainty that we would have lunch at some French bistro. I received a pleasant surprise when the limo pulled up in front of an authentic Chicago pizzeria. The pizza tasted really good, and most of our conversation centered on getting acquainted with Jim. After dinner, we went back to Chicago Records for the official contract signing. I saw a couple of new faces when we returned to Mr. Jennings's office. The company's attorney was a middle-aged guy who was completely bald and seemed to be sort of stuffy. He didn't smile much, and when he did, it didn't seem genuine. The other guy looked like he was in his early thirties, with black curly hair, and he had the greenest eyes I've ever seen. When he looked at me, it was as if he could see through me and into my soul. It was an eerie feeling, but he beamed a genuine and disarming smile my way. He reached out to shake my hand.

"Hi, Peter," he said. "I'm John Bell, and until you tell me different, I'm your attorney. I have looked over the contracts, and they look good. I took the liberty to change the wording in a couple of places so there are no misunderstandings. Also, per instructions from Tony, I have set up the trust for your friend Amy. All monies earned from that recording and any future royalties concerning the tune and lyrics are hers when she turns eighteen. Are you going to be her beneficiary?"

The question took me by surprise. I've never given any thought to the idea of Amy dying before me. For some reason though, and I am not certain why, my response came immediately.

"Please make her sister Kelly, the … uh … beneficiary."

The word felt thick on my tongue and felt odd to say. It was a most peculiar experience.

"Spelled K-e-l-l-y … and same last name as Amy's?"

"Yes, sir," I said.

He made a note on his legal pad, and then looked up with a smile. "Peter this may seem weird to you, but from here on out, I get to call you 'sir' and you can call me 'John,' if that's what you would like?"

Although I didn't know much about attorneys, I had a pretty good perception when it came to people and I felt sure I would like John Bell.

"I would feel really odd if you call me 'sir.' So, John, Peter will be fine."

I didn't think what I said was all that funny, but it got a big laugh out of everyone. Even the old bald guy chuckled. John rode the limo with Tony and me back to Tony's studio so we could talk in private. He told me exactly what Tony had suggested, that I needed to steer clear of Amy until she turned eighteen. He didn't make it too much like a lecture, but he seemed very concerned that I not get into a legal quarrel with Abigail Stevens.

"Ms. Stevens is a Tyrannosaurus in court. She is very good at making sure everyone involved gets eaten alive," he said.

I noticed he didn't smile when he said it, so I knew he was dead serious. Once we got to Tony's place, we said our good-byes to John, who insisted he had lots of work waiting for him at his office. It was good to finally have a break with just Tony and me, or at least that's what I thought. We had not even gotten to the door to the studio before we could hear what sounded like a party coming from inside. Tony swung the door open, and I followed him in, hidden behind his bulk.

"What the heck is going on in here?" he bellowed.

I had noticed that when Big Tony speaks, everyone stops, shuts up, and listens. This time proved to be no exception. I peered around the big man enough to see that the tiny reception room was packed full—and now quiet as a church. Every eye went past Tony's enormous presence and somehow zeroed in on me. I began to feel uncomfortable from the attention and realized that the room was full of musicians waiting to see me and not Tony. Without missing a beat, Tony made a path through the chaos and ushered me into his adjoining office and shut the door behind us. He went to his cluttered desk and somehow found the phone under a pile of papers and punched the intercom.

"Joelle, would you come in here please?" he asked politely.

A young pretty blonde came in from the reception room. I didn't even see her because of the crush of people. Joelle looked to be in her mid-twenties, with long, straight blonde hair. Her figure bulged in a sweater that in my mind looked at least two sizes too small, but I decided it wasn't a bad thing. A wave of embarrassment washed over me when she caught me looking a bit too long, and I could feel the flush heat up my face. She smiled, enjoying my embarrassment, and turned her attention to Tony. I felt relieved when she turned away. It was the first time I could remember noticing another girl in that way since Amy and I had started dating.

"Joelle, why are all of these people here?" Tony asked. "The interviews are not supposed to begin for another hour."

"They started showing up right after I got here. Some of them have appointments, but a lot of them just showed up. I didn't know what to do," Joelle said. It was easy to tell from her tone she was a bit flustered.

Tony chuckled and sat down. His black leather chair disappeared underneath him.

"It's okay. I guess we should have expected this turnout. It's the most exciting thing that's happened in music for at least a decade." He looked past Joelle to me. "See what you've started?"

I started to mumble an unwanted and unnecessary apology, but Tony interrupted me before I had a chance to speak: "I'm just kidding, Peter!"

As usual, I struggled with the sarcasm, but I did understand the gist of his humor.

Tony redirected his attention to Joelle and the problem in the reception room. After giving it some serious thought, he gave her instructions as to how to deal with it: "Okay, here's what I want you to do. Ascertain who has appointments and who does not. Ask the ones who don't have an appointment to schedule one, and in the meantime, they are to email us their resumes."

"Okay, boss," Joelle said.

She bounced out of the room and seemed happy to do Tony's bidding. Tony watched her with an odd sort of smile until she disappeared out of the room and the door closed behind her. He glanced up and realized that I had busted him ogling his receptionist. He straightened up stiffly and cleared his throat.

"Joelle's a good employee, but I have to tell her how to do everything," he said.

"Does she know how much you like her?" I asked before realizing the answer was none of my business.

Big Tony squirmed in the confines of his overburdened chair before answering me. "What... Joelle and me? She's smaller than my leg."

Even though I might have just been a kid, I could see the pain of what he thought was his own shortcomings in his eyes.

"Don't sell yourself short," I said. "You're a great guy."

He gave me a curious look. "How did you get to be so smart in the ways of love?"

I pondered his question, because in reality, I didn't really know anything about love. I knew that I loved Amy, but I couldn't evade the fact that it was my only experience in such matters. On the other hand, I was really good at observation. I noticed the things people do and their mannerisms, even though they didn't realize it themselves. Since I know I'm different than most people. I've spent most of my life watching people hoping to get some inkling as to how others act.

At any rate, my answer was simple: "I don't know much about love, but you seem to like her a lot."

Tony shook his head and smiled. "Suppose I do like her. I'm as big as a city bus. She, on the other hand, is petite and very pretty. There is no way she would ever be interested in me except for a paycheck. Besides, it would be inappropriate since she works for me," he said, his smile fading to a frown.

"Fire her," I said.

The wrinkled furrow on his brow moved back in the direction of the jovial qualities I had come to enjoy about Tony. He began to laugh, and as was often the case, I couldn't help but laugh with him.

"Perhaps I will do just that, Peter."

I got the impression that the subject was closing and that we needed to start interviewing for potential band members.

"How many interviews do we have this afternoon?" I asked.

Tony seemed grateful to have the focus back on the business at hand and shuffled through a stack of papers on his desk. "We have eleven auditions total, ten guys and one girl: three lead guitarists, three rhythm guitarists, two bass players, and three drummers. All of them are pros and have played in some really good bands—except the girl, and it's against my better judgment … but she is really good."

His remark made me curious. "What's wrong with the girl?" I asked, having no clue what he meant.

Tony leaned forward in his chair, then he put his elbows on his desk, folding his hands together, and plopped his bearded face into the newly made cradle. "There are two reasons. Number one, a girl in a band can be problematic on occasion. The other reason being she's Jimmy's daughter and my niece."

"How could a girl be a problem for a band?" I asked.

Tony sat up abruptly and chuckled. "Peter, you just went from being an intuitive young man to a dumb ass in less than sixty seconds. When you're on the road, you are going to spend a lot of time together. What if one of the band members takes a liking to Joni? Then they get mad at each other. Heck, it's hard enough to have no conflicts with four or five guys. A girl in the mix can be asking for trouble."

"Then why didn't you just tell her no way?" I asked.

"Joni is really hard to say no to, and like I said, she is really good. You could make it easy on me and just tell me to tell her no."

To me, I had nothing to think about. In my mind, I couldn't think of a good reason not to give her a chance, and besides, I really liked her dad Jimmy.

"Unless Jimmy tells us different, I say we give her a chance."

"I figured you would say that," Tony said. He shook his head with a sense of abject resolution. "Okay, you're the boss. All I am is a facilitator and your advisor."

"So when do we get started?" I asked.

Tony took a quick glance at his watch. "Actually, it's time for the first one right now. We might as well head to the studio." He picked up the phone and rang Joelle in the reception room. "Hey, sweet pea … I guess we're ready. Send contestant number one to the studio," he said and hung up.

"Did you say 'sweet pea'?" I asked.

"Don't start with me, Peter Shaw," he said in mock anger.

Regardless of what anyone might think, picking out good band members from a line of professionals is not an easy task. One of the hardest things is to ascertain whether they will be fairly easy to get along with. Down-to-earth qualities like being personable and easygoing are not common denominators in the world of musicians. I learned a lot over the next two days and realized in short order that getting along with the large egos would be a lot harder than making casual friends in high school. The saving grace for me was that, since it would be my band, I got to pick and choose. It didn't really make the choosing any easier, but in the end, if anything turned out to be a mistake, it would be my fault and no one else's.

An unexpected and refreshing surprise was Joni. Although I could tell that Tony did not seem real excited at the prospect, I really liked her. She was quite pretty and smart, but I liked her easygoing demeanor the most. Being young and naïve is a wonderful way to be in many regards, and deep down. Even so, I knew having a girl in the band might be trouble. After a lot of deliberation and a ton of advice from Tony, I picked a young lead guitarist named Johnny McManus. He was only two years older than me and could keep up with just about anything I threw at him. I suppose I identified with him because he seemed kind of shy like me. He had long blond hair that he wore tied back in a ponytail, along with blue jeans with more holes than denim, and a vintage ZZ Top T-shirt. Johnny looked like a throwback from the seventies, but he came across as a cool character and I liked him right off.

The rhythm and bass players came as a pair. They were fraternal twin brothers, Barry and Josh Thomas. Barry, the rhythm guitarist, kept his head shaved and sported a bright red goatee. He wore baggy khaki shorts along with a Hawaiian shirt. I learned later he wore the same thing whether it was summer or winter. He had an uncanny ability to follow a diverse range of music that I was quickly getting a reputation for playing. Josh played a modern five-string bass with extraordinary emotion and style. He had thick red hair about shoulder length, and was clean shaven. Much thinner than his brother, Josh dressed sort of preppy-like. I had no doubt in my mind that he was the best dressed of us all. The brothers looked and acted as different as night and day. However, when they played together, it was like they were Siamese virtuosos with imaginary attachments at the hip. They acted like true brothers in that they fought and tormented each other on a constant basis, but I could see that they always had each other's back.

Joni, for lack of a better word, ended up being an animal on the drums, and she didn't mind sweating to prove it. She wore her hair short, coal black, and she had on the tightest leather pants I have ever seen, it was hard to imagine how she managed to get into them. I found her to be professional, and really nice, but there was something about her that I couldn't put my finger on. In the end, even Tony agreed she was the best drummer that we interviewed, and she seemed to fit in like one of the guys. I didn't realize why until a few weeks later.

We made arrangements for the group to start practicing in one week. My parents and I had already talked about the direction of my newfound profession. They were okay with it even though I was still seventeen. McKinney High School approved my early graduation. I'm not sure if they did it for me or to quell the disruption I would have created staying in school. I had enough credits to graduate when I started my junior year, so it was more of a formality than anything. It helped that my school counselor liked me and pushed it through. Since I made straight A's throughout my entire school career, he didn't have too much trouble getting it done. The chain of events following that one day in the recording studio changed my life forever. Any thoughts of leading a quiet normal life were quickly disappearing.

As soon as I got home, I started packing. I hadn't folded more than two shirts before Mom came into my room and started crying about her baby leaving the nest. I knew deep down she felt proud of me, but nobody likes to see their moms get emotional. I'm pretty sure it's just what moms do, but it made me cry too. Dad came in a few minutes later and managed to find plenty of reasons why we should be celebrating instead of moping around. He could always find good in any situation, and pretty soon, he was teasing mom about when would she be moving to Chicago. He got a good laugh out of us on that one, since we all thought my stay in Chicago would be temporary. As soon as the band rehearsed and jelled and finished cutting a CD. We would be hitting the road for a long list of concert appearances.

My dad loved to describe my mom as pleasantly plump, and I'm not sure just how much Mom appreciated the term. Still, I learned one important thing from my mom and dad about family and relationships: they showed me every day what loving and respecting someone looked like.

Chapter 8
Amy

The dreariness of winter came to a close, and the new life of spring began to emerge from its slumber. Even so, I just couldn't seem to get out of the funk that had consumed me for the past several months. Being a senior in high school should be one momentous occasion after another. For many, it's the beginning of acceptance into adulthood and grown-up responsibilities. It's the last year of high school and time to prepare for college, work, or both. Not to mention the first telltale signs of independence, with the control of one's life sliding from the parent to the young adult. But, for me, I just wanted it to be over. I didn't socialize with anyone and spent most of my free time holed up in my room. Most of my friends were inundated with their boyfriends and what they would wear to the prom. For me, the whole affair had no meaning, nor did I have any interest. I refused several offers to go. I knew I would spend the whole time thinking about Peter, which would ruin my suitor's time as well as my own. I felt like that wouldn't be fair to them or me. Several months passed with no real communication with my mother. Sometimes I had to speak to answer a direct question, but I never allowed a conversation to ensue. It bugged Abigail to no end, but for the most part she let it be. We had one really tense moment during Christmas when I would not open the presents she bought me. She managed to remain nonchalant and donated them to Goodwill a few weeks later. Kelly wanted to support my rebellion by refusing her Christmas as well, but in the end, I could tell her heart was just not in it. I'm sure she felt relieved when I explained that it was my battle and that her suffrage would not help my case. Still… I don't think my defiance accomplished anything anyway. My mother managed to stay cool as a cucumber, and if I was getting to her, she never let it show. Mom's indifference coupled with my refusal to speak—drove the proverbial wedge deeper between us. Somewhere along the way, I began to wonder if she knew or if she even cared. So with graduation just around the corner, I started counting the days until I turned eighteen.

/////

I managed to get a part-time job assisting the high-school principal. Her name was Mary Rhodes. She reminded me of Mom—except that Mary was nice. She played the role of a dictator and enforcer quite well and had the uncanny ability to show up when it was least expected. Probing the halls for students roaming around without permission got her nicknamed the "Terminator." She was around sixty years old, and her two boys were grown with children of their own. On the occasions that we spent time alone, she was a virtual chatterbox, talking about her kids and grandkids. As time passed, we became quite good friends. One of my duties involved certain computer responsibilities that Mrs. Rhodes loathed. Due to the fact, she was computer illiterate. That's not my opinion; she admitted it in private. She explained that when she grew up. Only the government had computers, so she had never embraced the technology. Since retirement was close at hand, she had no intention of learning anything more involved than sending and receiving emails. So it became my responsibility to do the administrative drudgery. It came easy to me and more often than not took half the time that had been allotted. I found it interesting that an educator would not want to learn something new. Nevertheless, it gave me access to a remote Internet connection that my mother couldn't bug, so I didn't complain. I used the anonymous email account I had set up months earlier. Contact had been sketchy at best using friend's computers from time to time, but now. I stayed in touch with Peter on a daily basis.

Since I couldn't be there with him, Peter managed to send me pictures of the band as they hammered out their new CD. I felt connected once again and even got to know all of the band members. The only one I didn't like was Joni, and it was not from the lack of trying. She just remained somewhat aloof and never had anything to say, which I found to be odd because Peter said she was great and like one of the guys. As much as I hate to say it, somewhere along the way, I started to feel a little jealous of her. I never mentioned it, because I trusted Peter. But the nagging fact that she was there and I couldn't be… ate at me.

In just ninety days, they managed to record their first CD but couldn't agree on a name for the group. Peter's budding success had brought the band together in the first place, and he could have paid the members' salaries, but he chose to share—against Big Tony's advice. He wanted to give them an equal split, but Tony managed to convince Peter to see the good sense in having 51 percent, which gave him controlling interest and with that—the final say-so. So when the band members had arguments among themselves, it gave him the right to make final decisions, and to hire and fire band members if necessary. Peter didn't want a duty like that, nor did he relish the thought of having to be in charge. Tony's advice, though, turned out to be golden. The group's first major disagreement stemmed from naming their band. They had struggled through the long hours of rehearsing, and Peter worked double time composing music, without as much as a whimper. When it came to what they would be called, they argued and they argued. I actually found it kind of funny until

I realized what a toll it was taking on Peter. He was never one to take conflict very well. With everything else going on, the name just didn't make any difference to him. The fact remained, though: it did matter to his band members, so he labored over a decision. One afternoon, Peter and I were exchanging ideas, and I came up with PB & J, which included the first letter of everyone's first name. He pitched the idea, and I was amazed that they all loved it, even Joni, whom I still disliked more and more every day. My opinion wasn't fair since I had not met her and really didn't know her. The thing that kept bugging me was that all of the guys sent me emails teasing me about one thing or another, but she didn't, not one word, and that made me think that she had Peter in her sights. I managed to keep my worries to myself and not burden Peter with what I hoped were nothing but petty jealousies.

By the end of April, the CD was in stores nationwide and I was not surprised that it immediately hit the top ten. A week later, they went on tour. Peter was bubbling with excitement—something I had never seen in him. His mild mannerisms and even-keeled behavior were evolving. I couldn't decide if he was changing or growing. Email is impersonal. The intent is hard to decipher, and telephone conversations were nonexistent. His dark mood swings seemed to be nonexistent these days, which was a good thing. What really sucked was not being there to share these monumental times with him. I tried to remain happy and upbeat since the last thing I wanted to do was rain on his wonderful new life. Even though I felt miserable and left out I never complained. Peter was listed to play in what seemed to be every major city in the US—except anywhere near Dallas. It didn't change the continual distance between us, but I was lonely and felt disconnected.

Almost as quick as his new popularity, the advances of big money started to roll in. Speculation of their first recording alone was being estimated at over twenty millions dollars in gross sales, and that projection was for the first three months. Peter told me Tony thought that with the concerts and CD sales, the first years gross could be over 200 million dollars. Peter's share of the pie was slated to be around twenty-five million, minus Tony's fifteen percent, which amounted to just under four million. Another shocking piece of trivia came when I learned that that Peter had given me the royalties to the song that I wrote the lyrics to. The trust that Peter's attorney set up for me already had over thirty-five thousand dollars in it—and my mother had no clue about it.

The last few weeks of my senior year dragged by, and it seemed to me that it would never be over. The only thing that kept my spirits up was my daily job assisting Mrs. Rhodes. I even finally came up with a solution for the senior prom. Volunteer to be a self-proclaimed wallflower and serve refreshments. It really didn't surprise me when Abigail instructed Fred to drive and supervise me at the event; it was the icing on the cake. It made me glad, though, that I decided to not go with anyone. I felt embarrassed enough to have a chaperone as a party of one. I could only imagine what some poor guy would have thought if I had accepted a date. Fred and I had become quite close by then, so when he offered to stop by a local ice cream store on the way home, I accepted. It ended up being the highlight of the evening.

Graduation proved almost as uneventful. Kelly and Gina came to share my big moment, with Fred driving and supervising. Mom was yet again on the road involved in some big case in Los Angeles. After the ceremonious passing of our diplomas and pictures with friends, we made our way home. It was ironic, yet noteworthy, that many of my friends' families thought that Fred and Gina were my parents. I have to admit that I found myself wishing that they were. After all, they spent more time with Kelly and me than our mother did. A week later, Mom showed up in a good mood, which struck me as peculiar. It put me on guard that something was afoot. I suppose in her own way, it served as an apology for not being around much. For me, it was too late and not the correct avenue for mending the bridge between us.

Abigail announced a family meeting shortly after her arrival. She gave no preamble, also uncommon.

As soon as Kelly and I sat down, Mom said. "I have some wonderful news. We're going to spend a month in Europe together."

After the shock wore off and the reality of spending an entire month with Abigail set in, I asked, "Do I have to go?"

Mom smiled. "Well, yes, you do. It's a family vacation."

The depression hit right away. I realized that just when you think things could never get any worse, they do.

Kelly was excited and jumped right on the Abigail bandwagon. "Europe... cool! I can't wait. What countries are we going to see?" she asked.

"As many as we can," Abigail said.

There had been a time, maybe four or five years past, that Mom, Kelly, and I had talked about taking a trip to Europe. The concept of just us girls sounded appealing then, but a lot of things had changed. It struck me as really weird that Mom was either clueless or thought this one gesture would make a difference. What made her think the trip would make up for never being around for the last five-plus years? Or did she think it would make the humble pie she had served me for the past nine months more palatable? It seemed shortsighted even for Abigail and was beyond my comprehension. She made all the plans without even asking if I wanted to go. Not that we talked much anyway. But as I saw it, most of my friends, who actually liked their mom and dad, would not want to go on a month-long trip with their parents either. The idea of running away from home came to mind, as it had on many occasions. But I didn't even have a chance to do that. The arrangements had been made, and before I knew it, I was on my way to Paris, the city of love, with my mom and sister.

Paris is a beautiful city. We saw tons of cool places. Although I love my little sister, the allure of being there was for a different kind of love. So I daydreamed about Peter. Even Kelly said I seemed obsessed and should try to enjoy the moment. In a way, I knew she spoke the truth. There is a saying that absence makes the heart grow fonder of those not there. If that is the case, the absence of Peter from my life was making me fixated on wanting to be with him. Even I knew it was not mentally healthy to spend so much of my time dwelling on one thing, especially one person, no matter how much love is shared between you. I knew that I was plummeting into a bottomless spiral. Downtrodden by my mother and the world around me, my very essence began to change. I became the proverbial runaway train, and it seemed the harder I tried, the more depressed I became. It seemed almost funny that the feelings and happiness my mother tried to instill, were destroying me one piece at a time. I just had no outlet.

The last few months of school had given me the opportunity to at least have minimal contact with Peter, which had kept me on track. That little bit of contact, even though just a tiny thread, kept me believing and trusting that I would soon have my life and freedom back.

Our trip was, in fact, amazing, and many people would think I was being unreasonable and childish. Regardless of what anyone thought, including Abigail, it didn't change how I felt. We saw France, Italy, Greece, Spain, Germany, England, Ireland, and finished off the trip in Scotland—my personal favorite. I have no idea why I liked it best, perhaps, because it was the last on the list.

Kelly knew all about my dark mood, and she served as the silver lining to my gilded cage. However, if Abigail realized anything other than her own ambitions, she did a great job of concealing it.

McKinney had not changed a bit during our absence and was still the quiet little town we had left a month earlier. One day after getting home, Abigail left for New York with no estimate of her return. That suited me just fine, and it was the happiest day I had seen since graduation night. The restriction of home life had not changed, but at least I could sneak an occasional email from one friend or another's computer. The thought of waiting until November and my eighteenth birthday to roll around seemed to be getting harder and harder. Two weeks later. Peter told me via email that the band had just added a short-notice date to play in Fort Worth. For the first time in nearly eight months, I felt happy. The beginnings of a plan began to form. No way would I let this opportunity pass me by. I knew it would be an overwhelming risk for Peter, but I ended up giddy with excitement when I told him my scheme and he gave his adamant approval.

The concert would take place on a Friday night—less than a week away. The only hitch—he'd be in town for just one night before heading to Houston for a Saturday-night performance. That gave us a one-night window. Peter managed to send a backstage pass and some cash to a mutual friend. The money would cover my cab fare, and he promised me a discreet limo ride home. That was the easy part of the equation. The hard part was figuring out how I could be gone all night without anyone being the wiser. In the end, my little sister Kelly came up with a most excellent idea.

/////

We lived in the historic section of town, and our backyard featured a couple of huge oak trees, with one of them having a large playhouse built into it. Our dad had built it when I was little and Kelly wasn't even a thought yet. I think he had his sights on having a son somewhere along the way, since it was more like a fort than a playhouse for girls. When I was younger, Kelly and I played in it and loved to spend the night. The way into our retreat and the sanctuary therein was a rope ladder that could be pulled up. As children, it gave us a false sense of security. We learned that lesson the hard way. One time when we refused to come down, Dad had to get his ladder out. At the time, the punishment seemed to be cruel and unusual, but looking back, I had to laugh about it. We were grounded from the playhouse for two weeks. Our little sanctuary was completely closed in with walls, windows, and a roof that didn't leak too badly. Dad somehow managed to include some rudimentary luxuries such as water, electricity, and, just for us girls, a toilet. That was really cool, and I still find myself awed by his resourcefulness. I remember him telling me how challenging it was to include the utilities. Of course, at the time, I had no idea what he meant. He managed to add the amenities and hide the plumbing with such expertise that unless you knew about it, you would never realize it.

Kelly's plan was simplistic and yet genius for all intents and purposes. She put on a stellar performance hounding me relentlessly in front of Gina and Fred. The hassling went on for the next several days, and in the end, as planned, I gave in to my sister's demands and agreed to a night in the playhouse with her. Friday afternoon, we hauled food and various supplies to the tree house, with me complaining the whole way. Since we had all the luxuries of home, Kelly even packed several DVDs so she would have movies to watch while I was gone. Gina and Fred were completely convinced. Fred even took me aside and told me how nice it was that I conceded to my sister's wishes. I felt bad for creating the deception since they were just my jailers and not the judge.

What to wear was of paramount importance. What really sucked was that I had it in my mind to wear a sexy dress. Who knows why, considering the fact I'd never had one on in my entire life. The idea of shinnying down the tree in a short skirt after dark didn't seem that appealing. In the end, though, a girl's got to do what a girl's got to do. I felt no shame in the fact that I plotted and schemed to make this a night that Peter would never forget. I became obsessed with the idea that it might be my only chance to make him miss me until November rolled around.

Since I didn't own a dress like the one I had in mind, I solicited one of my friends, Jennifer, who always dressed on the fringes of our high-school dress code. I remembered that she had been sent home to change on numerous occasions. As I suspected, she had several dresses to choose from. Too many choices are always a challenge, and of course, I had to try them all on. After nearly two hours of "Is it this or that?" I acquiesced to Jennifer's advice. Luckily we were identical in size, except she was a bit taller. The little black leather skirt looked short on me, so I had to wonder how wicked it looked on Jennifer. She also had a mid-waist matching jacket (thank God) that covered a little and a sheer white blouse that Jennifer insisted completed the outfit. It should have been no surprise that she had matching black bra and panties to go with it.

"Amy, you cannot wear this outfit without this blouse and the bra and panties. It's the icing on the cake," she said.

Even so, I was blushing in several shades of rouge by the time I had finished modeling my ensemble. She also insisted on a pair of stylish stiletto heels, but I put my foot down on that. I opted for a more sensible pair of black patent-leather pumps. I couldn't walk in the stilettos anyway. Every time I took a step in them, one ankle would go opposite of the other; it was not pretty. After some additional scrutiny in the mirror, I recognized that I was falling well over the edge of looking like an underage hooker already. I didn't mind that too much. My goal was to look hot, not trashy, but I did want Peter's jaw to drop when he saw me.

After sequestering ourselves into the tree house, it took me nearly two hours to deal with my makeup and get dressed. I twirled around for my little sister and anticipated the worst before I had come to a stop.

"Oh, Amy … you're beautiful," she said. I don't think she would have said anything negative if she thought it, but it still made me feel pretty. "You look like a college girl," she added with a note of envy.

I didn't bother to tell her that in less than two months, I would be a college girl. Instead I relished the praise, knowing she meant every word. Kelly had been uncharacteristically quiet while I was getting ready. That luck would not to continue, and since it wasn't quite dark enough to make my getaway, I had to succumb to a round of questioning. Some of her inquiries deserved honest answers even though the truth was hard to tell.

"Are you going to spend the night?" she asked.

"I don't know. I definitely need to be back before daylight," I answered, somewhat shocked at the bluntness of her question. "What are you getting at?"

"Well ... I was just wondering," she said.

Kelly was not a very good liar, not to mention she had managed to embarrass herself, judging by the blush that radiated up her neck. She looked at the floor rather than me.

I took her chin in my hand and gently forced her to look at me. We made eye contact, and I could feel a twinge of shame spreading over my own face. I knew what she meant. She was wondering if I planned to have sex with Peter but didn't know how to say it. The word was unfamiliar to my vocabulary as well, so my reply was leading and vague: "Are you asking me what I think you're asking?"

"Yes," she said, barely above a whisper.

Releasing my hold on her chin, I needed to look away. All this time spent plotting for a night to remember, and even though I knew the evening could end up with the sacrifice of my virginity. I had not really confronted the reality of that decision. I loved Peter and in my heart always thought he would be my first and hopefully I would be his. Then it struck me. I was jealous of Peter's new life. Not because of the fame or fortune, but for what it could bring... other girls. I was preparing to battle an unseen and most likely nonexistent adversary. The truth of the matter was obvious. I was preparing to do whatever it took to ensure that Peter had aspirations for no one but me. For the first time in months, I felt uncertain of myself and the path that lay before me. Somehow I steeled my resolve and managed a smile for my little sister.

"Don't be silly. He's going to marry me for that to happen."

I didn't intend to lie. I believe the truth of the matter eluded me, maybe because I wasn't prepared to face it myself. Perhaps my reasoning was purposeful. After all, she was a little kid, and even though she was my sister, she didn't need to know everything. Whether deceit or conjecture, my answer granted the response we were both looking for.

"Thank goodness! You had me worried," she said.

Her remark came across as so frank that it surprised me and made me chuckle at the same time.

"Look, you're the little sister. I'm the one who should be worrying about you and giving you the advice," I said, laughing at her remark. "Now be a good lookout and make sure no one is watching."

She gave me a quick hug and stood back, holding my hands. "Have fun," she said. "I can't wait to hear all about the concert."

Kelly bounded to a convenient knothole that we had used for monitoring and protecting our privacy for years. "Aw crud, Gina and Fred are in the kitchen standing right by the sink."

The kitchen was in the back of our house, and the window over the sink looked into the backyard and had a direct line of sight to our tree house.

"That's okay; at least we know where they are. Time for plan B," I said.

Kelly picked up her cell phone and started dialing. The plan was simple. Either Fred or Gina would answer the phone and Kelly would ask for the other. For some odd reason, we only had one landline to our house, and it was in the den where the family desktop resided. I had always thought Abigail was either just mean or old-fashioned to not have cordless phones in every room. I had asked once back when we actually spoke. Her response was, "Why bother? We all have cell phones." It was easy for her to say, she had unlimited minutes, my sister and I did not. The den sat in the center of the house and had no windows. It was the perfect location for the distraction required, to have our devious little plan work.

"Hi Gina, its Kelly, could I please speak to Fred?" she asked, holding back a giggle.

Then, in a stoic moment of true professionalism, she put an eye to the peephole. Without a word, she gave me an "Okay" signal with her free hand.

"I love you," I whispered.

Moments later, I stood on the grass. Barefooted, I ran for the solitude of an alley behind our house. There I took the time to slip the pumps out of my backpack, and seconds later, I was speed-dialing Jennifer so she could call me a cab. A convenience store sat a few blocks from my house, and we had selected it as a good place for me to catch my ride. The cab showed up barely five minutes after I did. I guess the driver had seen it all and hardly looked at me as I got in.

"Where to, miss?" he asked.

"I'm going to Bass Performance Hall. The address is 555 Commerce Street, in Fort Worth," I said.

It was the backstage entrance. I planned to be there a little before nine o'clock, and security would be expecting me. My destination got an understandable reaction out of the cabdriver. He turned in his seat and gave me the once-over.

"Uh, miss … It's just a guess, but the fare is going to run around a hundred dollars, maybe a little more."

I guess he thought I would be shocked, but I already knew approximately what the trip would cost. Peter had sent plenty of cash with the backstage pass, via Jennifer, to cover my escapade. The driver didn't look old enough to appreciate being called "sir," so I scanned his license on display in a plastic folder on the divider between us. His name was Jerry.

"Thanks for the heads-up, Jerry. I'm aware of the cost. I'll be paying cash, and there's a nice tip in it for you if you get me there before nine o'clock."

"Yes ma'am."

In one fluid motion, he slipped the cab into drive and we were off. Jerry turned what normally would be an hour-and-a-half trip into an hour and ten minutes. Even so, it seemed to take forever. Once we got close to Bass Hall, traffic was a zoo. The media was having a field day reporting on the local kid turned superstar.

"Gee, who's playing tonight?" Jerry asked.

"Peter Shaw," I said.

"You mean that kid from McKinney?"

"Yes," I said, barely able to contain myself.

"Do you know him?"

"He's my boyfriend."

It just came out without really thinking. Needless to say, I felt crazy distracted, and the last thing I wanted to do was get into a personal conversation with a cab driver whom I had only met an hour before.

He glanced into the rearview mirror at me and smiled. "He's a lucky guy."

"Let's hope he thinks so," I said, barely above a whisper.

"What was that?"

"Thanks, you're very sweet, Jerry," I said, thankful for a break in the traffic that allowed us to get onto Commerce Street.

Jerry pulled up and stopped in front of the side entrance. A uniformed policeman working the area started towards us at a brisk pace, presumably, to send us on our way. Jerry hopped out of the cab to let me out.

"Sorry, but you can't park here," said the cop.

"Good evening, Officer. I'm just letting my VIP fare out," Jerry said.

Then Jerry opened my door and offered me a helping hand like I was royalty. I accepted his offer with grace and appreciated the gesture. I realized that my legs were shaking and I was trembling all over. My body had decided to have a concert of uneasiness that included a queasy stomach. The police officer looked me over, and it didn't take a rocket scientist to know what he was thinking.

"Unless you have a backstage pass, you'll have to go around front," he said.

I started to dig through my backpack for my pass and realized it was not a good match for my ensemble. It was an all-purpose accessory that went with me every day and I had snoozed on leaving it behind.

"Here's my pass, Officer Roberts," I said while scanning his nametag.

It was a skill I'd learned from Peter: "Make conversation with authority personal," he would say. The VIP backstage pass had my picture on it, so he couldn't doubt its authenticity.

"Okay, Miss Stevens, let me escort you to the security desk and get you checked in," the officer said.

"Thank you," I said and gave him the best smile I could conjure up. Then I turned and handed Jerry two one-hundred-dollar bills. "Thanks, Jerry."

He took the money and then looked at his watch. "It's ten after. We're late. The fare was only a hundred and ten dollars."

"Keep the change," I said.

Officer Roberts led the way to the side entrance, and I found myself thinking about what I could buy with ninety dollars. There I was, tipping like some spoiled rich girl, but I had to admit, it was kind of fun to play the part. An enormous man stood at the door. How I missed him when we had pulled up was a mystery. He looked at my pass and then looked at me with a scowl that soon turned into a big toothy smile. Then he offered a hand that totally engulfed mine.

"Hi Amy, it's really nice to meet you. My name is Eddie. I'm Big Tony's cousin."

He pumped my arm so hard I thought he would pull it out of its socket. But I knew I was home free.

"Hi Eddie, it's nice to meet you too. Is Jimmy the only scrawny one in the family?" I asked.

Eddie erupted into a laugh, which would run a close race to Big Tony's deep roar.

"Well, Amy, he's the runt of the litter and his kids are all just like him, but we love them anyway."

I giggled and immediately felt at home. Eddie tucked my free hand under his arm, which was as big around as either of my legs, and led me down a well-lit nondescript hallway that vibrated with the sounds of music from one of the opening acts. The narrow corridor seemed to go on forever, in part, due to the anticipation of seeing Peter, and because of the woozy feeling in my legs. We came to a dead end, and Eddie steered me to the right down another hallway ending with a door marked *Dressing Room*. That uneasy feeling seemed to get a little better and then the door swung open, all my self-confidence went away, in the blink of an eye. For a moment, I thought my legs would fail me: it was Peter. I hadn't seen him in almost nine months, and I almost didn't recognize him. He was taller and had filled out some. The awkward gangly kid I remembered had turned into a handsome young man.

"Amy," he said in a subdued tone.

I almost took his response as disappointed, but then he took two giant steps and picked me up and twirled me around with a strength I had not known him to possess. He then gently set me down, and the Peter I knew and had come to love, kissed me on the cheek.

I looked him in the eyes and decided he wasn't getting by with a peck on the cheek. I grabbed his face with both hands, stood on my tiptoes, and although I still couldn't quite reach, I pulled his lips to mine with an urgency I had never felt before. His response was all I needed. I knew at that moment he still felt the same way. Oblivious to Eddie or the world around us, we got lost in a kiss that did not last quite long enough. The duration of our moment did offer plenty of time to attract a crowd. I can't say I felt embarrassed, but I was definitely surprised that the hallway had gotten so congested. Tony stood just outside the door with Eddie behind us, which was a crowd in itself. Peeking around Tony's hulking form were four grinning faces that made up the rest of Peter's band. As I reluctantly released Peter, each and every one of them came up for their own personal hug just as though we were old friends. When in reality I had never met any of them. Joni came up to me first—and it really felt awkward because I was jealous of her. It struck me as odd that she seemed so affectionate, and it made me feel silly for harboring ill feelings toward her. Johnny the band's lead guitarist was last to introduce himself, then he turned to Peter and said. "Thirty minutes to ShowTime. And we still need to go over the song order."

"Uh, sure, give me just a minute," Peter said. "You guys go ahead. I'll be right there."

They all trickled back into the room, except for Tony, who just moved back a respectful distance from us.

"It's okay Peter," I said. "I'm not going anywhere. We'll have all evening to visit once the concert is over."

"I know," he said. "It just seems like it's been forever since I've seen you and…" He stopped long enough to give me a long appraising look, which I know embarrassed him as much as it did me. "You're beautiful."

Now it was my turn to be embarrassed, and I'm sure my color reflected the emotion. It was the first time he had ever said it like that. It is amazing how just two words can make you feel wonderful.

"Thank you," I said. "Now go take care of business. I'm expecting a great concert."

He smiled and boldly gave me a kiss on the lips, then hurried back into the dressing room. As I watched him leave, I became acutely aware of Big Tony's full attention. He wasn't smiling, nor did he appear angry. It seemed more like a look of concern. That felt disconcerting to me, given the high opinion I had for him. The look passed, and he held out his arms with a little smirk.

"What am I, chopped liver? Where's my hug?" he asked.

Being that Tony was about as big around as the tree that suspended my tree house at home, I found it somewhat challenging to hug him. I think my arms reached less than halfway around him, and in my mind, it felt something akin to hugging Santa Claus. I filed his worried look away into the back of my mind and tried to decide what to say. After our hug, I looked up at him and decided that blunt would be the best approach.

"Tony, I know what you're going to say."

"Actually, I really doubt that you do."

"Well… I know that we all agreed that I would not have any contact with Peter until I turned eighteen and that Abigail can cause us all a lot of grief."

"You're absolutely correct on both counts. I did go to the trouble of doing a little detective work on the side. Your mother is in Los Angles tonight and won't be returning home until after court on Monday. I am of course hopeful that you did a good job of ditching your nursemaids." The comment was serious in intent, and it showed on his face.

"Yes, I did. I know what's at stake."

"I have no doubt that you do." Tony hesitated then said, "Just so you know, I'm not against you and Peter being together. You're both clearly in love. It's hard to keep Peter focused on work since he's daydreaming about you all the time." He added a quick smile and a wink. "Peter needs to focus right now. In a couple of years, he will have enough popularity and money to deal with the Abigails of the world. What I'm more concerned with. is him being in love. You know much better than I that Peter has a fragile social persona. I know you would never hurt him intentionally, but my concern is simple things like spats." I guess he could see me take on a defensive posture because he held a hand up to stop my response. "Now before you start getting mad at me, I just want you to hear me out. Do you remember the first conversation the three of us had when you guys showed up in Chicago?"

"Sure, I remember."

"I told you that your lives would change forever if Peter's career took off."

"Tony, I know there will be challenges. There is no way anyone could have a relationship with Peter without realizing his societal challenges."

I could feel my anger beginning to subside, but I still didn't understand what Tony was getting at. I still felt perturbed, but it was easy to see Tony's concern about Peter's well-being. I couldn't in all fairness find fault in him for that. So I decided to cut to the chase.

"What are trying to say, Tony? Tell me what's on your mind and don't sugarcoat it."

His long sigh sounded deliberate, which helped cover the lengthy time it took him to collect his thoughts and voice the words: "It's about groupies."

"Groupies, this whole conversation is about groupies?" I asked.

"Not entirely but yes. It's about you dealing with Peter's groupies and knowing that, number one; he only wants you, and, two, he's going to have adoring fans. I'm afraid that you may become jealous of that aspect of his career. Trust me when I say this. It's a common problem. It takes a really strong relationship to deal with knowing that half the girls out there want to be Peter's lover. If you ever went off on him, I'm not sure where that would take him. The responsibility for Peter's mental health could be incredibly unfair and difficult for you. You may view this as none of my business, but I care about both of you kids and I want nothing but the best for each of you."

"And you have quite a lot at stake here as well," I said, butting in before he was finished.

His hurt expression made me regret my words.

"Yes … there are a lot of folks who have a lot of time, money, and effort invested in Peter," he said. "Besides all that, you know my intent goes well beyond business."

"Yeah, I know that, Tony. I didn't mean it the way it came out."

"Here's a perspective, maybe not a good one, but an analogy just the same. Peter is very much like a racehorse that is blinding fast. We all know he's the fastest horse out there, but he hasn't run the long race yet. Do you see what I'm getting at?"

"Yes," I said. "I suppose I do. No offense, but this evening is not starting out like I had pictured it."

I tried to pout for effect, but I'm just not the kind of girl to pull it off. It did make Tony laugh, and hearing him laugh always proved to be worth the effort, even if it was unintentional.

"Just think about it. We both want the same thing for different reasons."

He just started adding something else when the dressing room door opened, and with it, laughter and a ruckus spilled out from inside. Peter stood at the door, looking at us anxiously.

"Uh… Tony?" Peter said. "Joni and Johnny are at it again."

"Okay, I'll be right there." He turned back to me and quietly added, "All I'm asking is if you're going to love him, please trust him as well. He's worth it."

With that, he gave me another hug and a peck on the cheek and then hurried off to deal with whatever was going on in the dressing room. I followed him to the doorway. Peter seemed to be brooding with concern.

"What was that all about?" he asked.

I smiled, gave him a peck on the cheek, and said, "Oh … he was just telling me not to kill any of your groupies."

Peter just stared at me. I had been away from him for only a few short months, and in that short amount of time, I had almost forgotten that he had no grasp of levity. I hugged him, and when I felt him start to relax, I looked into his October-sky blue eyes.

"Just don't forget I'm your first fan and that I love you. And you will have groupies, but it's okay because I know you love me." I didn't give him a chance to analyze my comments and said, "How long before you go on stage?"

"Any minute now, Eddie will give us a heads-up for the ten-minute call. You have the best seat in the house, center-front in the VIP section. Eddie is going to sit with you with instructions to squash anyone who tries to bother you."

That visual made me laugh.

"I just can't believe I'm here with you," I said. "It seems like, it's been forever since I saw you last."

"How long can you stay after the concert?" The question reflected Peter's shy nature.

"As long as I'm home before daylight, my schedule is open," I said as demurely as I knew how.

I must not have pulled off the modest act very well or it had something to do with me being dressed like a teenage tart, but Peter's face began to flush—I imagined from the same anticipation I was feeling. Movement down the hall got my attention.

I recognized Eddie's bulk turning the corner. He waved and said, "It's ShowTime, Peter."

Peter gave me a sheepish look followed by another delicious kiss and sighed. "Guess I should go to work. Eddie will take care of you from here. The show will be two hours and sixteen minutes long. If we are encouraged to do an encore, it will add six minutes."

He started to give me the grand total of two hours and twenty-two minutes, but I stopped him before he had the chance. I put my index finger on his lips.

"It doesn't matter how long it takes. I'll be here when you're done."

I hugged him tightly and enjoyed his manly scent for a moment. Then I stood on my tiptoes and gave him yet another quick kiss.

"Break a leg," I said.

Then I turned to Eddie, who nobly offered a huge forearm, and led me to our seats.

Chapter 9
Peter

I watched Amy walk away with Eddie, and although I knew she would be safe enough in his care, I began wishing the concert was already over. She looked over her shoulder one last time as they rounded the corner that led to the auditorium, and waved. I waved back, thinking I should say something, but felt at a loss for words.

After ten months of no physical contact, I almost forgot about the emotions she stirred within me. Amy being close kindled a desire that had been quiet for a long time. Tonight the feeling was more intense than I could ever remember. She had dressed in a way that seemed different for her. While part of me liked the way she looked. Another side felt timid and uncomfortable. I thought Amy looked awesome no matter how she dressed, although I'm sure it's an observation that would not be appreciated. It bothered me knowing that other guys would see her and have the same thoughts that I did. Even so, I knew her appearance tonight was for me. Overall, it was a wonderful sensation that I was more than willing to enjoy.

Tony poked his head out of the dressing room and asked, "Did Eddie give us a curtain call?"

My mind still swam in a primordial stew of mixed emotions, and for a short moment, his question did not even register.

"Peter… is everything alright?" he asked.

I must have had a dazed look on my face as I focused on Tony and the two questions he just asked. I could see a distinct look of concern on his face. He knew full well my mind had gone elsewhere.

"Did you see how beautiful Amy looked tonight?" I asked.

Tony hesitated as if uncertain as to how to respond to my somewhat leading question. "Yes ... I did, but then, that was not a surprise. She's beautiful in more ways than one. I hope you had the good sense to tell her."

That made me smile and allowed me to remember the instant I told her a few minutes ago. "Yes, I did."

He walked to where I was standing and gazed down the empty hallway with me and said, "Well, that's good. You are a very lucky young man, Peter. If you think you can come back to planet earth for a couple of hours, maybe we can get this concert behind us, then you can have some time to be in love."

I looked at my big friend and thought about his comment. "Is it love, that I'm feeling right this moment?" I asked.

Tony's laugh rumbled down the hallway like a Texas thunderstorm in July. "Yes ... Peter, there is absolutely no doubt in my mind that you two love each other. There are some other forces at work here as well, and I'm sure you will have a great time sorting through them. But you're not out of the woods yet. We still have to keep you off of Abigail's radar for another four months."

He paused for a second. I don't think he was looking for a response as much as to collect his thoughts. I had come to respect and appreciate Tony's opinion. Sometimes I didn't necessarily agree with him, but I always listened. He put an arm around my shoulders and led me back to the dressing room.

"Come on, lover boy," Tony said. "Let's go play Amy some music."

I still had not gotten used to the audience cheering and the applause. Every time I walked out on stage, my stomach churned. Some people called it butterflies, but for me, it felt more like a buffalo stampede. The rest of the band seemed to not be as affected as I was. Of course… they would all admit in private that it felt unsettling in some manner or another. For me though, I experienced sheer terror. Put me in a studio and I was in my element and comfortable, for the most part. On stage, I was scared stiff. Sometimes I would have to force my legs to carry me to the piano. Once settled in at the keyboard, I could block out my surroundings and focus on my music. I guess the piano had become my sanctuary and when I played. I could lose myself in the magic of music. I tried to explain to Amy and Tony what it felt like, but so far, it has been a personal experience that I have been unable to explain. When I get the music just right, I feel colors. How do you explain that to someone? After all, no one feels color; they see it—everyone I've ever met … that is, except me.

We were standing just offstage waiting for the lights to come down, which was our cue to come out. My stomach stampede had already hit full swing and if anything, it felt worse since I knew Amy was out there waiting to see me play. The lights came down, and we picked our way through the equipment. The crowd noise quieted down in anticipation.

I sat down and scanned the front row for Amy while the rest of the band took their places. Once the lights came up, I knew I wouldn't be able to see much from the glare of the spotlights. It was easy to see Eddie's hulking figure on the front row, and there to his right, I could just make out Amy's tiny form.

We didn't usually start with the song that Amy had written the lyrics to, but the band didn't seem to mind when I made the request. Of course, they all knew why. It was a small thing to them but a big deal to me. With Amy's blessing, I had named the song, "Make Them Smile." It seemed appropriate and she liked it. It hit number one on the charts not long after it was released and stayed there for over four months. As the lights came up, I heard a deafening roar as the audience's excitement increased in intensity. The electricity of a frenzied crowd is a unique thing. I found it easy to get caught up in the excitement. What's even more noteworthy is how easy performers get caught up in the fans' adulation. Most of the band had already been affected at some level or another. To me, it felt embarrassing and still made me feel uncomfortable. The only praise I cared about was whatever came from Amy.

When the lights started to soften and the stage and spots came alive. I finally felt like I could relax. You would think that would be the moment when anticipation of the performance would be at its highest. Perhaps for some, that is the case, but not for me. I guess it's due to the fact that a crowd becomes surreal after I start playing and it's easier to pretend they're not there. Joni started the beat; it was a very light sound of her drumsticks clicking together and was barely audible. I started into the piano intro and, as was usual for me and soon. I became lost in a swirl of color and music.

The next thing I remember with distinction was when we finished out the set and went offstage. We didn't go far; as we had come to realize that an encore would be expected. The audience worked itself into another frenzy, stomping their feet so hard it seemed that the whole building would collapse upon us. We waited about three or four minutes until Tony gave us a nod to suggest we go back on stage before the crowds' jubilation turned to anger. We played two more songs, finishing with our original first hit "Amy's Song." As we took our bows everyone was on their feet. The concert was another success, but I felt more excited about it being over. I couldn't wait to spend the rest of the evening with

Amy. I was already somewhat bummed out knowing that half the evening had disappeared and I would not see her again for several months. I pushed the negative thought aside to allow myself the chance of having a fun evening. I knew if I dwelt on the downside too long. It would change the nature of our time together. I wanted tonight to be as perfect as possible.

The afterglow of a concert, as I call it, begins when you walk off the stage. After performing for two to three hours, you're bombarded by the electricity created by the audience. The high is heightened by the intensity of the performance, especially when you know it was a good one. When we finished a show, the band would be giddy with excitement. The experience still felt new to me, but Tony said it was a common byproduct for most musicians and actors. It's hard to explain, but simply put, it's an intense feeling of self-satisfaction that is shared with the group you are working with.

The band had already settled into a routine, which for the most part was silly, but it had become our way. It started off with high-fives and congratulating each other on another fine concert, then the band would start picking on each other's performance. It was little stuff: a missed key by a micro-second, a vocal harmony that may or may not have been a little flat or sharp. I think it was just banter, and usually it never got out of hand. Johnny, our lead guitarist, said the reason they never picked on me was because, so far as any of them could tell, I never slipped up. I heard everyone's mistakes, including my own. It was due to Tony's good advice that I did not participate and point out everyone's shortcomings. In my mind, it was a curse: even when everyone else thought things went perfect, I recognized every minute mistake. The fact that we live in an imperfect world is not a foreign concept to me. Nonetheless, my mind just won't stop, and the only way I can turn it off is by replacing my thought process with something else. Often times, I would go watch some TV, if there was one around, or put on my headphones and listen to some classical music. Tonight my deterrence was Amy and I decided to wait just offstage. Knowing it would be the path she and Eddie would take to the dressing room.

Moments later, she appeared with Eddie in tow. I had missed a lot of things about Amy, but what I missed the most was how she seemed to be happy all of the time. Even when it seemed there was no way she should be, she was. Tonight proved to be no exception, and she nearly knocked me off my feet when she jumped into my arms.

"Oh, Peter, you were wonderful tonight."

"Thanks. I'm glad you enjoyed it."

"Of course I enjoyed it. You were awesome." She kissed and hugged me with an intensity I had never seen.

The embrace lasted for quite some time, not that I was about to complain. In my peripheral, I could see Eddie trying to look the other way while patiently waiting for instructions. I pulled her away so I could see her face.

"Do you want to get out of here?" I asked.

She nodded her head and smiled. "Yes ... that would be nice."

"Eddie, would you please have the car brought around to the freight entrance?"

"It's there waiting for you as we speak," Eddie said. He beamed with a distinct look of satisfaction for anticipating my request.

"Thanks, Eddie. I should have known you would be a step ahead of me."

He stood a little straighter. "That's my job, Peter. If you two would follow me, I'll lead the way and make sure you manage a clean getaway."

He took off down the hallway. I offered my hand to Amy and looked at her with a certain sense of trepidation. Without hesitation, she took my hand, and I believe she would have dragged me down the hall if I had not picked up the pace. That simple action told me that she was where she wanted to be and was with whom she wanted to be with.

We walked in silence for a short time, the sound emanating from our shoes echoed down the hallway. "So what's the deal with having the limo pick us up at the freight entrance?" She asked.

I laughed because I remembered how dumbstruck I had been the first time the band got shuffled off to a secluded rendezvous to catch a ride without fans lurking about.

"Well … I would like to say it was my brilliant idea for maintaining anonymity, but the truth of the matter is that performers do this sort of thing all of the time. It's to avoid paparazzi and errant fans looking for a picture or an autograph or worse."

I probably should have left off the last two words, because I was rewarded with an obvious questioning look that was followed by an awkward silence.

"What do you mean by 'or worse'?" she asked after the short pause.

The question sounded innocent enough but the answer was not, and I realized that I had stepped into a quagmire with both feet. I knew that the best approach was always to just be truthful, but the truth seemed embarrassing, and even though I was guilty of no wrongdoing, the discomfort was still there.

"Well … it's to avoid … you know."

There was no doubt that I had her full attention, but I noticed a certain amount of mischievousness in her mannerism.

"I'm not sure I understand what you're getting at," she said.

Eddie laughed out loud and coughed into his hand, trying to cover up his outburst. I knew I was caught between a rock and a hard place, and there was no way out.

"Groupies," I said quietly.

"Groupies?" she asked.

Her tone sounded judgmental at first, and the only thing that came to mind was to look away, embarrassed beyond belief. Then I noticed she was snickering just as we came to the door leading out to the underground freight delivery area. Eddie turned and shushed us with a finger over his mouth, but his face looked as red as Santa Claus. I had no doubt that he was about to explode. The whole entourage was amused time and time again by my discomfort with the adoring fans and the groupies.

"Let me go first and take a look around," Eddie said.

Then somehow he slipped his 350-pound bulk through what seemed like a crack in the doorway.

Once we were alone, and without missing a beat, Amy tugged on my arm for attention. Having fans made me feel uneasy enough; the fact that some of them adored me made it even worse. With reluctance, I made eye contact.

"Peter, I know you are struggling with all of the attention. The fact that you don't buy into all of the adoration coming your way is endearing. We talked about this with Big Tony in Chicago months ago. I know what a groupie is, and I know what a lot of them are willing to do just to meet you. I also know that you love me and that you would never do anything to hurt me. That being said, they are your fans and you shouldn't ignore them all of the time. If you do, it will hurt your popularity."

"You of all people know that I don't do crowds. Most people I would just rather not deal with, especially the ones that have some sort of simple-minded agenda. The rest of the guys—heck, even Joni—are inviting girls up to the hotel after some of the shows," I said.

My comment put a confused look on her face. "Why would Joni invite girls to the hotel?"

"Joni's gay. I thought you knew that."

"Oh… that explains a lot," Amy said, and then a peculiar smile crossed her face.

The door opened without any preamble, and Eddie stuck his head in. "Coast is clear and the limo is here."

He pulled the door open and made room for us to pass. The black stretch limo had parked a few yards away, idling, and the driver was holding the door open for us so we could make our quick getaway. Now I was the one almost dragging her as we raced to the seclusion of the luxurious backseat. We piled in, and the door shut behind us. In seconds, the driver whisked us away.

We gawked at the melee as the limo hit the streets. The off-duty police that we hired to work our venues were worth every dime. Barricades were moved to let us pass and then put back in place to block anyone from following us. Soon we were away from it all. I watched with idle curiosity as Amy poked and prodded every cubby-hole in the limo. She squealed with delight when she managed to get a flat-screen TV to appear and disappear by the touch of a button.

A little past midnight, we pulled into the Rosewood Mansion on Turtle Creek, which Tony had said was a really nice five-star hotel in Dallas. In the past few months staying in really nice places had become commonplace but as soon as we pulled past the main entry to the discreet side entrance, I knew I had outdone myself. The driver stopped, opened the door for us, and handed me the room keycard.

"Mr. Shaw, you are in a Master Suite. The elevator is just inside. Take it to the top floor, and then take a right out the door to the end of the hall. Please call when you want me to come back. I'll be here waiting within twenty minutes." He handed me his card, which had his cell number on it. "Is there anything else I can do for you?"

Noting his nametag, I said, "Thank you, William. I'll be calling you later tonight for a trip to McKinney."

I discreetly put a five-hundred-dollar tip in his hand, which he palmed like it happened all the time. Money was one thing I didn't care about. I sent a lot of what I made to my dad, which he in turn invested. The rest I just spent for frivolous things like excessive tips. There were times I would give some random homeless guy a couple of hundred dollars until Tony caught me doing it and scolded me: "Peter, you just can't give that much money to those people at one time. A lot of them are alcoholics, and that much booze at one time could kill them." I remember being shocked but took what he said to heart and only gave big tips to working people from that time on. I still gave money to needy folks, but I kept it to twenty dollars at a time.

"I've lived in McKinney all of my life, and I didn't even know this place existed," Amy said.

I unlocked the outside entrance with the keycard and let her go in first.

"I know, neither did I. Tony found it and made the arrangements."

"When will the rest of the band be here?" she asked.

"Oh, they're not staying here," I said, and then I started second-guessing myself, hoping that Amy didn't read some sort of motive into the arrangements.

"Good ... then we'll finally be alone for a while."

I think I gulped and had to concentrate on just breathing for the next few seconds. Her comment should have made me more at ease but it only made it worse. I knew my face was turning red from embarrassment, and I felt grateful when the elevator door opened right away. The ride up seemed to take forever even though there were only three floors. It looked very nice as far as elevators are concerned. There were mirrors all around and what appeared to be granite floors, and it was trimmed out in a dark cherry-wood finish. I pretended to scope out the décor and did my best to avoid eye contact with Amy, not because I didn't want to look at her. I just felt embarrassed. It was the first time I had ever taken a girl to a hotel room alone. And what little confidence I had concerning the evening seemed to be waning fast. I was grateful when the door opened, and I even managed to remember my manners and let her step out first.

We took a right as directed and a short walk later arrived at the door. Under the fancifully written room number, it said, *Master Suite*. Talk about intimidation; my breathing started to increase, and it seemed that the temperature had increased by several degrees. I guess I froze at the door for a bit longer than I should have. Amy turned my face toward hers so that I had to look at her.

"What's the matter?" she asked.

"Nothing," I said.

"Peter, you will never be able to hide your emotions from me. You should know better. Would you give me the keycard please?"

I envisioned the stupid look on my face as I handed it to her. She deftly opened the door and let us in.

"Oh, Peter, it's beautiful! Check it out."

The living area of the suite was enormous and just to the right of the entry stood a huge stone fireplace. Straight ahead were sliding glass doors that went out to a terrace with a stunning view of downtown Dallas. In the center sat a big leather sofa and chair, but what really got my attention was the grand piano tucked into the corner beside a door that I presumed went to a bedroom. I felt quite relieved that we hadn't walked into a room with a huge round bed with mirrors on the ceiling. To the immediate left, I saw a small kitchenette and a granite bar stocked with several liquors that I didn't recognize since I didn't drink. I meandered to the kitchen area and found a variety of soft drinks.

"Would you like a Coke?" I asked.

"Sure, that would be great."

I watched her as I fixed us a couple of Cokes. She walked out onto the terrace and looked around, then came back in with that bubbly smile I had grown to love. Then she went to the closed door by the piano, opened it, and peered in while reaching for the light switch. The resulting illumination was a good indication of her success, and she disappeared through the doorway. It seemed like a lot of time passed, but I waited, not really wanting to go into the bedroom. Finally, I got my voice back: "Hey ... your Coke is ready."

"Cool. Would you bring it to me?"

I can't explain why, but all of a sudden, my feet felt like they were weighted down with lead. It was a struggle to just put one foot in front of the other as I made the trek to the bedroom. When I got there, I almost dropped the Cokes. Amy had kicked her shoes off and was lying on the huge king-sized bed.

"Peter, put the drinks down and come lay down with me."

I complied obediently, but I wasn't sure if I was ready for what might come next. I went to the unoccupied side, lay down, and closed my eyes. I felt frozen. Like slab of meat in the freezer. A short time later she poked me in the side.

"Open your eyes, silly," she said.

I turned to her voice and opened my eyes. Her eyes were full of mischief, or perhaps excitement. I couldn't tell which. I started to speak, but I couldn't think of what to say. Lucky for me, she read me like a book and put a finger on my lips.

"Look at the ceiling," she said while pointing up with her finger.

I cast my eyes upward, dreading the mirrored ceiling that I knew had to be there—and was pleased to be wrong. "Are those cherubs?" I asked.

"Close, but I think the bows and arrows make them Cupids. So … do you have a clue as to what I want you to do now?"

All I could muster up for an answer was, "No."

She giggled and sat up. "I want you to play for me. I know you have been playing all night, but will you play for just me?"

I sat up and rolled to my feet. Her request was something that I was comfortable with and good at. She jumped up, grabbed my hand, and led me out of the room to the piano bench. I had been working on a few new tunes that I hadn't played for anyone yet. This seemed to be the perfect time to give them a go.

"Would you like to hear something new?"

"Oh yes, absolutely! I was hoping you might be working on some new stuff."

She clapped her hands together in a happy fervor of anticipation and excitement that overflowed onto her face. The stress of the unknown subsided and I was in my element. I sat down and prepared to play the four tunes that I had been working on.

"I haven't put any words to these yet, so maybe you can come up with something," I said.

"That's okay, just play for me."

So I played and watched her as she stood next to the piano. She closed her eyes and moved in small subtle movements to the tunes. After I had played through them, she asked me to play them again, but this time, she sat down next to me, then put her arm around my waist and leaned against me. The distraction was a pleasant one, but I did make a few mistakes. When I finished, she didn't move, and for a minute, I thought she had fallen asleep. She stirred and looked up at me. Her eyes were misty but not from tears. I saw a look on Amy's face that I had never seen before.

"It's getting late," she said, "but before I go, there is something else we need to do. I want you to make love to me… Peter."

She put her fingers on my lips, signaling she wanted no response, and then led me to the bedroom.

Chapter 10
Amy

The limo ride home was quiet, and I was thankful the driver made no effort to be chatty. I was happy, content, and confused. The confused part was what I dwelt on most of the way home. The evening had gone just the way I had planned it—right down to the last detail. Even though I had no idea how to seduce someone, nature filled in the gaps where I lacked experience. I'm sure I wasn't all that good at it, either, but I realized that what I've heard is true: men are quite easy when it comes to sex. I suppose it's just nature working its wiles. I had indeed seduced Peter, and in reflection, I don't feel sorry for what I did. After all, I loved him, and I knew he loved me.

I snuggled into the plush leather seat to savor and relived the evening. I didn't enjoy myself for very long because the first thing I did… was to judge myself. Not that I could change anything now if I wanted to. It came down to two things. I wanted my wedding night to be the first time I made love. Now that choice is a moot subject. So now… my biggest concern is. Will Peter think less of me for dressing like a tramp and enticing him into the bedroom? Knowing how sweet, innocent, and gentle Peter is. My brazen behavior could create problems I hadn't considered. I felt guilty remembering how reluctant he seemed. He was nervous. I got that. So was I. What was surprised me and I'm sure Peter as well. I took the lead throughout our encounter. The surfacing of that trait taught me something about myself that I didn't know. The fact that neither of us knew what we were doing didn't help, but we did figure it out. Still, I just couldn't get it out of my mind that he seemed so hesitant.

It was five thirty in the morning when I asked the driver to pull over and let me out just a block from my house. I had already taken my makeup off and put my pumps into my backpack. Being as quiet as possible, I made my way to the tree house in my bare feet. Once I made it back undetected. I would be home free. The house and tree house were dark, which I took as a good sign. I knew if Abigail was home, that would not be the case. Still... as I crept up the ladder to my sanctuary, I tried to be as quiet and discreet as possible.

Sunrise was minutes away and the early morning glow offered just enough light to see Kelly curled up in her sleeping bag fast asleep. I felt tired. But there was no way I could sleep. A lot had happened... and it was all too fresh on my mind. I changed into an old T-shirt and sweatpants that served as my standard sleep attire. I curled up close to Kelly, being mindful to not wake her. My mind instantly went back to making sense of what I had done. Why I had chosen that path, and what happens now, weighed heavy on my mind. It wasn't regret that had me in a melancholy state of mind. On the contrary, I had designed the evening to be something we would both remember—and I have no doubt that I had been successful in that regard. So why did I feel bad about it?

I retraced the last part of the evening and soon became aware that my heart rate and breathing had quickened. I may have only been seventeen, but that morning. I was as much a young woman as any other.

The memory of Peter's face when he kissed me good-bye surfaced and that made me smile inside and out. Still I brooded about the choices I had made and the more I thought about it, the more confused I became. For the life of me, I couldn't decide if he was happy, sad, or indifferent. His mannerisms were unchanged. He told me he loved me like he always did. But his expression was one I had never seen before... and it was disturbing. I found myself second-guessing my actions and started to cry. I pulled my legs into a fetal position, buried my face into my hands... and hoped I could keep to keep my tears to myself. I thought I was doing a pretty good job of being quiet, when all of a sudden, Kelly stirred and sat up.

"Amy, what's the matter? Why are you crying?" she asked in a whisper. I didn't answer her right away. Because I didn't know what to say and I knew it would be impossible to convince her that everything was fine. "Is Mom home? Did you get caught?"

"No," I said. "Well, I don't think so. The house is dark and quiet."

"Well, if she was here, we both know that would not be the case."

Kelly's matter-of-fact statement struck me not only as correct but very funny. I laughed, and it felt good. I had been blubbering for long a time and the emotional change lifted my spirits. In the meantime, Kelly had moved over next to me and taken my hand in hers. She didn't say anything at first, maybe not sure if she should, but a twelve-year-olds curiosity is relentless and it was just a matter of time.

"So... why were you crying, sis?" she asked.

I thought about it and tried to be as honest as I could: "I'm not sure why."

Her face screwed up in the way it does when she gets mad. "He didn't break up with you, did he? That bum! A little fame and us little country girls aren't good enough for the big star!"

"No... he didn't break up with me," I said, interrupting her soon to be epic tirade on the evils of boys.

"Okay..." She hesitated and then asked, "Did he hurt you?"

136

"No… I really don't want to talk about it. Can you just give it a rest?"

"Oh my God, you did it, didn't you? You let him have sex with you, didn't you? And you're hurt, aren't you? What can I do, sis? Should I boil some water and tear up some sheets?"

Before I could stop her, she got up on her feet, cavorting in a frantic pantomime that would have been funny if it wasn't making me mad.

"Sit down … and be quiet, for crying out loud! I'm not having a baby."

I snapped at her before taking the time to realize that her intentions were good. My little sister felt concerned and, at her age of innocence, had no idea what the repercussions of a first-time sexual experience might be. Heck … I was quickly realizing that, even at the ripe old age of seventeen, I had not thought my actions through.

"Sissy, I'm fine. I'm not hurt."

I tried to sound as reassuring as I could but realized too late that I had not denied anything. I never was very good at keeping the truth from Kelly since she and I had always been so close. As a rule, I could stay a step ahead of her and avoid a topic that I didn't want to discuss. However, I already had a certain amount of personal guilt consuming me. My guard was down and I'd left the door open for her prying curiosity. She sat back down and managed to stay quiet while I considered what would be appropriate to share and how far to go with my explanation. After a brief moment of contemplation, I decided that I would tell her the truth— excluding certain details that she didn't need to be privy to. That proved to be a dilemma. How do you explain that sort of intimacy to a twelve-year-old? The experience was, on many levels, confusing. I expected it to be enjoyable, and I guess it was. The truth of the matter and yet another mystery, it didn't last long enough to be sure. Why did everyone make such a big deal out of it? I'm not sure if sharing the experience with my little sister was the right or the wrong thing to do. There were a few times though. I had to stop, to refrain from laughing at her various expressions. Her brown eyes grew to the size of chocolate moon pies and her mouth would open to say something, and then close without a word. It's uncommon to see Kelly unable to speak. When I finished and made it clear that I would not divulge any additional information. She was very supportive and mature, in her own way.

"Okay... that was pretty gross and I have no idea what you were thinking," she said.

I really wasn't in the mood to hear a long sermon about why I shouldn't have done what I did. But I listened anyway.

"I understand that you love Peter and you were worried that you might lose him to some groupie bimbo. But if he really loves you, he would have waited." As she paused, I was already wondering who was more mature between the two of us. "The good thing is I know you were smart enough to have him wear a condom."

That comment hit me like a bomb. Neither Peter nor I had even thought about it. I managed to tell a convincing lie though. "Well of course we did. I'm not stupid." I didn't think I sounded all that convincing, so I berated her: "What do you know about condoms? You're too young to even know what they are for."

"Listen, Amy... I know you think I'm just a little kid but I know more than you think. You remember the girl in the class ahead of me, Patty Lawrence? You know... the girl we all hated because she was so pretty and got her boobs before anyone else? Well... we all thought she had the flu really bad but turns out she's pregnant."

"No way," I said.

"Oh yes way... her sister told me. Their family is having a major meltdown because they are very religious and are trying to decide whether she is old enough to have the baby."

"She's only thirteen. She's too young to have a baby."

"Sorry to give you a science lesson, big sister, but if you're old enough to have a period... you're old enough to have a baby."

Kelly was up on her feet at this point, hands on her hips, pacing back and forth in the tiny confines of our tree house, posturing herself like a middle-school health teacher. As much as I wanted to criticize her rant, she was absolutely correct on all counts. Just a few hours earlier, I'd had unprotected sex. I took a breath to prop up my waning confidence and told myself that the chances of getting pregnant from one encounter were nonexistent.

"I realize now that I didn't really think it through," I said. "It's too late to change anything now, and it won't happen again until we're married. I'll bet that girl Patty had been carrying on with her boyfriend for some time and it finally got her into trouble."

"According to her sister, it just happened one time at summer camp with an older boy."

I was glad the conversation had shifted away from me—but that statement made me feel a few butterflies.

"Just once ... Wow, that's a bummer."

I couldn't think of anything else to say, and in the back of my mind, I wondered. *What would I do if that happened to me?*

"Well, thank goodness you are smarter than Patty."

"Yeah ... Good thing I thought ahead," I said. While reassuring myself, that everything would be fine and hoping that what happened to Patty wouldn't happen to me.

I can't remember being as thankful for an interruption as I was when I heard Gina yell up at us: "Hey … you campers interested in some breakfast?"

It didn't take much of an assessment to realize I felt starved, and one look at Kelly told me we were on the same page. I opened the door, and we both stuck our heads out together.

"We're starving," I said.

"Well, come on down to the kitchen. I have waffles cooking as we speak," Gina said with a smile and then headed back to the house.

I gathered up my backpack and started down the ladder. My confidence was coming back, and I thought that, all things considered, I'd had fun seeing the concert and Peter, and couldn't wait until November and my eighteenth birthday. Then I would be with Peter all of the time.

/////

It was a typical north Texas summer: hot and humid. The weeks drifted by slow and I spent more time than usual with Kelly. Since I wasn't interested in any boys... she didn't cramp my style. We went swimming at somebody's house almost every day. Most of my friends thought I was crazy hanging out with my little sister so much. I guess somewhere along the way, I realized she would be my friend long after my high-school buddies had come and gone.

Abigail flew in on her broom every so often, and I always felt relieved when she left. I had learned, though, the best way to handle my mom was to go along with her without making it too easy; after all, I didn't want to arouse her suspicion. She had already planned my college education and pre-enrolled me into the Texas Woman's University in Denton for my first year of college—only about a forty-five-minute drive from our home. She selected generic classes that I would need for pretty much any degree. Abigail was consistent, I'll give her that. She never considered what I thought or wanted. I complained just enough to make things seem normal and avoided her as much as possible. I had no doubt that she wanted me in school and close by so she could keep me living at home—under her thumb.

Around the middle of August, right about when I was getting my class schedule worked out, I realized I was late for my period. What I had put aside as something that would not happen to me was proving to be wrong. Nature often times doesn't ask permission to follow its course. Although I had never missed a period since I'd gotten my first one, I had heard that it could happen, so I waited and hoped.

September came and I realized that life had thrown me an unexpected twist. I managed to buy an in-home test kit without anyone knowing and cried to myself in the bathroom when I tested pregnant. Still in denial, I managed to sneak off to a clinic near the college campus that would keep it anonymous. They confirmed that I was indeed with child and guessed me to be about eight weeks along. I counted the weeks to myself since I knew the exact day of conception and wondered how they could be so accurate.

While I walked back to the university grounds and my next class, I cried. I just couldn't stop. In my mind, I always thought being pregnant with my first child would be the happiest day of my life—and that made me cry even more. The realization of the responsibility that had just landed in my womb was overwhelming. I skipped class and sat under a big pin oak tree and blubbered until I had nothing left inside me. A lot of students walked by and I know they noticed but no one stopped to ask what was wrong. In a way, it made me happy that no one asked.

I did the math and figured I would become a mom in late March or early April. I wondered what it would be like to have a baby. How much would it hurt? I had no one to confide in and was scared. The thought of being a mother someday, had been appealing, until it became a reality. I guess I wanted to prove that I could be a better mother than my mom. Clearly, though, not only was I not ready to be a mother and I had no idea how Peter would react when he found out he would soon be a father.

We managed to stay in touch by email and occasional phone calls. But I didn't want him to find out that way... so I kept it a secret. You can't see someone's reaction over the phone any more than you can via an email. So I lived with the guilt and kept telling myself it would be better to tell him in November, on my birthday. I felt deceitful for not telling him but I just couldn't do it. One thing was for sure. I was having a baby and I could only hope that Peter and I would be raising it together. I had two months to go before I turned eighteen, and I would be four months along by then. All I could do was hope that I wouldn't be showing too much by the time November rolled around. I soon learned the joys of pregnancy and started throwing up every morning and eating like a football player.

Chapter 11
Kelly

Ever since my father got killed riding his Harley. Mom had been the family breadwinner. I suppose that's a good excuse to have no time to be a mother. She told me on more than one occasion that she's never had time to grieve or to feel sorry for herself. Mom had a pre-law degree before she was married. So when my dad died, she decided to go to law school and become an attorney. She does find time to tell me every so often that she is really good at what she does. Her specialty is keeping the firm's rich clients out of trouble. According to Mom, the music industry seems to thrive on decadence and most of her patrons are, in some way, shape, or form, in that business. For some reason, of which I'm not sure, the subject came up yet again this week. The intro is the same every time, and then she continues into her job description, which I know by heart and is as follows. Keep her clients out of court whenever possible and when that fails... out of jail.

She never used to discuss the details of her cases. For some reason... that changed over the last few months. Now every time she comes home, she vents and tells me everything. Her cases dealt with everything from drug charges to having sex with minors and just about anything you can imagine in between. She would finish up with some variation that always concluded with how she finds that particular part of her job to be somewhat disgusting—but it pays very well. My take on the subject, although I have never voiced it to anyone, is that it's all about the money.

Mom scrolls through her list of justifications like it was a script for a play. I guess it's to make her feel better... because it sure didn't make me feel any better. I just want a mom and to feel like a normal family. I just couldn't figure out. Whether she was clueless of how anyone else felt or if she just didn't care. One thing is for sure. I am too scared of her answers to ask any questions. As a result, she could continue uninterrupted about how we were much too young to realize that all the nice things we have. Are due to her hard work and that work requires travel. The next segment goes on to observe that we must hate her because she is so tough on us.

Today I got cornered on the way out the door to a friend's house for a swimming party— this time our chat took a different direction.

"Kelly," she said. "You are the youngest but you are self-reliant, more mature, and easier to deal with than Amy."

This dialogue was a repeat and first hit the stage about a year ago when she and Amy had their meltdown. I'm not certain if Amy had been her favorite before the Peter incident. However, since I was the only one who would have a conversation with her. I had moved to the top of the list. My elevation *to most favored child* status had only happened because Mom held a bigger grudge than the one my sister harbored. Even though it had to be obvious that the whole subject made me uncomfortable, Mom still vented to me.

"Ever since their adolescent romance, she thinks she can't live without him. I know he's a very smart young man with considerable musical talent. The thing is. I deal with people just like him all of the time. He's not the right guy for Amy. I knew she would be mad at me for forcing them apart. What surprises me is how long she has resented me for it. I know someday she will thank me for doing what was best for her."

She paused for a bit and looked through me, rather than at me, and I knew that she was using me for a sounding board. I had no idea why and even though it was for all the wrong reasons. It made me feel like an adult.

Her pause was brief before continuing her rant. "Amy is clueless as to what life would be like living out of a suitcase. She is the poster child for a homebody and would hate it in less than two months. And Peter, in the end, is like any other guy who has girls chasing him from one town to another. As soon as she decided to stay at home and not travel with him, he would be with the first groupie that came along. Men can't help themselves; it's what they do—and musicians are the worst. I thought the months' vacation in Europe would snap her out of the melancholy state of mind that has rendered her listless. When I was her age, I would have thought I had died and gone to heaven for a trip like that. But it didn't seem to help. That's why I was forced to take charge of her college plans. Once she gets a semester under her belt, she'll come around and get on with her life. It's clear she needs some guidance and direction. I knew being close to home would be best for her. In time, she'll get focused and realize that she needs to have her own career. Amy's pretty and will have no problem meeting another guy. I just hope he will be more appropriate for her to date. I learned the hard way that life is rarely fair and you have to be ready to roll with the punches. It's a man's world, and even an educated woman has to work harder to be successful."

I don't think she ever took a breath throughout her Amy dissertation. Awkward as the conversation was, that impressed me. I knew I had a talent for talking, and I could see where I'd gotten it from. The moment of conciliatory pride was short lived, though, because just when I thought Mom couldn't say anything that would embarrass me, I discovered I was wrong.

"I don't date much, although I do get asked out from time to time. I generally refuse. Most of my colleagues think I'm gay. I see the looks and the condescending smiles but it makes things easier to let them think what they want. Guys have to put you in some sort of unreachable category to make them feel better about themselves. The thing is. I really don't care what anybody thinks, whether they are men or women. I'm good at what I do and around the office I keep it, strictly business. Oh, I get in the mood for male companionship like any other woman. Since I spend so much time in hotels, it's not easy to meet a guy that's not affiliated with work. Besides that I don't have time for a relationship and if I did. I wouldn't make the time. It's just not worth it to want something and then lose it again."

I guessed she'd finished because Mom paused... then peered at me with a peculiar expression on her face.

"You can close your mouth now," she said.

I complied without comment. The conversation had taken a turn that definitely made me more than a little uncomfortable. Mom had been talking to me like we were friends, not mother and daughter.

"Guess that's a little more than you wanted to hear about your mom," she said.

Then... without a smile or expression of any kind, she started to say something else but her cell phone rang. Never have I been so grateful for a conversation to be over.

"Hello, this is Abigail," she said and took off in the direction of her office.

I made my escape. By the time I came back from swimming, Mom had left again. There had been no discussion about my thirteenth birthday that was only three days away, but I did find a gift on my bed. An attached note said. *Do not open until your birthday. Something came up with work so I may not be home for the big day.* I knew that meant she would not be back and by the time she did get home. My birthday would be a distant memory. I sat down on my bed and picked up the package and shook it a couple of times to determine if the rattle sounded like a video game or something equivalent. Tears welled up in my eyes, but I fought them off.

Abigail has missed the last three birthdays, so why should this one be any different?

Then I realized that for the first time I had thought of my mother not as *Mom* but as *Abigail*, just like Amy did. At that point, I couldn't help myself. More tears came and with it anger. I threw the gift across the room and bounced it off the wall and thumped onto the floor. I buried my face in my pillows and bawled like a little kid. Thankfully no one was around to hear me. Fred had taken Amy to Denton so she could get her class schedule in order, and Gina had gone to the grocery store. I'm not sure how long I cried but I felt exhausted by the time the tears quit coming. I tried to figure out why it had bothered me so much. After all, it wasn't anything new. Abigail managed to be around for most of the major government holidays. Of course that was because the courts were closed. It was unsettling that soon I would soon be thirteen—a teenager and a young woman.

I'm not sure if it was emotion or a predetermined moment in nature's big scheme of things, but the very next day, I got my first period. Needless to say, Abigail wasn't there. Amy was and she patiently walked me through my first steps into puberty.

She threw me a great birthday party too. This year... no boys were allowed. Some of my friends grumbled a little but my sister managed to turn the affair into a slumber party and even got a couple of her college friends to join us. That made my party the coolest and most grown-up birthday party ever. We stayed up nearly all night and even though the house was a mess. Gina and Fred were unruffled by the whole affair. They had become the closest thing to a family structure that Amy and I had. So we both pitched in to clean up when everyone left the next morning. We were about halfway done when Abigail showed up. She walked around, quietly assessing what had occurred in her absence and then sat the four of us down. First she griped at Amy and me for talking the hired help into doing our bidding. Then she sent us to our rooms so she could yell at Gina and Fred. What scared me the most about the whole deal was the fear that she might fire them. I was quickly realizing that as soon as Amy turned eighteen, she would be gone and I would be left to deal with the warden by myself. I did not relish knowing exactly what would happen when that news hit the fan.

We learned later that Abigail had given Fred and Gina a couple of days off without pay. Our sentence was for Amy and me to clean the house to her specifications. Three days later, she left for work again, this time for nearly two weeks. I guess it never occurred to her to ask if I had a fun birthday party. The subject about my new monthly visitor also never came up. That was not much of a surprise since we'd hardly spoken the whole time she had been home. I decided that I had no good reason to tell her since it seemed that Abigail only had an interest in her needs and not anyone else's. The whole puberty thing felt embarrassing to me. So I had no trouble keeping it to myself. The distance between Abigail and me—and Amy and Abigail—seemed to increase every time we were together. I was glad that Amy and I continued to get closer. However, the fact that Abigail was maintaining her status as public enemy number one didn't feel right.

The next few weeks, Amy and I stayed busy with school. Since she had begun college, our class schedules—for the first time ever—didn't sync up. I saw very little of her except on weekends, and those occasions seemed to be shorter as the weeks swept by. Even so, I noticed subtle changes in my sister's behavior. At first, I didn't really think much of it. I thought about talking to Gina about it but decided to keep it to myself. I noticed that her bathroom time increased. When you live with someone and have been sharing a toilet all your life. You tend to notice infringements on your time schedule. I was puzzling over the phenomenon one day and realized that her lengthy stays had started sometime in August. Being generous is a good character trait for siblings and now that I had become a young woman, I decided to overlook the violation. Of course, the whole idea is, if you give, you get back somewhere down the road. Trust me, it's not like I'm the perfect little sister. I didn't think much more about it until one morning when I thought I heard her throwing up. Still sleepy I got up and walked to my door, which connected our Jack and Jill bathroom. We each have our own vanities, so the only part we actually shared was the shower and commode. With only a door between us, I could hear Amy puking her guts up—and it sounded really gross. I rapped on the door softly.

"Hey, sis … you okay in there?" I asked.

"Go away!" she replied.

Unwilling to be sent away without good reason, I stood my ground. "What's the matter? Do you have the flu?" I asked with as much sympathy as I could muster so early in the morning.

"I'll be fine. Could be a little dose of food poisoning," Amy said.

She didn't sound very convincing, and the next sound was an eruption that sounded like some sort of dying moose call. There came a pause, and then the toilet flushed. I waited and listened to the water running in the sink. After what seemed like an eternity, she opened the door.

"See, I'm fine. Now will you leave me alone?"

"You don't look fine. You look like crap," I said as a whiff of my sister's vomit floated to the doorway. "Oh ... that smells disgusting."

I stepped back, waving my hand in front of my face trying to make the vile odor go away. Only an involuntary step back from the doorway saved me from gagging. Then I noticed that Amy was wearing the pink pajamas I'd bought her last Christmas. They had fit her fine then. Now I could see her bulging in the middle and putting quite a strain on the buttons.

"Dang, sis, you're getting fat. You had better get yourself on a diet or Peter won't know you next month."

I added a little giggle in there thinking what I said sounded kind of funny. Without any warning, Amy began to cry. I expected her to throw something at me but I darn sure didn't expect her to start crying. That was an oddity because Amy rarely cried about anything. Then the proverbial light bulb came on in my head. I started to acknowledge that I understood but I didn't know what to say. Instead I wrapped my arms around my big sister and hugged her like there was no tomorrow and cried with her. I'm not sure how long we carried on but probably not as long as it seemed. Amy pushed me to arm's length with one hand and brushed some of my tears away. It made me feel stupid.

"I'm the one who should be wiping your tears away," I said.

"You did in a way, sis. Just the fact that I don't have to keep this secret to myself already makes me feel better."

"Why didn't you tell me sooner? You know you could have and that I would still love you."

I thought she was going to start crying again but she took a deep breath and shook it off.

"I didn't tell you because I lied to you that morning in the tree house."

It didn't take a rocket scientist to fill in the blank spots. Although I don't know much about the subject, I understood the general idea that resulted in my sister being pregnant.

"Well, I figured that part out." I said.

I'm not sure if it was the way I said it or just a release of stress that Amy had been harboring for two months, but she laughed. It happened somewhere in the middle of an actual laugh and blubbering. It was the closest I had felt to her since school started.

The early morning commotion brought Gina to my bedroom door. I barely heard the knock before she stuck her head in. "What's going on up here?" she asked.

Even though Gina acted serious, she had a playful demeanor that meant she was mostly curious rather than being nosy. Without thinking, I stepped in front of Amy, shielding her from view.

"Nothing is going on," I said.

The remark, not to mention the gesture of using myself as a human shield, proved worthy of suspicion without a doubt. Gina, being a veteran parent, just shook her head and rattled off something in Spanish that translated roughly into something about crazy young women.

Once she closed the door, I turned back to Amy and gave her a quick once-over. I put my chin in my hand, closed my eyes, and shook my head in disapproval.

"We need to go shopping, and I mean today," I said.

Amy looked somewhat perplexed and apparently didn't really understand my thinking. "I don't need any clothes right now. Heck, in a month, I'm leaving with whatever I can carry." I heard a tone of indignation in her voice that told me she was clueless of my objective.

"Sis, you are busting out of your pajamas, and they were loose on you six months ago. I'm going out on a limb here and guessing that most of your clothes are getting snug too."

My hands had gone to my hips for effect. I guess it worked, because she got it.

"Yeah… most of my jeans are getting pretty snug."

Her observation came out like she was thinking out loud to herself and had just realized that she was getting noticeably bigger.

"How could I be so stupid? I'm pregnant. Before long, I'll be a big whale waddling around. I probably won't even be able to tie my own shoes. I guess I better get some slippers and a big fuzzy robe."

I almost laughed, thinking how funny she was being but managed to keep it under control long enough to realize that she seemed to be on the verge of tears again. I didn't know anything about being pregnant and it was becoming abundantly clear that my sister didn't either. I decided a good perusal of the Internet that night would be helpful. For now though I knew Amy needed my help because she was a basket case.

"Okay … this evening, as soon as I'm done with school, we are going to the mall and do some shopping," I said.

"I can't go buy maternity clothes! It will be a dead giveaway the first time Abigail sees me."

She looked like she could lose it again any second.

Crap, how many times can you cry in less than ten minutes? I thought to myself.

She looked around, her head lolling like she would soon pass out. I grabbed her and hugged her, then gently separated us enough that she could see my face.

"Sis, we are going to get through this and everything is going to be okay. We are not going to buy maternity clothes, but we are going to get some stuff that is a little looser fitting."

She started crying again. This time though… it was the good kind, she managed to get it together in short order.

"How could I have ever gotten through this without you?" Amy said.

"You've been taking care of me for as long as I can remember. I guess it's my turn. Besides, it's a great excuse to go shopping," I said.

Amy started to say thanks, but she must have realized what time it was. "Crap … I've got fifteen minutes before I have to leave—and you have less than that," she said.

Then she headed off to her bedroom, mumbling something about not having time to look pretty today.

I washed my face and the other needful things before hurriedly jumping into some clothes. About halfway down the stairs, Gina appeared at the bottom, presumably to announce our desperate lateness.

"Breakfast is on the table. Does your sister know she is running late?" she asked.

"Yep … she does. She'll be down in a minute. I'm starving. What are we having this morning?"

"Waffles…and they are getting colder by the minute," Gina said.

She had a fake sternness plastered on her face that melted instantly when I kissed her on the cheek. I brushed by her without another word and attacked the Belgian waffle topped with blueberries and whipped cream. It looked delicious but in lieu of my lateness. I gobbled it down so fast I can't say that I tasted much. I heard a honk from the street outside, which told me my best friend Susan's mom was outside waiting to take me to school. We carpooled because my house was on their way to school and her mom insisted on picking me up. It was nice of her and I got a lot less ribbing from friends than I did when Fred drove me. Now he had to accompany Amy to college every day and shadow her there. Fred kind of looked like a secret service or bodyguard type; he always wore a dark suit and drove a black SUV. He was devastatingly handsome and even though he had been around for several months. I still got tongue-tied every time I saw him, so, it was by far less embarrassing to ride with my friend.

Susan and I had been friends since kindergarten. It took her less than two minutes to see that something weighed heavy on my mind. She badgered me for answers. I knew that loose lips sink ships and my first responsibility was to Amy. Besides being a top-secret commitment to my sister, it felt like an uncomfortable truth and one that I really didn't feel like sharing. This bomb had gone off less than thirty minutes ago and I wasn't sure exactly how I felt about it.

Am I ashamed of my sister's choices? I wondered. *No, I would never feel that way about Amy. She's in love and it is too late to worry whether or not it had been a bad choice. The deed was done.*

For the first time in my life, I felt a weight of responsibility that I had never know before. I didn't know for sure if it was a bad feeling or a good one. I've never had anyone depend on me for this level of support. Even though I felt troubled by the whole sordid mess, it also made me feel needed and more grown up than I had ever felt. Susan continued to badger me until I acquiesced and lied, telling her that I'd had a fight with Amy and that I just didn't want to talk about it. That seemed to satisfy her curiosity and the subject changed to our usual morning banter.

After school, Amy and I went shopping and found some jeans and blouses with a little extra room for her—all on sale to boot. We bought stuff that Amy would normally wear so it wouldn't put up any red flags, if by chance Abigail happened to peruse her closet. The trick was to buy stuff a little bit bigger without looking like it was. Even though we were under constant scrutiny, we both enjoyed an allowance that would be enviable to most and trivial to some. Amy and I were both pretty frugal with our money. So when we pooled our resources, we had plenty for the task that lay before us. We had no idea if Abigail looked through our closets to see what we spent our money on. So it seemed prudent to not get carried away. Amy insisted that I buy something for myself as well. With everything that had transpired, we still managed to have fun together and I realized how lucky I was to have a big sister who would actually spend time with me. Circumstance had created our dependence on each other and I liked being her confidant. No matter what, we were closer as a result of that trust.

Chapter 12
Peter

The concert schedule had been brutal, so it was no big surprise when we had a two-week break in October. The band went in five different directions. Even Barry and his brother Josh went their separate ways for a short vacation. I didn't really have any place I wanted to go. So I went home. Money was already rolling in so fast that I was getting financial advice on what seemed to be a daily basis. I had been discouraged from giving too much money to my family because they would have to pay taxes on anything over a gift of twelve thousand dollars. I landed in the highest tax bracket and already paid more in taxes than most people could imagine having for an income. My closest advisers encouraged me to buy things and let my family use them.

My dad grew up on a farm in Missouri and loved the idea of having a ranch. The whole idea didn't appeal to me. But I knew it had always been a dream of his. As a surprise, I bought a thousand acres and some horses. The ranch sat about thirty miles north of McKinney, which put it pretty close to Lake Texoma. The location was perfect since Dad loved to fish and the lake was well known for its striped bass population. The main house was over eight thousand square feet and even had a wine cellar. Dad never cared for wine much but would have an occasional beer. It surprised me to find out that he and Mom did like some of the red wines Big Tony had sent them, over the last few months.

Mom walked through the house but pondered for a very long time in the kitchen. She loved to cook and the gourmet kitchen looked to be a chef's paradise. It was oversized with lots of cabinets and granite countertops. The refrigerator, freezer, six-burner gas stove, dishwasher, and sink were all restaurant-quality, commercial-grade stainless steel. I think she touched everything as she went through it with a fine-tooth comb.

Dad had gone outside with Tom Parks, the previous owner, to get a firsthand tour of the property and livestock on horseback. Tom was a native Texan and the ranch had been in his family for over a hundred years. His wife had died a little over a year ago, and his kids were all grown. They lived in Dallas and had no interest in country life and Tom was getting too old to take care of the place. He had about three hundred head of Black Angus cattle and thirty-four horses. Most of the horses were quarter horses, but he also had six thoroughbred mares that were registered and came from big-name racing stock. None of that meant much to me. Dad however, seemed like a little kid on Christmas day.

I am what most people would call a loner. Making friends has never been easy for me. Except for my Mom and Dad, the friends I did have were far and few between. When Amy came along, it was the first time that I ever connected with someone. Now it was early October and thirty-two days before she turned eighteen. I was daydreaming about that when Tom came in with Dad, who jabbered away about what a nice place it was. Mom and Dad didn't know I had already bought the place. They thought I was just looking at it mostly as an investment. Tom was happy to play out the façade so I could be the one to spring the surprise. When the attention centered on me, Mom was the first one to speak her mind. She had always been the family penny-pincher. So it was not at all surprising to hear what she had to say.

"Peter, the house is lovely, and it does have a remote location that I'm sure is appealing to you. You may want to consider though, since you have all of this newfound popularity, something in a gated community. This place is just too big for one person. You would need full-time help just to keep it clean."

She made the comments while looking around and gesturing for effect. It seemed quite funny to me, and I had a hard time not laughing.

"Your mother is right, son," Dad said. "This ranch would take daily supervision, even if you hired help, just to do the everyday chores. This place is huge!"

Dad's last remark also included the use of his arms in a big circular motion for effect.

I had to be careful not to look at either one of my parents in the eye or the illusion would have been seen through. My folks knew me all too well. So I walked to the sliding glass door that overlooked the horse pasture behind the house.

"You have to admit," I said, "it is a really nice place and the realtor insists that any land purchase is a good investment. The paper-pushers are telling me I need to put my money into something substantial."

Dad, the man I had grown up admiring my whole life, walked up and put a hand on my shoulder. "It's a beautiful place son. One like I have always dreamed of, but you have never expressed any desire to have a ranch. I think you should consider some commercial property in town."

I just couldn't keep the cat in the bag for much longer, so I looked at Dad and winked with a big smile and whispered the words, "Merry Christmas, Dad."

My dad loved to talk so it was a rare occasion for him to have nothing to say. There was no doubt that he understood my meaning. He stood there speechless, his eyes moistened as the realization of a lifelong dream became a reality. Dad's reaction immediately affected me, and I began to tear up as well. It made me wonder why human beings could cry about something joyful as energetically as something sad. I can't control the fact that my thoughts have a tendency to stray and usually it's at the wrong time. I was brought back to the moment when Dad gave me a big hug. That told mom that something was amuck and that she was not privy to understanding what was happening.

"What's going on, you two?" she asked. Her first steps were slow and uncertain, but as she neared us... Dad and I turned toward her. "What's the matter? Why are you crying?"

Dad offered an arm as she joined us and brought her into a three-way hug with her in the middle between us. "Well Margaret," he said and then paused for effect. "Our son here has just informed me that this place he's been pretending to be interested in buying is in reality an early Christmas present."

"Well, that's a mighty big present. Who in the world do you think is worth a gift like that?" She said it before she had put everything together and then it dawned on her. "Oh... Oh my... John, we can't accept it. Even from Peter... We couldn't afford the taxes on this place."

Dad glanced at me with a questioning look. It was time to explain myself and hope that they would be good with the truth.

"Mom, here's the deal. I've already bought the ranch. The accountants have set up an account to pay for the day-to-day expenses that include everything from feed for the livestock to utilities and, yes, even property taxes. If I give it to you, then you would have to pay taxes on it and it wouldn't help me out. As they explain it to me, it will be a tax shelter. I need somebody I can trust to look after it. So I thought you and Dad would be interested in taking on the task."

Mom frowned at Dad and then softened up a little when her gaze went to me. "John, have you been a part of this charade?"

"I just found out moments ago," Dad said.

"Well, I suppose we could look after the place for a while and see if it's a fit or not," Mom said. She looked away scanning the kitchen again. When her eyes returned to me, they had tears of joy in them as well. "Peter, you are a marvelous young man. I'm very proud that you are my son."

I'm not sure but I think old Tom may have been crying a little bit too. Then I had a quick discreet conversation with Dad, and we agreed to ask Tom to stay on as a consultant.

"Mr. Parks," I said, "my father and I would very much like it if you would stay in the area and be a consultant on the inner workings of the ranch."

"Yes, I would be happy to," he said with noticeable enthusiasm. "As a matter of fact, since you gave me my asking price, I bought a house with a dock on the lake just fifteen miles from here. If John will find time to go fishing with me. I'll teach him everything I know about ranching."

I knew that my dad was living the dream, and he answered for me before I could squeak out a word. "You'll have to accept a salary to make this an acceptable trade," Dad said.

"Sorry John... that's just not the way we do things around here. Peter tells me you're a class act when it comes to fishing. I don't know beans about it because I never had the time. You teach me all of your tricks concerning the fine art of angling, and for that, I teach you about ranching and racehorses. Do we have a deal?" He held out his hand for a shake that would close the arrangement.

Dad shook Tom's hand and slapped him on the shoulder with the other. "It's a deal Tom, but I'll warn you right now,

Peter may have stretched the truth a little as to my fishing skills."

"Stretching the truth is part of fishing," Tom said.

They both laughed while mom and I rolled our eyes at each other. The good thing was that my dad and Tom had seemed to really hit it off. The bonding made the ranch deal go a lot easier from my end since I wouldn't have to look for an authority on ranching who was interested in a part-time job. Not to mention the fact that I would never find anyone who cared as much about the place as Tom did.

I could tell there would be a long conversation about the inner workings of the property and Mom was already caught up in thinking about decorating the house. So I took the opportunity to take a walk and check out the place. Tom suggested that I walk down to the lake. Turns out my new ranch had a twelve-acre lake on it—who knew? I followed his directions, which were about as easy as it gets. There was a well-worn road that ran straight south behind the house. It was fenced on either side with a hedge of mature trees on the west side. It was midafternoon, so shade covered the road.

Autumn in Texas usually comes late fall, it had been a pretty dry summer, so the leaves were turning colors early. The temperature was in the high seventies making the day very pleasant. I grew up in the city and had very little exposure to country life. The first thing I noticed was the quiet. A soft breeze stirred a mixture of organic aromas into the air. Their pungent smells were quite different from the city. I had to admit though, it was kind of nice and without a doubt much different than living in the city.

Chicago was noisy twenty-four hours a day, seven days a week. I had one more week before I had to be back to the studio to start recording our next CD. I already had most of the music in my head, but at some point in time, I knew I would have to go through the drudgery of actually putting it on paper.

If the band could read my mind, it would be a lot faster.

The notion was a ridiculous idea, and it made me chuckle to myself. My thoughts turned to Amy—nothing new. It seemed sometimes that I thought of little else. The last night we had been together still weighed heavy on my mind. I wasn't sorry about what we did. In fact, it had been wonderful. My only reservation, and one that came to mind every time I thought about Amy, was: why? It was a special night, but it would have been special whether she had given herself to me or not. I had considered the course of events that led to the last part of the evening in my mind over and over. I didn't want to come to the same conclusion every time I thought it through, but I did. Amy must have been afraid of losing me. The idea seemed so bizarre to my way of thinking that I just couldn't help but dwell on it. Amy had always been my anchor. She was unwavering and solid in her opinion and, I thought, in confidence. I can't really explain why that bothered me. The guys in the band managed to be with a different girl in every city we played in. I got why most girlfriends would be worried about the solidarity of a relationship, especially when it came to popular musicians. I guess I felt like she didn't trust me a hundred percent and wanted to prove she would be worth the wait. I hoped as soon as we were together, we would have a conversation to clear the air. Amy was very intuitive when something was troubling me, and she would have me talking about it in short order.

I had no idea how long I'd been walking, all of a sudden the lake came into view and it was spectacular. I had no concept of how big a twelve-acre lake, it surprised me. It was huge and shaped like a crescent moon. The long part ran more or less north and south, while the road ran across the east side, which was the dam side and higher than the rest of the lake. The west side featured loads of cattails, and a pretty big population of ducks swam in and out of the shallows. I'm guessing they were hunting for tidbits of food, because every so often, they would plunge their heads into the water. I sat down and watched them for a while. It probably sounds a bit loony, but it was fun. For just a little while, I managed to not think. That's not an easy task for a guy like me. I'm not sure how much time had passed before I heard something and looked up to see my dad walking up. He just gave me a nod and sat down beside me and got into watching the ducks. After a short while, he broke the silence.

"Do you want to talk about it?"

I considered saying "Talk about what?" but I knew my dad had been figuring out my moods long before Amy had come into the picture. I viewed my dad as a great guy. He was smart, caring, and fun to be around. I felt lucky to have a dad like him. I truly wished I could be just like him, but I knew that would never be the case no matter how hard I tried. Dad was a really sharp fellow, more so than your average guy, he had an uncanny amount of common sense. That's where our differences began. I suppose some would say I was a genius or perhaps a prodigy. Music and mathematics were simplistic for me. Music gave me joy, whereas math just seemed to satisfy my ravenous hunger for knowledge. Most people probably believe that being so smart would have been a godsend. I suppose it was, but at the end of the day, it seemed more like a curse. I eyed Dad and saw no indication of judgment; he did have a curious sense of mirth to his demeanor.

"I'm not sure where to start, Dad. How much time do you have?" I asked.

I forced a smile in an effort to bring some levity to the moment. I guess, smart as I am, it didn't work.

"I have as much time as you need. There has been something on your mind ever since you got home." He paused before continuing. "Why not just start with the first thing that comes to your mind?"

"Amy is on my mind most of the time."

I kind of just blurted it out. Dad smiled and shook his head.

"Women … can't live with them and you can't live without them," he said.

It wasn't the first time I had heard my father make that observation. I knew… according to Dad at least, the words had been voiced by men over a millennium.

I chuckled. "Do woman have a similar saying for us guys?" I asked.

"Probably, I'm guessing they never voice it because they already know we can't make it without them. Men have always been the hunters and providers. The women were gatherers who most likely fed everybody with nuts and berries when the hunt didn't go well. They also nurtured their families and kept home a place that we wanted to return to. I suppose the world is changing these days and there are role reversals, but it's hard to change instinct."

"I saw Amy in July after the concert in Fort Worth."

"Yeah, I figured as much. I was pretty sure wild horses couldn't keep you two apart. I'm guessing you pulled it off without getting caught since Abigail hasn't called the police."

"No, we were very careful about that. But something happened that night after the concert," I said, so softly I wasn't sure if he heard me.

"Yeah, I figured that would happen sooner or later too."

I waited for him to add to the comment, to expound or to judge me, but he didn't. I guess I shouldn't have been surprised. Dad never passed judgment on anything until he heard the whole story. I wasn't sure why I'd brought it up. It was awkward to talk about, even to a guy as cool as my dad. Still… it was my dad. Clearly, though, I had dug a hole, and now I faced finishing the conversation or clamming up. Difficult or not, I wanted answers about something that I knew very little about, so I opened up.

"Amy showed up to the concert, and she looked unbelievable. I've never seen her so… dressed up."

I looked at dad so he would know it was his cue to explain that part to me.

"She dressed up for you son. That part is not rocket science. I'm certain she loves you as much as you love her and she wanted you to remember the night."

"Well there's no danger of me forgetting the evening, that's for sure." I shocked myself, but the conversation seemed comfortable enough and Dad made me feel like it was just everyday stuff. "We were apart for over ten months and I thought about her every day. When she came to the concert, I didn't have any expectations for that evening except to see her."

"Do you think she was trying to seduce you?" he asked.

"No… Well… I don't think so. Ah heck, I really don't know."

"Did you initiate the encounter… or did she?"

"I don't know. It just sort of happened but it just seemed like it was planned. You know what I mean?"

"Yes, I do know what you mean. Why does that bother you?"

"I don't know. It seems like maybe she did that because she was insecure about us and about me."

"Is she pregnant?"

"No... she couldn't be. It was just one time."

"Did you use a contraceptive?"

"No... I didn't. I'm not sure if she did. We didn't talk about that; it just happened."

I think Dad knew I was close to being an emotional wreck. He put his arm around me and gave me a hug.

The ducks were getting braver and filed by quacking in unison, while dad considered what to say next. "I'm guessing that Amy wanted to seal the bond between you. I think you are reading too much between the lines here. Heck, a hundred years ago, she would almost be considered an old maid." He punched me in the side and managed to get a smile out of me. "You are without a doubt the smartest individual I have ever known, so it's hard for me to realize that you still have very little in the way of life experiences to draw answers from. The two of you are at the most fertile age of your lives, which means yes. She could get pregnant from only one time. Now I'm not so old-fashioned to say you should have waited and been married first but you both should have given the consequences a lot more thought. So you are telling me that you're not sure if she seduced you or not? Correct me if I'm wrong: she didn't make you do anything that you did not want to do?"

"No, she would never do that!"

Dad had hit a nerve. I realized by the tone of my voice that I was defending Amy's character. Dad had an odd sort of smile on his face. It was an expression that I had never seen and wasn't exactly sure what it meant.

"When are you going to see her next?"

"She turns eighteen on November fourteenth and is coming to Chicago. We are going to get married."

"What if she shows up pregnant? Would you still want to marry her?"

"Of course I would. That would be all the more reason for us to get married."

"Let me put it in a different way. Don't get mad and please give it some honest consideration. If she were pregnant, would you feel like she had trapped you into marriage?"

The question was asked in a calm and constructive manner. I took a breath and considered my answer with care. The question-and-answer session had come full circle and I was beginning to understand what he meant.

"I would have to say the timing would be less than perfect. But I've known ever since I met Amy that I wanted to spend the rest of my life with her. No matter how hard it was or what challenges we faced. Without her—my life would be empty and have no meaning."

Dad smiled. "I think you may have just answered the questions to your dilemma. If you're willing to accept what life hands you with open arms and can do so without blaming your partner. Then you have a good foundation to build a relationship upon. Being in love is a very important part of marriage. To have a lasting bond you have to be best friends as well."

"You've been telling me how smart I am for as long as I can remember. If I'm so smart, why do I ask questions about stuff that's not complicated?"

It had been a long time since I had heard my dad laugh so hard. I could not figure out what I said that was so funny. As a rule, it hurt my feelings when people laughed at me. At least in this case, it wasn't malicious, but it still bothered me. Dad only chuckled for a short time. I knew he picked up on my mood right away.

"Okay… I know you're not laughing at me. What's so funny?" I asked.

Dad managed to choke off his amusement and then wiped some tears out of the corner of his eyes. "Relationships and women are harder than rocket science, music, or mathematics, for all mortal men. Believe me when I tell you that I am regularly confounded by your mother. They keep us guessing because they can. It's the spice of life, I suppose." He stood up and dusted his trousers off, then offered me a hand up. "Come on, let's get back before your mother sends out a search party for us."

I took the hint, knowing it was getting late. For some reason a piece of me wanted to linger. There was something about this spot. I made a mental note to come back and spend more time at a later date with Amy. I took Dad's hand. Hopped to my feet and gave him a hug.

"Thanks, Dad… I appreciate the talk. Do you like the ranch?"

We started up the dirt road to the house and Dad switched gears to the new conversation.

"I love it son. This place is like a dream come true for me. I hope when you have the time. You'll take a moment to slow down to the ranch life crawl and enjoy some of the simple things in life."

"You mean like the ducks?" I motioned back toward the lake so he would know what I meant.

"Yes… like the ducks, and much more," he said. "Did you know that we are the proud owners of six thoroughbred mares and that two of them are descendants of Secretariat?"

"I remember a movie about Secretariat but I guess I didn't realize it was about a real horse."

"Oh yeah, he was a real horse alright. He was the last horse to win the Triple Crown, back in the seventies.

Anyway, those two mares that you acquired with this ranch have Secretariat in their bloodlines. With a little research, we could have them bred to a champion stud. Who knows, we might be in the racehorse business."

"Are racehorses something that you're interested in?"

"Well… it would be expensive. I won't lie about that, but sure, working with horses is a passion that's been with me since I was a kid. I really never thought I would get an opportunity to do it again. It would be a ton of work and fun. If we got really lucky and produced a winner, it might pay for the ranch at some point down the road."

I figured Dad had no idea that I had just given Tom twelve million for the property, livestock, and equipment. I planned to keep it that way and had asked Tom to keep that part of the deal to himself. The glow and passion on Dad's face was worth every dollar. I didn't buy the place expecting to make anything, so I had no expectations. One of the big things I respected about my father. When he made up his mind to do something, he usually did it. So he talked and I listened to his ideas on our way back to the house. Mom was waiting outside, talking to Tom when we got back. She scolded us for taking so long.

We all shook Tom's hand, exchanged pleasantries, and then loaded up in the new Range Rover that I had just bought for Mom and Dad. It was a short ride and Dad babbled about raising racehorses all the way. I settled into the backseat for the ride home. Wishing I could see Amy. Even though we managed to share some sporadic emails and a couple of quick phone calls over the last three months, I was definitely getting impatient. Amy had convinced me that we shouldn't take any chances since her birthday was just a few weeks away. Being in the same town and knowing that Abigail was out of town made that decision sheer torture. After waiting a whole year, another few weeks would be doable, but the last days of a long wait are always the worst. The visit with mom and dad filled in the gaps of loneliness, and before I knew it. I was on my way back to the Windy City.

The remaining weeks of waiting were not as bad as I thought, because once the band reunited. We went to work on our new CD. I put everyone through a brutal schedule so we could be done on November 13, the day before Amy's birthday. I left nothing to chance and I decided to pick her up in style. We finished recording late on the night of the thirteenth, and Big Tony took me to the airport early on the morning of the fourteenth.

I chartered a small business jet with plans of picking her up at the McKinney airport. She would pretend to be sick and sneak away from her house. I wasn't sure exactly how she would get away from Fred and pull it off. She assured me, though. It would not be a problem. Tony wanted to come along but I insisted on going alone. So it was just me, the pilot, and copilot. They both seemed like really cool guys and once we made it out of the restricted airspace. The copilot let me take his spot for a few minutes and I got fly for a little bit. I had fun doing it, but my mind kept wandering and made it a bit of a challenge. I went back into the cabin and snuggled up in one of the big leather chairs and somehow nodded off. The next thing I knew the pilot announced our descent into McKinney and that we would be landing soon. We had left Chicago at seven and I noted the time was now nine thirty.

"Wow... two and a half hours," I mumbled to myself.

I thought about how long it had taken Amy and me to drive it just a little over a year ago and how we had to scrape money together for gas.

The bump of landing and a chirp of the tires announced our arrival. I peered out the window, straining to see her. It's a small airport, so it only took a few moments to taxi up to the FBO—fixed base operator. The pilot told me and that we would take on some fuel while we pick up our passenger. As soon as the copilot opened the door, I bounded down the stairs. It felt cooler than it had been a few weeks earlier but I hardly noticed. My anticipation of seeing Amy was all I could think about. I didn't see her at first and my expectation swiftly turned to fear. What if she didn't show up? Had she changed her mind? And then I saw movement behind the shaded glass of the FBO office door. When it opened there she was. An older man held the door open so she could step through. Amy had on a knee-length winter coat with a hood that was pulled up over her head. I almost laughed when she looked up at me and waved.

"Peter!" she squealed with delight.

I guess she was trying to be incognito, because she had on the largest pair of sunglasses that I had ever seen. It seemed funny to me since anyone who knew Amy would have realized it was her. I took off in a trot. She mimicked my lead and we spun into each other's arms midway.

"Oh, Peter! I didn't think this day would ever come. I've missed you so much."

I can't think of a moment that I've ever been happier. The look on Amy's face told me... she felt the same way. I kissed her and wanted to linger on her lips but neither of us wanted to take a chance on a confrontation with Abigail. "Come on. Let's get out of here." I said.

She beamed a big smile and said. "I can't wait! I've been dreaming of this day for a year."

We hurried to the plane and boarded while her luggage was loaded. I plopped down into one of the oversized executive seats, and Amy sat in my lap. She kissed me with a ferocity that sent my male instincts into a primal frenzy. I was on the edge of one of those moments where a guy's mind goes almost feral. Somehow—I heard a harrumph and then another one much louder than the first. I looked in the direction of the sound and realized the copilot was trying in vain to get my attention while still managing to keep his eyes averted. I'm sure I looked dazed and confused but managed to acknowledge him.

"What's up Teddy?" I croaked.

"Uh, Mr. Shaw, there is another young lady here who's insisting you know her. Do you want me to send her away?"

I looked at Amy, wondering who it could be. The crew was aware of a possible confrontation with Abigail and had seen a photo. I knew it wasn't her. I glanced out the nearest porthole and in short order realized who it was.

"It's your sister," I said, looking back at Amy, and then motioned to the copilot. "It's okay. Let her in."

Kelly ran up the air-stairs and took one short but all-encompassing look at her surroundings and bounced up and down, squealing with obvious delight.

"This is so awesome, you guys! A Learjet 45XR, Way to ride in style," she said dropping into the seat facing us.

"Sis, what are you doing here? How did you get away from school?" Amy asked.

"A friend's older sister brought me. I just had to come say good-bye to you both."

"Uh, we already had a very long good-bye that. If memory serves me, started last week," Amy said.

I thought she sounded a little grumpy with her little sister but wisely chose to not get involved.

"I know," Kelly said in a low, sort of whiny voice. "I promise I won't stay long. The guy fueling the jet said he would need at least five more minutes to top off the tanks."

"Wait," I said. "Before, you said this is a Learjet 45XR. How did you know that?"

My soon to be little sister-in-law looked at me as if I were simple minded. It's not a look that I get very often. I felt more amused than offended.

"Because I like airplanes and I want to be a pilot when I get old enough to get out from under this rock in Texas," she said, sounding a little perturbed.

She hadn't directed it toward me, I knew; it was her situation in general. I totally understood since she was still trapped in an unpleasant home life that for her would not be changing anytime soon. Sadly neither Amy nor I could do a thing about it. Kelly came out of the momentary gloom as fast as it had arrived, though.

"Since I won't be able to be at your wedding," Kelly said, "I wanted to tell you both how happy I am for you. I hope that once the deed is done, the warden will accept the fact that you guys love each other and we can be a family again."

A sniffle came out of Amy, and before I knew it, they were both crying. Amy got up and hugged her sister, then said, "We are and always will be a family, no matter what."

I remember thinking that I would never live long enough to figure out why girls cry about the oddest things. Then I understood the full impact of what Kelly had said. Her father was dead and she had a mother who made up for her absence by being overbearing and controlling. To make matters worse. I was taking the only real family Kelly had away from her. I guess at that moment. I reached some level of understanding. I began to get weepy eyed as well. There was no way any of us could know what life had in store for us. It was a special moment that I will always remember. The sisters parted from their embrace, and I handed them both tissues. Luckily I had located a box of Kleenex to dry my own eyes before they noticed.

They both got it together and almost as quick as the tears came. They seemed back to normal. Except for the red swollen eyes and runny noses, another of the many phenomena that I have at some time or another wondered about. Why does your nose run when you cry? It's just kind of weird.

"Did you tell him yet?" Kelly asked. The question was obviously for her sister, but needless to say, it sparked my interest.

"No... shut up," Amy said.

"Tell me what?" I asked.

I saw Kelly pantomiming, *sorry,* with her lips and redirected the conversation. "Well, I guess I had better get going so you guys can leave," Kelly said as she stood up. She gave her sister another hug and then came over and gave me a kind of quick but awkward version. "Bye, you guys. Stay in touch, sis." And then she waved and left.

The copilot reappeared from outside and pulled the door shut behind him. He smiled at us and said, "We're ready to go. You two need to get your seat belts on for takeoff."

He disappeared into the cockpit and pulled the door shut. A few minutes later, we were winging it to Chicago. We lounged in each other's arms and kissed and talked about how hard the past few months had been. The conversation was light. We were happy to just enjoy being together for the first time since July. The two-and-a-half-hour flight passed in what seemed like minutes but we managed to catch up on the past few months. The pilot's voice came over the intercom and announced that we would be landing in about ten minutes and that we should get our seat belts on for landing. We sat facing each other, and for some reason, the comment that Kelly had made came back to me.

"What was Kelly talking about when she said? Did you tell him yet?" I asked.

Amy's face went from jovial to serious in an instant. Clearly the subject hit a nerve, and needless to say, that unsettled me. My mind ran rampant with a variety of scenarios, but none of them prepared me for the answer. She looked out the window, pretending to be interested in the Illinois urban countryside. She still wore the knee-length coat that she'd arrived in. Earlier, when I encouraged her to take it off, she said she was kind of chilly. That seemed odd to me at the time since the climate in the Learjet was a comfortable seventy-five degrees—at least I thought it felt comfortable. She hugged herself and sighed quietly, then looked at me.

"This is not how I wanted to tell you. I had hoped for a better time, perhaps a better setting. I guess you deserve to know now rather than later," she said, then stopped. Her pause was more than I could handle.

"Tell me what?" I asked. I sensed a level of suspense and a certain amount of dread in the air coming from Amy. My mind was screaming *"Tell me!"* but at the same time, I felt afraid she was going to inform me she had changed her mind.

"I'm pregnant."

She said it blunt and as a matter of fact. At first, the word didn't register. The statement was out of the ordinary and not the kind of conversation that we would ever have. It took me by surprise. I didn't know what to say. I felt so relieved that she hadn't dumped me that I took a bit too long to respond. Her eyes were burning a hole through me, and all of a sudden, I realized that she was nervous and anticipating my reply. I started to say, "Are you sure?" and knew right away, that would be stupid. Of course she knew or she wouldn't have said it. My mind went briefly to when Dad and I sat by the lake a few weeks earlier and he asked me how I would feel if something like that happened. As luck would have it. I had pondered that thought at great length and although this was not the time I would have chosen. I was going to be a father. I unbuckled my seat belt and went to my knees directly in front of her and took her hand in mine.

"I guess we'll need a bigger apartment," I said with an awkward smile. Realizing a more appropriate response for the moment, I quickly added, "I love you and there is nothing in this world that will make me happier than to have a family with you."

"Oh, Peter… I was so scared you would be mad. I love you so much."

The tears came, and this time, I didn't try to hide mine. It was just us, and we were caught up in a special moment that we would never forget.

"I love you too," I said.

The tires chirped and I knew we had landed and our new life in Chicago was about to begin. I got back in my seat but sat on the edge so I could still hold her hands.

"I'm guessing that's why you wore that heavy coat all the way from Texas?"

I thought she would start crying again and realized. I had a lot to learn about pregnant women. That made matters more complicated because I didn't understand them when they weren't pregnant.

"I'm fat and I didn't want you to see me until you knew why." I could tell the change she was experiencing was taking an emotional toll on her. So I chose my words as wisely as I could for an eighteen-year-old young man with no clue.

"You are beautiful, and you'll still be beautiful even when you can't see your toes."

I probably could have used a better combination of words, but it was how I felt. I hoped it would make her feel a little better about herself.

"You're not just saying that, are you? In a few more months, you'll have to butter me up to get me through the door."

That visual was funny to both of us and I guess it broke the tension. As we laughed, I thought about putting butter on her and embarrassed myself.

"Why are you getting so red in the face? Peter Shaw, are you blushing?"

I think her noticing made me even more self-conscious. My thoughts betrayed me. I had to come to grips with the fact that I was looking forward to touching her again. Then without preamble I said.

"Well ... I was thinking about you being all buttered up."

As soon as it came out of my mouth, I wished I hadn't said it.

"Oh," she said, realizing the intent of my statement.

Then it was her turn to blush. We were both saved by the plane coming to a stop in front of a private FBO at O'Hare International. The engines wound down to a stop and seconds later, the door opened up. The plane wobbled noticeably just before Big Tony poked his head inside.

"Hi Amy, welcome back to Chicago," He said.

Amy bounced out of her seat, nearly knocking me over in the process and gave Tony a big hug.

"Hi Tony, how's my second favorite man in Chicago?" she asked.

"So there's still a chance for you and me?" he asked.

"If Peter runs me off, I am all yours," she said and then giggled.

They both looked in my direction and even though I knew they were just picking on me. I felt a little twinge of jealousy.

"So Dad, are you ready to get married?" Tony asked.

I was a little taken aback. "Am I the last one to know that I'm going to be a father?"

"No, I'm sure there are a few folks that don't know yet," Tony said.

He was trying to be funny and I knew it, still. I guess my demeanor didn't reflect the humor. Tony had known me long enough to understand the eclectic nuances of my personality and promptly changed the subject. "I followed my instructions from both of you and have everything arranged for you two to get married. In Illinois, there are no blood tests, which mean you can get your marriage license on the same day you apply. You're both eighteen years old so parental consent does not apply. There is a one-day waiting period. I suggest we get the license and go underground until tomorrow."

"Abigail is not due home for a couple of days, so she won't know I'm gone until it is a done deal. Besides that... I'm eighteen. There's nothing she can do to stop this now," Amy said, obviously annoyed that she was still under her mom's thumb.

"Whether you want to believe it or not, your mother is extremely smart and connected," Tony said. "I have talked to Peter's attorneys, and they both agreed that it will be harder for her to give you guys any grief after your married. That being said, time is your friend, the longer we can have you two disappear, the better." Tony paused and looked at me for a moment, apparently trying to decide what to say next and then asked. "Have you discussed the honeymoon with Amy yet?"

Amy gave me a most curious look, one laced with almost no emotion. "Have you made plans for our honeymoon, Peter?" she asked.

The question caught me off guard. I was a rookie as far as relationships went, but I felt pretty sure this was one of those times when you are a romantic hero or it has the opposite effect.

"I did make some plans for our honeymoon. If you don't like the idea, we can go somewhere else," I said.

"Okay." She said.

She seemed somewhat apprehensive but remained patient and gave me the moment I needed.

"I was talking to Don Henley a couple of weeks ago. He suggested that we go to Fiji. There is a small island called Turtle Island. It's what they call an all-inclusive resort and is very private," I said, hoping the last part would make it as appealing to her as it did to me.

"You were talking to Don Henley? Like… the Don Henley from the Eagles?" Amy asked. Her tone had an unexpected amount of animation, and then I realized why. So I decided to be funny.

"Are you interested in our honeymoon or do you want to talk about a drummer I met?" I asked.

Tony chuckled, but Amy's face took on a look that told me she was confused by my response and dismayed that I didn't just answer her question? I understood though. She was awestruck that I had met a performer she really liked. I on the other hand, saw him as a regular guy who had been nice to me. We shared a passion that made having a conversation easy. Even so, I tried to quell her curiosity.

"Tony introduced us at one of the studio functions. He was a really nice guy. We talked about music, and you, my two favorite subjects," I said with a smile.

"Oh… So tell me more about our honeymoon."

I knew she was still busting with questions about the famous Eagles songwriter, vocalist, and drummer, but I felt happy to change the subject back to us.

"It's a small island resort in the South Pacific that has a maximum of twenty-eight guests at any given time. They even have a private beach that we can have for the day that would be for just us. Anything we need or want is available, food, drinks, water toys, scuba diving, and swimming."

"It sounds very expensive. Are you planning to spoil me with frivolous luxuries?" she asked.

"I've been waiting a whole year. I want to do anything you want, but mostly I just want to be with you."

I guess I was getting better at the relationship thing, because that comment got me a hug and a kiss.

"It doesn't matter to me where we go, Peter. I love you."

We were interrupted by someone clearing their throat. The copilot peeked through the door and could just see past Tony's hulking figure.

"I'm sorry to interrupt, but we have another client coming in about an hour, and we need to clean and prep the plane for a trip to New York."

"That's okay. We have a busy day ahead of us," Tony said.

He headed out and down the narrow stairway. Amy and I followed Tony out. I stopped to thank and tip the crew. I had already learned it was expected and that it affected how you were treated the next time. Performers and celebrities were in many ways like everyone else. Most of them were very likeable, but a few were not. Since I constantly worried about fitting in and being liked, I went out of my way to project a good image. Tony had coached me on the subject. He pointed out that a big tip doesn't make up for being an ass. It made total sense to me, and it cost less in tips.

Someone had already loaded Amy's bags into the limo, and soon we were on our way downtown to a nice, out-of-the-way hotel that Tony had arranged for us. I thought it was silly not to just stay in the penthouse apartment that I was living in. Tony had wisely suggested that it might be in our best interest to stay somewhere off the beaten path, as he put it.

It felt good to hear Amy say, "Wow," when we pulled up to the Hotel Sofitel on Chestnut Street in downtown Chicago.

"I booked a suite that has a view of Lake Michigan. I hope you like it," Tony said, more for Amy's benefit than mine.

We gave Amy an hour to freshen up. According to Tony, it was a courtesy that in his experience most women appreciated after a long trip. I thought it was kind of silly since we had spent two hours in a luxury business jet and a thirty-minute ride in a stretch limo. But I conceded to my friend's expertise on the matter. I have to admit that Amy did seem to enjoy the time to make her nest ready for later. In what seemed like two hours later. The three of us headed down to the Cook County courthouse and got our marriage certificate. The court clerk was very nice and told us we could see a judge the next day. Or if we wanted to use a local justice of the peace, she would give us a name. We decided on the second choice and got the address. They had a small chapel, and Amy thought it sounded better than getting married in a judge's chamber. It turned out to be a perfect location since it was not very far from the hotel. We called and made an appointment for two o'clock in the afternoon the next day.

ALLEN HIVELY

Once all of the plans were made, we went back to the hotel.

"I have a ton of stuff to do so I'll see you two tomorrow." Tony said. We said our goodbyes and we were finally alone.

"What do you think about calling room service for dinner?" I asked.

"Sounds great I don't want to go anywhere tonight."

I can't remember what we ate or even eating it for that matter. What I do remember is how pretty Amy looked, and that the additional glow made her even more so.

"You are even more beautiful pregnant." I blurted it out rather than thinking through the words. She seemed embarrassed and obviously shy about the subject. Her face became even more flushed than normal, and I struggled to form the words that would better convey what I meant. I could write a love song on a napkin while having breakfast, but in the heat of the moment, words eluded me. We were quiet for a time as I tried to sort out my thoughts. I wasn't sure what Amy was thinking, and that complicated my thought process. I didn't realized what I was doing until she shifted her position from apparent discomfort.

"What's the matter, Peter?"

She asked the question so quietly I almost missed it. When I looked up into her eyes, I realized that I had been staring at her tummy. My eyes and mind were working in unison once again and had a wonderful thought.

"Nothing is wrong, everything is right," I said.

Her candor eased some, but I could tell she was waiting for me to fill in the blanks. I smiled and reached out to touch her belly, which was in the beginning stages of showing the baby—our baby. She almost recoiled but allowed me to touch her. I could feel the quiver of her nervousness and thought

182

about the new life growing inside her. Our child, whether turning out to be a boy or a girl, would be a little part of each of us.

"What I was trying to say is that you are beautiful. I love you. And I love our baby who is at this very minute growing inside you. I'm looking forward to the joys and tribulations that life has in store for us. Being married and having a family with you is what my dreams are made of." I was careful and very deliberate and sure that I said it exactly as I meant it.

"I was so worried that I when I showed up fat and pregnant that you would feel like I was a burden to you and your career."

The words came out slurred because a full-on cry was on its way. I knew this one came from relief and happiness.

"You're not fat; that's our baby," I said, meaning every word, but it still perpetuated the flood of tears.

As beautiful as Amy looked that night, I have to admit that no one looks good crying, whether it's a happy cry or a sad one. The only difference is the emotion of happy thoughts as opposed to bad ones. She went to the bathroom to blow her nose, which ran about as much as her tears. A few minutes later she reappeared with a semblance of composure. With the exception of her swollen red eyes and smeared eye makeup. Even though, it struck me as somewhat funny. I wisely decided to not mention it. We ordered dinner from room service and had a nice quiet meal alone. She disappeared into the bedroom afterwards and I started to get nervous. Even though we had made love the one time, it still felt very awkward. Seconds later, she reappeared carrying my backpack and handed it to me. I took it from her, wondering what was happening. I felt fairly sure the evening had been going well. At least in my mind it had. She smiled and kissed me, then handed me a keycard.

"You're not sleeping with me tonight, not on our wedding night. It's a tradition. That also means you will not see me until we get married tomorrow at two o'clock."

"Okay, I've waited this long. I suppose one more day can't hurt," I said with a smile.

Even though I still felt a little confused, I realized that I was actually a little bit relieved. The nervous tension that had plagued me earlier evaporated. She kissed me again. A much better one this time and I started to think maybe staying would be a better idea, tradition or not. Amy, however, had made up her mind and began pushing me toward the door. She kissed me one last time at the door and opened it. I knew then I was leaving for sure.

"What room am I in?" I asked.

"It's the next door down on the same side as this one." She paused for a moment, smiled, and continued. "We're doing the wedding tomorrow out of necessity but I assure you that I expect a proper ceremony in the not too distant future." Without further ado, she shut the door.

Chapter 13
Amy

As soon as I shut the door, I had second thoughts. I really wanted Peter to stay with me so we could just talk and be together. I felt uncertain about a lot of things, and although it was unlike me to be needy or to need reassurances. Tomorrow I would be married without having my sister or friends there to share the moment. I gave up the only family, if one would call Abigail family. I've ever known to have a life with Peter. Kelly was not only my sister. She was my friend and a big part of my life. I already missed Kelly and felt empty inside knowing. I wouldn't see here anytime soon. I didn't regret my decision. I just felt alone.

Peter and I had been apart, except for our one encounter, for more than a year. Now it almost felt awkward to be around him. I knew the feeling would pass; even so, it was scary. I had no doubt that I still loved him. And I knew it would take some time getting used to being together again. After being apart for so long I suppose I needed reassurances that everything would be alright. And that the three of us would be happy. The reason I asked Peter to stay away tonight had nothing to do with tradition. In reality—it was embarrassment. It's probably silly. I just didn't feel very comfortable with the idea of spewing into the porcelain throne on my first morning back with him. The morning sickness had subsided somewhat but still snuck up on me when I least expected it. Since I had no relationship with my mother or anyone else old enough to understand the changes I was going through. I relied on what I could glean off the Internet.

My night was restless and my morning began early. And yes, I got sick. By the time I got out of my steaming hot shower, I felt ravenous. It seemed to be another side effect from being with child. I was hungry all of the time—and very concerned that I would be as big as a house by the time I had my baby. I heard a knock at the door and my first reaction annoyed me. Peter must have thought. I wasn't serious about no contact until two o'clock. The hotel supplied big fluffy robes, so I pulled one on and wrapped a towel around my wet hair and headed to the door with an attitude. I slung the door open just as a second knock began... still not sure what I would say. But it wasn't Peter. It was Big Tony—and a woman I had never met before. My thought process revolved around what I was going to tell Peter. Instead my mind went blank and I stood there like an idiot... with no idea of what to say.

"I know it's early. Should we come back?" Tony asked.

I could see that Tony sensed my awkwardness.

"No... not at all," I said while trying to figure out what he was up to.

In that quiet interlude, my mind thought up all kinds of bad scenarios. Peter had changed his mind; my mother was here, and so on. I guess somehow he sensed my concern, because before I could ask, he intervened.

"Amy, nothing's wrong," he said, then hesitated before looking at the woman who had accompanied him, then back at me. "This is Janet... my sister-in-law. She's married to my brother Jimmy, who you met last year."

I instantly remembered Jimmy because he had taken a knee and apologized for what Tony thought was some inappropriate language when Peter and I first went to the studio over a year ago.

186

"I remember Jimmy. He was very nice to me, a real gentleman," I said.

"Is she talking about the same Jimmy you and I know?" Janet said while punching Tony in the ribs with an elbow. Her voice had a thick Northern accent that seemed to slide out the side of her mouth.

"Since you're new in town and you don't have any friends here yet. I thought Janet might help you feel welcome," Tony said.

He acted as though he had more to say but Janet interrupted him. "I think us girls can handle it from here. Why don't you run along before you end up putting your foot in your mouth?" Janet said, chuckling out loud.

Tony looked visibly relieved and didn't protest, which seemed a little odd. I felt uncertain as to what the pair was up to but figured I would know soon enough. Tony gave me a quick hug.

"I'll be back to pick you up at one thirty," he said, then turned and bolted for the door.

It was almost comical how fast he made his way out considering that Tony weighed over three hundred pounds. The door closed with a thud and I turned my attention to Janet. For lack of a better way of putting it, she seemed pleasantly plump—not skinny and not fat. Her hair was black, cut short, and she had piercing dark brown eyes. I suppose she knew I was sort of sizing her up. She managed a smile and stepped over to the window, taking a moment to enjoy the view. I knew she had teenage kids, including Joni, so I figured her to be in her late thirties. She was very pretty and seemed to have an air of confidence about her. Just as I began to feel a little uncomfortable with the situation, she turned away from the window and back toward me.

"I know you're wondering what the heck is going on here. I don't blame you a bit. First of all, I'm very happy to finally meet you. I hope we'll become great friends after we get to know each other. Just so you know. I'm a blunt no-nonsense kind of gal and have no problem speaking my mind. It may have been better if we had met socially and become friends the old-fashioned way, but we're going to fast-track the process. Feel free to stop me if I go too fast or overstep boundaries that you feel uncomfortable with."

She rattled the words off so fast I could barely keep up. So I pretty much just nodded my head and said, "Okay."

"I'm guessing you don't have a physician lined up for when the baby comes?"

"No."

"I figured as much. I asked Peter, but like most men, he's clueless. Men can be so stupid sometimes. I mean, my God. What do they think? That's a rhetorical question honey. They think we're supposed to go out by the nearest tree, squirt it out by ourselves, and chew the umbilical cord with our teeth. And then be home by five to cook dinner."

At that comment, I laughed, but Janet was on a roll and continued.

"You know I'm joking, right? Anyway... the big lugs do have some redeeming qualities. That Peter of yours is a sweetheart. Let me give you some really good advice though. Keep that young man on a short leash if you know what I mean. He's a looker and popular and rich."

"Peter would never cheat on me."

I surprised her and myself by the way I blurted it out. It even stopped Janet's whirlwind analogy of pregnancy, marriage, and men, but only for a minute.

"Honey... you have a lot to learn. He's a man, isn't he? Men can't help themselves. It's the way God wired them.

Trust me, if you don't keep an eye on your man, he'll break your heart. Didn't your mother teach you anything?"

"No, she didn't. We don't talk at all," I said, turning away trying to stop the tears before they started.

"I'm sorry, sweetie. I knew that you and your mom were not getting along. Here I am carrying on, running my mouth about the pitfalls of life on your wedding day."

She knew she had hit a nerve and softened some by offering me a hug. It actually seemed a bit weird. Since less than five minutes ago, we were perfect strangers. I guess I needed it. I started crying and couldn't stop. There was a vacuum in my life and at that moment. I realized how much I needed a mom. In her own quirky way—Janet filled that need. She petted my head and just sort of rocked me and let me cry. Peter would have tried to figure out how to make me stop crying. Abigail would have told me to get over it and be strong. Janet knew I just needed to get it out. Motherly compassion was something that had not been present in my life—and it felt good. I made a pact with myself that I would not let my baby grow up without a nurturing bond between us.

"Guess you needed that," Janet said.

The way she said it sounded kind of funny. Somehow, even though I was having an emotional episode, Janet managed to make me laugh again.

"Why don't you go dry your hair and get some clothes on and I'll order some breakfast from room service?" she said. "You have got to be starving. Growing babies is hard work."

"Thanks, that sounds good. I am really hungry," I said and headed to the bathroom.

By the time I had finished drying my hair room service was knocking at the door. Janet signed the check and sent the young man away.

"I didn't think to ask what you liked, so I ordered a variety of choices," Janet said.

"It all smells delicious."

"Well, you better get after it, then, while it still does."

I nodded in agreement, knowing exactly what she meant. One minute I could be hungry as a horse; the next, not so much. We both sat down and I ate while she watched.

"There's way too much food here for me to eat it all. Please have some," I said.

She eyed the platters of Belgian waffles, pancakes, fruit, and cereal. I could see a look of indecision in her eyes.

"The day starts early at our house," she said. "The kids have to be up for school and Jimmy works as a carpenter during the week. I had breakfast almost two hours ago." She paused for a second, perhaps to consider a second breakfast, thought better of it, and continued. "I took the liberty of scheduling some people over to get you ready. A hairdresser and makeup artist will be here around ten o'clock. Tony arranged for a lady to bring some dresses by." She looked at her watch. "She should be here any minute."

"You mean they are going to come here to the hotel room?"

"You better believe it. It's just a matter of money and with Peter being an instant sensation, there is no shortage of dollars. So my advice to you honey is... enjoy."

I giggled at her comment then stuffed a huge chunk of waffle in my mouth and dug into the plate for a second bite. It wasn't very ladylike to talk and eat but Janet made me feel comfortable. "I didn't grow up poor by any stretch of the imagination but having so much will take some getting used to." I said.

"Well, just don't go and become some spoiled little rich bitch who thinks she's a princess."

190

"I have a feeling I have a new friend who'll let me know if I'm getting out of line."

"You can count on me to tell it like it is honey."

If I like someone, it doesn't take long to decide if they're a potential friend but this had to be a record. Janet was cool.

We heard a knock at the door and Janet hopped up to answer it. It was the dress lady. Complete with two assistants and three racks of wedding dresses on wheels. She introduced herself as Amanda and led me to the couch to sit and chat about what I wanted.

"I wasn't sure what you wanted… so I more or less brought the store," she said.

I could hear no emotion in the comment. Amanda conducted herself in a stuffy professional manner you would expect from an upper echelon clothier store. Even though time was short, I couldn't help myself and tried on several. Janet did a nice job of grounding me and her taste seemed somewhat similar to my own. In the end, it came down to two dresses on totally opposite ends of the spectrum. They both felt a little snug so I needed to decide which one. Would I look better in? The simpler of the two looked very basic, but it had better shape for my blooming figure. It was a white linen dress cut about knee length. The collar had small pearls beaded into it and sheer lacy arms that ended mid-forearm.

"How much is this one?" I asked.

"Oh, let's see, that is one of the less expensive ones. I think it's around one," Amanda said.

"Cool, only a hundred. I would have thought it would have been a bit more. It's very pretty," I said.

"No ma'am… I meant around a thousand." Amanda said curtly.

I tried to keep my composure. Not wanting to look like a complete idiot. As calm as I could, I said, "Okay…" And then I asked, "How much is the other one?"

It was a beautiful traditional wedding dress made out of white satin and lace, with a short train. It was definitely my first choice, even though I knew it would be a bit too much for the little chapel wedding we had planned. It was a fairy-tale dress, to be sure.

"This one is designed by Maggie Sottero and is a very nice choice Amy. With accessories, it will run around twenty-five hundred. As you can see, it is a strapless, full A-line design, and it has a dipped neckline and corset closure. The style creates a beautiful hourglass shape in the bodice. The skirt is corded lace with a full length that is finished with a scalloped edge. It's called the Primavera, and the color is diamond-white. It is one of our best sellers, and you will look beautiful in it."

I knew full well that both dresses were way out of line for the affair at hand. I had twenty dollars to my name. And there had been no discussions between Peter and me about money. I didn't think it would be a good idea to start off our marriage spending money like it grew on trees. I guess I seemed to be in a daze or a loop going in a circle, because Amanda cleared her throat.

"So Amy, which one do you like?" Amanda asked.

"We'll take them both," Janet said.

She paused for a moment, and just as I was about to say, *Are you crazy?* She added, "Please include all the accessories as well. What size shoes, Amy?"

"An eight, I think," I said, still reeling at what had just happened.

I managed to get my act together and led Janet aside for a private discussion.

"Are you crazy?" I said. "That'll be nearly four thousand dollars by the time she gets done adding stuff."

"I know! Ain't it great?" she said with a giggle.

I guess she could see that I was angry about her jumping in and spending Peter's money. She regarded me with a sort of subtle curiosity.

"Look, honey, Tony told me—and I quote—'No limit.' They're just lucky we didn't have time to shop. So you like both dresses, right?"

"Yes."

"Great! Then you can wear the plain one for today and the really nice one when you do the real McCoy," she said.

"It's really okay? Tony said its okay with Peter?" I asked, still trying to get my mind around spending that kind of money.

"Amy... yes... its okay. Girl, you're getting married in less than..." She paused to look at her watch. "Three hours. You don't have time to shop around or to establish a budget. Do you have any idea what a traditional wedding costs these days—I mean a big one in church with a big guest list?"

"No, I don't have a clue," I said.

"My little sister had a medium-sized affair two years ago, and it was over ten grand. I thought we were going to lose my dad on that one. And the family even pitched in and did all of the food."

"Wow. I always thought I would have a big wedding but now... I don't know. I told Peter last night that I still wanted one."

The thought almost made me cry. Kelly would not get to be there today and Abigail might forbid her to come to the big wedding too. I guess Janet saw the mood swing on my face.

"Look... Peter loves you and I have a feeling he would marry you ten times if you wanted him too," Janet said.

"You think so, really?" I asked.

"I know so honey." She said giving me a big hug.

For some reason, I felt better and somehow. I knew everything was going to work out just fine. I thought how ironic it was that a hug at the right time could make a bad situation a little brighter. Except for my sister, that simple gesture hadn't been a part of life in my family. I'm not sure why... but Abigail just didn't hug. It was sad but true. Janet felt like the mom I never had and it only took her an hour to make me feel that way.

She noticed the negative look that crossed my face. "What's the matter? You're not going to start crying again, are you?"

"No... I'm okay. In some ways, better than I can ever remember, I just wished Kelly was here."

"It'll be okay honey. Hey... I have a great idea! Why don't we videotape it? Sometime down the road when an opportunity presents itself. You can show it to her," she said.

"That's a great idea!" I said. Squealing with delight I hugged her neck.

I guess Amanda was becoming impatient; she cleared her throat loud enough to interrupt. I had forgotten about the dress lady and her assistants in tow.

"How would you like to pay for the dresses?" Amanda asked.

Janet came to the rescue once again as I contemplated the realization that I couldn't even afford the tip. She produced a credit card from what seemed to be out of thin air.

"Charge everything to this card. We need that dress and the accessories within two hours," Janet said, pointing at the linen dress.

Amanda got an odd—almost disgusted look on her face. "This isn't Wal-Mart. This sort of stuff takes time."

"Look, Amanda, we have a wedding in less than three hours," Janet said. "Make it happen and there will be another five hundred in it for you."

"I believe we can accommodate you," Amanda said. Her tone changed and she was all smiles. "I'll have the dress altered and have one of my people bring it back with the accessories."

Then one of her assistants measured me around the middle and my feet to ensure the correct shoe size and they all scurried out.

"I guess money does talk after all," I said after the door shut.

"Yes indeed my young friend... it does," Janet said.

Before I could even ask whose credit card she used. The door rattled again. This time it was two guys who knew Janet.

"Hey girlfriend... how's my favorite Italian hot mama?" The one in the lead said. He was devastatingly handsome—and obviously gay, which was okay by me. It irritated me a little, though, that his nails looked better than mine ever had. He dressed sharp, too. He looked at me and said, "Honey, when I'm done with you, everybody in Chicago is going to want to marry you."

"Amy... this is Francis. He is a little full of himself... but he is the best in town and that is a fact," Janet said.

"That's why I love you," Francis said, giving Janet a hug.

"I don't have what it takes for you to love me," Janet said with a chuckle.

"Honey... I may not want to marry you. But you are my favorite girlfriend."

They both started laughing and the banter continued for a while. I just stood there realizing that I was not in McKinney anymore. When they finally stopped Janet twirled me around while Francis looked on, holding his chin in his hand while tapping his foot.

"You have two hours to pull off your usual miracle," Janet said.

"Two hours! Are you crazy? I can't do it in two hours. Her hair is a mess; it will take that long to straighten that out. Her nails are a mess and then there's her makeup. It just can't be done."

He ended his last words in a huff, rolling his eyes for more effect. *Talk about a drama queen*, I thought, resisting the urge to laugh.

"Francis, you have two hours," Janet said. "And it has to be perfect. Now get busy."

I thought she was a bit harsh for them to be such good friends.

"Read my lips, Janet: there's no way!" Francis said. "You're crazy! I have my reputation at stake here. When she walks out that door, everyone's going to know it's my work. This is art Janet... you just can't hurry art. It's like good food. We're not talking burger-joint stuff here. We're talking ... filet mignon and I'm the ... cordon bleu." He paused to take a breath but was interrupted.

"Francis," Janet said, "you can save the dog-and-pony show for your high-society clients. We'll double your fee since it's a rush job."

"Dog-and-pony show, do you think that's what this is?" he asked.

"Yes, that's exactly what it sounds like. Now do you want the job or not?" Janet asked.

"Oh yeah, sure, I can do it. It will be tough, though. Don't for a minute think this will be easy," he said, pausing for effect or deep contemplation.

I presumed he was trying to figure out what to do with my hair.

"I guess I need to work on my sales pitch some," Francis said. "Was it the delivery? Or did I just get too carried away? It was the filet mignon line, wasn't it?" he asked.

He seemed so perplexed and worried. The whole thing struck me as funny. I couldn't take it any longer and started to laugh. Janet soon joined in but Francis looked dead serious.

"That's okay... laugh at Francis," he said. "Who cares if his feelings get hurt?"

He feigned a stoic pose in the process, which made it even harder to stop giggling. I had to turn my back and look away to get a grip. Janet once again stepped in.

"Francis, your pitch is fine but I know you—and you do this every time. You are without a doubt the absolute best hairdresser and makeup artist in Chicago. That's why you get the impossible tasks... because you can do it," she said.

"Well of course I can do it!" He snapped. "Can't a guy just get a little respect and appreciation for his craft?"

"You're awesome," Janet said and gave him a hug.

"See... that wasn't so hard now was it," he said, then looked to his assistant. "Timmy, get my things set up. We have a lot of work to do."

I watched the exchange with subtle amusement, although I did laugh out loud a couple of times. I tried not to be too obvious, since at first, I didn't feel real sure how much was serious and how much was for fun. Janet told me later it was a little of both and that Francis was a bit of a prima donna but he was the best. He stood a little less than six feet tall, had a slender build, and sported long brown hair tied back with a leather thong. Everything about him looked impeccable, right down to some of his odd mannerisms. I guessed that he worked really hard to convey that royal air he seemed to encompass himself with. Though Francis was a bit full of himself, once I got to know him, he was a pretty nice guy. It was the first time I had ever talked about men with another man, and boy did he have a lot to say. On more than one occasion, my face reflected my embarrassment.

The two hours flew by. What with the entertainment that accompanied the service. When I wasn't blushing, I was in stitches. The waiting drove me crazy because. He wouldn't let me see a mirror until he was completely finished.

"This is art, Amy. There's no reason to look at the canvas until the rendering is complete," he said.

When he finished at last and finally stopped doting. He brought the mirrors out to let me see. I have to admit I was shocked. I've always known I was pretty. However, I was very proud of the fact that I didn't go around with an attitude and thinking. *Look at me! I'm so pretty. I'm a princess.* I had friends who were like that and that quality didn't appeal to me. The wholesome approach worked better for me. It just seemed less fake and more honest. Why go through life pretending to be something that you are not? I have to admit, though, as I looked in the mirror, I saw someone I had never seen before. Francis was… the best.

"Amy… you are as beautiful as an angel. Would you mind if I took a picture for my portfolio?" Francis asked.

Janet interrupted, not giving him any time to gloat. "Maybe next time, Francis. She's incognito this time around. We can't have any pictures floating around just yet."

"So who is she marrying? Your secret is safe with me. I won't tell a soul," Francis said.

"Tell you what," Janet said, "I'll tell you next week and you'll be the first one to know outside of Big Tony, myself, and of course the bride and groom. And Francis," Janet said, motioning him closer.

"Yes," he said, barely above a whisper.

"It's big news, really big," she said.

He didn't say anything at first, then smiled, and started hopping up and down; clapping his hands like a kid on Christmas day.

"You promise? You're going to tell me first?" he asked.

"Yes, I promise. Now pack up and get out of here. I have to get her dressed and to the chapel in less than thirty minutes," Janet said.

Francis took on the look of a dejected puppy and said. "You're the best, Francis. Hurry up, Francis. You're a miracle worker, Francis. But as soon as you're done with me, it's, get the hell out, Francis. Really, Janet, I don't think you appreciate me."

"I'm appreciating you with a five-hundred-dollar tip. Now hurry your butt up!" she said.

You would think the money made absolutely no difference, because he snapped at Timmy to hurry up, and they headed to the door. Janet led the way and opened the door for them. She stopped Francis with a gentle touch on his shoulder. He stopped but refused to look at her.

"Francis, you are the best... and if you weren't gay, I would leave Jimmy and rock your world," she said, as serious as a heart attack.

"You'd rock my world? Oh, Janet, Janet... Janet. Honey, you couldn't handle this stuff," he said, pointing at himself.

"See you later—and try to stay out of trouble," she said, closing the door and not waiting for an answer. "Wow, he was in rare form today."

"Is he always like that?" I asked.

"Yep, pretty much all of the time. He's a real character... and you might as well say part of the family. Big Tony and Jimmy's dad found him living on the streets when he was around ten years old. He took him in and got him placed with a foster home. Francis is really smart. He went to college and was a computer whiz. Somewhere along the way, he decided he didn't love it as much as doing makeup and hair. I think he made the right decision. It's definitely his calling. It's impossible to see him without getting an appointment made a month or so out, and he doesn't do house calls except for friends."

There was another knock at the door, and Janet answered it. It was Amanda's assistant delivering the dress and accessories.

"Perfect timing," Janet said. "I'll take the dress and you can put the rest of it on the couch. Thank you."

"Yes, ma'am, you're welcome. Let us know if we can do anything else," the girl said and then let herself out.

"Okay," Janet said, "let's get you dressed. We have a wedding to get to."

I looked at the clock and realized that I only had forty-five minutes before I was to be married. All of the activity had kept me from thinking about it too much. All of a sudden, it hit home. The time had come and I was nervous, to say the least. Janet must have been psychic or a mind reader or something.

"Hey, don't worry," she said. "Being nervous is normal. At the end of the day, you're going to be happy as a clam."

"How is it that you seem to know what I'm thinking almost before I do?" I asked.

"Well, I'll let you in on a little secret. I really don't know any more than you do. I just have a little more experience in life. I come from a large family, which means. I've been around several marriage ceremonies. Trust me, for the most part; they are all very much the same. Only the characters are changed, to protect the innocent," she said, chuckling to herself.

"Thanks for taking the time to be here with me. I can't tell you how much it means to me. There is no way I could have pulled this off."

"Oh sure you could have. It's not rocket science, but I have to admit. When Peter sees you, he may not be able to think straight. I think we are all done here."

There was a full-length mirror in the bedroom, and I looked at myself, turning from side to side. It just didn't look like me. I guess I looked older and that was hard to get used to.

"You really think Peter will like it?" I asked.

"Amy... honey, you are beautiful. He is going to be speechless. I guarantee it."

We heard another knock on the door but this one sounded a little heavier than the others. I held my breath every time the door opened worried that it could be Abigail. Janet opened the door and the frame was filled with Big Tony dressed in a nice black tux. I didn't know they made them that big. He looked great.

"Tony, you look very handsome," I said. "Thank you for making this a special day for me."

"It's a special day for all of us sweet pea. But hey, you still have time to ditch the bum and marry me instead," he said with a big smile.

"Well, if he doesn't show up, you just never know." I said. Partly teasing and dreading how I would feel if I was stuck at the altar groom-less.

"I don't think there is any worry about that. I cuffed him and hauled him over to the chapel about a half hour ago," Tony said with a chuckle.

"Oh you did not," I said. Not really sure if he was joking.

"Amy… he is as nervous as a cat in a room full of rocking chairs. I assure you. There's nothing that would keep him away. Shall we?" he said, offering his leg-sized arm.

I felt like a little kid next to him. He was tall and almost as big around. I couldn't remember ever feeling better or safer.

We arrived twenty minutes later and still had a few minutes to spare. Since I had already been there, I knew that I wouldn't have a private room to sequester myself. The chapel looked nice, it was small and as a rule—did several ceremonies per day. Tony got out of the limo to check on the timing while I waited with Janet in the car. We didn't talk; I just felt too nervous. She sat holding my hand that was shaking like a leaf in the wind. Only moments passed before Tony came back out and opened the door for me.

"Looks like they're ready for us," he said, offering his arm again.

"Okay," I said.

Taking a deep breath to gather my resolve, I stepped out. For the first time that day, I noticed the strong winds. The sun was shining but it felt really cold. The temperature mixed with my bundle of nerves created a spontaneous shiver that made my whole body shake. I leaned most of my weight onto Tony because I didn't trust my legs to hold me up unassisted. I guess my added burden didn't bother him, because he moved unaffected to the door. The chill was replaced by a blast of warm air as the door shut behind us.

The wedding chapel was a single room with a few pews and an altar. It was over a hundred years old and had that musty old smell that historic houses shared. Originally it had been a local Baptist church. It had an open high-pitched ceiling that revealed the heavy timbers of the A-frame structure. There had long since been buildings built on either side, blocking the sunshine from the stained-glass windows. The day before, I remembered thinking how pretty the windows must have been years earlier. Much to my surprise, someone along the way had thought to light them from behind. They looked beautiful, at that moment, much of my anticipation faded. I realized that it might not be the big church wedding. I had always imagined, however, it would be perfect for the need at hand. I knew even if we had a bigger ceremony down the road. This would be the one I would always remember.

My thoughts and emotions were still jumbled as my gaze scanned the room. There were a few people seated in the pews. My eyes stopped though, when I saw Peter standing at the altar. With the old pastor who ran the chapel. Peter wore a black tux similar to, but a much smaller version of, the one Big Tony wore. It was the first time I had ever seen him dressed up and he looked very handsome. The nervousness started to come back when our eyes met, his mouth dropped open just enough that I was sure. I made the impression that every bride wants to make. The trembling increased with every step and forced me to hang onto Tony for dear life, as we made our way down the aisle. The band was all there, and even they had all dressed up for the occasion. I saw a handful of people within my peripheral vision that I didn't know. As I got closer to Peter though, it seemed like we were the only two people there.

I'm sure Peter wanted to say something. The nervousness showed on his face and somehow that made me feel better. The pastor cleared his throat and began. It was something of a blur after that. I vaguely remember repeating the words at the appropriate times and hearing Peter stumble through his.

"You are now husband and wife. You may kiss the bride." The pastor said.

Peter kissed me, and it was a much more subdued version than how we both felt.

"May I present to you Mr. and Mrs. Peter Shaw," the pastor said.

It sounded weird hearing my new name. But it felt good knowing that our baby had a father and we were a family. A massive weight had been lifted off my shoulders. I guess I had not realized how much I had been worried about something happening or going wrong to prevent us from getting married. Just the fact that we managed to be married without Abigail interfering was a huge relief. I felt happier than I had been in over a year. Even so, a part of me was saddened by the fact that I had to do it all on the sly.

I hadn't noticed Peter's mom and dad until we were walking out. Peter's mom, Margaret, had tears in her eyes when she hugged my neck and kissed me on the cheek. I could tell her feelings were genuine and that she was happy for us.

"You are so beautiful, Amy. Welcome to the family," she said.

Peter's dad, John, was next. He hugged and kissed me as well. "Congratulations, Amy. I'm glad Peter was lucky and smart enough to make it work out for you two."

"I'm not sure who the lucky one is. Right now, I'm feeling pretty lucky myself," I said.

There was some shoulder slapping and whatnot from the band, and of course they all took their turns giving me a kiss including one, a little over the top, from Joni. We had our reception in one of the hotel's banquet rooms, and the restaurant did a wonderful job considering the short notice. After all of the stress of the day, I realized how hungry I was, so when the food came, I didn't talk much. I felt like a pig, but I was starving. After dinner, we toasted with alcohol-free champagne since at least half of us were too young to drink the real stuff, at least in public—plus I was pregnant. I suspect some of the band members had been imbibing in secret, though, because they were having just a bit too much fun. Being a small affair, it was over in a couple of hours, and I have to admit I was glad to be alone with just Peter and myself.

We both felt awkward because we had been apart for so long and neither of us knew what came next. That created some apprehension and a little tension. I suggested we changed into some comfortable clothes and a bit later ended up on the couch, in our suite.

"Today's the first time I've ever seen you dressed up." I said. "You looked great."

I was trying to break the ice, knowing how Peter could clam up at any moment if he began to feel self-conscious.

"Oh… yeah… thanks, the dress you picked out was very pretty. I think your hair and makeup made you look older," he said.

"Is that a bad thing?" I asked. I wasn't sure if I was offended or flattered by the comment, Peter could be very vague sometimes.

"No… I didn't mean it like that. You are very beautiful. I guess I like the regular you best."

I could tell he was trying to decide if he had just said the wrong thing and whether he should file an appeal.

"Thanks," I said. I kissed him lightly on the lips. "That has to be the best compliment a girl could get."

"Really?" he asked with surprise.

"Yes, really… at least if your meaning is that I'm beautiful without makeup and my hair fixed up."

"No… I mean, yes, that's exactly what I meant."

"You do need to know that girls like to get dressed up now and then. So you are forewarned that, once in a while, I would like for us to both get dressed up. And... it doesn't have to be a special occasion, like getting married, to do so," I said.

Then I slid over as close to him as I could, knowing there was only one way to get over the clumsy feelings we were both having.

"Do you want to go to bed?" I asked.

He looked around for the time and I almost had to roll my eyes.

"It's not even nine o'clock," he said, obviously clueless as to my meaning.

"Not to sleep, silly." I said, trying to be as casual as I could what with my heart pounding.

"Oh, is that okay to do? I mean, we're married but... well... you're pregnant," he said, finally getting it out.

"Well, I can't get pregnant again."

I shocked myself due to the fact I just kind of blurted it out. I wasn't surprised that I needed to take the lead. I did hope, though, that some of Peter's shyness would wear off in time.

"We are supposed to consummate our marriage," I said. "And no... you can't hurt me, if you're gentle."

It was a wonderful night. Even though neither one of us had a clue as to what we were doing. Peter was very gentle, and I knew that I had chosen my soul mate well. I was very happy that against all odds. We had turned a potential bad thing into a good one. Being pregnant with no marriage and no connection between us could have been a tragedy. But our union would give our unborn child the family and loving home that I'd never had. It was all I had ever hoped for. Any uncertainties that I had for disobeying my mother's wishes were behind me. Peter, our new baby, his family, and Kelly were my family now.

We lounged around the room all morning and ordered room service for a huge breakfast. Midday, there was a gentle rap on the door, and Peter answered it. It was my new surrogate mother, Janet.

"Good morning. How are my two favorite newlyweds today?" she said.

"Hi Janet, we're doing great," Peter said. He looked at me, knowing this social call was mostly for me.

"Good morning," I said. I could tell she was on a mission but for the life of me. I had no clue what it might be.

"If I'm butting in please send me on my merry way. Here's the deal. Amy, I talked to Dr. Lawrence. He's my gynecologist and he will take you as a patient," Janet said.

"Oh, that's great. Do you like him?" I asked.

"He's great or I wouldn't recommend him. He delivered all three of my kids, which brings us to the purpose of my visit. I asked his office to do me a favor and they said he could see you today at two o'clock. I took the liberty of making the appointment since I knew you two might be leaving on a honeymoon."

I looked at Peter. "What do you think?" I asked.

"I think you should see him. We have our whole lives ahead of us, what's a couple of hours? Besides, I'm coming with you."

"Really, you want to come?" I asked, somewhat surprised.

"Yes I do," he said.

"Great," Janet said. "The limo will be by to pick you up in about forty-five minutes. The doctor's office is not far from here. Oh… and Peter, Big Tony asked that you give him a ring and let him know if you guys want to book the trip to

Fiji. I think he told me there was a flight leaving in the morning or you would have to wait a few days to make the right connections. See you two soon," she said and then left. The whole conversation had taken place without her stepping into the room.

Janet was on the way to being my best friend ever. Dr. Lawrence was awesome. Finding a good gynecologist is heaven sent; I've known that ever since I got my first period. I supposed someday it wouldn't be so embarrassing, but it is not just getting your blood pressure checked. It's way more personal. For that reason, I decided Peter didn't need to be present for the actual exam. Knowing he was easier to embarrass than I was. I did ask for him to come in for the ultrasound. We got to see our baby for the first time. It was the coolest moment of my life.

"Do you want to know if it's a boy or a girl?" Dr. Lawrence asked.

"No, I want it to be a surprise… but I'm sure it's a girl," I said.

"Fair enough, I will tell you that your baby is healthy and everything looks like a normal pregnancy. I'll see you next month," he said and then left, shutting the door quietly behind him.

"A girl huh, what makes you so sure?" Peter asked with a smile.

"I don't know why. I just know. Will you be disappointed if it's a girl?" I asked.

"No, it doesn't make any difference to me. But I don't know about having two Amy Shaw's in the world. That's a little scary." He said, laughing.

I punched him hard enough to make him wince, but I'm sure it was just for a little dramatic effect.

"Scary? I'll show you scary, Mr. Shaw." I said. I just I couldn't be serious long enough to chastise him.

We laughed, and he kissed me. I couldn't remember how long it had been since I felt enough joy to really laugh. It felt good to be happy.

On the way back to the hotel, Peter's cell phone rang. "Hello... Hi Tony, what's up?" There was a really long pause and I could tell that for some reason. Tony had a lot to say. "If that's what you think we should do. Then book the flight." I was bursting with questions because Peter's face reflected that the conversation was not a good one. "Okay... yeah, we can be ready in a couple of hours. Thanks Tony," he said and shut off the phone. "Tony said Abigail called his office a few minutes ago and that she is in town and really mad. He thought it was best to not tell her just yet about us getting married. He says the longer we are married before she tries to challenge it, the better off we all are. And he told her that he has no idea where we are. Considering how resourceful your mother is, we should consider getting out of town for a while. He booked us a private flight to LA, and from there, we can go commercial to Fiji."

"I can't believe she could do anything anyway. We are both old enough to be married without parental consent," I said.

"I know that and you know that. Tony says there are loopholes in the law and that is what your mother is really good at. She could say that you were brainwashed or drugged or God knows what. Tony checked again with our attorneys, and they agreed that the best thing we can do is disappear for a while and let her cool off."

"I have no doubt its good advice. I guess I knew all along that it might come to this. It's appalling that she just won't let it go," I said.

The tears were coming, and there was no stopping them. Peter was sweet. He didn't try to fix it. He was smart enough to know that no one could do anything, so he held me until I got it together.

Two hours and ten minutes later, we were headed to Los Angeles on the same plane that had brought us from McKinney to Chicago.

Chapter 14
Peter

Amy fell asleep about thirty minutes after we took off for LA. I suppose the stress of being four months' pregnant, getting married, and her mom's unannounced visit had taken a toll on her. I quietly watched her sleep, knowing she probably needed the mental break. My thoughts returned to the phone conversation I'd had with Big Tony. I left out most of what he told me to spare Amy the grief because I knew she would try to shoulder the responsibility of her mother's meddling. Abigail was filing a complaint in Chicago court, citing wrongful abduction and coercion, along with a long list of legal jargon that I didn't quite understand. Since we both had passports, thankfully we could easily leave the country on a moment's notice.

We arrived at LAX in a little less than three hours and just made the daily flight on Air Pacific to Fiji. The only seats left were first class. I was getting used to the upper-class amenities. Amy on the other was still a bit awestruck. We landed on the main island of Fiji at Nadi International Airport ten hours later. The airport looked larger and more modern than I had expected for an island in the middle of the Pacific. I later learned that it had been in existence since before World War II and was now a main hub with over a million passengers a year.

We found the Turtle Island office just a short walk away. I felt somewhat surprised that there was nothing fancy or pretentious about it. The walls were covered with pictures of the resorts, beaches, rooms, flora, and people who appeared as if they were having a great time, which totally made sense because every picture looked like a postcard. A very large, happy woman in a brightly flowered dress sat behind a desk. She perked up the minute we came through the door.

"Welcome to Fiji. You must be the newlyweds, Peter and Amy," she said in perfect English. "My name is Mary."

Somehow she dislodged herself from behind the small desk and gave both of us a lingering hug to welcome us to the island. It was the first time Amy really relaxed and smiled since we had left Chicago. I already didn't want to leave.

It's an uncommon experience to meet a total stranger and within a few short minutes feel like you've know them all your life. Mary was one of those people. For some reason, I expected an island name, but within twenty minutes, we learned a short life history. Mary was a proverbial open book.

"You're probably surprised that I have an English name. I am a native of Fiji. I do have an island name but most people have such a hard time remembering it. I started using Mary." She laughed an infectious belly laugh that made her whole body jiggle, and then she continued. "There is only one flight a day to Turtle Island, and you missed it by a couple of hours. I took the liberty of calling your agent Big Tony to see what kind of accommodations you would expect for tonight. I booked you a one-bedroom villa at the Tokatoka Resort Hotel. It's very nice and I'm sure you will be happy there. I have a limo waiting for you and the driver will help you with your bags."

"Thank you very much, Mary," Amy said. "Is there any place to buy some island-appropriate clothes? We just left Chicago with snow on the ground. I don't even have a bathing suit."

Mary beamed an understanding smile. "Just tell the driver and he will take good care of you."

About a half an hour later, we checked into the hotel. It seemed nice enough in my mind to just stay there. The villa had its own private balcony adorned with real plants, very private and nice. The floors were all tiled, and the room looked bright, cheery, and felt very relaxing. I sprawled out on the bed to relax for a minute and quickly got a scowl from Amy.

"Don't get too comfortable," she said. "We don't have much time before the shops all close—so we are going shopping." She had her arms all folded up and had a tough school principal look on her face.

I reached up, laughing, and tried to pull her down with me. She pulled away in mocked distress.

"Oh, no you don't," she said. "You'll get none of that until you take me shopping, Mr. Shaw."

Lucky for me, I was a quick study, and I learned female behavior on the fly. Five minutes later, we were driving into Nadi for some shopping. We drove through an endless sugarcane field that stood so high, the only other thing you could see was the Sleeping Giant Mountains in the background.

Aside from the tropical theme, Nadi seemed much like any other city. It was built in 1947, so it didn't have what you would call a historical section. Between the two of us, we made a lot of the local merchants happy. By the time we finished. We had to buy two new suitcases to have something to pack it all into. We soon made it back to the hotel, exhausted. We ordered some room service and afterward I took a shower. By the time I was drying off, Amy was already asleep.

The following morning, we were up early and off to the airport once again. The driver took us to a remote area where the seaplane service was based. Although it looked to be in pristine condition, the single-engine de Havilland Beaver looked like something out of the distant past. The color scheme was akin to what you would expect to see on a South American tour bus. The antique seaplane sat on large pontoon floats that had small wheels built in so it could take off and land on a hard runway.

The pilot was a portly middle-aged man who appeared to have noticed my uneasy stare. "Don't worry, mate, she's fit as a fiddle," he said in a thick Australian accent. He patted me on the back for reassurance and grabbed our bags to load them.

Beaming with anticipation, Amy gave me a quizzical look. "What's wrong, mate? She's fit as a fiddle," she said.

Even though it was a terrible attempt to copy the captain's accent, it made me laugh and quelled my hesitation. She wrapped her arm around mine, and we followed the pilot to our Turtle Island transportation.

Once the baggage was loaded to his satisfaction, the pilot turned, gave us a quick appraisal, and smiled. "My name's Jack," he said while offering a hearty handshake to each of us in turn.

"I'm Amy, and this is Peter, my husband."

"Okay, yeah, you're the newlyweds." His smile caused deep furrows to appear on the brow of his tanned face. "Welcome to Turtle Island airlines. One of you can sit up front if you would like. There's just the two of you this trip."

"Do you mind if I sit up front?" Amy asked me.

"No, go for it," I said.

We got in and buckled our seat belts while Jack distributed a couple of headphones for the ride.

"The ole girl is a beaut, but she's a bit noisy. The microphone is voice activated, if you have a question or want to talk, feel free. Just hold the chatter down until we get out of here and I'm done with those clowns in the tower," Jack said.

He went through his preflight check and fired up the old radial engine. It started with a loud pop as the fuel and air mixture ignited in the cylinders. There was a huge puff of black oily smoke that worked its way down the fuselage like a smokescreen. He tested the controls until satisfied, then called the tower, asking permission to taxi. The old airplane seemed awkward as it rolled on the tiny wheels below the huge aluminum floats. In every direction, we were dwarfed by the commercial airliners that studded the airport landscape. Slowly we worked our way down to the end of the runway and waited for our turn to take off. Jack throttled the engine up and checked all the controls one last time while waiting for permission from the tower to depart. He eased out onto the runway and lined up on a white stripe that seemed to go on forever, and then pushed the throttle to maximum.

There is something really cool about the sound of an old radial engine. We lumbered down the runway for a very short time before the powerful seaplane broke ground and we were off. Once the old bird was flying, she became as graceful as any creature of the sky.

The view was almost like a fantasy world from our perch high above the South Pacific. The water had a color of blue that a photographer or painter would be hard pressed to capture. The wind seemed calm and the water looked so clear that you could see some of the larger sea creatures hanging around the shallow reefs. The hour trip went by fast. Before we knew it, the island showed itself on the horizon. A few minutes later, we splashed down into a quiet lagoon and taxied to a pier that came out into the water. Jack leaned the fuel mixture and the big radial engine came to an abrupt halt. We slowed moving on nothing but momentum, and stopped about two feet from the dock. It was obvious he had practiced the maneuver many times. There were six people waiting for us and as soon as we deplaned. They took turns hugging us and making introductions. Everyone seemed so friendly, and it felt like they meant it. Not because it was a high-dollar resort.

After introductions, they escorted us to our villa, or bure, as the islanders called it. There were only fourteen on the entire island, which meant no more than twenty-eight guests at any given time. Each one was built by native craftsmen and designed to be traditional, authentic, and eco-friendly. I didn't know exactly what to expect, but I felt somewhat relieved that it wasn't thatched huts with a couple of hammocks strung up inside. I could see by Amy's mannerisms and the animated sparkle in her eyes that she was delighted.

Every couple was assigned a personal concierge called a "bure mama," whose mission was to provide guests with a perfect stay.

"I am Mama Lai," your bure mama. She said, as we walked up the path to our bure. "Anything you need while on the island please don't hesitate to ask."

She was very nice and went out of her way to show us around our bure and to be sure we knew about all the activities available to us. I didn't want to be rude, and she was so nice that I just didn't have it in me to tell her that we just wanted to be alone. Since Amy seemed so attentive and captivated by Mama Lai's every word. I wasn't really sure if she shared my sentiment.

Then, out of the blue, Amy interrupted the well-rehearsed introduction to the island. "Mama Lai, you're wonderful and you have made us feel very welcome. I hope you won't think this is rude, it's been a really long couple of days, and Peter and I are newlyweds."

Mama Lai clammed up and managed a knowing smile. "Of course you are. Will salad, fresh fruit, and seafood, be okay for lunch and dinner?"

"Sounds delicious," Amy said with a smile.

"Lunch will be in a couple of hours, and dinner is usually served around five. It will be served on the patio. I'll just knock to let you know it's ready. Will that be okay?"

"Yes, that will be perfect," Amy replied.

I just stood there hoping I looked somewhat intelligent, realizing how much I missed Amy's ability to handled situations like these. She conveyed what we both wanted, which was alone time. With a social ease way outside of my expertise. The best part was that she wanted the same thing that I wanted.

Except for the wonderful meals left on the patio, we didn't venture outside until the next day. I guess some guys would find it odd that some of my fondest memories of that first day and night were the times spent talking. We covered everything from my career, to Amy going back to school, to our hopes for our unborn child. The idea of being married didn't bother me since I had given it lots of thought in the past year. Wondering if I would be a good parent and what being a parent really meant. Felt almost as scary as learning that I was going to be one. A perplexing thing about Amy was that she seemed to be able to read my mind. It was common for her to answer a question or probe for one before I even voiced it. That took some getting used to, but we had shared that connection soon after we started dating. Somewhere along the way, I became accustomed to her clairvoyance, and now I relied on it. It filled in the gaps when I struggled to articulate a point. That first twenty-four hours in Fiji made me realize that Amy was indeed my soul mate who would forever be entwined in my life. Later that night, we did consummate our marriage again, several times.

By the next day, we felt restless and ready to explore and see what Turtle Island had to offer. Though a privately owned island, it was a little over five hundred acres in size, not all that big in the grand scheme of things, but it took most of the day to see the highlights and to schedule activities. We decided to experience everything available, which included hiking trails, sailing, horseback riding, bicycling, fishing, scuba diving, and sunset dinners on our own stretch of private beach. It's funny how the first days of a vacation are lazy and slide by so slow. Then towards the end, it speeds up and all of a sudden it's over. Nevertheless, that is exactly how our two weeks in Fiji went, and before we knew it, we were on the seaplane headed back to Nadi. Leaving was the hardest part; it seemed that the entire staff took the time to see us off at the dock. We jabbered excitedly about all the stuff we did to Jack, all the way back to Nadi.

"You probably get tired of passengers telling you what a great time they had," I said.

"No, not really," he said. "A lot of people who come to Fiji and Turtle Island are privileged and somehow unimpressed with the beauty. I've never really figured out how they miss that. More often than not, they'll complain about this or that more than what a great time they had. You kids are genuine and have been a pleasure to meet."

"Thanks, Jack," Amy said. "You've been a lot of fun and a pleasure to meet as well."

"Why thank you, Amy," Jack drawled. He seemed to add a little extra to his already thick Aussie accent.

He looked back at me since I once again sat in the backseat. I just couldn't tell Amy "No" when she asked to fly in the copilot seat again.

"I was wondering if you would sign my copy of your CD, Peter," Jack said.

I felt a little taken back since I had not said anything about music, much less that I had recorded anything. I did manage a nonchalant answer: "Sure, Jack, it would be my pleasure. I'm just surprised you knew who I was."

"Ah, make no mistake about it mate. You are very popular in these parts. I think the whole island knows you're visiting the area," he said.

"Oh," I said. I guess my tone signaled my discontent. I had been hoping for two weeks of anonymity.

Jack picked up on it right away. "No worries Peter. I cut the local paparazzi off at the pass. I gave them just enough information to make them believe me."

"What did you tell them?" I asked.

"I spread it around that I did take you out to Turtle Island and that a yacht was supposed to pick you up from there. I accidentally let it slip that Thailand was your next destination. I called the folks out at the resort so they would collaborate with my story."

"Do you think they will do that for us?" Amy asked.

"Oh sure… we do this stuff all the time. There're a lot of folks that like to blend in and not get noticed. I've already heard my story go full circle and come back with some interesting embellishments," Jack said with a chuckle.

I didn't ask what they were. I just sat back with a quiet sigh of relief that Jack didn't notice, but Amy did. She smiled back at me, winked, and gave me a reassuring look. Big Tony had suggested that we leave our next destination a secret and not tell anyone. He also suggested that we wait and buy the tickets with cash on the day we wanted to leave. I thought at the time it had been overkill, but now I realized how easy it might be to find us. It seemed kind of funny that Amy and I had talked about going to Thailand but had decided on Hawaii instead. After landing, we taxied to another remote part of the airport that I noticed looked different from the place we'd left from.

"This isn't where we took off from, is it?" I asked.

"No worries, Peter, just doing my job to keep you guy's invisible as promised," Jack said.

Paranoia started to rear its ugly head, but I relaxed when we stopped and I saw the limo parked nearby. I recognized the driver as the same guy who drove us when we first arrived to Nadi. Jack handed me his copy of my music and started unloading our stuff. I solicited a pen from Amy and signed the CD jacket for him.

"Give me your business card, and I'll send you a copy of the new one when it comes out," I said.

"Thanks, mate ... I'd like that very much," Jack said.

The driver joined us and busied himself loading our bags into the trunk. When he had finished, he abruptly dragged Jack off to the side and whispered something to him, then handed him something. Jack came back over to us with a lopsided grin and flashed a handful of CDs.

"I am embarrassed to ask, but Moe wanted to know if you would sign these for him. He's a good guy, and for what it's worth, he's also in on keeping your travels quiet," Jack said.

"No problem," I said, then took the CDs and shook Jack's hand. "I hope our paths cross again in the not too distant future."

"I would like that, Peter. You two are a couple of really nice kids. Don't let the fame ruin that," he said.

"I won't." I said.

He got a hug from Amy. "Thanks for everything, Jack," she said.

We loaded up in the limo, and on the way to the Tokatoka Resort Hotel, I asked Moe who the CDs would be going to so I could personalize each one.

"You'll do that for me?" he asked.

"Sure, Moe ... I'll be happy to. Just give them to me one at a time," I said.

He gave me the names. Some of which I had no clue as to the spelling, and when asked, neither did Moe. By the time I was finished with that task, we were pulling into the hotel parking lot. Moe pulled us around to a side entrance stopped and handed me a key.

"It's the same room as before. Thanks for signing the CDs. My friends will love it," he said.

"You're welcome."

I tried to give him a tip, but he refused it, then jumped out of the car, and took our bags up to the room. He started to leave once we were settled in.

"Moe," I said, "do you have time to take me to the airport in about an hour? I need to make some changes concerning our flights."

"I would be happy to Mr. Shaw, but I'm sure you can do it over the phone," Moe said.

My mind raced for a believable reason, and I went for the first thing that came to mind. I took Moe outside. Closed the door, and pretended our conversation to be a secret. "I don't want Amy to know where we're going next. It's going to be a surprise," I said.

"Oh ... okay. I'll be back for you in an hour," he said, turning to leave.

"Thanks, Moe."

I could tell by the confused look on his face that he didn't understand why I didn't just go down and use the lobby phone. Even so, I had no need to explain my desire to pay cash for the tickets or that we didn't want to leave a trail to our next destination. I went back in, and Amy gave me an amused look.

"Did he buy in to your story?" she asked.

"I don't know. He did seem a little confused."

"Well, you could have just told him the truth instead of the cloak-and-dagger story."

I'm not really sure why her comment hurt my feelings, but it did. I learned a lesson about myself that day that I've regretted ever since.

"If you want to take care of the arrangements so we can stay a step ahead of your mother, then… by all means."

It's one of those things that you say and wished you could take back, but it was too late.

Amy's eyes went wide. "As a matter of fact, Mr. Shaw, I can take care of the arrangements. Just because I'm a woman and pregnant doesn't mean that I'm incapable of staying a step ahead of my mother or anyone else for that matter!" she snapped, and then stomped through the door, slamming it behind her.

I stood there, dumbstruck, and ran the conversation back through my brain a couple of times to figure out what had just happened. My indecision delayed me a minute or maybe two before I bolted out the door. I didn't want to continue the argument that sprang from poorly chosen words or to discuss the pregnant female hormones that I was just learning about. I just wanted to say I was sorry.

When I reached the parking lot, I saw two black SUVs, four men who looked like NFL football players, Amy, and her mother. Two of the men were holding Amy's arms and trying to maneuver her into one of the SUVs while Abigail calmly watched.

"Hey! Let her go!" I shouted and took off in a run toward the melee.

"Peter!" Amy managed to scream just as the two huge men forced her into the car.

A third man jumped into the driver's seat, sending a cloud of sand and dust into the air as they sped off. The other guy stepped in between me and Abigail just as I reached them.

"What are you doing? Have you lost your mind? Amy and I are married. Why can't you just leave it alone?" I shouted.

I had never been so mad, ever, in my life. It didn't matter to me how big the guy was, my brain and my body had disconnected. I took a swing, and the guy he didn't even try to stop me. It felt like I hit a tree trunk. I kept doing my best to pound the guy to a pulp but only succeeded in wearing my anger down. He finally grabbed both of my hands to stop me, but I squirmed and twisted enough that I managed to kick him. I guess it hurt him because he slapped me with his shovel-sized open hand and almost knocked me out. I staggered and somehow stayed on my feet, realizing that I didn't have a chance with this mountain of a man. I did manage to look up at him and glare in defiance.

"You just pissed off the wrong guy, mister," I said.

He gazed down at me with what looked like either regret or pity. I wasn't sure which.

"Look, son," the man said. "I'm just doing my job. Now calm yourself down before I have to hurt you."

I took a deep breath and relaxed. I guess he realized the fight, at least for the moment, was finished, so he let me go. Abigail put a hand on his shoulder.

"That should be all, Felix," she said. "I'll handle it from here. I'm sure Mr. Shaw doesn't want to face assault along with all of the other charges that I have filed against him."

"Charges... against me? You really are crazy, Abigail!" I said with more belligerence and disgust than I knew I could speak.

Her smirk wavered for a moment but was fast to return.

"Peter, here's the deal. I am not going to allow you to ruin Amy's life. I've worked with people like you in the music industry for a long time now, and you all end up the same. Oh, I know you're a nice young man right now, for the most part, but I know that will change. Fame and money have a way of turning good people into bad ones. For example, just minutes ago, Amy came running out into the parking lot crying. Did you hit her?"

"No! I would never hit Amy. I love her."

"Ah... that may be but you did have an argument bad enough to make her cry. What happens six months down the road when you're out doing concerts and some groupie sneaks up to your room making offers of the body? Will you resist?"

"We're married and I wouldn't violate our trust." I meant it and in spite of the futility of the moment. I actually hoped I could convince Abigail that she was wrong.

"Oh, I'm sure you mean well, and you might even remain faithful for a time, eventually though, it always ends the same."

"How is it that you have such a low regard for everyone's feeling and needs except your own?"

"Experience... Peter. I'm going to leave now because you're not going to change my mind, and I'm sorry to say there is no way to change yours. Two can play the cat-and-mouse game," she said with a smile.

"What's that supposed to mean?"

"It means that until Amy comes around to my way of thinking, I intend to isolate her so you can't find her or be an influence. Rest assured, Mr. Shaw. I'll spend every dollar I have to make sure you will never see her again."

Her face took on a dark and twisted expression. It looked almost like a smile, however the gesture held no humor. It was a mixture of contempt and personal superiority conveyed in a glance just before she turned to walk away.

"Abigail ..." I said.

She stopped and looked back.

"I have more money than you ever will. I assure you that I will not stop until I find Amy. When it's all over but the crying, you'll be the one with no family." I managed to keep my words controlled, although I'm not sure how. Never in my life had I experienced so much anger and I didn't like the newfound emotion. She wavered just long enough for me to realize that I had struck a nerve in her resolve. I saw her confidence buckle for a brief moment before she turned and walked to the car. Felix followed close behind. As she rounded to the passenger side of the SUV, he chanced a quick look back toward me before opening the driver side door. It seemed like regret on his face. I watch them drive off and could not believe what had just happened.

I felt numb but somehow in a few moments came to the conclusion that no matter what. I would not give up without a fight. I packed all of our stuff in record time. Including the memorabilia from our trip and booked the first flight back to Chicago. I don't remember much of the flight home. Amy and I had drunk a bottle of champagne during our stay on Turtle Island. I'd never really cared for alcohol. Now though, I guess it was part depression and part anger. I got drunk and slept most of the way home—even though I was only eighteen. Flying first class out of country follows a different set of rules. It was a course of action that my head really regretted the next day.

Big Tony was waiting for me at Chicago's Midway International Airport terminal. His bear-like hug was familiar and needed. It took about all I had not to lose it completely and sob out my emotions. I steeled myself and maintained some semblance of composure.

"I'm not going to ask how you are because I already know the answer," he said.

We walked in silence to the limo and got in while the driver took care of the bags.

"First thing for you to know is that there are no charges against you," Tony said. "Abigail came to town and created a legal nightmare, but it was short lived. She used her connections here and tried every underhanded trick imaginable to annul your marriage with Amy. As a result, a short impromptu court hearing materialized, which we were expecting and ready for. There was no short supply of witnesses willing to testify that Amy was of sound mind, willing, and not coerced. So in accordance to the laws of Illinois, Abigail lost—and she was a very bad loser. That happened about a week ago, right before she just disappeared."

Tony stopped. I could tell that he had something to add and was struggling to say it. His eyes were misty, and he looked away for a second before continuing.

"I thought we had won and it was over. The attorneys patted each other on the back, and we all went out to a nice victory dinner. I should have called you. It's my fault she found you."

"No... it wasn't your fault. This is all about Abigail. I've given it a lot of thought on the way home and pieced together conversations that Amy and I've had. Abigail has a tainted view of people in the music industry, which is largely due to the cases and clients she defends."

Tony held up a hand before I could finish. "It sounds like you're defending her actions."

"Not at all, I am trying to understand her. I think if we can do that, we might be able to figure out where she took Amy."

"You're a bigger man that I am, Peter," he said.

I cocked an eyebrow to his response, and he smiled.

"I wasn't talking in terms of physical size."

He paused for a moment, waiting to see if I had anything else to say before continuing.

"I took the liberty of spending a big chunk of your money and hired four private investigators to track Amy down. I'm sorry to say we have hit nothing but dead ends so far. What we do know is that Abigail chartered a jet from Hawaii to Fiji. On the way back, they made a fuel stop in Hawaii and filed a flight plan to Seattle, Washington. The pilot closed the flight plan about an hour before their arrival. We're not sure where they landed."

"Isn't that kidnapping and illegal entry into the United States?" I asked.

"Yes. The good news is that's helping us get the feds involved. The bad part is there is no record of them landing in the US."

"So we have no idea where the flight landed?"

"Our best guess at the moment is that Abigail used a foreign charter service, which makes them a lot harder to track down. I hate to be the bearer of bad news, but they could be anywhere in the world by now. She's smart and probably knows that, legally, she'll lose control of Amy and could go to jail for kidnapping."

Tony's cell phone rang. He paused and stole a quick glance at the caller ID.

"It's our guy in Hawaii," he said before answering the call. "Mr. Sato thanks for getting back to me so soon. I know it must be very early there."

The initial greeting became a one-sided conversation as Mr. Sato shared his latest update. I was bursting to know what was being said while Tony nodded and said "Yeah" every so often. Only two or three minutes passed, but it seemed like it took forever.

"Call me as soon as you know. Thanks, Mr. Sato. Good-bye."

"Well, what did he say?" I asked.

"He said they chartered a Japanese-owned business jet to Canada. He's still following some leads, but he thinks they landed in a small airfield in British Columbia."

Tony paused.

"He had to have more to say than that," I said.

"PIs spend a lot of time telling you how many favors they've called in and that they're working as fast as they can. It's a dog-and-pony show to justify a bigger check."

"Tony, you know I don't care about the money. What does he think?"

"He's pretty sure they landed at Kelowna International Airport in British Columbia. It's going to take him a few more hours to confirm it—which, and I am quoting Mr. Sato, by the time we know for sure. They will probably be long gone."

"Then we shouldn't wait. Let's book a flight and go right now."

I figured that Tony would argue with me and was prepared to explain why, but he surprised me: "I agree. It's worth checking it out." He paused and gave me an appraising look. "It'll be much quicker to have somebody who already lives there check it out. Let me pursue that possibility first. In the meantime, will you please go home and get a little sleep? You look exhausted and in no shape to be searching the Canadian countryside."

It wasn't exactly what I wanted to hear, but I knew he was right. The only sleep I had gotten had come from an alcohol overdose on the flight home.

"Okay... but I'm not taking a backseat on this." I said. "As soon as we know something, I'm on the first plane available to Canada."

Tony visibly sighed and gave me a halfhearted smile.

"I'll let you know the instant I hear something," he said.

The limo came to a stop in front of my thirty-two-story high-rise apartment building. My place was on the top floor. Seeing it made me realize that Amy hadn't even been there yet, that bummed me out even more. I guess Tony noticed as my mood darkened.

"You want me to go up with you and hang out for a little while?" he asked.

"No, but thanks for everything you're doing. I wouldn't have had a clue what to do or where to start."

"We'll get through this. Now try to get some rest and I'll call you as soon as I have some answers."

He got out of the limo with me and gave me another quick hug. I went up, took a hot shower and got in bed. The last thing I remembered before falling asleep was wondering what Amy was doing. Then there was a noise. I struggled against the fog. Trying to figure out where I was and what was going on. Slowly I realized the phone was ringing, and my wits swiftly came to focus.

"Hello," I answered.

"They landed in Kelowna about twelve hours ago and disappeared again. Our guys here are looking for some local help to track them down. At least we know they're in Canada."

"Thanks for the update, Tony. You know where I'll be. Call me when you have some news."

I hung up the phone, thinking Canada is a big place.

"It'll be like finding a needle in a haystack," I said to an empty room.

Chapter 15
Amy

My captors were gentle for the most part. I couldn't kid myself about their resolve though. They were very efficient. The way they conducted themselves suggested a military background. Not that I knew anything about that sort of thing except what I'd seen on movies. After a short ride to yet another remote airport location. They hustled me into a modern but secluded hangar. I half-expected a barren aircraft storage facility, instead they ushered me into a plush waiting area furnished with black leather chairs and couches. I saw a full bar to the left as we walked in. Glass covered two walls from the floor-to-ceiling, giving a panoramic view of the Nadi airport. Just outside—a private jet, noticeably bigger than the one Peter and I had taken from Chicago to Los Angeles, sat on the tarmac. I wandered around the room, racking my brain for a way out of my predicament; however, all the exits were guarded. A few moments later, the door opened and yet another very large well-dressed man entered the room. I thought he had been there at the hotel, but it all happened so fast. I wasn't sure. In any case, I felt a sense of authority that came in with the man, which was easy to recognize even for my untrained scrutiny. His eyes surveyed the room, making contact with the other men. No words were spoken, or needed, to know he was in charge of the goon squad. He walked straight over to me and introduced himself:

"Hello Amy, my name is Felix."

"I know my mother hired you to kidnap me. If you let me go right now, I'll forget this ever happened and I won't press charges," I said.

A painful expression crossed his face that intrigued me as very peculiar. It gave me the distinct impression that his assignment didn't sit well with him. The empathetic features disappeared and were quickly replaced with the lackluster expression of a professional. I positioned myself, knowing how stupid my next action would be and that it would invite retaliation. It would change nothing except to leave a lasting and mutual impression. I kicked him squarely where it hurts a man the most. He didn't go down, which scared me, but I knew it had hurt—and that satisfied me a great deal. I thought about all those years of playing soccer and then beamed him a polite demure look. That's when I wondered, a little late, if he would beat me for my indiscretion. Felix's expression fell somewhere between anger and pain. I hoped his irritation would be focused inward for allowing it to happen in the first place. Rather than punishing me for taking a cheap shot at him. Once my brain caught up with my own anger, hindsight of my action and how foolish I had been became clear. The baby growing inside me meant there were two lives to think about now. Then I did something that surprised me yet again. Felix was a very large man. He had not moved except to bend over and put his hands on his knees, and was doing his best to take long deep breaths. I put a hand on his arm.

"I'm sorry," I said. "You didn't deserve that."

He looked up and winked. "Sometimes unpleasant things come with the job," he said quietly.

There was no smile or indication of it, but somehow I knew Felix was a nicer guy than I had thought. He stood, straightened some imaginary wrinkles from his suit, and looked around. Nobody laughed or joked about him getting his clock rung by a little girl. I wasn't under any illusions of being tough again. I had too much at stake. I knew the identity of the puppet master in all this. Abigail had not shown herself since our confrontation at the hotel, but I knew it would just be a matter of time.

And then, right on cue …

"Amy that's not very ladylike."

I turned to see my mother in the doorway.

"Well… it's not like I've ever had a decent role model Abigail." I said with as much contempt as I could manage.

She shut the door behind her and strolled toward me like she was the queen of England. As she got closer, her facial features became more apparent. Abigail had her courtroom face on, but underneath, I could see that she had changed. She didn't show anger now; it was contempt, the sort of regard one would have for something vile. At that moment, I felt more afraid of her than all of the hired muscle in the room. Even so, I had been repressed by her for way too long.

"Your control over me is over," I said. "Not that you've been around long enough to notice—your little girl has grown up. I'm of legal age and happily married. You are the criminal in this kidnapping."

I wasn't done but she interrupted me: "Amy… honey, this isn't about controlling you. It's about saving you from yourself. Oh, I know you'll be mad at me for a while… but this is what's best for you."

"I don't care what you think or what you want. This is my life and I want you out of it, permanently." I didn't manage the cool and calm demeanor that Abigail maintained, but I didn't care and I was getting louder and madder as I went. "Peter will find me, and when he does, it will be the last time you will ever see me. I hate you for this!"

The tears started, and I knew deep within myself that my pent-up anger was turning into hatred for my mother. I'd hoped that in time we would manage some sort of connection and have a chance at a normal relationship. Abigail, though, seemed intent on following a self-serving path, and she left no way for us to reconcile our differences.

"Look at you," she said, "you're a mess." She paused and appraised me in a critical way that had become so familiar over the past year. "In three months, Peter will have forgotten all about you. Surely by now you know there is no shortage of groupies and bimbos just waiting to fill in when you're not around." She reached out to touch my shoulders in a feeble effort to become maternal. Repulsed—I shrugged her away. "My goodness, the good life has already taken its toll. I'll bet you've gained ten pounds since I saw you last. You know, Amy, rock stars don't like chubby girls. You've always been so pretty and petite. How long did you think he would stay with you? Him, out on the road ten months a year, and you, sitting home eating chocolate and getting fat?"

It took all the restraint I could muster not to refute her comment with, *I'm pregnant, you stupid bitch.* But I held my tongue. I really wanted to say it even though I had never used that word in anger toward anyone. Yet a portion of me didn't want to lose that tiny bit of innocence. More important was the fear of how she might react to that news, and I wasn't taking any chances. I knew Abigail expected a response from me. She was pushing my buttons in hopes of forcing me to say she was right. Then she could win her argument and be self-satisfied in being correct. That was not going to happen.

"The thing is, Abigail. Not only are you a pathetic excuse for a mother. You can't even get a boyfriend—and for some unknown reason, you blame me. You hate the fact that I can be ten pounds overweight and still turn heads. Not to mention the reality that I'm young and pretty and you're not and will never be."

The comment was mean. But in my mind, she deserved it, and I had a lot of pent-up anger in me that was finding its way out. What happened next was something that I'd never seen. Abigail lost it. Her face reddened, almost like someone blushing, she was furious. She was somebody that I've never seen before. Her eyes glassed over and she slapped me so hard that I saw stars. We had been in some really big arguments but Abigail never lost control—not even the first time she slapped me months earlier. I could see the disconnected look of insanity in her eyes. Even though my face still tingled from the assault and I tried to maintain my defiance. But when I saw her face contorted with rage, and could see her doubling up her fist for the knockout punch. I cowered and tried to cover my face from the next blow. It didn't come. When I peeked through my arms, I saw why.

"Ahh!" she screamed, and then growled some guttural noises while writhing about like a crazy person.

Felix had stayed the blow with one hand and somehow calmly took the kicks, jabs, and scratches that she was dishing out on him. The fit of rage ran its course in ten or fifteen seconds, it seemed longer though. I realized then and there that my mother was crazy enough that I needed to be smarter with my mouth. Then she stopped, collecting her composure almost as quickly as she'd lost it.

"You may let go of me now, Felix," she said so calmly it was eerie. He released her, and she looked up at him and said in the same calm voice: "Don't ever touch me again, or you'll be unemployed and that little problem I agreed to fix for you will get worse."

Her gaze returned to me, and I withered like a dying flower. I had felt a lot of things toward my mother, but for the first time in my life. I was afraid of her.

"Perhaps… given a little time, cooler minds will prevail," she said, then looked back at Felix. "Let's get loaded up and get out of here."

That was it. She walked by me without another word.

"Thanks, Felix," I said.

"Sure... it would probably be best if we go now," he said, then paused and watched Abigail walk through the door. "Do you love him?"

The question was quietly spoken and unexpected.

"More than my own life," I said with new tears welling up in my eyes.

He studied my face for a few brief seconds. "Yes, I believe you do. Do you believe that our lives are destined?"

"I always did... until today."

"Have faith, Amy," he said and then walked away, giving orders. "Let's wrap this up, gentlemen. We're out of here in five minutes."

The room turned into a flurry of activity, and five minutes later, we were in the air. A couple of hours later, Felix brought me a sandwich and a can of Diet Coke. My defiance was gone for the time being, and I was real hungry. I devoured the lunch, and a few minutes later, I felt sleepy.

I woke up feeling groggy; a head full of cobwebs, and my mouth felt like it was stuffed with cotton balls. My surroundings didn't make any sense to me. It almost felt like a dream, but I knew it wasn't. I tried to sit up and realized I couldn't move. My blurred vision was slow to return, and when it did. I realized that I was strapped to a bed and still on the plane. I tried wiggling free and felt a slight sting in my arm. There was an IV attached, it became all too clear as to what had happened. They had drugged me and planned to keep me that way until we reached our destination. I raised my head enough to see Abigail sleeping in a seat in the back. There was a stirring behind me, and Felix came into view. Even though he had served me the drugged meal, I knew who had orchestrated the act. He glanced at Abigail to make certain she was still sleeping and held up a note: *Blink, if you're thirsty. Don't talk.* I blinked as instructed. He disappeared, then returned and lifted my head enough that I could take a sip from a curved straw. I finished that cup and two more, blinking between each one. I mouthed a "Thank you" and received the slightest hint of a smile in return. He wrote another quick note and held it up for me to read. It had two words on it: *Stay asleep.* I pieced together the meaning to be that if I woke up, Abigail was likely to have me sedated again. So I closed my eyes and tried to think about Peter and the fun we'd had in Fiji—while also hoping that whatever they had hooked me up to wasn't hurting the baby. It wasn't long after that I could tell we were descending. Shortly after, we landed with a thump and a squeak of the tires. I heard movement in the cabin, and I felt her presence.

"Well, Sleeping Beauty is still out. Perfect. Customs won't be a problem. I know everyone here. Once we have her loaded into the car, it's off to Grandma's house," she said.

I knew I couldn't react, but at least now I knew that we were in Kelowna, Canada.

Mom's parents were born and bred Canadians. Kelly and I had spent several happy summers at their lake house until seven years ago when my grandfather, Clyde Henderson, died of a heart attack. We never went back after that. Grandma Mattie never dealt with the loss very well and mentally deteriorated within months. Abigail brought her to Texas and put her in an assisted-living facility. I've heard that when a couple has been together for a long time and one dies, the survivor seldom lives long afterward. Clyde and Mattie had been married for sixty years, and even though I had been just a kid. I'd never doubted that they still loved each other. I often wondered why Abigail didn't bring Mattie home to live with us. At the time, she was still sharp minded and the opportunity to look after Kelly and me would have given her some purpose. Within three years. She barely knew who we were. Now dementia coupled with old age had rendered her into a blank canvas. She would just sit staring off into whatever world she lived in. Rarely speaking and making very little sense when she did. Once in a while when we would visit, she would start talking to her husband Clyde, just as if he were sitting right there next to her. Sometimes I felt that, at least in her mind, he was.

Abigail had not mentioned the house in years and I assumed it had been sold. It didn't take long before the curvy roads and lying down with my eyes closed gave me motion sickness. The car had an old musty smell that almost seemed familiar. I cracked my eyes open just enough for some visual reference, hoping it would help deter the nausea that steadily grew worse. I realized right off that it was Grandpa's old Cadillac. Unfortunately I was being monitored at that precise moment.

"Hi sleepyhead," Abigail said.

Her tone made it sound like we were out on a Sunday drive. At least she seemed to be in a good mood. I opted to not make things worse, at least for the time being.

"Where are we?" I asked, trying to sound sleepy even though I was wide awake.

I sat up, pretending to rub the sleep out of my eyes. Silence seemed to be the best course of action, so I waited. Abigail was bursting with things to say, only a couple of minutes passed before she started filling in the blanks.

"So, Amy, you're an intelligent girl, it shouldn't take much brain power to figure out where you are." She paused but only long enough to realize I wasn't answering. "As you know, Grandpa's house is a good five-hour drive from Kelowna when there's no snow on the ground."

As if on command, we turned a corner and pulled up to a waiting helicopter. I was still wearing the light tropical clothes from Fiji, and the frigid air cut like a knife when we got out of the warm car and transferred to the waiting Bell Jet Ranger. Helicopters are inherently noisy, and even though there were headsets available, Abigail remained silent. I considered making a scene but decided to make use of my most valuable assets—my eyes.

I tried to commit the countryside to memory. However, it didn't take long to realize that after a while, it all started looking the same. If I did try to escape, I would be lost and probably freeze to death in a few hours. I overheard the pilot telling Felix how it looked like it was going to be an unusually cold winter.

It was the first of December and the spring thaw wouldn't come until late May. I started counting off the months to myself; the revelation was not a good one. I would be due in March or April and much too pregnant to hike out of the wilderness within another few weeks. Despair began to overwhelm me, and it took all I had within me not to cry as I watched the rugged terrain drift by. About an hour and a half later, we sat down in a little clearing about fifty yards from the Henderson lake house. It looked different from what I remembered. The lake was frozen over, and I noticed nothing but snow and ice as far as I could see.

I was a bit surprised when the pilot shut the helicopter down and came into the house instead of dropping us off and leaving. The house felt toasty warm inside and looked just like I remembered it. The whole place looked rustic. Like you would expect wilderness hunting or fishing lodges to be. One wall in the great room had an impressive collection of trophy sized deer, with a huge moose head mounted in the center. On the opposite wall hung lake trout and pike that Grandpa had caught. In the center was a large two-story rock fireplace with a cozy fire blazing inside. The mantle had a variety of pictures, knickknacks, and memorabilia that belonged to my grandmother. Smoke scented the air with a woodsy aroma. The only thing missing was the smell of fresh bread that seemed to always be baking when we visited. While taking my little walk down memory lane, I hadn't noticed that Abigail had dispatched the two men, leaving us alone. Our eyes met and all I could think about was how much I hated her. Instead of voicing that thought. I did my best to look subservient. I suspect I didn't have to try hard to look the part. Never in my life had I felt so hopeless, alone, and out of control.

"I'll make this short and sweet for two reasons," she said. "One is because I have to go back to work and pay for what you've put me through." Luckily she didn't pause long enough for me to respond to that one. "The second reason is that no matter what I say, even though I'm right. You won't listen to me right now. In time… you'll come around. My guess is when Peter dumps you in a couple of months. This unpleasant business will be over with and all will be forgiven." She smiled and patted me on the cheek, then walked toward the door. "Johnny, I'm ready to go. We can just make it back to Kelowna before dark." She said, leaving the door open behind her.

The pilot appeared from the kitchen, carrying a Styrofoam cup, spilling little puddles of coffee as he hurried out the door. A few minutes later, the drone of the helicopter faded away and there was an intense silence. I could hear the wind blowing outside and the tap of a big pine tree slapping against the cabin. Felix walked in from the kitchen with a mug in each hand.

"Would you like some hot cocoa?" he asked.

His eyes were almost as sad as I felt, but I wasn't in the mood to be nice anymore.

"Which bedroom do I get?" I asked.

"You get the master bedroom and lucky me gets a bunk bed in the guest bedroom." He tried to smile. I knew he was trying to make the best of an unpleasant situation.

"Don't misunderstand my apology in the hangar," I said. "I was sorry for my conduct; maybe you deserved it, maybe you didn't. One thing you can be completely assured of: you're not my friend. We're not going to sit around and play Old Maid together. And when this is all said and done, you will go to jail, hopefully with Abigail. You'll make a cute couple. I hope they don't split the two of you up."

I turned on my heel and followed the still familiar path to my grandparents' room, slamming the door behind me as loudly as possibly.

Boy, I showed him, I thought, then lay down on the bed and cried.

Chapter 16
Kelly

Christmas hadn't been much fun around the Stevens house for quite a long time. This year was proving to be the worst yet. Mom rolled into town the week before in such a foul mood that I didn't even bother to mention my hopes for a new laptop. I didn't know much about high finance, being thirteen; I was more into what I wanted at the moment. That whole thing about ignorance being bliss was true after all. I found myself wishing to be five years old again. My mother's monetary trouble was self-inflicted, but the stark reality of her actions could never be measured in just dollars. I was about to get a quick lesson concerning our household budget instead of a new computer for Christmas. And to make a bad day worse, I would soon realize that my mom was losing her mind.

For as long as I can remember, every time Mom asked for a family meeting, it was always something bad. I showed up five minutes early. I'd learned the hard way when it concerns an official family meeting, it's always better to be early than late. I sat in the solitary chair across from the couch so Mom couldn't sit too close. I didn't know why. I was wary of this impromptu meeting. Maybe because it was the first one since Amy had left. Looking around the family room, my eyes stopped on the antique Steinway grand piano that took up a large corner in the family room. Images of my twelfth birthday came flooding back and I could almost see Amy and Peter sitting there on the bench. I could still remember his mischievous smile when he asked if he could play me a tune for my birthday. The memory of my embarrassment put a brief smile on my face. So much had happened in the past year. I wondered if things would ever be the same.

I couldn't see Gina, but could hear her chopping away at something in the kitchen in preparation for dinner. She had been acting out of sorts all morning and didn't have much to say, very unusual for her. An eerie stillness loomed in the house, which, for some reason, just felt wrong. The clicking of Mom's high heels on the hardwood staircase echoed through the house and announced her arrival. I took a deep breath to relax, but my heart pounded in anticipation.

"Ah… good you're here. Thank you for not being late," Mom said.

I felt a little bit sad that her greeting wasn't something like, *Hi, honey, how was your day?* Most of my friends had families that spoke to each other like that, not the case in our house. Amy always said. *It is what it is.*

"Hi Mom," I said, being careful not to have any kind of attitude in my tone.

For some reason, perhaps for the first time in my life, I had an epiphany. Most of our family meetings in the past had started off with a confrontation between Amy and Mom. The reason had been due to Amy's tone, according to the warden. I smiled for a split second, remembering Amy's nickname for Mom. God, I missed her so much.

"Want to let me in on the joke?" Mom asked.

"Oh … Ah, no, I was just thinking about something Amy said a long time ago. I really miss her," I added, hoping for some civility to come back my way.

"Well, I miss her too. She'll be back when she's better."

Mom looked through me like I was a window. Her mind somewhere else as she spoke. The comment surprised me, since the best we could ever hope for would be a visit, and that wouldn't happen unless there were some fences mended between the two of them. Mom cleared her throat to speak. I sat and listened in amazement as she shared what had transpired in the past few weeks.

"When I became aware that Amy had run away from home, I knew I had to intervene. Your sister has always been compulsive and never thinks things through. Rather than weighing the pros and cons of a decision, she's always been one to jump in with both feet, with no fear of the consequences."

"Amy's been in love with Peter for a long time." I blurted it out before considering the rebuttal. None came though.

"Honey, a year or two may seem like a long time to a teenager. But I assure you, in the big scheme of things, it's not. Amy would have ended up pregnant and discarded. You forget that I have defended several rock stars over the past few years. I know how show business turns people into users."

"I don't think Peter is like that. He's a really nice guy."

"No one starts out that way, but money corrupts. Once they get used to having lots of money and the privilege that goes with it. Using others becomes easy. If Peter had used his gift in another way, he would have stayed a nice guy."

Mom stopped and waited as though she knew I had more questions.

"So where's Amy now?" I asked.

"I think it's better that you don't know just yet."

Her lips pursed, her expression signaled that she had a pretty good idea. I knew more than I was admitting to.

"Why are telling me this?" I was afraid to know the answer, but curiosity compelled me.

"You're the smart one, that's why you've always been my favorite. Cut to the chase and no beating around the bush.

244

I'm telling you because my decision to save Amy came with a price and it will affect us all. The price tag for rescuing your sister to date is a little over three hundred thousand dollars and the meter is still running. That's not including the fact that I haven't worked in nearly a month. So how does that affect us?" She paused long enough to ponder her own question, and then continued. "I think you're smart enough to realize I don't have that kind of money lying around. I gave Gina and Fred notice; their last day is this Friday. I put the house up for sale this morning, and the realtor is pretty sure she has somebody who is interested in buying a house like ours."

"What? Where will we live?" I asked.

We had lived in the same big old house in the historical part of town for as long as I could remember. The thought of moving from everything familiar began sinking in—and it was scary. Even worse was losing Gina and Fred. They were, more often than not, my only family.

"I'm looking at some apartments on the other side of town. You'll be closer to school and most of your friends."

I guess she added that part to make me feel better. It didn't.

She managed a halfhearted smile and then asked, "Do you have any more questions?"

"No... I guess not."

"Okay, good," she said, then turned and walked away without another word.

I couldn't help but wonder if mom realized her actions would cost much more than money. There would be a terrible price to pay. I knew Amy would never forgive her for meddling. She may have thought she was doing the best thing for Amy. The thing is, I had little doubt that it would backfire. As I replayed our conversation in my mind, a certain reality became crystal clear: Mom didn't know that Amy was pregnant.

Not only did I not get the laptop. I didn't get anything from Mom for Christmas that year. Not even a card. I did get a nice card from Gina and Fred with a fifty-dollar bill in it. I thought about giving it back, but heck, it was my total haul from ole' Saint Nick. The house sold on December 28, and the buyer was eager to close. By the middle of January, we had moved into a three-bedroom apartment on the other side of town about four blocks from school. During that span of time, Mom and I hardly spoke. It seemed funny in a way, because to the best of my recollection, she had not spent so much time at home in years. She appeared to be in a bad mood most of the time. So I did my best to stay invisible.

On the last Sunday of the month, Mom called me into our living room, which was too small for all of our stuff. It felt cramped, and maintaining any distance from the warden was difficult at best. I guess in some ways I was smarter than Amy. She always spoke her mind regardless of the consequences. I kept my tongue in check for the most part, and that skill served me well most of the time. As always, Mom started off the meeting and I listened.

"I have to go to New York and will be gone for a few days. With any luck, I'll be back by Friday. Since you have proven yourself to be the sensible one in the family, I am taking a chance on you. The house rules have not changed and you know what they are. I'm not going to waste time going over it again. I will take the time to tell you that if you disobey my trust, we will be talking about boarding school. Are we clear on this matter?"

"Yes," I said.

Short and sweet has been my savior; don't fail me now, I thought.

"Good," she said.

"Mom."

"Yes."

"Is Amy okay?"

"A little better every day," she said and then paused.

I think she was considering saying more but clammed up. I knew the conversation had ended.

Mom left the next day. The more I thought about it, the more I had to know what was going on, so I made a decision. I asked a few friends at school if I could borrow their cell phone. On the third try, I got lucky. One of my well-to-do friends, who had unlimited minutes, let me borrow hers and didn't even ask why. After school, I went straight home and started making phone calls. I had a pretty good head for numbers, especially when it mattered to me, so it only took two tries to reach Big Tony.

"Hello... Tony. This is Kelly Stevens."

There was a short pause before he responded. "Hi Kelly, you're Amy's sister, right?"

"Yes... I'm calling because I found out a few weeks ago from Abigail that she kidnapped Amy and took her somewhere."

It felt weird calling Mom by her first name. Like my sister always did. I guess it was my attempt to sound older than I was.

"Well, that appears to be the case... but all we know for sure is that Amy was abducted in Fiji," he said.

I knew he was being guarded with his response.

"Look, I'm sure you know Abigail did it. I also know you're trying to be politically correct. Maybe because you think I'm a kid and shouldn't know the facts. Mom told me everything in detail." There was a long pause this time, and I was just about to say, "Hello... anybody there?"

"Kelly, do you know where your sister is?" He asked the question carefully and then there was another pause.

"No, I don't, and trust me. If I did, I would tell you. I want to help find her. I know Amy's pregnant, but Mom doesn't."

"That's good to know. We were hoping to find her before that fact became too obvious. I know your heart is in the right place, Kelly, but it's probably better for you to not get involved in this mess."

"Look, I may only be thirteen, but like it or not, I am involved in this mess. Will you give me Peter's phone number so I can talk to him?"

"I'm really sorry. I don't think I should do that. It could cause Peter more grief with Abigail."

It wasn't the answer I was looking for. I had no doubt he was trying to look out for Peter's welfare. Even so, I wasn't giving up that easy.

"Mom's gone to New York for a week. I'm home alone with a borrowed cell phone. Will you at least take the number and ask him to call me?" I was pleading; there was no denying it.

There was an audible sigh, then he asked, "Where's Gina and Fred?"

"Mom had to let them go and sell the house to pay the kidnapping fees." I wasn't trying to be funny, but that got a chuckle out of Tony.

"Okay, I'll call Peter and give him your message. If he doesn't call back, just know that he's really in a bad way."

That comment perked my interest.

"What's wrong with Peter?" I asked.

"Let's just say he's not taking very good care of himself at the moment."

"Thanks, Tony," I said and hung up.

I sat and waited. I had no reason to think that Peter would jump on the phone and call me, but I hoped he would. Time can almost stand still when you're an impatient teenager. I cooked a TV dinner and ate it without even noticing what it was. Our new tiny living room didn't offer much space for pacing; it didn't take long for it to feel more like jail than a house. Every so often, I glanced out the window. The sun continued to drop into the horizon until there was nothing left but an orange hue. It had been two hours since I'd called Tony. It was getting dark and for the first time in my life, I felt really alone. No Amy, no Gina or Fred, and of course, as always, Mom was gone. It's funny how you can be expecting a phone call any minute, but when it comes, the ring scares the crap out of you. It took about a millisecond for the shock to run its course. I dove for the phone and knocked it off the coffee table, fumbled with the answer key and took a deep breath.

"Hello," I said.

"Hi Kelly," Peter said.

"Peter! Oh my God. Thanks for calling me. Look, I want to help find Amy."

"Any help would be appreciated, but we have some of the best private investigators in the business looking for her and have had no luck." His voice cracked, it didn't take a rocket scientist to figure out he was emotionally exhausted.

"Okay look, Abigail told me everything except where they took Amy. Do you have any clues?"

"All we know is they landed in Canada." He sounded frustrated; it echoed in his voice. "Thanks for wanting to help, but unless you can get Abigail to spill the beans. I'm not sure what you or I can do."

He sounded so sad, it became infectious. Then it hit me. A revelation so plain it had to be true.

"What part of Canada were they seen last?" I asked.

"Heck, I don't remember. They landed in some little town in British Columbia."

He had a little slur to his words, and I thought about asking him if he had been drinking, but something familiar clawed at the back of my mind, nagging me, and that was more important.

"Tell me the name of the town, Peter. It could be important."

My mind reached for the answer to the blurry puzzle forming in my brain. Then came a pause accompanied with a deep sigh.

"Hang on a minute. I have it written down somewhere."

He sounded a little bit condescending, but I could hear him rustling through papers. After what seemed like forever, he came back to the phone.

"Kelowna is the name of the town where they landed."

"Why have I heard of that name before?" I asked. It was more of a question for me than it was for Peter, then I remembered. "Our grandparents had a cabin up there! We used to go there when I was little."

I felt so excited; I had figured out the puzzle.

"Kelly, this is very important: do you know what the address is or about where it was?"

Peter's voice was no longer lethargic. He sounded excited. I knew for sure that this was new information. I tried to divine a location or some useful information out of my brain, to no avail.

"Heck, I was a little kid when we went up there. I remember the house and a big lake, that's about it."

Disappointment hit me hard. There I was the great sleuth. One moment of grandeur and it was over. I could feel the tears welling up in my eyes. Peter must have heard it in my voice.

"Don't cry," he said. "You've already told me more than anyone else has." He managed a soothing voice, even though, I knew he was just as frustrated as I was.

"I feel like an idiot. It's just... well... I'm worried about her."

"Yeah... I am too. Listen, did you ever write letters or get any from your grandparents?"

"Oh, heck yeah, lots of times! Granny was always sending cards. Good thinking. Stay on the line; this might take a few minutes."

"Yes, go look. I'll hang on. Go... go!" he said with a new level of excitement in his voice.

I kept the phone with me but ran to my bedroom and dropped it onto the bed. If I still had any of Granny's cards, I knew right where they would be. Mom tried several times to get me to throw my box of keepsakes away. I'd refused. I found the box. It was penned with a bold magic marker that said *Kelly's stuff* on the top. I ripped it open and dumped the contents on the bed and frantically started searching. I found the bundle of envelopes wrapped by a rubber band. A Christmas card sat on top, and in the upper left hand corner written in a beautiful cursive hand was my grandparents' address. I scrambled for the phone and didn't have to ask if he was still on the line. I knew he was.

"It just says Trout Lake, Canada. I remember the name now. It's a really long narrow lake and is well known for its trout. There's no street address, though, and I don't think there is any." I blurted it all out so fast I wasn't sure if he heard me.

"Kelly, you are the best. I'll let you know when we find her. Love you, sister." He hung up abruptly, and the line went dead.

I spread out on the bed and made the biggest snow angel I could in my pile of memorabilia.

"I did it," I said.

I don't think I've ever been as proud as I was at that moment. I thought about how the conversation had gone and basked in the glow.

"'Love you, sister,'" I said, remembering his words out loud for my own ears to hear, "I have a brother."

Chapter 17
Amy

December was a blur, and Christmas would have gone by without notice except that Felix made me a popcorn necklace. It was dumb, but I have to admit I liked it. Spending a month alone with someone and trying to avoid them is a very difficult thing to do, especially when you're snowed in. I had nowhere to go and the old movies got older pretty quick. There was no Internet, cable, satellite, and no antenna, which would have done no good anyway since we were miles from a city big enough to have a TV station. The only connection to the outside world was an AM radio. So in the end, I did exactly what I said I would not do.

My compromise came about very slow. I wanted to dislike Felix because of what he represented. After all, he did contribute to my being kidnapped, and in my mind, I considered that an inexcusable act in itself. There is something to be said for being lonely. When you're truly isolated from human contact, almost anyone is better than nobody at all.

We started off playing cards once in a while until that bored me to tears. About mid-January while snooping around the house, I found an old chess game in the attic. I had been rummaging through stuff, mostly being nosy, and partly for something to do. I found the attic through a pull-down ladder in the hall. It was dark, dusty, and, for lack of a better term, smelled old. Every place I stepped left footprints that were like the first steps in the dust on the moon. It was a time capsule of memories packed into cardboard boxes and antique trunks. I found some old pictures of my grandparents and Abigail from years gone by and was surprised that she seemed so happy and sweet. Off in a corner, by itself, sat a big ornate trunk. I guess it had been closed for a long time and took quite a bit of persistence to get it open. Inside and stacked on top was an old chess board with a cigar box filled with the pieces and some more old photos. I found a picture of Dad and Mom playing chess; the date on the back made it over eighteen years old. She was clearly pregnant—with me. I cried.

I'm not sure why I brought the game back down with me from the attic that day. I left it on the dining room table and forgot about it. I saved the pictures as well but hid them in my personal effects. A week later while making my usual rounds from one side of the cabin to the other, I noticed that the chessboard had been set up. Felix was in the great room tending to the fireplace, which is where he seemed to always be.

"Why did you set up the chess board?" I asked.

"Well, I just assumed that you brought it down from the attic so we could play."

Several hateful comebacks came to mind, but I knew it would be a waste of effort and accomplish nothing.

"I don't know how to play," I said. "I think it belonged to my dad."

The emotions I had experienced that day in the attic resurfaced. I turned away so he couldn't see me on the verge of crying. I'm not sure why it mattered. Perhaps I didn't want him to see how vulnerable I felt. A couple of deep breaths helped me get a grip on my emotions while the realization set in as to how bizarre it was to worry about his opinion in the first place. Of all the tribulations at hand, the fact that I could cry for no apparent reason should have been the least of my concerns. The few conversations I'd had with Felix revealed he had been in the military. That part, I'd already guessed, but he didn't talk a lot and I didn't feel like asking many questions. The notion that he was hiding something interested me. Being the curious girl that I am, coupled with the fact I had nothing else to do. I decided to see what I could learn about my abductor.

"I could teach you how to play," he said to my back.

"Okay."

I turned to him, just in time to see a fleeting look of surprise before his customary unreadable features returned. He gestured for me to pick a spot to sit, and I got my first chess lesson. After learning the nuances of how the pieces moved and some basic strategy, we played. He beat me the first four games in less than ten moves, I'm pretty sure he wasn't trying very hard. The main thing that kept me interested, rather than just getting mad and quitting, was that he explained everything in detail. How my moves triggered his and how I could avoid being beaten that way again. It wasn't obvious at first, but the ice between us started to melt.

"So where did the game of chess come from?" I'm not sure why I asked.

"Chess originated in India somewhere around 600 AD. They called it 'chaturanga.' It was divided into the four known military divisions of the time infantry, cavalry, elephantry, and chariotry. Those eventually became pawn, knight, bishop, and rook, respectively. The game was introduced to Persia, and then spread through the Middle East after the Islamic conquest of Persia." He paused, "More than you wanted to know?"

"No, please continue." He had surprised me. For one thing, it was already more than he had said in a month—and I did find it interesting.

"The game spread from the Middle East to Russia and by the tenth century had expanded throughout Europe. By the end of the fifteenth century, it survived several prohibitions decreed by the Christian church and took the shape of the modern game we play today."

"That's interesting. I'm surprised you know all that."

It came out wrong and I started to apologize, but he actually laughed. It seemed like a good way to smooth over my comment so I did to.

"Don't tell anyone," he said. "I'm trying to keep it a secret."

"I didn't mean it the way it came out." My words even surprised me. Here I was, saying I'm sorry to someone I loathed the day before.

"It's okay Amy. If I were you, I'd hate me too." He held my gaze long enough that I knew he was being sincere.

"I guess in a way," I said, "we're both pawns in the game that Abigail has set us in." Even as I said it, I realized that I had begun comprehending the bigger picture. "So, Felix, I know why I'm in this game. Why are you? And don't tell me it's for the money, because I have a feeling there is more to it than that, especially after what Abigail said that time after you kept her from hitting me again."

He smiled. The question put him into deep contemplation for a while, and he rapped on the table with his sausage-sized fingers, trying to decide whether to answer, or what to say. Then he took a deep breath and nodded.

"I was the lieutenant of a SEAL team platoon at the beginning of the second Gulf War, or as the brass liked to call it, Operation Iraqi Freedom. Our job was to ferret out the supposed weapons of mass destruction. We were working our way into a small village about forty miles outside of Baghdad. Resistance had been light for the most part, so when all hell broke loose, we were caught off guard. An IED—improvised explosive device—went off and took out four of my men in the blink of an eye. One minute they were there, and then they were just gone." He paused. I could see that he was reliving a moment that in my mind was nothing short of horrific. "A firefight ensued, which put us in a crossfire situation. Two more of my guys were dead and three wounded before we could take cover. Out of sixteen men, I had six dead and three wounded in thirty seconds. The team managed to neutralize the threat in short order. From beginning to end, the whole engagement lasted no more than five minutes."

"I imagine five minutes is a long time when you're being shot at."

"Yes, it is."

"So what happened then?" I asked, suspecting there had to be more to the story.

"We secured the village."

"What does that mean exactly?"

"It means we went through each and every house, hut, and barn, removing threats. The last house, which was where most of the opposition had come from, wouldn't give up. I called in an F-16 for an airstrike. Turns out there were six kids in that house, and none of them were over fifteen years old. The press had a field day. It didn't matter that the house was full of weapons and that I had six guys dead. When the politicians got heat, they turned it on the higher-ups in the military, and it ended up around my neck. I ended up with a dishonorable discharge. To make a really bad situation worse, now the Iraqis are trying to bring me back to stand trial. Since the whole deal is unpopular for everyone involved, good ole Uncle Sam decided to throw me under the bus."

"Our government is going to let you take the blame for doing your job?"

"Yeah … that's about the size of it."

He stood up and walked over to the fireplace, poking at the logs.

"So that's how you became an indentured servant for Abigail," I said. All the pieces of the puzzle began fitting together in my mind.

"You're smarter than you act, too."

"Don't tell anyone. I'm trying to keep it a secret." I smiled, and for the first time, it seemed like my captor relaxed a little.

"Does Abigail know you're pregnant?"

The question came out of nowhere, and I wasn't expecting it nor did I know what to say. I looked down at my belly and knew the secret was out.

"No... not yet anyway."

I caught his gaze, and he smiled back with reassurance.

"Don't worry," he said, "I'm not going to tell her but..." He paused in midsentence and seemed to have a private conversation with himself for a few moments then continued. "She's planning to be back up here the first week of February."

I wasn't sure what the exact day was, much less the date, but I knew it had to be the latter part of January.

"Oh no ... What's the date today?" I asked.

"It's the twenty-ninth."

"She can't see me pregnant! She'll make me give up the baby."

The tears started welling up in my eyes, and I had no chance of looking brave. Felix walked over to me, and I could tell he felt undecided as to what he should say or do. I didn't take time to explain it, and I have no idea why, but I put my arms around him and sobbed. I barely came to his chest, and Felix seemed as big around as the Texas pin oak tree in our back yard. My dad wasn't a big guy, as best as I could remember, so the two had nothing in common except for how he made me feel. The paternal sanctuary had been missing in my life ever since my father died. I cried until his shirt was wet and then cried some more. He didn't say anything. He just patted my back and let me get it out.

I didn't expect a revelation or a sudden change in loyalties, so when my emotional breakdown ended, it was just awkward. The hard truth of reality came back as I gained control and I pushed myself away from him.

"I'm sorry... I got your shirt all wet," I said. Not really wanting eye contact, I pretended to look at the floor.

"It's okay. It'll dry... I think."

Even though he made a small attempt at humor, I could tell it was a weird moment for him as well.

"I'm going to go lie down for a while," I said.

I couldn't think of anything else to say, and for the most part, I just wanted to be alone. I tried to sort things out that night but had no clue as to a way out of my predicament. All I could think about was the baby and how Abigail would react when she found out.

The next morning when I woke up, I noticed there wasn't the typical smell of coffee in the air that I had become accustomed to. I didn't need to get dressed since I was still in my clothes from the previous day. The fact that I smelled like a farm animal crossed my mind as I wandered out into the family room. It seemed more quiet than normal, and the fire had almost burned out. I noticed a big mound of fiery red coals but no fresh wood in the fireplace. That was unusual. Ever since we had been there, Felix had never let it burn down. I poked my head into the kitchen. It was empty, and I noticed the coffeepot was not on.

That's weird. Well, maybe he stayed up late and is still asleep, I thought.

I wasn't an everyday coffee drinker, but for some reason, it sounded good. Once it was brewing, I chucked a couple of logs on to the fire and prodded it with a poker. I had no clue what I was doing but the hot coals made short work of the new fuel. Pretty soon, the logs were blazing and giving off a substantial amount of heat. Satisfied with my efforts, I poured a cup of coffee into one of my grandfather's big porcelain mugs that had always been my favorite. I went to the old leather couch, sat down, and wrapped my feet in a comforter that had been in the same spot as long as I could remember. Outside, I saw that snow was falling, but that came as no big surprise. It was always snowing. By the time my drink turned cold, I started to get the feeling that something was not as it should be. I went to the spare bedroom door, which was closed, and rapped on it softly.

"Hey, are you awake?" I asked.

No answer came, which made me hesitate, but I decided to knock quite a bit louder. There was still no response. I turned the handle and rapped on the door again as I opened it. The room was empty; it looked as though the bed had not even been slept in. A feeling of dread crept into my brain. The thought of being alone and abandoned in the middle of nowhere scared me.

Why would he just leave me? I wondered.

Then I heard something in the distantance, getting louder. It sounded like a motorcycle. I disregarded that notion, knowing it had to be a snowmobile. It got louder until it sounded like it was right outside the front door. That bad feeling came back. It was unlikely that Abigail would show up braving a snowstorm when she could wait a couple of days and waltz in, enjoying the warmth and comfort of a helicopter. The motor shut off, and I heard footsteps. The door swung open before I could react from my last fleeting

260

thought: *What if it's a stranger?* Terrified, I shrunk back from the heavily clothed man wearing a helmet with a full face shield. He shut the door and pulled off his headgear. It was Felix.

"Oh... you scared the crap out of me! First you're gone. Then you barge in here like some sort of mountain man. What's wrong with you?" I didn't feel like crying this time; I was mad.

"What's the matter? Did you miss me?"

The jovial aspect of his response caught me off guard, but I still felt pissed, so without thinking, I threw Grandpa's mug at him. It was a good throw or bad, depending on your point of view. It would have hit him in the face, but somehow he caught it with one hand. He inspected it, looked up, and smiled.

"This is your favorite mug. You could have broken it."

Then it dawned on me. He was in a good mood. He hadn't been in a good mood since I met him.

"What's up with you? Why are you in such a good mood?" I asked.

"I've made a decision that I should have made weeks ago and I feel good about it."

He stamped the snow off his feet, pulled the parka off, and walked over to warm up by the fireplace.

I was clueless where this conversation was going, so I asked the only question that seemed obvious to me. "You wanted to take a snowmobile ride? I wished you had done it sooner. It's improved your mood."

He laughed. It was a deep and hearty laugh, and his face wrinkled around his eyes. I wondered how long it had been since he had experienced a happy moment.

"I have an idea to share with you. If you think it's crazy, or something you don't want to do... well, no harm, no foul."

He paused for me to respond. So I said the only thing that came to mind. "Okay… I'm listening."

"This whole deal between you and your mother is wrong. I'm not judging or taking sides. The thing is you're pregnant and it's obvious you want to keep your baby. Whether that call is right or wrong is academic. Some kids turn eighteen and are still just kids. Since I've been around, you've acted way more mature than your mom. Maybe someday you two will make up. Right now you need to be close to a doctor. The Canadian wilderness is no place to have your first baby."

His smile disappeared with the comment. I realized that he really cared and that made me feel good. I also got the gist of his real meaning. So far… my pregnancy was going easy and normal. What if that changed?

"You know I agree. So what do you have in mind?" I asked.

"This snowstorm is a big one. According to the radio, we're going to get two or three feet of snow in the next two or three days. That means even if we could get to a road, it would do us no good for several days. We don't have an airplane or helicopter, but I did find us a nice shiny new snowmobile and plenty of fuel."

"Wouldn't it be crazy to take off in this storm?" I asked, looking outside, knowing the answer before he could reply.

"That's the tricky part, and yes, you're right. We need to leave before it quits snowing so our tracks are covered. Timing will be critical. We can't leave too early or we might get lost in this blizzard and freeze to death. If we leave too late we'll leave tracks and Abigail will find us. If we leave too early, we might not make it. Are you still interested?"

I knew my decision affected not only me but Peter and our unborn child as well. The storm looked to be getting worse outside. I watched the wind blow the heavy snow in a swirling motion out the front window while I weighed my two options. The circumstances that had brought me to this place were fueled by Abigail's interpretation of what was best for me. What I wanted and felt did not matter to her. There was just one choice since I didn't trust Abigail with the future of my baby. The hard part was the unknown outcome of braving the weather on a machine that could quit on us anytime.

"How long will it take to get to some sort of civilization?" I asked.

"We'll go cross country, so that will save time. I'm guessing, but I think we can make it in a day, maybe two. The days are short, and I won't take a chance of traveling at night."

"Have you done anything like this before, like while you were in the military?"

"No... not really, I spent most of my career in the desert."

He wasn't laughing or cavalier about our jaunt through the back country of British Columbia.

"Well, that's comforting," I said.

"I'm not going to lie to you. It's not going to be a walk in the park. You're going to be cold and miserable the entire trip."

"Now you're sugarcoating it." I was joking, but he wasn't amused.

"I'm sure you noticed on the helicopter ride out that the terrain is mountainous most of the way. The good news is I found a map, and the machine I borrowed is almost new."

"You mean, the machine stole," I said.

"It was the only cabin that I could find within five miles of this place, and there was no one home. From the looks of the place, it's been a while since the owners have been around. Anyway, I left a note and promised to pay for it—which means your hubby can take care of that." On that, he smiled.

"I guess you looked for a radio or telephone?"

My question didn't rate an answer; all I got was a scowl.

It snowed for the next two days. About the time I was wondering if it would ever quit, the weather forecast on the radio predicted the storm would end the next day, early in the afternoon. As luck would have it, we had no shortage of warm clothes. Felix encouraged me to overdo it because, as he put it, "You can always take some off, but you can't put more on." I took that as meaning to take lots of clothes.

"No, I meant to take all the clothes you can wear," he said.

Then he proceeded to discard most of the things I had piled up to take with.

"We're not taking an SUV on this trip," he said. "Where do you think we would put all this stuff?"

He seemed amazed at my lack of understanding on the subject and that I thought there would be room. Once the final pile was settled on, I understood. There were two old smelly down-filled sleeping bags, two tarps, food and water for three days, and three plastic five-gallon gas containers.

"Where are we going to put all this stuff?" I asked.

"Now you understand how limited we are for space. To answer to your question, take a look outside."

I saw that he had an old toboggan tied to the back of the snowmobile.

"Where did you find that?"

"It was in the boat house hanging on the wall."

It took Felix nearly a half-hour to load the sled to his satisfaction. Then he came back in to the cabin to warm up one last time. I filled a stainless steel thermos with boiling hot coffee, hoping it would stay that way for a while, then took one last look at what had been my prison for two months. Five layers of clothes later, I felt as ready as I ever would be.

"I'm ready," I said.

He was trying without success to tune into a last-minute weather update. "I guess we're not going to get a forecast," he said, giving up the effort. Then he looked up at me. "You look like the Michelin man." He chuckled.

"You said—"

"I know, I know. Alright, daylight's a wasting."

He headed for the door with me waddling at his heels. The snowmobile started on the second try, and we were off. Within the first hour, I felt glad for every stitch of clothes I had on. Luckily I had Felix for a windbreak. I could only imagine how cold he had to be.

We tried stopping every hour to warm up but after the third time we decided, it really didn't help. After that, Felix would only stop when he needed to consult the map and take a swig of the coffee. The snowfall quit just before we stopped for lunch. The canned chili was cold, and I would have been happy to do without. Felix insisted that I eat. By late afternoon, I felt numb from exposure. We couldn't go very fast, which was probably a good thing since every so often we would have to stop and backtrack due to cliffs, obstructions, or mountains going almost straight up. I wanted the trip to be over and was not looking forward to camping in the woods overnight, but when we finally stopped for the evening, I was glad. I have to give credit where it's due. My companion was everything I was not in a wilderness environment. Within twenty minutes, which is a really long time when you're freezing to death. He had a fire going and the beginnings of a shelter built with the tarps he had brought along. The fire felt good—there was no denying that—but there are a couple of annoying things about campfires. The smoke follows you no matter where you sit… and you cook on one side and freeze on the other. Still, I wasn't about to complain. At least not out loud.

Dinner was beef stew out of a can. Felix was pretty clever when it came to improvising. He fashioned some tongs out of sticks so we could heat the stew up and retrieve the hot can without getting burnt. I'm generally kind of a picky eater, but I ate two cans of the stuff and would have had more if it were offered. I felt nature's call, and after a few uncomfortable minutes, I knew there was no putting it off.

"Uh … I need to go," I said as delicately as I could.

He turned and rummaged through a backpack and pitched me a roll of toilet paper.

"Don't go too far," he said.

I shed some clothes before heading to a private spot in the trees. I was freezing again by the time I made it back to the fire. I put a couple of layers back on until I felt comfortable and warm again. Felix hadn't said much since we had left, and I began to wonder if he was having second thoughts.

"Are you regretting your decision?" I asked.

"No… no regrets, I'm just beating myself up for getting involved in the first place. It was a bad job and I knew better." He doodled in the snow with a stick for a while, and then said. "I'm sorry."

"You know what, Felix, there's another way to look at it. If someone else had taken this ill-gotten job, I'd probably still be stuck in the cabin waiting for the warden to return."

"Thanks," he said with a chuckle. "I guess that is a better way of looking at it." He started to say something, then reconsidered and fell silent again.

"Do you have a girlfriend or a wife?" I asked.

He grinned, considering the question just long enough that I wasn't sure if I would get an answer or not. "Yeah, several girls, I guess I haven't met the right one yet. Maybe someday I can stay in the same place long enough."

"How do you feel about Chicago?" I asked.

"Why do you ask?" he asked.

I could tell he had no idea what I was getting at.

"I can't promise you would be in one place, but if you're interested in a steady job with excellent pay and benefits, I have an offer you might want to consider."

"I'm sorry, but I'm not following you."

"Gee, you've seemed so smart up to this point. I'm offering you a job as head of security for Peter's band."

"I appreciate the thought. What makes you think your husband would be so gracious after all that has happened?"

"If I ask, I'm sure he'll do it."

"Yeah, I bet he would at that. We'll see how it goes. We're not out of the woods yet. Then there's getting you out of Canada without a passport."

"Just get me to a phone and keep us incognito long enough for Peter to pick us up and we're home free."

My passport had been left in Fiji, but I knew Peter would have brought it home with him. The problem was whether Abigail would be looking for me by then and if she had any of the local officials in her pocket. I felt certain she did, it would be stupid to underestimate my mother again.

"It's going to be a long day tomorrow, so you might want to get some sack time. I'll keep the fire going and take the first watch. In four hours, I'll wake you up."

"What are you watching for? There's no way Abigail could find us this soon."

"Not her... I'm more concerned about wolves."

He was dead serious, and I had thought the only thing we had to worry about was freezing to death.

"Oh crap. I didn't think about wild animals. There could be bears too."

I looked from side to side trying to listen for animal noises.

"No worries about bears this time of year. They are all hibernating someplace warm and cozy." I guess he realized I seemed to be on the verge of freaking out. "Hey, I'm probably just being worrywart. Old habits die hard."

He smiled and tried to act nonchalant, but the seed had been planted. I crawled into my sleeping bag thinking dreamland would never come. The long day, in the cold, had worn me out. The next thing I knew Felix was shaking me awake.

"Oh, has it been four hours already?" I asked, still half asleep.

"It's been more like six, you lazy bum. Wake me if you start dozing off, and don't let the fire go out. I've gathered plenty of wood so you won't have to go looking for more."

He pointed to a big pile of branches a few feet from the fire, then stretched and disappeared into our makeshift shelter. In less than thirty minutes, I was bored out of my mind. I added wood to the fire, poked it with a stick, mostly for something to do. The stars lit up the sky, in a myriad of brilliant specks of light. I tried to recognize some of the constellations, without much success, and thought about how great it would be to see Peter again. The fire felt nice and toasty. There was just enough air moving in the right direction that the smoke stayed out of my face.

I woke up with Felix's hand over my mouth.

"Be quiet and don't make any sudden moves," he said softly.

Waking up with a hand over your face is disturbing, to say the least. I blinked my eyes, trying to adjust to the darkness, and heard panting. Three wolves stood on the other side of the nonexistent fire that I had let burn out. Their eyes had an eerie red glow that looked unnatural. The two smaller ones stood closest and seemed more curious than dangerous, but the other one standing back a few feet was big.

"What are they doing?" I whispered.

"Trying to decide how hard we'll be to eat," he replied, easing his bulk out of the makeshift tent. I glanced in his direction and saw him wrapping one of my extra sweatshirts around his left arm. "Don't take your eyes off them," he said. "It's the only thing making them cautious."

It all happened so fast, it was nothing like you see at the movies. For such a big man, Felix moved fast. He didn't wait for the wolves to attack; he went straight for the two smaller ones. One went for the left arm that he seemed to offer as the other one tore into his leg. He dropped his right arm behind the wolf's head and pushed with his left. I heard a sickening crunch when the animal's neck broke, along with a subdued yelp. Then it fell into a pile on the ground and didn't move again. The other one was still viciously ripping away at his leg and didn't seem to care as Felix calmly picked up a branch as big around as my leg. Sensing danger, the animal let go to back away, but the big man's swing was already in motion. The blow connected with such force that the wolf did a complete flip in the air. It tried to stand up but whimpered softly and collapsed. The big gray one stood motionless watching... waiting. Felix roared like a crazy man, shaking the tree branch in the air.

"Come on, big boy!" Felix shouted. "Let's see what you've got."

The wolf lingered, I guess to prove it could, then turned and trotted off into the darkness.

"Are you okay?" I asked.

"I'll make it."

He limped over to the woodpile, grabbed an armful, and then dumped it on the bed of coals that was faintly flickering in the darkness. He bent down and blew repeatedly until some yellow flames appeared. As the fire grew, so did the light, it exposed a gruesome scene. I saw blood splattered all over the recent blanket of pure white snow. I had to close my eyes and look away so I wouldn't throw up.

"I'm going to need your help," he said, sitting down beside me.

"Um... sure, what can I do?"

I turned my focus to him and realized where most of the blood had come from. He removed my bloody sweatshirt, revealing two deep gashes in his arm that he briefly examined, then wrapped it back up. Then he gently eased his boot and sock off and pulled his pant leg up. His ankle was ripped up real bad. It was the grossest thing I'd ever seen. I turned my head and threw up.

"Amy... I know this is going to be hard for you, if you don't help me. I will bleed to death." He said it in such a calm way that it didn't dawn on me at first what he meant.

"I don't understand. What do you mean?" My nausea seemed better, but I still averted my eyes.

"The bleeding from my leg is pretty bad. I need you to do a field dressing for me."

"I don't think I can do it," I said, sniffing back the tears that were trying to come. I was ashamed because he had just saved my life. "I'm sorry, Felix, but—"

"No buts. I can't do it, and if you don't, I'll be dead before the sun comes up."

"I don't know how, and—"

"I'll walk you through it. Get my backpack and get the first-aid kit out."

I did as I was told and dug the box out, opening it up.

"Okay, those big packages are gauze pads; you'll probably need two of them. In that little rectangle box is a roll of gauze wrap. Grab that and the tape." He lay down and scooted closer to the fire. "I need you to look the wound over to see if the blood is pulsing or if it's just a steady flow."

"Why?" I asked.

"Pulsing means artery damage, but a steady flow is veins or capillary injury."

"If I look at it, I may throw up."

"Well, try not to throw up on me. I might end up with an infection as well." He managed a chuckle but I could tell he was in a lot of pain. "I need to know if it's an artery, Amy. If it is, we'll need to rig a tourniquet."

I knelt down beside his leg and took several deep breaths. He slid his pant leg back up, and I did my best to examine the wound. It was the nastiest injury I had ever seen, really gross. I guess though, once I realized I had to do it, or Felix would die. Something clicked.

"Its bleeding a lot, but I don't see any pulsing."

"Okay, that's a good thing. Now strip off a couple of pieces of tape and stick them on your shirt so you can get at them easy. Open up the pads and gauze. Put the pads on the worst areas and then wrap the whole thing tight with the gauze and tape it."

A few minutes later, I had finished my first field dressing and then smiled. "I did it."

"I never once doubted that you could do it. Now dig out one of the ACE bandages and wrap it again, making sure it's snug but not too tight."

When I had finished, he looked at my handiwork.

"Excellent," he said. "Now if you don't mind repeating the same procedure one more time…"

He offered his arm, and I made short work of bandaging it up. As I washed the blood off my hands in the snow, the first glimmers of light peeked over the horizon. We ate some more canned food warmed by the fire and loaded up to leave. Felix was moving pretty slow, so I did everything I could to help, by sunrise we were on our way again.

Chapter 18
Peter

The conversation ended with Kelly and I was dialing Big Tony seconds later. I shared the phone call with Amy's sister, and on at least two occasions, he asked me to stop, slow down, and repeat myself. I felt alive for the first time. In nearly two months.

"Slow down and tell me again," Tony said.

I took a deep breath and started from the top. "Kelly thinks Abigail took Amy to their grandparents' cabin. She dug out an old Christmas card and found an actual address. It just said Trout Lake but that's closer than all of British Columbia."

Once I got the message across, Tony sounded as excited as I was.

"This is huge, Peter. I'll make some calls to our people up there and charter a jet. Pack some warm clothes amigo. We're going to go get your wife. I'll call you back in a few minutes. Good-bye."

I hung up. Giddy with excitement. Two months of being told. *We're doing everything we can. Sooner or later new information will surface.* Just came across to me as excuses. My immediate task at hand was to get packed. I looked around for my backpack and realized where depression had taken me. The apartment looked like a disaster. Clothes, empty food cartons, beer bottles, and an assortment of trash were scattered around the living room.

Ah crap... Amy is going to be really pissed when she sees this mess. I'll never hear the end of it.

The thought was so random. I laughed out loud—a sound that had been foreign to my place for too long. I pondered on the piles of beer bottles and realized that I had been drunk more often than not since returning from Fiji. It struck me as ironic considering I've never really liked alcohol and beer was on the bottom of my list. My spiral downward into a pit of hopelessness happened without knowing how I got there. I made a vague promise to myself that I would never let that happen again. I found my backpack buried under a pile of clothes. My search for something clean to wear didn't go very well. So I opted for how wrinkled they were and how bad they smelled. The truth of the matter, so it seemed, everything smelled. A quick sniff located the source. It was me. The phone rang and I fell over the piles of garbage trying to get to it.

"Hello, Tony," I answered.

"Hi Peter. Okay... I've booked us a charter to Kelowna and contacted our guys up there. The bad news is they're having a blizzard. The airport is shut down. They're saying it may be a day or two before we can even get in there."

"We could drive," I said. It was a foolish comment. I knew it as soon as it came out of my mouth.

"We'll be able to fly in sooner than we could drive," Tony said. "They're expecting over three feet of snow. All we can do is put everything into place and go the instant they open the Kelowna airport. In the meantime, I'll find a place to charter a helicopter and a local pilot who knows the area. You should use the time to clean up your apartment and take a shower. I can smell you over the phone." He chuckled at his joke. "I'll call you as soon as I know anything. Good-bye."

"Good-bye," I replied, then pitched my cell phone on the bed, scratched my head, and took a cautious whiff of my armpit. "Oh... that's bad. It's definitely time for a shower," I mumbled to my empty apartment.

274

After the shower, I started a load of clothes and started bagging up the assortment of trash. Sixteen big garbage bags were stuffed full when I was done. I felt ashamed that I had disintegrated to such a level of body, mind, and spirit. I watched it happen, in a disconnected sort of way. The thing is I did nothing to stop it. Being bummed out or sad is one thing. I gave the word *distraught* a whole new level of meaning.

My best efforts to do a rudimentary cleaning job seemed lacking even by my standards... so. I decided to have the maid service come in and do a deep cleaning. I knew I would never get it clean enough no matter how long I worked at it. It was something I had heard from my mom on several occasions. *That's not clean;* she would say and then methodically point out the little spots of this and that. Once pointed out. I would admit she was right. The thing is. I never understood why I couldn't see it in the first place.

It's amazing how a shower and clean clothes can make you feel better. I wasn't ready to conquer the world but my overall outlook had improved. I called Tony for an update.

"I don't have any new news yet," he said.

"Yeah, I figured as much. I was calling to see if you can round up the band. Might as well get some work done while we're waiting for the blizzard to blow itself out."

There was a pause, an audible sigh—no doubt from relief—and then Tony said, "That's great news, Peter. The guys will be thrilled to get started on your next CD. In fact, they are all at the studio as we speak. Would you like me to send a car to pick you up?"

"No... I'm ready to go. I'll just grab a cab; it'll be quicker."

"Okay, uh, great. I'll see you there. Good-bye."

"Good-bye," I said.

Tony had been my best friend through the whole ordeal and took care of everything while I felt sorry for myself and stayed drunk and mad at the world.

He was already there by the time I arrived wearing shorts and a Hawaiian shirt big enough for a two-man tent. It was below freezing outside so I figured he must have showed up in what he had on.

"Hi Peter. I called first to make sure everyone was still here. Good thing too. They were about to leave because Barry and Josh have been arguing for the last two hours, according to Joni."

"What are they fighting about now?" I asked.

"Who knows, they're brothers. It's what they do. Let's see if we can get these knuckleheads to work."

He had an ear-to-ear smile that must have been infectious. It had been so long since I had anything to smile about, it felt unfamiliar. Tony became serious and gave me a Giordano hug. If the hug didn't crack ribs, the slap on the back from his meaty paws would. I came back from a dark place and we both knew it.

"Welcome back," Tony said. "We've—I've missed you."

"Yeah... I'm sorry." I was going to include some excuses, but he interrupted me.

"Hey... it's okay. We all understand, and mark my words; we will get her back—and soon! Now let's go get some work done."

He led the way to the studio. The band seemed to be in good spirits and that made me feel really good. I deserted them for nearly two months, hadn't worked on anything and, to be honest, thought about nothing but Amy. Joni, however, had written a tune that sounded pretty good. It was great to have someone else take the lead for a change. All I had to do was work out my part of the melody on the piano and harmonize with her on the vocals. A few hours later, we managed to hack out her song. It felt good to get the creative juices flowing. By the time we were feeling good with our results. A new tune began wandering around in my head.

Tony promised to keep an ear out for the phone and told me not to worry about missing the call for our rescue mission. We worked long hours for the next two days and got an amazing amount of work done. Counting Joni's, we hammered five new songs for the band. The last two needed quite a bit of work but we were interrupted. The phone call finally came.

We left Chicago a little after three o'clock and landed in Kelowna just after dark. The snow banks were piled so high on either side of the runway; it gave the illusion of landing in a tunnel. Our Canadian private investigator assured us that Abigail had not been around. Although some of his sources thought she was due back sometime in early February. I noted that tomorrow would be the first of February. The clock was ticking. Our local contact introduced himself as Jack Smith, which I found enormously amusing. I guess he caught on and assured me that it really was his name. Jack recommended that we leave as little of a footprint as possible. He had taken the liberty to rent a couple of rooms at one of the local inns under his name. The helicopter chartered for the next day had been ferried in from Vancouver to further protect our anonymity.

"Is it just me," I said, "or are we being a bit too cloak and dagger? If Abigail's not here, we should be in and out before anyone knows the difference."

Jack considered my thoughts but was spot on as to why we should proceed with care. "The thing is... what we don't want is a confrontation with the mom. I know its Canada but it's still a foreign country. The best thing we can do is to get in, find your wife, and get out. The last thing you want is to get the local authorities involved."

"This is your backyard Jack," Tony said. "If that's how you think this should go down, then we are in agreement."

Tony looked at me with a raised eyebrow to see if I approved. I closed my eyes and nodded.

"Whatever you think," I said. "I just want to find Amy."

I didn't sleep much, if any that night. By five o' clock, I was up, dressed, and ready to go. The anticipation of what the day had in store was driving me crazy. I tried to watch TV. Gave up and ended up pacing back and forth in the room. At six, Tony rapped on my door.

"Oh... I guess it was stupid on my part to think that you might still be asleep," he said, stepping in as I opened the door.

"I'm not sure if I slept or not. I got up about an hour ago."

Tony gave me a wink and said. "Jack's having a doughnut and coffee in the lobby. By the time we get to the helicopter. It should be getting light enough to head out."

I pulled on my jacket and led him out the door. The ride to the airport was uneventful. It was still dark so we couldn't see anything anyway...except snow.

"Is it always so cold here?" I asked.

"Yeah, it is this time of year. The arctic cold front that brought all the snow has made it even colder than normal," Jack said.

We parked by what appeared to be the hanger of a small FBO. I couldn't really tell since most of it was covered with snow. A path to the front door gave just enough room to get into a nice and toasty waiting room inside. The helicopter that we chartered spent the night outside in the below-freezing temperatures. There were two guys braving the cold with a machine that had two big flexible tubes running from it to the helicopter. The pilot stood inside. Watching the hired help scurry around his aircraft. He introduced himself once we were all in, and the door shut.

"Hi… I'm Jim Rutan," he said, offering handshakes all around.

Once the greetings were out of the way, I motioned outside and asked, "What are they doing?"

He gave me a curious look before answering, "You don't get up this way much, do you?" It was a rhetorical question and I knew he didn't expect an answer. Instead I got my first lesson in extreme cold-weather aviation. "When the temperatures are this cold, the lubricants are so thick they don't do much good, so we preheat the engine. If we do a cold start, it will cause unnecessary internal damage. Since we can, we heat it up first."

One of the guys outside turned and waved to Jim.

"Gentlemen, it looks like we're ready to go. Shall we?"

As soon as we got into the Bell Jet Ranger, I realized that all the heating had been reserved for the mechanical portion. It felt as cold inside the aircraft as it was outside. Jim fired up the turbine engine and scanned the gauges until he was satisfied. Five minutes later, we took off. The first rays of sun were peeking over the horizon before the cockpit had warmed enough to slip out of our jackets. An hour and a half later, we were skimming over Trout Lake. Even though we didn't see many cabins to reconnoiter, it was still a painstaking process. We would land and Jack would go up and bang on the doors. If no one answered, he would test them to see if they were locked. Surprisingly enough, most of them were open and empty. On the fourth try, Jack reappeared and waved for me to join him. My heart leapt to my throat in anticipation as I trudged through the waist-deep snow. Fortunately for me, Jim landed as close as he could and Jack had already made a path. I burst into the cabin out of breath, expecting Amy to jump into my arms but was disappointed by a cold and empty room.

"There's no one here," I said.

"No… but I think there was and not very long ago. The fireplace is full of ashes, and the kitchen sink has recent dirty dishes in it."

Unconvinced, I looked around hoping for some hard evidence that Amy had been there. My eyes came to rest on a chess game set up on the dining room table sitting beside it was an old cigar box. I opened the box and found some old pictures. I handed one of them to Jack.

"That's Abigail and Amy's father. This has to be their cabin, but where are they?" I asked.

A wave of disappointment hit me. Amy was not here and it seemed as though we were no closer to finding her. Jack disappeared into another part of the house and came back a few moments later carrying a small white blouse.

"That's Amy's," I said. "She was wearing it in Fiji the day Abigail took her."

He handed it to me. I held the blouse close to my face, and the memory of that day came rushing back. I noticed a faint scent of her perfume still lingering on it. I folded it with reverence and found an inside coat pocket for it. Jack seemed unsatisfied and wandered outside looking for clues.

I watched from the porch while he scanned the snow just a few feet from the house. He took a deep breath and exhaled sharply. The warm breath created a misty cloud of vapor that lingered while he looked around the porch. He saw a snow shovel, grabbed it, and began removing a layer of snow from the area that had caught his attention. Within a few moments, he hit a hard-packed layer and knelt down. After carefully brushing away the powdery snow, he examined the results of his handiwork and stood up. He dusted the sparkling crystals off his clothes while exploring the terrain with his eyes, then glanced back at me. In the barren sea of white, I could only hear the whine of the helicopter while it sat at idle. I noticed that Tony was battling his way through the deep snow, puffing great clouds of smoke from the exertion.

"What's the verdict?" he asked, gasping for breath.

"She was here, Tony," I said. "Jack thinks up until a couple of days ago."

Tony's reaction appeared much like my own—disappointed.

"I have a theory if you want to hear it," Jack said.

"Absolutely, what is it?" I asked, eager for answers.

"There were two people staying here. We've confirmed that Amy was here, and I'm pretty sure there was a man with her."

I had an uneasy feeling as to where the conversation was going but said, "It makes sense that someone would be here to keep an eye on her. So what are you getting at?"

"I think they left here on a snowmobile about two days ago. You can see the tracks right there," he said, pointing to the area he had dug up.

"You think they left in the middle of the blizzard? That would be crazy!" I said.

"Not if they wanted to cover their tracks. Look, Peter, I'm not sure, but it could mean that Amy convinced her captor to take her home. Leaving while it was still snowing would have covered their tracks, and Abigail wouldn't know which way they went. It's a long shot, but it's the only answer—unless…" He stopped.

"Unless what?" I asked.

"Unless… for some reason, one of them needed medical attention."

I could tell he regretted the comment as soon as he said it, but it was too late.

"She's pregnant," I said.

"How far along is she?" he asked.

"She is going on seven months. Jack, we have to figure out which way they went."

"Kelowna is the closest city of any size. I believe they would have headed that way," Jack said.

"Why do you think that's the direction they'd take?" Tony asked.

"Because that's what I'd do. It's your call, Peter," Jack said, looking around to see that I had already started running toward the idling chopper.

Chapter 19
Amy

Dawn gave way to sunrise. The sun peeked through the trees to reveal a beautiful blue sky without a single cloud in sight. It didn't feel any warmer, though, and our progress seemed slower than it had the day before. Felix stopped several times. Referring to the topographical map that he'd found with the snowmobile. I felt cold, frustrated, and impatient. If I had known what bad shape he was in at the time. I would have been afraid as well. Just before noon, we came to what appeared to be, a very large frozen lake. It was the first barren landscape we had seen since leaving the cabin at Trout Lake. The trees and mountains that bordered the other side seemed miles away.

"That's Arrow Lake," Felix said, "which puts us about here." He pointed to a spot on the map showing me our precise location. I was clueless as to why he thought I needed to know but it took my mind off the cold. "It's about four miles to the other side of the lake. Once we get there. We'll take this pass right up through here." He pointed to a dent between two mountain peaks that were jagged and uninviting.

"It looks like we're only halfway." I whined.

"The hard part is over short stuff. We can go faster now that we're traveling in a straight line. Once we get through that pass, most of the terrain will be rolling hills and meadows. We'll be sipping hot chocolate before dark."

Although the map didn't tell me everything that Felix's trained eyes saw. Three hours later, we were heading down the backside of the pass. Just like he described it earlier, the lay of the land looked smoother. Off in the distance, I could faintly make out a city. I pointed over his shoulder and he nodded in response. He slowed to a stop and got off to stretch.

"That's Kelowna," he said. "It's about fifteen miles away."

He stepped back to the sled for a gas can and refueled the snowmobile while it sat idling. I noticed him wobble a little. I thought he had just lost his balance.

"I'm going to leave the sled here," he said. "It's just slowing us down at this point."

"Need some help?" I asked.

"No… I got it," he replied.

I stamped my feet and rubbed my hands together trying to stay warm, salvation was just a few miles away and inklings of deliverance restored my resolve. I heard a thump and turned to see Felix crumpled into a pile on the snow. Caught up in my own discomfort and thoughts, I missed the fact that he was still bleeding. I saw a good-sized puddle of frozen blood on the snowmobile and blotches in the snow everywhere he had stepped. It took all the strength I had just to roll him over. He was unconscious but breathing. I shook him, gently at first, then harder.

"Felix! Wake up! Don't you quit on me now. I was just starting to like you."

I was yelling and shaking him as hard as I could. His eyes flickered open, and he managed the beginnings of a smile.

"Looks like I may have to decline on your job offer," he said.

"No… you're not getting off that easy, mister, not after all we've been through. I have intentions of making life miserable for you for a long time to come."

Tears were welling up. I knew this time I had to be the strong one.

"Amy... I'm not going to make it. If you don't leave me and go, you won't either. Follow the map like I showed you and just go."

"Let me tell you something, marine, I'm going to unload the sled and you're going to help me get you on it. Then we are getting out of here together. So what do you have to say about that?"

I had stood up over him in defiance, making ready to start the unloading process. He raised his arm and gestured me closer with his forefinger. I bent down so I could hear.

"Not a marine... Navy SEAL," he said.

I stomped over to the sled and began unloading and was madder than I'd been in two months. "Fine, you want to be a sailor instead, fine. Frankly I don't give a crap about your macho labels. You want to prove to me a Navy SEAL is better than a marine, then get your happy ass on that sled, soldier."

I finished my rant and had an empty sled at about the same time. I looked back, expecting a response, and saw that he was up on one elbow trying to get up. He was weak, and I knew I'd never get him on the sled by myself. I hurried over to him and tried to get him on his feet, but he was too weak and I wasn't strong enough to compensate.

He slumped back onto the snow and said, "Disconnect the sled."

"No! I told you I'm not leaving you."

He shook his head. "Disconnect the sled and bring it over here by me, then roll me on to it."

This time I got his meaning and it made perfect sense. It would be much easier than trying to drag him. It wasn't very far but I was fighting a losing battle. If he passed out on me, I didn't know if I would even be able to roll him. Lucky for me, the sled was attached with a simple carabiner and was easy to disconnect. The snow was deep and every movement proved to be a struggle, but I managed to maneuver the sled in beside him.

"Okay, big shot, time to show me some of that Navy machismo."

He managed a weak smile. "You're worse than my drill sergeant."

On the second try, with his help, I rolled him onto the sled. I tied him and the last jug of fuel to the sled with the tie downs we used for the supplies. It took me quite a while to figure out how to operate the snowmobile and to maneuver it close enough to reattach the sled. The carabiner snapped shut and something moved in my peripheral vision. About thirty feet away stood the big gray wolf.

"You've got to be kidding," I whispered.

Somewhere in the back of my mind, I remembered our first encounter and that Felix had said to keep eye contact. Every time I made a small move backward, the wolf took a step toward me. It was a cat-and-mouse game—and I was the mouse. The deep snow was almost as much of a hindrance for him as it was for me. My next step backward bumped into the idling snowmobile and I felt pretty sure that when I moved to get on it, the wolf would make its attack. I took a deep breath, said a little prayer, jumped onto the saddle, and twisted the throttle full on. The tread spun, covering Felix with snow. My heart jumped into my throat as I realized we were crawling along rather than speeding away. The machine started to pick up speed and I chanced a looked back. The big gray loped through the deep snow with long strides and got close enough to nip at Felix's boots before we started to outrun him.

A few minutes later, the wolf was a speck on the horizon. If I had been paying closer attention to my driving instead of worrying about the wolf, I would have seen the tree in time.

My resulting maneuver avoided the tree but I ended up hitting a boulder buried in the snow. I did a beautiful front flip over the handlebars and landed in a snowdrift about twenty feet away. Any other day it would have been funny since the only thing hurt was my pride. I dug myself out and trudged back to the crash site. The sled had jack-knifed and rolled Felix to the side instead of crushing into the back of the snowmobile. One of the skis that steered the machine was bent double, which meant. I would be walking and pulling Felix on the sled. The prospect of that had just set in when I saw the big gray again. He stood looking at me, his tongue lolling out to one side. It seemed as though he was laughing and the joke was on me. Aside from being tired and cold, I felt helpless. I started to cry, put my hands on my tummy, and thought about my unborn child. That's when I realized the stark truth.

"Amy…" It was Felix. His voice sounded faint but controlled.

"It would have been better if you had stayed unconscious." I said, trying to sniff back the tears.

"Go for the tree. If you can get up high enough, you'll be safe."

"What about you?" I asked, knowing the answer.

"Don't worry about me. I won't make it through the night anyway."

I knew he was right and might be. The only chance my baby and I had. Fear hit me. My legs felt like lead, and all of a sudden, the prospect of outrunning the wolf seemed impossible.

"I'm too tired. I just can't do it," I said.

"Amy, listen to me. You can make it. I didn't bring you all this way for you to quit on me and your baby."

Something happened to me at that moment. I'm not sure what but I knew I would fight for my baby with every breath and ounce of courage I could muster. My mind flitted back to the first wolf attack and how Felix beat them away with a stick. The fact I had nowhere near his strength never crossed my mind. Plumes of vapor came out with every breath as I looked side to side for something I could wield as a weapon. I kicked around in the snow and hit something hard. Keeping my eyes on the wolf, I reached down, groping and hoping it would be something I could throw or swing. It was a stick not much longer than my arm. I would have cried if I hadn't been so angry.

"Amy, get the fuel can," Felix said.

"What?" I said, having no clue what he meant.

"There's a gas can on your right just a little behind you. Pour it out in a circle and light it."

I looked over and saw the red plastic fuel can and I understood. *Fire!* With stick in hand, I hedged over to it and tried to remove the cap. My fingers were so cold the feeling was almost gone in them.

"I can't unscrew the cap! My fingers are too cold."

"Yes, you can. Put the stick down and use both hands," Felix said.

I looked back at the big gray, who stood mystified at what I was up to. He seemed ever so patient. I stuck the branch of wood in the snow so it stood straight up and gripped the cap with both hands. It came open.

"I got it!"

"Good. I knew you could. Now pour it in a circle around us."

It felt heavy so I retrieved my stick and dragged it closer to where Felix lay.

"That's close enough. Start pouring."

I followed directions. The snow wasn't very deep there, and as I poured the gasoline out, it melted a trench as I went.

Halfway through my second pass, the container was empty. That's when I realized I didn't have anything to light it with. Tears welled up in my eyes, and the wolf took a few steps closer, tired of my little show with the red jerry can.

"Amy!"

"What?" I said, looking back at him.

"Here," he said.

He was holding up his torch lighter. I eased back and took it out of his hand.

"Keep your face back as far as you can when you light it. It's going to be quick when it ignites."

It took a few tries, and our tormentor was now walking up unafraid. The explosion was sudden, and the flames singed my face. The circle of fire ignited immediately, and the heat felt overwhelming. I cringed back and huddled with my face down by Felix. He had what looked like a smile on his face but had passed out. A few minutes passed, and the flames started to diminish. The gray had ran back a few yards but hung around.

"Go away and leave me alone!" I screamed.

That lolling smile stayed on the wolf's face, and he just stared at me. The fire was almost nonexistent when the gray's attention turned away, he seemed distracted. He cocked an ear, and that's when I heard something too but couldn't quite make it out. The wolf shifted his feet and looked uncertain of his next move. A few seconds ticked by while we stayed entrenched in our standoff. Then the sound became loud enough to recognize.

It was a helicopter. *Abigail!* I thought. *Nothing like trading one wolf for another... At least she won't eat me.*

The beat of the rotor became distinctive and clear when the chopper popped into view. It looked like the pilot tried to land on the big gray, and his tactic worked. The lord of the forest turned tail and loped away. I dropped to my knees and started sobbing. After all the misery, I was right back where I had started from. The jubilation of living through our ordeal seemed bittersweet. I could barely feel the snow kicked up by the helicopter since my face was so numb. A blurry figure flung the door open and jumped out before the oversized skids hit the snow. Over the noise, I heard my name.

"Amy!"

The voice sounded familiar—and it was not Abigail. I squinted trying to make out the figure through the manmade snowstorm.

"Peter?"

I couldn't believe my eyes. His last lunge landed him just a foot away, and he stopped.

"Oh, Peter, it is you!" I dove into his arms crying with joy and knocked him over, burying him in the snow. "How did you find me? I thought it was Abigail. Did you see the wolf?" I talked a hundred miles an hour and gave him no chance to speak. "Can we go home now?"

"Yes... absolutely. I've missed you so much. I thought about you every minute of every day since Fiji. I'm sorry for what I said. I didn't think I was ever going to find you," he said. Rambling just like I did, once he got the chance.

I kissed him—a long and luxurious kiss that I had dreamed about every night while at the cabin. Then I heard a loud throat-clearing, and then another familiar voice boomed over the idling aircraft.

"I know you two are kind of happy to see each other but wouldn't this reunion be a little nicer somewhere warm?" Big Tony said.

We struggled to our feet, laughing, and then I remembered. "We've got to get Felix to a hospital. He's bleeding to death. He got hurt protecting me from a wolf attack last night. We have to save him," I said.

Minutes later, Tony, Peter, and another guy, who introduced himself as Jack, carried Felix's near lifeless body to the waiting helicopter. The flight took about ten minutes, and I was just getting warm when the airport came into view. It was a welcome sight. Thanks to some quick thinking and experience in emergency situations, the pilot radioed Kelowna General Hospital on the way. The emergency-room staff was waiting with a gurney when we landed. I began unbuckling my seatbelt to follow them in, but Tony stopped me with a gentle hand.

"We need to go straight to the airport and leave," Tony said.

"But I want to make sure he's okay," I said.

We had headphones on, which made it easier to have a conversation over the thump of the rotor's blades.

"Amy... we can't stay," Tony said. "We can't afford to take the chance of getting caught up in the bureaucratic red tape. There'll be questions about how he got hurt and why you were in the wilderness. It's all explainable but Abigail could show up before we could leave."

"I'll stay with your friend and take care of the local questions," Jack said. "As soon as I know anything, I'll let you know. Tony's right, though, you should leave."

Jack got out and shut the copilot door and gestured to the pilot to lift off.

"Hey Jim, would you radio ahead and let our corporate pilot know we want to leave as soon as we can?" Tony asked.

"I've already made the call, big guy," Jim said.

I snuggled up as close to Peter as I could and said, "I've grown some since you saw me last. You may want to trade me in."

I meant it as a joke. But the seed that Abigail had sown must have been lingering in the back of my mind. I've never been an insecure person; if anything, more the exact opposite. It may have been the stress, being pregnant, or the experience as a whole. Either way, as soon as it came out of my mouth, I could see that Peter saw no amusement in my comment.

"You know that I was just kidding around... right?" I said.

He smiled, and the brief shadowy look disappeared. I took it as a gentle reminder for me to be mindful of the fact that Peter didn't understand sarcasm. I'm pretty sure he knew a cynical comment when he heard one. The problem was more aligned to the notion that he didn't understand why anyone would use a negative term to be funny.

"I sort of went off the deep end these past two months," he said without elaboration and then fell silent.

Since we were still on the headsets, our conversation was public to everyone in the cockpit. My eyes found Tony's. He did a slight nod and winked. I had no doubt that Peter's anguish during the past two months had, in some ways, been worse than my own.

"I can't wait to see the apartment and be home," I said.

"As long as we're together, we are... home. I love you," he said.

"I love—" I stopped.

The baby's first noticeable movement triggered a wondrous sensation. I put Peter's hand on my tummy so he could feel it.

"Can you feel her?" I asked. "It's the first time she's kicked!"

"Yeah... I can."

We both grinned from ear to ear.

"You still think it's a girl?" he asked.

"Yeah, I'm not sure why; it's just a feeling."

We landed just a short distance from what I guessed to be our ride home. Tony and Peter both had backpacks, and all I had was the multiple layers of clothes on my back, so our transfer to the jet was quick. The engines were at idle, making it too loud to talk. Just before I went up the stairs, I looked around to satisfy myself that Abigail wasn't going to accost us at the last minute. Once we were airborne and could move around, I got up to make a beeline for the lavatory. Peter followed me to the back of the plane.

"I don't think there's room for both of us in there," I said.

Peter blushed and chuckled. He reached past me to retrieve a small bag stashed in the rear of the plane.

"I brought you some clothes and makeup and stuff," he said.

"You're going to be the best husband a girl could ever want."

I had never been more truthful in my life. Restrooms in airplanes are pretty small, but chartered jets are built for comfort. I looked in the mirror, grimaced, and thought. *Oh my god, I look hideous.* I started stripping off the layers of clothing. The first to come off were several sizes too big and not very attractive. Even though they had served their purpose well, it felt good to get out of them. As the pile on the floor grew, I realized the clothes had been masking my stench. *Oh I smell disgusting.* I thought. Hot water and baths had been in short supply at the cabin. The last thing to come off was the gray wool ski cap. I put my hair into a tight bun the morning we left the cabin. Surprisingly, my impromptu hairdo had stayed in place, but it looked and felt like a grease pit.

"Yuck," I said and put the beanie back on.

I did the best a girl could do with nothing but a little water and a wash cloth. The small overnight bag that Peter brought for me was the same one I had taken to Fiji. It was just a simple tote bag that held a lot of stuff, and it was packed full. I wasn't sure if he picked out the contents or had some help, but either way, it was perfect. I giggled with delight. The outfit was pink sweatpants and a matching top. The sweatshirt was embroidered in light blue and said *BABY* with an arrow pointing down. In addition, I found my makeup kit, deodorant, tennis shoes, and socks all piled neatly in the bottom. I promised myself to always remember how joyful just a few simple things can be.

We landed in Chicago three hours later, and it looked just like it did when I'd left. I'm not sure why that idea crossed my mind—perhaps because I had lost two months of my life—but I reveled in the satisfaction of being back in civilization and was thankful that no one greeted us when we got off the plane. My grungy feeling would only go away after a shower or a nice long soak in the bathtub. The prospect of seeing anyone until after a good cleansing of body and soul was not an appealing thought.

When we stepped off the plane I was shocked to find out we had to clear customs. "You have to be kidding." I said, disgusted that I would have to be seen in public. Peter just smiled and handed me my passport. An hour later, the three of us loaded up in a waiting limo for the short ride to my new home.

Tony cleared his throat and said, "I probably don't have to say this, but I don't want to see either of you for at least a week. That being said... I've taking the liberty of setting up some new security measures. You both know my cousin Eddie. He insisted on watching over you two and proclaimed it his personal mission to see that you will not be disturbed. I explained to him that he would have to sleep sometime, so he agreed to find a couple of guys that we have used before on tour. Eddie has a good heart and a simple mind but rest assured no one will get by him. We should get you in to see the doctor sometime tomorrow. I'll call you in the morning and let you know what time." I hugged Tony's neck. "Thanks for everything. I can't tell you how much you mean to both of us," I said.

Tony averted his eyes and squirmed in his seat. I could tell he had more to say but was uncomfortable with saying it.

"Okay," I said, "there's something else. What?"

He exhaled a Tony-sized sigh and continued. "Our attorney wants to file a restraining order against Abigail, just to be on the safe side. I wanted your blessing before he did it."

"Wow," I said, "just when I thought I couldn't be surprised." I looked at Peter for an opinion and saw that he wasn't going to volunteer one unsolicited, so I asked him, "What do you think?"

"I guess under the circumstances that it would be the smart thing to do, at least for now. Maybe in time, after the baby comes, your mom will come to her senses," Peter said.

"Yeah... it would be nice to at least get along so I could see my sister. It's hard to say how Abigail will react to being kneecapped, but I agree. This control thing that she is obsessed with has to end now."

"Okay," Tony said, "I'll tell him to start the paperwork. Once a judge signs it, she'll risk going to jail if she bothers either of you."

We pulled to a stop in front of the high-rise apartment building that was to be my new home. I hugged Tony again and gave him a quick peck on the cheek.

"Bye," I said. "Thanks again for everything."

Peter tried to introduce me to the doorman but didn't get a chance: "You must be Mrs. Shaw," the man said.

I smiled and offered a handshake. "I don't mind 'Mrs. Shaw,' but I'd prefer you call me 'Amy.'"

He smiled and nodded in what I perceived as appreciation for my casual demeanor.

"Thank you, Amy. I'm Phil. If you ever need anything, I'll do my best to help."

Peter was fumbling through his stuff with no apparent success. "Phil," he said, "looks like I misplaced my card for the elevator again. Would you key us up?"

"Sure Peter, not a problem."

Phil inserted his card in a slot and pushed the call button. It must have been on the ground floor, because the doors opened immediately. Phil stepped in and repeated the procedure, pushing a button marked with a large P on it.

As soon as we started up, I had to know. "What's the 'P' stand for?" We were alone, but I asked in a whisper. One thing about my new husband that I could forever be certain of was that he would never find humor at my expense or my naiveté.

"It's the penthouse floor."

A quick wink accompanied his comment. The thing is I already felt like a hick for asking in the first place. In Peter's mind there's no such thing as a dumb question, if you're sincere in the asking. It was one of the many reasons that I loved him. I was thankful he found his key on the first try, and I got the first glimpse of my new home.

As bad as I needed a shower, I couldn't resist taking a quick tour of the apartment. It was big. The living, dining, and kitchen areas were interconnected as an open floor plan with hardwood floors throughout. The kitchen was set up with oversized stainless-steel commercial appliances and granite countertops. The sink was located in a bar overlooking the living room and six black leather swivel chairs. There was a black Steinway piano, which was no big surprise, and black leather furniture. I decided right on the spot that the place had too much black stuff for my taste, even though it was really nice. I knew at some point in time, it would have to go. The breathtaking feature was the glass wall with sliding glass doors that looked out on to the patio and commanded a spectacular view of Lake Michigan.

"Oh, Peter… this is awesome."

"Yeah, it's pretty cool."

The master bedroom looked spacious, with luxurious thick carpet and an oversized king bed. There were glass doors and another patio with the same lake view across one entire wall. I wandered into the bathroom and couldn't believe it.

"This looks like a bathroom out of a home-and-gardens magazine," I said.

Peter didn't reply; he just smiled, knowing that I was very impressed. The two his-and-hers closets were both bigger than my whole bedroom had been in our old house back in Texas. My eyes fixated on the one thing that was going to make the next hour or two simply heaven: the Jacuzzi tub, built for two.

As I prepared for my needed bath, I realized that it felt a little awkward disrobing around Peter. I knew it was silly. After all, we were married, but we had been apart more than together. Peter averted his eyes when I got into the tub. Knowing that he was a little embarrassed as well somehow helped me not feel so foolish. There was no hiding the baby anymore, and my bulging belly didn't help me feel very pretty. Peter sat by the edge of the tub while I tried to turn myself into a prune.

"On my God, this feels so good," I said.

Peter chuckled and shook his head. "That's the third time you've said that."

"Well, it does. It's been two months since I've had a decent bath. The water heater didn't work right at the cabin."

"I've been so depressed. I didn't care if I took a shower or not." He looked away to avoid my eyes.

I knew for certain that Peter had been so miserable and worried that he could not function. Most people, if they lose someone they love, do get over it eventually. Peter, on the other hand, lived so close to his sleeve. I worried that he would not be able to deal with tragedy if it came to visit.

"Peter, what would you have done if Abigail had been successful and you never saw me again?"

"I don't know. Judging from my behavior these past two months, it would've gotten worse before it got better. I stayed drunk a lot." I found no smile in his eyes now, and he was clearly reliving the pain of his inability to cope.

"We all go through life hoping that misfortune doesn't lash out at us. But you have to have the resolve to work through problems. Will you promise me that you'll think about that?" I asked, knowing full well it just wasn't in him to do it. I lolled back in the tub, and my tummy bobbed to the surface. "Oh, I'm getting fat as a cow." I pouted.

"You're even more beautiful than you were in Fiji."

I knew he really meant it. That's just Peter. As for myself, I wasn't sure if I felt exactly the same way, but it sure felt good hearing it from him.

"So you like me fat... cool. No dieting and no exercise nothing but cake and ice cream."

I laughed and splashed water at him so he would know I was joking. With Peter, you had to be crystal clear with the intent.

"Gosh," I said, "it's still hard to believe the nightmare is over and we're back together."

"It won't be long before we'll be three. When things calm down, I want to take you to Mom and Dad's ranch. You haven't got to see it yet," he said. The smile and good mood returned as though it had never left.

"I can't wait. I think we should plan to go as soon as the baby is old enough to travel."

"Sounds good to me, let's plan on it."

"Well, I guess I'd better get out of this tub before I really do turn into a prune." I flipped the drain open and stood up. "Hand me a towel, Daddy."

I was over the bit of embarrassment that I had suffered from earlier. Peter's crimson face was priceless. He was clearly not quite ready to see his uncovered pregnant wife. He recovered, though, and fetched me a towel.

"Do you have any chocolate ice cream?" I asked.

"No, but I can have some delivered."

"You can get it delivered, really?"

"Anything you want, and quick too," he said. Clearly he had used the perk before.

"Is it the same people who clean the apartment for you?"

"How could you know I used a cleaning service?" He looked baffled.

"Peter, there is no way you could keep this place so clean. It's so clean, it looks like a laboratory," I said, laughing.

"Oh... No, the delivery folks are different," he said, clearly not getting my teasing.

"Can we get some pizza, too?" I asked, realizing I was really hungry and guessing he had no food in the house.

"You want pizza and chocolate ice cream?"

"Never question a pregnant woman when it comes to food. Your wife has been living in a shack, in the middle of nowhere, for two months. Don't make me get rough with you." I tried to look serious, but just couldn't pull it off, and laughed. I did get the desired results, though.

"Two large veggie pizzas and a gallon of chocolate ice cream are on the way," he said and then hurried off to place the order.

I dried my hair and rummaged around for some clean clothes. The few clothes that I had were in my closet, but of course, none of them fit. Fortunately I found an old, stretched-out set of sweats. It wasn't a fashion statement, but they were clean.

I ate pizza and ice cream until I was so full I could barely waddle around. We lay on the bed and talked about baby names and Peter's new CD until exhaustion overtook us.

The next day, like clockwork, Big Tony called around noon to let me know that my doctor would make a house call and come by around five o' clock. The afternoon went by slow, and we enjoyed being lazy. The phone rang. "Hi Tony," I said, when I recognized his voice.

"Sorry to call again but I just heard news about Felix. He's going to be in the hospital for a few days and will make a full recovery. According to the doctors your field dressing saved his life."

"Thanks for calling Tony, that's good news." I hung up and told Peter the news. The doctor came by and said that the baby and I were doing fine. He still wanted me to come into his office in a week so he could do an ultrasound. Our week of personal alone time went by too quick, but we couldn't be hermits forever. As nice as the apartment was, it was time to get out and about. The hard part was convincing Peter to go to the studio without me and get back on track with the band. Janet showed up unannounced and helped my cause.

"Oh, look at you, you're beautiful," she said.

I loved Janet. She really was the mother I had never known.

"But you need some new clothes," Janet said. "You can't spend the next two months locked away in this apartment wearing sweatpants and eating ice cream."

"How did you know about the ice cream?" I asked, giving Peter a suspicious look and wondering if he was sharing my eating binges with everyone.

He shook his head, mouthing "No" with his lips.

"Amy, you're not the first pregnant woman to have food cravings. I guessed about the ice cream 'cause, heck, who doesn't like ice cream. My second baby, it was rocky road. Sometimes in the middle of the night, I had to have a pickle. One time, we were in bed and I made Jimmy go out at midnight to get me a jar of kosher dill pickles. He was not very happy, but he did it." She stopped, gave Peter a quizzical look and asked, "Don't you have music to make and money to earn? She'll be here when you get home. Don't worry, Eddie and those two security goons Tony hired are going with us."

Peter finally gave in and nodded. "You're right. We have a lot of work to do at the studio. Go shop and have fun. Oh yeah, you'll need this." He dug his wallet out and thumbed through its contents, then pulled out a couple of cards and handed them to me. "These are yours; I forgot to give them to you."

It was a picture ID and a credit card with my new name, Amy Shaw. It was my first credit card, and it earned Peter a big kiss.

The shopping trip was a blast, but it was odd having bodyguards following us around the clothing stores. After a while, though, I decided for the time being it would be a fact of life. Every so often, I would get a little panic attack when I would see someone who looked a little like Abigail. After a while, the worries of confrontation passed. It felt great getting some clothes that actually fit, and it turned out that the bodyguards had a second use: they carried all of our purchases. About the time I felt I had a sufficient wardrobe, Janet suggested we look for some baby clothes.

"So what do you think? Is it going to be boy or girl?" Janet asked.

"I feel like it's a girl, but I don't have any reason to know for sure. I told the doctor I didn't want to know."

"I think you're right, but let's shop for stuff that will work for either."

I think it was more fun shopping for the baby than it had been for me. The days following, Janet and I burned a hole in the credit card buying baby clothes and baby accessories. After that, we started looking for baby-room furniture and kitchen stuff since we had nothing to cook with or to eat off of in the apartment. Our new place started to feel like a home, and I even started cooking instead of ordering carry out all the time. I couldn't contact my sister, because her cell didn't work. It took a little time to figure out a way, but I finally contacted one of her friends and gave her my cell phone number. My phone rang ten minutes later.

"Where are you? Are you okay?" Kelly asked.

"Hi, sis, sorry it took me a few days to get in touch, but your phone didn't work."

"Yeah, the warden had it shut off—said we needed to cut every corner we could. Did Peter tell you she sold the house?" she asked.

"Yeah, I heard. If she hadn't spent so much money kidnapping me, she wouldn't have put herself in the poor house. I'm sorry you're suffering for it." I felt awful about my sister being caught in the middle of the war between Abigail and me.

"Don't even worry about that," she said. "You're happy and with Peter again."

"It's all because of you that he ever found me, sis. You were a genius to figure it out."

"Ah, it was easy once I was able to talk to Peter and find out you were somewhere in Canada."

We talked for over an hour. I told her the whole sordid story. She freaked out about the snowmobile ride and the wolf attack and had to know every detail. I happily provided the long version of my adventure.

"How's the baby?" she asked.

"The baby is fine, and I'm getting as big as a house," I said.

She laughed.

"Listen," I said, "as soon as the baby is old enough to travel, we will be coming to Texas. Peter bought a ranch for his mom and dad up by Lake Texoma. We need to figure out a way to see each other then."

"Mom is gone most of the time now, so that shouldn't be too hard to do. I'm not sure if she even knows you've flown the coop. There hasn't been a nuclear explosion reported yet," she said with a chuckle.

"We got a restraining order against her, so when she finds out about that and my escape. I'm afraid she may lose it. Be careful around her, sis, and don't say anything that will aggravate her."

"Don't worry about me, I'll be fine. I guess I better sign off here. Can I call you every day?"

"Absolutely… I love you."

"I love you, too. Good-bye."

We managed to talk almost every day. About a week later, she informed me that Abigail had come home angry and sullen but kept to herself as to why. Of course, I had no doubt that my escape had gone full circle. The good news was. She didn't take it out on Kelly, and for that, I felt greatly relieved.

February and March seemed to fly by. The time had come when I couldn't see my feet, unless I was sitting down with them propped up. Peter and the band had finished the CD and would be going on tour again at some point, so he was spending lots of time at home with me.

We went to see the doctor on April 3. It was a beautiful spring day. My due date was supposed to be around April 15. The checkup went fine and he said everything looked like it would be a normal delivery. He told Peter to pack an overnight bag and explained why when he saw that my husband was clueless. It was such a nice day that I convinced Peter to walk home. It was only about a mile, and he reluctantly agreed. Of course, Eddie insisted that he and his two assistants come along. It seemed silly to me, but I went along with the idea, as long as they would give us a little space. I just wanted to have a nice walk with my husband without the entourage that accompanied us everywhere we went. We held hands and talked while Eddie and his men hung back a ways.

"Isn't it a beautiful day?" I asked.

"Every day is a beautiful day with you."

"Peter … I love you more than anything in the world. You know that, right?"

"Sure, and you know I feel the same way. What are you getting at?"

"I've been thinking a lot lately about how you would get along if something happened to me."

"Nothing is going to happen to you!" he said, suddenly agitated.

"Peter, I know. Just hear me out. After learning what happened with you after Abigail kidnapped me. I haven't been able to stop thinking about this. If something did happen. I need to know you would be okay and take care of our baby."

"I promise our baby will never need for anything. You have my word."

He still seemed to be somewhat uptight with the conversation, so I decided to let it go. I figured I would ease him into it again, another time. I knew he was so entwined with me that if something happened, he would not do well. For some reason I felt the need to prepare him for something that would never happen. With the baby just days away and the looming shadow of Abigail still in our lives. I worried about him and what would happen if Abigail pulled another stunt.

I changed the subject and asked, "Have you heard anything about Felix?"

"Yes. He's fully recovered and will be in Chicago next week."

"What about his legal problems? Have you heard anything from the attorneys?"

"Turns out, the firm that we use has connections in the Senate. They managed to get the Armed Services Committee to look into Felix's case. It looks like he's going to be cleared of any wrongdoing and will end up with an honorable discharge."

"That's great news. Are you still okay with the idea of hiring him to be chief of security for us?"

"Sure, he already saved your life once. That makes him alright in my book."

"Good, I'm glad we can help him out."

We chitchatted about what to have for dinner, and then had a vigorous debate on names for the baby. I still thought it was a girl, so those were the names we talked about the most. He liked "Rebecca Ann," after his grandmother, but it just didn't feel right. I wanted to name her after my sister Kelly. It was the first time we had ever disagreed on anything. In the end, I guess it didn't really matter.

We were almost home, just a few steps from the entrance to the apartment, when Peter said, "Abigail."

"You've got to be kidding!" I said. "There's no way our baby girl will get that name."

"No… Abigail," he said, pointing her out.

And there she was. Wearing a dark gray suit and heading our way with purpose. I didn't notice anyone with her but she was the last person I wanted to see.

"Well, I see you've been busy doing exactly what I suggested you should not," she said, stopping just an arm's length away. "I was hoping to try one more time to talk some sense into you."

In spite of the mix of emotions I felt within. I tried to calm myself. "I'm sure you're aware of the restraining order against you," I said. "After the last kidnapping, you gave us no choice. Since you don't want to be a part of my family, you can go away and leave me alone."

"I am your family, you insolent little twit!" she said, reaching out to grab my arm.

Peter stepped in between us and said, "Abigail, this conversation is over. If you leave right now, we won't press charges, and maybe someday you two will reconcile your differences."

"The only thing I'm desperately trying to do is to keep my daughter from cavorting with a musician that is an autistic time bomb just waiting to explode. Now get out of my way before I have you arrested for assault!"

Her threat caught Peter off guard. By the time he realized that she was being the aggressor. She had shoved him away and gotten a hand on me. I shrugged her off and stumbled backward toward the street. The last thing I saw was shock on Abigail's face.

Chapter 20
Peter

The scene would play over and over in my head for years to come. I know I couldn't have done anything more. But every time I viewed it in my head. I blame myself. Abigail shoved me aside and grabbed for Amy's arm. I watched helplessly as she shrugged away and stumbled into the street. A city bus was coming to a stop and barely moving when it struck her. The combination of her being off balance and the momentum of the vehicle spun her around and propelled her toward a parked car. Her head struck the bumper with a sickening thud. The accident seemed to run in slow motion and ended with her slumping onto the ground unconscious. I remember yelling out her name. "Amy!"

What happened next are bits and pieces of a nightmare rather than an accurate recollection. I ran to her, wanting to pick her up but afraid to touch or move her. A pool of blood had started to flow from her head.

Panic stricken, I yelled. "Somebody call 9-1-1... please. God... don't let me lose her."

I looked up at the crowd of onlookers circled around. Even though they all seemed sympathetic, no one moved. I didn't know what to do. I could feel tears running down my face, dripping onto her cheeks, gently someone touched my shoulder.

"I'm a nurse; let me take a look." She was an older lady with a kind face.

I nodded. "We need an ambulance," I said.

"I've already called one. They'll be here any minute." She looked at Amy briefly then at me. "Do you know her?"

"She's my wife and she's pregnant. Oh God, this can't be happening. Not now!"

"What's her name?" the nurse asked.

"Amy... Amy Shaw."

The ambulance arrived after what seemed like an eternity, and the EMTs took control right away. All I knew for sure. She was still alive. They loaded her up and told me which hospital they would be taking her to.

"I'm going with you," I said.

"Sir ... we're not supposed to allow that," the driver said.

The nurse who had taken the time to help stepped up and whispered something into his ear.

"Okay," the driver said. "Get in the front."

The hospital was just a few blocks away, and we were wheeling Amy into the emergency room entrance just minutes later. At that point, they took Amy into a trauma room and me into an office to collect information about her. I answered the questions and filled out the paperwork, still numb from shock. When I was done, they asked me to go to the waiting room and said that a physician would be in to see me as soon as they knew something.

When I got there, Big Tony was already in the waiting room pacing the floor. "How is she?" he asked.

"I don't know. They won't let me in there. They said a doctor would be out as soon as they knew something."

Tony put an arm around me and walked us over to sit down.

"There's nothing you can do to help now, Peter. Don't take this the wrong way, but you'd just be in their way."

"Abigail caused this and I want to have her locked up." The shock had begun wearing off, and in its place, anger took over.

"Well… as for being locked up, she already is. When Eddie caught up to you, he and his men tackled Abigail to the ground and sat on her until the police arrived. You know that couldn't have been pretty," he said with a chuckle. "I also called your folks, and they said they would be here as soon as they could get a flight. I hope that was okay?"

"Huh? Oh… yeah, thanks, Tony. I didn't even think about it."

My mind kept going back to Amy, and I found it harder to concentrate on our conversation. Sometime later, Janet came in and asked if we knew anything. We still didn't. So we all waited together. The band trickled in one by one offering their support. With us all together, it wasn't long before some people started to figure out who we were. Then the media showed up. If it hadn't been for the fact that Eddie and our security team showed up about the same time, it would have been horrible. They kept the reporters away from me until a couple of patrol cars arrived. The Police soon had control of the melee and we ended up in a private waiting room.

I lost track of time, the ensuing media circus made the situation even more challenging for me to deal with.

"How long have we been here?" I asked.

Tony looked at his watch and said, "I've been here about two hours."

"It seems like it's been much longer," I said.

Everyone nodded in agreement but said nothing. A few minutes later, the door opened, a tall thin man with pale skinned emerged. He looked tired.

"Mr. Shaw?" the man asked.

"Yes," I answered and stood up.

"Could I have a word with you?" He asked

He held the door open for me, and we stepped out into the hall.

"How is she?" I asked.

His solemn expression didn't look encouraging. I had a terrible sinking feeling and waited for the bad news.

"Mr. Shaw... the trauma to the head was severe, her neck is broken. We put her on a ventilator so we could keep her alive long enough to deliver your daughter. The baby is healthy and doing fine. Amy has a severe hematoma from the injury. She has no brain activity, and the vent is the only reason she is still alive. It's your decision whether you want to turn it off or to wait until she goes on her own."

I heard the diagnosis, but his answers made no sense. I guess. I just stood there. I don't know for how long.

"Mr. Shaw... you don't have to decide this minute," the doctor said, bringing me back into the conversation.

"Can I see her?" I asked.

"Of course you can."

"Is the baby with her?"

"No, we took the baby to the nursery. She was almost full term, so we don't anticipate any problems. It's just routine procedure. You can see her too, when you're ready."

He led me down a long hallway, stopping at the last room.

"Can she hear me or know that I'm here?" I asked.

"Science would say no... but I believe she's still here. Just not in this body. Take as much time as you want and talk to her. We'll be close by." He motioned to the attending nurse to leave with him.

Amy lay on a bed in the center of the room. I noticed an array of equipment attached to her and a tube in her mouth. I could hear a slow *beep... beep... beep* that I guessed to be her heartbeat. The only other sound in the room was the pumping of the bellows machine that did her breathing for her. The rhythm was slow and methodical. I walked up close enough to take her hand and started to cry. I'm not sure how long, when I stopped. I pulled a chair close to her bed and started talking.

"Why did this happen to you instead of me? You're much more capable of carrying on than I am. Amy, I love you so much. Everything I am is because of you. How do I survive without your love and support? I can't bear the pain of losing you." I laid my head on her arm and cried until there were no tears left, then talked to her some more. "Amy... it's a girl just like you said. I haven't seen her yet, but I'll bet she looks just like you. Her name is Kelly Ann. I don't know anything about babies, but you know I'll do my best. I'm taking her home to Texas so she can grow up in the country at our ranch. I promise our daughter will grow up like any other regular kid. I guess Abigail was right after all. The music business has been nothing but a curse. All of this could've been avoided if I'd just gotten a regular job."

As she lay there, I felt something inside me dying with her, and I knew I couldn't stop it. I wanted to say more, really I did. I just couldn't think of anything else, so I sat and watched and listened. There was no reply. In my heart, I knew there wouldn't be, but I waited and hoped anyway. For me, time stood still, in reality, it continued to pass—for how many hours. I had no clue. The nurse came in from time to time to check Amy's readings then leave. A gentle knock came at the door, and it opened quietly. It was Mom and Dad. Mom pulled a chair up beside me and sat down. She didn't say anything for quite a while.

"We talked to the doctor Peter," she said softly.

I looked at her, then Dad. I could tell they felt my pain along with their own. Amy was the daughter they'd always wanted, and they never had a chance to really get to know her.

"He said that she's already gone; that the machine is all that's keeping her body alive," I said. "I think they want me to let them turn it off. But I just can't bring myself to actually do it."

"Would you like to know what I think?" Mom asked.

"Sure, Mom... I don't know what to do."

"I know its hard honey... but you have to let her go."

She took my hand and cried with me. I didn't think there were any tears left inside me but then they came again.

One hour and thirty-four minutes later. I gave the nurse my consent to turn off the ventilator. Somewhere in the back of my mind, I really thought the staff was wrong and that Amy would continue breathing. She did not, in a very short time. The beeping stopped and went to a constant flat tone.

It's ironic that you can be so happy one moment, and seconds later, it's taken away. My parents led me out of the room and back to the waiting room. It was an uncomfortable time, and everyone tried to convey their sympathies. Even though every word was in earnest, to me it meant nothing. No words were going to change what had happened. In my mind, guilt was festering, and every minute that passed. I managed to blame myself a little more.

"Why don't we go see your daughter?" Mom suggested.

I realized that I had forgotten all about Kelly Ann. "Yeah... I would like that," I said.

My sense of responsibility grew with every step, and with it, a new anxiety began to rear its ugly head. How could I ever raise a child without Amy? How would I explain to my daughter when she was old enough to understand that my ambitions played a part in her mother's death? By the time we found our way to the nursery. I had convinced myself that my new child deserved more than I could offer as a single parent.

The exterior of the nursery was a long row of windows, on the other side, rows of cribs with babies. I don't think I had ever seen so many newborns, in one place, at the same time. Mom found the one with our name on it. One of the nurses held my daughter up to the window. She was tiny and fragile and had some of Amy's features.

"Oh, Peter... she is beautiful," Mom said.

It was the second happiest moment of my life, and Mom was right. She looked beautiful. But the heartache of knowing she would never know her mother was almost unbearable. From that moment, I knew that whatever it took, I would learn to be a dad and no one would ever take her away from me.

Two weeks later, Mom, Dad, Kelly Ann, and I left Chicago for Texas. I expected more grief from everyone who had something to lose due to my decision, but it was a quiet parting. Tony and Janet were the only ones who saw us off that day, even though we promised each other to stay in touch. I knew it would never happen. I was an empty shell, falling into a dark abyss of misery, and nothing could stop it.

Chapter 21
Kelly

Eleven years later:

It was early March, and Texas got a late snowstorm that even surprised the local meteorologists. It wasn't a ton of the white stuff like the northern states get on a regular basis. Dallas is just ill-equipped to handle a foot of snow when it accumulates so fast. Everything just shuts down. I didn't mind missing a day of work. Except that March has always been a gloomy month for me. Sitting in my apartment watching it snow and sulking wasn't helping to cheer me up.

Years have passed since Amy died, and every spring. I go through this depression. Even though it's been a long time, I still miss my sister. Some years were worse than others. For whatever reason though, this year had me at an emotional crossroad. When I was younger, I never understood funerals or memorials. To me, it seemed to promote sadness. Now, years later, I realize it also means closure. It took me a long time to understand, it was the one thing I never managed to have.

I remember Mom coming home looking like she had spent a few nights in jail, which apparently she had. Disheveled and stripped of her arrogance. She never uttered a word about what had happened. She locked herself in her bedroom that night.

The computer had been my sanctuary and only vent available for some time. It also was where I learned that my sister had died. I contacted Big Tony in the hopes of discovering what had happened and to find out if the online stories were true. It seemed understandable the he was reluctant to fill in the spaces for me. My insistence prevailed, and I got the unadulterated story. I can't say that I was surprised, it all made perfect sense once the whole sordid story came out. Even though I'm quite sure there was no love lost between Tony and my mom. He was good not to judge. He promised to stay in touch and said that he was pretty sure Amy had willed something to me. I asked if the baby was okay and how to get in touch with Peter. That's where the conversation lost momentum.

I left for school the next day, when I got back home, Mom's room was still locked. I knew something was wrong, but my mom being the private person that she was. I knew better than to bother her when she was in a mood. The next morning—a Saturday—I decided to bang on her door, I got no response. I didn't know what to do, so I called a friend of mine whose dad was a cop.

Mom had overdosed on sleeping pills and alcohol. No note, no fanfare, and no explanation. My life had changed in a way I could have never imagined. I tried unsuccessfully to contact Peter and Big Tony. After that life got in the way and I had to prepare for what fate had dished out.

The only relative I had was my dad's brother, Jason, who lived in Austin with his wife and two kids. I don't think they were excited to inherent another child, but they did their best to make me feel at home. About six months after I moved in, the checks started to appear. The song that Amy wrote the words to had been in the top ten for the better part of a year and still hung in the top one hundred for almost two years after that. The first check came with a letter from Peter's attorney. It explained that Amy and Peter had gifted the royalties from that song to me. The money had been set up in a trust and invested, which turned out to be kind of a bummer—no spending sprees, but I always had pocket money. Every month, I received a four-hundred-dollar check until I graduated from high school. When I started college, I would have additional funds to pay for tuition, books, and room and board.

I gave my uncle Jason two hundred dollars a month to ease his financial burden and quickly became his favorite niece. Uncle Jason and Aunt Julie were nice to me. They became the closest thing to a family I'd ever known except for Amy, Gina, and Fred. However, as soon as I turned eighteen, I felt more than ready to move out.

I turned into a loner long before I started high school, and spent most of my time on the computer. My one outlet was band. I was a drummer, and I loved it. The music and choreography for parades and football games appealed to me. It was a lot of fun. The few friends I had while living in Austin were from band class. So when it came time for college, I majored in computer science and minored in music. I continued to play the drums. I guess it just felt good to beat on something. Even though there were a lot of good universities to choose from. In the end I picked Texas Tech. It was a good college—and I liked the band uniforms.

School was pretty easy for me. I studied, but not too much, and still ended up on the dean's list every semester. Since the money had been tucked away for my education, I stayed with it until I got my master's degree. As time passed, I got to be more and more of a loner. I didn't date much throughout college and when it came time to get a real job. I applied for an IT position at Hewlett-Packard in Dallas. Texas was the closest thing to home I knew, so even though I was overqualified for the job. I took it.

IT allowed me, for the most part, to continue being a hermit. I did most of my work in a secluded cubicle that rarely required physical contact with my coworkers. I spent a lot of time on the phone, so after work, the last thing I wanted to do was talk to anyone. It became a trend that I knew wasn't healthy. I realized that I should do something to change my behavior. It just wasn't in me to do it.

The past eleven years had not been all bad. In fact, I'd had some good times along the way. But now, as I sat with my third glass of wine watching it snow, I could only reflect on the bad times. As a rule, my solution for depression was to surf the Internet and live my life vicariously through others. Once in a while, I would get drawn into a Facebook chat conducted by the handful of acquaintances that I communicated with from time to time. It seemed almost laughable to me that I had over three hundred *friends*, but in reality. They were just my links to humanity. I glanced at my laptop sitting idle on the coffee table. It beckoned to me like a nicotine craving or a bottle of wine that needed to be consumed—an unusual metaphor, considering I didn't smoke and rarely indulged in alcohol to excess.

Today though… would be an exception to the rule. My mission was to have a private little memorial for my sister and, yeah, even my mother. I knew that, if left to my thoughts. Another bottle of wine would be coming off the rack and I would feel bad for it tomorrow. So I grabbed a bottle of water out of the refrigerator and booted up the computer. Surfing the internet for entertainment is what I did, rather than doing something real. After a couple of hours, just as I was getting ready to log off, I saw an unusual posting from one of my acquaintances at work. Her name was Judy Christy. She was a vivacious little redhead that all the guys in the office drooled over and all the girls hated. In some ways, she reminded me of Amy. I guess that's why I didn't dislike her. On her Facebook page, she told the world about her day at a place called Skydive Dallas and about making a tandem parachute jump. Curiosity compelled me to follow the snippets of her day and how much fun she'd had. I learned that when you make a tandem jump, your harness is connected to the harness of a professional skydiver who basically takes you on the e-ticket ride of your life from thirteen thousand feet. I even found a link to watch the video of her jump, it looked pretty cool. It had been a long time since anything had perked my interest. The pages on the Skydive Dallas website were very interesting. I lingered on the site, reading and looking at pictures for another half an hour. Then the fuddy-duddy in me reared its ugly head, and I decided it was an immature and childish endeavor. I laughed at myself while shutting down the laptop and then began settling back into the safe private little world I had built for myself. The intrusive little seed had been planted, though. That night, I went to bed wondering what it would be like to fall through azure skies with puffy little cotton-candy clouds all around.

The next day, enough of the snow had melted for me to go to work. I decided it would be better for me than staying at home alone. Lunch rolled around and I went to the company break room. I was in the process of microwaving a Healthy Choice Café Steamer when Judy Christy herself walked in.

"Mind if I join you?" she asked.

"No… I mean, sure, please do," I said.

"Do you like those?" she asked, pointing at my lunch.

"Yeah, they're pretty good."

"I should bring something for lunch like that, but I always seem to forget about it until I'm hungry."

I wasn't sure if she was baiting me to share my meal or just making conversation. If you've ever seen a Café Steamer, it's just about the right size for lunch, but the portions are a bit small.

"I have another one in the freezer if you want it," I said.

"That would be great, thanks," she said.

I waited until she finished nuking it and sat down.

"I really appreciate it, Kelly. Tomorrow we'll go out. Lunch is on me."

"Oh... no, you don't have to do that. These things are cheap."

"I insist, besides you're about the only girl here who will give me the time of day. No offense, but it doesn't seem like you have many friends here, either."

I started to come back with something like, "I have plenty of friends and everybody likes me," then caught myself, realizing she was right. I hadn't made any friends since college. I had fallen into the routine of eat, sleep, work, and then get up and do it all over again.

"I suppose you're right," I said.

She gave me a quizzical look for an instant, and then frowned. "I didn't mean it in a bad way. I know the women don't like me because the guys do, and that makes it hard to have some girl time."

She paused as if waiting for me to respond, but I couldn't think of anything except, *Yep, you're right about that.* Since I couldn't think of something positive to say, I kept it to myself.

"Can I ask you a question?" she asked.

"Sure, I guess so."

"I'm trying to figure you out. You're hands down the prettiest girl in our whole division, and yet you just keep to yourself. Are you married?"

"No ..." I said, almost choking on the big mouthful I had just shoveled in. I took a big gulp of bottled water and managed to get the bite down without spewing.

"Gay?" she asked.

"No... not gay either. I just like to keep to myself."

The painful truth of the matter, I couldn't figure myself out, so explaining what made me tick to someone else, felt intimidating. For whatever reason, though, I found myself liking Judy. She didn't beat around the bush when she wanted to know something, and I liked that. Most people are so worried about being politically correct that they often times remain guarded, which is why I think most people are covertly hostile. Judy, on the other hand, lived on the borderline of blatant. Not only did I find that refreshing, it stirred something in me that had been dead for a long time. Spontaneity had been missing from my life for about eleven years. I knew why. After all there was a huge black hole in my life. I never realized how depression had ruled my life. Even after all these years

"You just don't seem like the hermit type," she said.

"Oh… well, I wouldn't say I'm a hermit, but I guess 'loner' isn't far from the same thing."

"What you need Ms. Stevens is some excitement in your life, to get that stale blood circulating again."

Her self-induced excitement animated her to a level that in my opinion should be illegal, but that was the fuddy-duddy in me trying to come out.

"I suppose you think I should jump out of a perfectly good airplane like you did this weekend," I said.

"Ah… so you do Facebook. I figured as much. You sit back and endorse a conservative lifestyle. In the safety of your own home and experience your thrills through others."

I should have been mad, but she hit the nail on the head. I laughed instead. "Yeah I suppose I do." The humor at my expense made me feel better than I had in a while.

"I'm sorry, that was over the top," she said.

"No… it's okay. You're right; even so, I'm not gutsy enough for the skydiving thing."

Even as I said it, I knew it wasn't about whether I felt brave enough for the adventure. It was me crawling back into the cave I called life.

"Look… if you were on Facebook. Then you already heard me rant about how much fun it was. There was something else about my experience that I didn't include, mostly because it has taken a couple of days to sort it all out in my mind."

"That it was too freaking cold to be playing in free fall?" I said.

"Very funny, but, yeah, it was really cold. I think it will be a lot more fun next weekend when it warms up."

"It snowed yesterday. Get a grip." I said.

"How long have you lived in Texas?" she asked.

"All of my life."

"Then you know Texas weather changes from day to day. It's supposed to be in the seventies on Saturday. I've already signed up for another tandem, and if I still like it. I'm going to take the accelerated free fall course."

"What's accelerated free fall?" I asked.

"It means that they teach you how to skydive without being attached to an instructor. You learn to open and fly your own parachute. In other words, it's like learning to drive instead of riding in the passenger seat."

"I don't know if I could do that."

"Heck, I don't either. All I can tell you is it's a lot of fun. The regulars who skydive every weekend know how to have a good time and they're an interesting group of folks. It's not cheap, so most of them come from the professional world and…" She leaned in close and whispered, "it's about 70 percent men."

"Yeah, I don't know. I'll have to look on my calendar. I think I've got something going on this weekend." I lied about having something to do, and she saw right through me.

"If you don't want to go, just say so. I'll bet you a week of lunches you have no plans this weekend. Come with me! It'll be fun. Look, let's just go spend the day and you can check it out while I make my jump. If you decide you're interested. I'll come with you when you schedule yours. The worst thing that could happen is you miss a day in hermitage."

I had to give Judy credit where it was due. She was good when it came to spinning a solid pitch.

"You missed your calling," I said.

"Huh?"

"You should have been a used-car salesman."

She laughed. "My dad owns a used-car lot. It was my first job. You're funny when you try to be. So does that mean you'll come with me?"

"Yes... I'll come," I said. Not sure what I had gotten myself into.

"Great... I'll pick you up on Saturday around noon. My jump is at two o'clock. The instructor said it would be the warmest time of the day."

We exchanged phone numbers and email addresses on the way back to our respective cubicles.

"You're not in IT. What do you do here?" I asked at the elevator.

"Sales and marketing," she said.

"I think I've been duped," I said as the door opened.

"It's going to be so much fun. See you later!" she said.

By the time Saturday rolled around, I had all but forgotten about the day trip to Skydive Dallas. Judy on the other hand, had not. She called me about ten o'clock to remind me that she would be over to pick me up around noon.

The ride from Dallas took us up Highway 75 through McKinney, where I'd grown up. Even though I lived close, I avoided taking the walk down memory lane, and hadn't been back since I'd left for Austin.

"Hey, earth to Kelly. Where did you go?" Judy asked.

"I used to live in McKinney. I guess I was reminiscing."

"Judging by the look on your face, reliving the Spanish Inquisition sounds more like it. You want to talk about it?"

"Another time perhaps, it's pretty depressing stuff and I don't want to ruin our day."

"Sounds like a two-bottle wine night. You can tell me yours and I'll tell you mine, deal?"

"Yeah... deal."

I settled back in the seat, thinking that it would be good for me to share my life's chronicle. *Who knows? Maybe I'll feel better for it.*

Skydive Dallas is about five miles south of a little Texas town called Whitewright. I pointed out a posted sign but Judy knew exactly where she was going. It seemed as though she began driving faster the closer we got. The last turn onto the private airport turned out to be a nice paved road with speed bumps about every hundred yards.

"The regulars tell me the owners had to put the bumps in to keep everyone's speed down," Judy explained.

"If they're like you, I totally understand. You've been going faster and faster the closer we got."

"You're probably right. I can't wait. Yahoo!" she screamed while stamping her feet and shaking her head like a lunatic.

"Look at all the cars. There must be a lot of people who want to make a tandem," I said.

"What will surprise you is how many of them are regulars who come out every weekend to jump. It's kind of like boats, motorcycles, and racecars. They're fanatics about their sport."

We pulled into a parking spot and walked to a huge metal building owned by Skydive Dallas. The double glass doors opened into a café full of people eating at picnic tables. Judy led me through a door where I saw T-shirts and a glass counter with what I presumed to be skydiving sundries.

"Cool, a gift shop," I said.

"It's the pro shop. Don't act like a whuffo," she said.

"What's a whuffo?" I asked, not knowing if I had been insulted or not.

"I'll tell you in a minute."

Judy got in line, and a few minutes later, she made it to the counter and paid for her jump. We went back into the café, ordered a couple of hamburgers, and found a place to sit.

"So… what's a whuffo?" I asked. I made every effort to be discreet since it seemed like a sensitive subject.

"A whuffo is a non-skydiver who shows up and asks. Why do you jump out of airplanes?'"

"Okay, so… what's so bad about that?" I asked.

"Well nothing really, but we don't want to act like a couple of rookies."

"Well, I am a rookie, and you have one whole jump, so I'd guess you are as well."

She acknowledged my comment with a frown, so I figured it was best to change the subject. One wall of the café was glass, and the other side there was a large room filled with skydivers. Several of them were wearing different colored suits and seemed to be doing some sort of choreography.

"What are they doing?" I asked.

"I think they call it dirt diving. They practice what they want to do in the air while on the ground. Hey, that one is kind of cute." She pointed the guy out, and then looked around, hoping her remark hadn't been overheard.

"What's the deal with the outfits they're wearing?" I asked.

"Those are called jumpsuits. They have them custom made. That's why his butt looks so good in it."

"Did you bring me out to ogle the guys or to learn about skydiving?" I asked.

"Well… both, I guess. Heck, as long as we're here, we might as well look at the menu."

She giggled, and I felt my face warming up. I'm not sure, I may have blushed—and that hadn't happened in a very long time. Our order came and we ate our burgers in silence. So far, the outing with Judy had proven to be entertaining. She was a chatterbox and the few minutes of peace and quiet couldn't have come at a better time.

My eyes roamed back out to the hangar floor and watched the jumpers do their dirt dive. I was interested but didn't understand what I was watching. When they were done, I noticed a guy who seemed familiar. He had long curly brown hair and a short-cut beard that seemed to be the current style for men. For some odd reason, it seemed ruggedly attractive. Then I thought. *Who wants to kiss sandpaper?* The guy turned and looked right at me. I started to turn my head and pretend I wasn't looking, but his eyes captured my gaze. I couldn't make myself turn away. They were a beautiful deep blue and seemed… sad—very sad. His face looked devoid of emotion, almost disconnected. I recognized the look as the same one I saw in the mirror every day.

"And who are you ogling?" Judy asked.

There was no hiding the truth, and I looked back at Judy, guilt written all over my face. "He looks familiar. Do you know who he is?" I asked.

"No idea, but it's a friendly bunch. Go talk to him."

"Oh… no… there's no way. He's a perfect stranger."

The conversation ended abruptly when a tall, nice-looking guy came to the table. "Hey, Judy, you really did come back to make another jump. Cool!" he said.

"Hi Jim, yeah, I think I'm hooked," Judy said.

I could easily guess that part of her new interest in skydiving could have something to do with the fact that Jim was a hunk. I managed a quick yet tactless wink conveying my thoughts. She got it loud and clear and gave me that frown I saw earlier, and then smiled.

"Jim… who's the guy standing there in the black-and-white jumpsuit?" Judy asked, pointing with shameless intent.

Jim looked back at the group and nodded. "His name is Allen Shaw—quiet guy, kind of keeps to himself. He's fairly new. Been in the sport a couple of years and has already made several hundred jumps. I took him on his first tandem. Why?" he asked.

"Oh… this is my friend, Kelly. She thought he looked familiar," Judy said.

"He's a day trader—and brilliant at it, at least according to the folks out here that have money to invest. They say he's rolling in the dough, but you wouldn't know it to talk to him. The guy is as humble as they come and the nicest person you could ever meet. He comes out every jumpable Saturday and goes home at sunset."

"He doesn't stay for your famous deck parties?" Judy asked.

I wasn't sure if she was asking for me or for her, but for some reason, I was curious for the answer.

"Nope… I think he has a little girl. He always goes home after jumping. So… are you ready to make your skydive?" Jim asked.

"I can't wait!" Judy said.

"Well… let's go get you suited up then. You're welcome to come to the back hangar and check it out if you want to Kelly," Jim said.

"Thanks." I said.

We followed him out through the hangar and into another attached room that looked equally as large. Half of the space was occupied by people packing parachutes on blue carpet, and the other half, designated by a maroon color, provided the space for tandems to be staged. Judy made her jump and I got so caught up in the excitement that I signed up for a tandem class for the following weekend.

I watched Allen Shaw's activities throughout the day. Hovering on a thin line between observing and stalking, my little obsession just wouldn't go away. I wanted to ask him if he knew Peter, or if he might even be his brother, although I didn't recall Peter having a sibling. By the time I worked up the courage to say something, he had already left.

Chapter 22
Peter

I don't remember many details of the trip home after Amy died; the misery that began with her abduction, spiraled back into depression after the accident. I flew home with my parents and new baby girl after the arrangements were made for Amy's cremation. As soon as we stepped off the plane at DFW fans seemed to come out of the woodwork, all wanting an autograph. I tried to be appreciative and even signed a couple, it didn't take long for me to realize though. I just couldn't deal with it. That's when I decided to become anonymous and drop off the radar. I apologized to would-be fans, explaining that I was not Peter Shaw and introduced myself as Allen Shaw, no relation. Some complained that I was stuck up and some just walked away. They all knew I was lying.

I didn't leave the ranch for several months, weight loss, longer hair, and a new beard changed my appearance. My behavior changed due to alcohol abuse and personal neglect. About a year later, I changed my name to Allen K. Shaw, and after a few years of practice, I believed it myself.

The first couple of years after Amy's death, I was not a pillar of society. I drank daily and didn't quit until I managed to be drunk. Kelly Ann and I stayed at the ranch with my mom and dad since I couldn't take care of myself, much less a baby. If it hadn't been for my parents, I would have lost my daughter to the state and ended up dead in a gutter somewhere. Those were the darkest days of my life. I plunged headlong into an abyss of despair.

Dad walked in on me one Sunday morning while I was pouring my first scotch on the rocks of the day. It was 8:00

a.m. Even being hammered from the night before, I was still cognizant enough to have my wits about me.

"Peter… would you sit with me for a few minutes? We need to talk," he said.

Dad and Mom refused to use or accept the name I had invented for myself. It didn't bother me since home was my sanctuary.

"Sure, Dad… what's up?" I asked.

Not one time since we had come home from Chicago could I remember either of them judging my behavior. He gestured for me to sit at the dining-room table. From the time I was old enough to remember. All of our family meetings took place at the kitchen table. So when Dad asked me to sit, I knew he had something important to talk about.

"Son… your mother and I have been sitting on the sidelines raising your daughter and watching as you destroy yourself. I have to tell you it's not been pleasant to watch. We knew you needed some time for closure. Then a year went by and a second, now we're going on a third. Peter… if not for us, do it for your daughter. At the rate you're going, you're going to drink yourself to death, and Kelly Ann will never know either of her parents. Who's going to tell her about her mother? Heck, son, I hardly knew Amy. And what's worse, you're living in the same house and your daughter doesn't even know you."

Dad didn't talk much, and even though I had spent a lot of time dazed and confused, I loved and respected him. Somewhere inside, I wanted to show that, but I felt somewhat baffled as to why this conversation was so long in coming.

"Why now?" I asked.

"What do you mean?"

"If this has been on your mind all this time, why bring it up now? It's a little late, isn't it?"

"Peter... we've had similar conversation on many occasions. I couldn't even begin to count them. You really don't remember, do you?"

"Was I rude to you, Dad?" I asked.

A few tears trickled down my cheeks while I realized that I had no recollection of last week much less the month before.

"No, son, you've not been rude or violent to anyone except to yourself. We talked to a psychiatrist a few months ago; he thought you should be hospitalized. Your mother and I decided to give you a little more time, hoping you would snap out of the funk you're in. If you continue down this path, you could lose custody of Kelly Ann. Are you with me so far?"

"I think so," I said. But doubt hung in the forefront of my mind.

Will I wake up tomorrow and be clueless of the conversation I'm having today? I wondered.

Why this heart-to-heart ended on a positive note, is anyone's guess. The reality check though, came in loud and clear. I looked down at my glass full of whisky with its three half-melted ice cubes and realized I wanted to change. I walked over to the sink and poured the swill down the drain, it disappeared in slow motion. Dad was standing beside me when I looked up. He gave me a hug like he did when I was little. I'm not sure how long I cried. A lot of emotion had been pent-up for too long. He guided me back to the table, indicating that our conversation was far from over. I heard something behind me and felt a presence. Mom and I shared a connection, at least when I was sober. The experience is hard to explain, but over the years, I got use to it.

"Good morning, Peter," she said.

"Hi, Mom," I said.

A hush took over the table, and I recognized a concerned look between parents, then Dad smiled. "Well, Margaret… I believe our son is back from the dark and lonely place he's been residing."

She looked at me with a hint of tears that did not come. "Have you told him yet?" she asked.

Dad shook his head and took a deep breath. "No, there was no point unless I was sure where the conversation was going."

"Tell me what?" I asked.

He glanced back at Mom, then me. I knew that look. He was collecting his thoughts, which meant he wouldn't be sharing good news.

"I guess the best approach is straight on. Peter… you… we… are broke," Dad said.

It took a little while for it to soak in. My mind raced back in time, two years ago, which I could still remember for the most part.

"I paid cash for everything. How could we be broke?" I asked.

"Yes, you did, and that's one of the reasons we're still living here. The problem is taxes. It would have been sorted out if you had continued in the recording business. When you decided to quit music, the big paychecks stopped. Not long after that, income and property taxes came due. It was a staggering amount of money."

"I thought the royalties would see us through," I said.

"I think you know that the music industry and their fans are fickle. The royalty checks are the only cash flow you have, and they have kept the day-to-day bills paid. Those dollars are still coming in, but they are slowing down. The biggest revenue-producing song was '*Make Them Smile,*' and you gave the rights to Amy's sister. Don't get me wrong; it was the right thing to do. The ranch has produced a couple of pretty good horses that I sold, and that helped, but not enough. By my best guess, you have about six months to a year before the IRS steps in and starts taking stuff. If you put the ranch up for sale now and get a decent price for it, maybe we can solve the tax debt and salvage some cash."

It was the longest conversation that I could remember having with my dad for a very long time. Discussions with him were generally short and to the point. Clearly I had been disconnected for way too long. I looked around the room, it seemed like I was seeing it for the first time. My scan stopped and lingered on the half-empty bottle of scotch on the counter.

"I guess I've picked a hell of a time to quit drinking," I said.

I was serious, but the comment broke the tension. Mom and Dad laughed long enough that I was able to understand the humor.

"It's your call son. What do you want to do?" Dad asked.

I pondered his question longer than most people would. I suppose. Since I was just coming out of hibernation this was all new news to me.

"Give me a couple of days to think. I'm not going back to music. I just can't do it," I said.

"Peter… would you mind starting off by taking a shower and burning the sweatshirt you're wearing?" Mom said.

Except for "Good morning," it was her only comment to me throughout the entire conversation, so I figured it mattered to her. I took a sniff and understood her implication.

"Seems like a good place to start," I said with a sheepish smile.

The shower that morning seemed almost ritualistic. In many ways, it was a cleansing of body and soul.

///////

That talk with dad took place almost nine years ago and the outcome created quite a chain of events. Most importantly, I quit drinking and have been sober ever since. The alcohol abuse began as an escape from misery, in the end, it fueled my depression, taking good traits and giving nothing in return. I guess somewhere in the back of my mind, I still blame the music industry for Amy's death, when in reality. Abigail created the chain of events that led to the accident. Even so, I still feel guilty and have never forgiven myself. I could have made a nice living just writing music and selling some tunes, life just didn't play out that way.

The two things I've been blessed or cursed with, depending on the point of view, were music and numbers. I found school boring, and regardless of how smart you are—and even though you can test through a lot of stuff—there are hoops to jump, to get a degree. With the IRS poised to take everything away, I didn't have the luxury to spend time in school.

The day I came out of my alcohol-induced haze, I got on the Internet and discovered day trading. At the time, I still had about fifty thousand in cash, so I gambled it on the stock market. As luck would have it, I made some good choices. In the beginning, I probably benefited from a good helping of luck since I really didn't know what I was doing, but I had a natural talent for analyzing trends in the market. I mortgaged the ranch for additional capital, and within three months, I tripled my money. Within a year, I turned my investment into a million dollars. The influx of cash kept off the wolves long enough to save the proverbial farm. Part of the luck was that I got into it at exactly the right time. Nine years later, there is still money to be made, but it's slower and caution is a virtue.

Once I was on the right track and my money issues had been alleviated. I slowed down enough to smell the flowers, so to speak, and took some time to look at myself. I still felt depressed and thought about Amy every day. Her ashes were laid to rest by the lake under a big marble headstone. Kelly Ann and I go there on a regular basis and I tell the same stories about her mother over and over. I still cry every time.

Over the years, I managed to acquire the credentials necessary to share my skills with a select few clients, and everyone knew me as Allen Shaw. Peter, in my mind and everyone else's was dead. About three years ago, when I first started accepting a few clients, I connected with one of them and we became friends. His name was Luke Anderson and he jumped out of airplanes for a hobby. I felt intrigued—but skeptical. He never pushed me to give it a try. I guess for whatever reason, that made me more interested. One day I decided to go see what it was all about.

Skydive Dallas was cool for many reasons, but I liked the people most of all. They came from every walk of life, from mechanics to physicians, for the most part, treated each other the same. They loved their sport like scuba divers or sailors, and I felt a camaraderie shared by everyone involved.

The fascinating part was that the professional skydivers, the competitive skydivers, and the fun jumpers all treated people new to the sport like old friends. It was a connection that I had never made in my entire life. I'm a little different than your average bear so having a circle of friends didn't happen. The old adage, a round peg into a square hole, is me in a nutshell. I made a tandem, was hooked, and soon thereafter signed up for the AFF—accelerated free fall—program. The program, as a rule, takes twenty-five to thirty jumps in order to become a licensed skydiver. It took me thirty-five, but I loved the fact that, for the first time in my life, I found something that didn't come easy for me.

It's not a natural environment plummeting through the air at a hundred-twenty miles an hour toward the ground. Luke suggested a skydiving wind tunnel. It would give me a chance to work on some of the maneuvers that were proving difficult for me. Vertical wind tunnels are exactly what they sound like, a vertical column of air that you can practice in and improve your skills. The bit of coaching I received at the ifly tunnel in Frisco, TX was the little push I needed, and the next weekend. I got my A-license which meant I could jump with other skydivers and was the beginning of a beautiful relationship.

I would never be a professional or competitive skydiver. I liked just showing up when I wanted to and make some jumps for fun. Last weekend was one of those days when I showed up to see my friends and make a few skydives. We had just finished practicing a dirt dive—choreography done on the ground before skydiving—when Luke walked up.

"Hey, have you noticed the girl over there in the tandem area?" He asked pointing somewhat discreetly.

"Huh? No… not really," I said.

"Dude, she has been staring a hole through you. I think you should go over and talk to her."

"Really?"

I looked over his shoulder and saw the girl. She was in her early twenties, with long reddish-blonde hair, very attractive, and vaguely familiar. The moment she realized I was looking at her, she averted her eyes. I figured it was just a coincidence.

"I think she's just looking around."

"I've been watching her watch you for a while. Just keep her in your peripheral. She'll look again," Luke said with just a hint of a smile.

Sure enough, a few seconds later, she looked at me again.

"I guess you're right," I said.

"Go talk to her. She's pretty," Luke said.

"No... I don't think so."

"Okay, suit yourself," he said and left to finish packing his canopy.

Several things went through my mind. The first was the notion that she might have been a fan of Peter Shaw, but I rejected that idea since she would have been a kid back then. I couldn't shake the feeling that we had met. It bothered me enough that I decided to leave early. I packed up my stuff and left without saying good-bye to anyone. Only about 10 or 15 percent of the people who make a tandem like it enough to return and make another jump. The math made it simple to conclude that by next weekend, she would be gone and I wouldn't have to worry about an unwanted encounter. Anonymity had been my friend and protector for a long time, and the last thing I wanted was to have my real identity revealed where I liked to play.

Eleven years and I had not dated anyone—and really didn't want to. The thought of losing someone again deterred me from getting close to anyone. Besides, I still loved Amy. It seemed unfair to have a relationship with someone new, knowing I was still in love with my dead wife. Every time I thought about it, the whole concept felt too mind boggling for me, so I kept myself busy with work, and my daughter. I convinced myself that next Saturday the girl would be gone, even so, my thoughts continued in a loop, and no matter how much I tried to distract myself, the feeling that I knew her just wouldn't go away. A week later, as I drove out to Skydive Dallas, she still lingered on my mind.

Chapter 23
Kelly

"I think it's awesome that you signed up to do a tandem next weekend," Judy said. "We can come out together again if you want to. I decided to take the AFF course. This skydiving thing is just too much fun."

"Yeah, let's plan on it. I'd rather come out with you than to come alone," I said.

"Did you ever talk to that guy?"

"What guy?"

"You know who I mean. I saw you staring at him several times."

I knew she wasn't going to buy into my act of indifference, besides that, it was a forty-five-minute ride home. The little time that I had spent with Judy told me she was like a little pit bull and she would not let go until I fessed up or made something up that she'd believe.

"No... I didn't talk to him. By the time I worked up the nerve to say something, he'd disappeared. You know how sometimes you see someone that seems familiar?" I asked.

"Yeah..." she said.

I didn't think Judy did one-word sentences. I knew she was drawing me out to open up.

"I don't know... there was something about him and those blue eyes. Like... October-sky blue... oh... no... There's no way," I said.

The revelation hit me hard, as obvious as it was—even with the similar name—I still hadn't made the connection, beyond wondering for a fleeting moment that he might be Peter's brother. And I was positive that he had no siblings, so...

What if it's actually him? No ... It just couldn't be. I thought.

"What? Tell me!" Judy said.

It seemed clear that if it was Peter, he was using a different name, grown a beard, and wore his hair longer to hide his identity. I thought back to when Amy had died and my short conversation with Big Tony. He said that Peter had just disappeared. But, if this guy was Peter, then that's not what happened at all; he just blended back into familiar surroundings. That meant there was a good chance my niece was living somewhere close by.

Since Peter is a savant, maybe he's delusional... and this is his way of protecting himself from the pain of losing Amy. I thought.

"Earth to Kelly... hello!" Judy said. "Are you out there? Where did you go, girl? Hey, this guy must be big news. So come on, spill the beans."

Until I had a chance to think at length on the subject, I couldn't possibly tell Judy what I thought to be the truth, so I lied. "I thought he was one of my sister's old boyfriends. It couldn't be him. I was mistaken; the guy I was thinking of was shorter and stockier."

"I didn't know you had a sister. Does she live around here?"

"She's dead."

"Oh crap... Open mouth and insert foot. Kelly, I am sorry."

"It's okay. She's been gone for eleven years, but I do still miss her."

"Hey... we talked about getting together tonight, so let's do it. We can go get some sushi and a couple of glasses of wine, my treat. I still owe you lunch."

"It was a frozen dinner. Sushi is expensive."

"Don't worry about that. I want to get better acquainted. After all, we're going to be skydiving buddies pretty soon."

"No," came to mind at first. I just wanted to go home and sort out whether I had seen Peter Shaw or if it was a figment of my imagination. *If it was him and we cross paths again, what will I say?* I wondered.

A part of me felt angry, because his daughter was the closest thing to my sister I would ever know and he had closed the door. I could understand his resentment toward Abigail, and maybe it never dawned on him that I would want to stay in touch.

Or perhaps it's not him and I'm just nuts.

Either way, I had to know.

"Okay, sushi and wine sounds like a great way to finish out the day," I said.

"Great! My mission is to remove you from the boring, sedentary life you've been living and show you how to have some fun."

Judy seemed more excited about improving my lifestyle than I did, but I had to admit that spending the day with her was the most fun I've had in a long time. Dinner was indeed a better choice than going home to an empty apartment. Judy seemed like a breath of fresh air, although it was early to know for sure, she seemed like a really nice person and someone who would make a great friend. We went to a little pub after sushi and shot some pool. She knew a lot of people there, so in just a few hours. I made a bunch of new acquaintances. I vowed on the ride home, at least what I remembered of it, to get out more. The next morning, I had a booming headache and decided that the excessive intake of spirits did not have to go hand in hand with socializing. After feeling like crap all day I decided that moderation truly is a virtue. I tucked the concept into the back of my aching brain for reference at a later date.

Monday at work started out as a whirlwind. I wondered at one point if it was solar flares, aliens, or planetary alignment that caused glitches in the company's software. I spent more time at work than at home most of the week. Saturday rolled around, and I was comfortable and loving my bed with no intentions of getting out of it anytime soon. The first time the phone rang, I managed to just ignore it. Voice mail would pick it up, no worries. The next two times, I thrashed around my nest groping for my tormentor. Unfortunately I'd left the cell phone on the kitchen counter to charge and had not thought to mute the ring. By the fifth or sixth call, I was wide awake, angry, and had quite enough of whoever thought it necessary to call me over and over again on my day off.

"Hello," I said.

"Kelly? Good grief, girl, wake up," Judy said.

"Ha-ha, very funny. Just so we're clear on the subject, if you want to be my friend, you don't wake me up early on my day off."

There was a short pause, and I'm pretty sure she was snickering. "It's eleven o'clock. Have you forgotten about your tandem jump at two?"

"Oh crap! Yes, I completely forgot. When are you coming by?"

"So sorry, so sad, princess, I'm already here. I had to show up early for the AFF class. I've been calling you all morning. You remember how to get here, right?"

"Yeah, no problem, I'll see you in about an hour."

It was hard to pin down why the Saturday appointment at Skydive Dallas escaped my conscious mind. As busy as my week had been, I thought about the mystery of what happened to Peter Shaw several times. That subject weighed heavier on my mind than the idea of making a tandem jump.

A quick shower, fresh clothes, and light makeup had me on my merry way. The drive gave me a little time to think about jumping out of a perfectly good airplane, instead of concerning myself with whether or not I would run into my late sister's husband. It had been years since my last epiphany, but this one without a doubt had gotten my attention. The whole skydiving thing sounded like fun when someone else was doing it. I started thinking about what if scenarios, and as I got closer, the fear factor got worse and worse. I saw a little country convenience store about five miles short of my destination. I pulled off, telling myself that I needed gas, but when I stopped at the pump and glanced at my fuel gauge, it was almost full. As a kid, I had always been a daredevil, but as an adult, the draw of being a thrill seeker had gone away.

I squeezed $6.14 into my tank and went in to the store to kill some time. The cashier sold me a candy bar (something I never eat) and a bottle of water while continuing to chat with her coworker. Determined not to let a little case of stage fright deter me, I continued on, and ten minutes later, I was in the Drop zone parking lot, sweaty palms and all.

An attractive young woman named Genifer motioned me over as soon as I walked in the door. "Are you Kelly?" she asked.

"Yeah, sorry I'm running late."

"No, you're fine. Just go into the pro shop, get weighed, and sign in. Then we'll all go upstairs together and watch a short film about safety and what to expect on your tandem jump."

I felt a little numb by then, but did her bidding, and a few minutes later, I sat through a video about making a tandem.

After our short film, we were shuffled back down to the main hangar and instructed to stay close by and wait. Every so often, they called out some names over the intercom and suited them up for their jump. It was a well-oiled machine, and even though my nervousness remained, it helped that everyone who left on the airplane returned with a gentle parachute landing, bubbling with excitement.

The moment of truth came when they called my name. My tandem master's name was Ernie; he assured me that even though it was my first time, he had made a couple. To be honest, his levity didn't sound very reassuring. Judy came out of an adjourning classroom for a bio-break and stopped to wish me a good jump.

"You are going to have so much fun," Judy said. "Who's your tandem master?"

"Some guy named Ernie. He seems nice enough."

"Wow, you lucked out. He's in charge of the whole school and, from what I understand, has over eighteen thousand jumps."

"Better than… a couple," I mumbled.

"What?" she asked.

"Nothing, how's the AFF class going?"

"Great, there's a lot more to it than I thought, lots of safety stuff."

Judy didn't seem as excited as she had been the week before. "I don't know anything, but it seems to me the safety stuff would be very important," I said.

"You're right—and I know that. I guess it's the realization that if something happens, like my parachute doesn't work, it's up to me to do the emergency procedures. On a tandem, you're just a passenger and the person in charge has lots of experience."

"Do you want to know what I think?"

"Sure I do."

"I came out here scared as hell, but after being out here a while. I think everyone here is a little scared. That's the attraction and why people keep coming back. Somehow they are able to manage their fear."

"Wow, that's pretty insightful for somebody I had to drag out of bed this morning."

She smiled, and we watched the Cessna Caravan pull up and take on the next load of jumpers. The turbine engine made it hard to hear for the few minutes it was on the ground. She hugged my neck as it left.

"Thanks for the pep talk. It was just what I needed. Everyone here had to start somewhere," Judy said.

"You'll do fine. Just pay attention to the safety stuff," I said.

My tandem master returned with a blue jumpsuit and handed it to me. "I think this one will fit you," he said.

It wasn't as becoming as the custom suits worn by the experienced jumpers, although it did serve the purpose of being an extra layer of protection. Once it was on, he started getting me into my harness, which was separate from his. Ernie explained that he would attach my harness to his once we were in the airplane. I have to give credit where it's due, the professionalism of the staff made me feel safe.

We boarded the plane, and the early part of the ride up was filled with most of the jumpers joking around about one thing or another. One guy asked Ernie if he had remembered to take his medication this morning. Another asked how his first jump went yesterday. It was all in good fun; the joking made me feel more relaxed, and took my mind off what I was getting ready to do.

The jump ended up being an amazing experience. I expected the free-fall to be like an elevator drop or some sensation of falling, it was more like floating on water, except for the wind blast. I opted for a photographer who shot stills and video of the jump. He was right there in front of us the whole time. That was pretty cool. The free-fall ended at about five thousand feet and the parachute opened. Then it was completely quiet.

"How are you doing so far?" Ernie asked.

"This is a blast," I said.

"Enjoy the ride. We're going to do a series of turns so we can land close to the hangar. The camera guy opened lower so he can be ready for our landing. Don't forget to smile."

"I'm sure that won't be a problem. I think there's one glued on my face."

It felt like being on a mountaintop. Everything looked miniature, the cars, houses, and as we got lower, I could see the ant-sized people. The landing came too soon, but the adrenaline high lingered, it was easy to see why people come back to make more.

On the drive out, I thought I would just make my jump and go home. The excitement of day changed my mind. So I decided to hang around and watch Judy make her first AFF jump. I got out of the gear then headed for the restroom to brush my hair and make sure I was somewhat presentable. That's when the worlds of two broken hearts collided.

"Oh... excuse me," I said.

"No... it's my fault," he said.

It was the guy from last weekend. Standing up close and hearing him speak confirmed who he was.

"I know this is going to sound weird, but could we talk?" I asked.

"Uh... sure, what's up?"

"I'm Kelly Stevens. Do you remember me?"

He paused, either trying to remember or deciding what to say. "Hi, I'm Allen," he finally said.

"I'm Amy's little sister."

Until I knew his side of things, I wanted to play along with his cover, but he persisted.

"I think you have me confused with someone else."

"Take a walk with me," I said.

He took the comment as I meant it. I wasn't asking; I was telling him. On the south side of the hangar was a large deck where, according to Judy, after-jumping parties occur. At the moment, it was deserted and the perfect place to have a blunt conversation.

"I played along with you in the hangar. This is your playground and you've gone to a lot of trouble to be anonymous. The thing is you spent way too much time with Amy for me not to recognize you."

He didn't say anything at first, maybe judging whether to continue the charade or come clean.

He took a deep breath, shook his head, and said, "How did you figure me out after all these years?"

"The long hair and beard threw me off, but not many people have the same shade of blue eyes as you. That and your voice, as soon as you spoke, I knew it was you. What's up with the masquerade?"

"I don't know where to start. In the beginning, I just wanted to be left alone. After a while, I just became someone else. I've actually made a few friends out here that like me for who I am."

"Look, a part of me understands. Another part of me is really pissed off. Do you think you're the only one who suffered a loss? I lost my sister, my mother, my brother-in-law, and my niece, who incidentally I've never had the privilege of meeting. So explain to me why you shut me out of the only family I have?"

I had been carrying around a lot of anger for a long time. It felt good to let go of it, and I was far from finished.

"It never occurred to me that you would want to have anything to do with me or Kelly Ann."

That took the wind out of my sail. "You named her after me?" I asked.

"It's what Amy wanted. She never got to see her, either."

He started to cry and so did I. For some reason, I hugged him. It just felt like the thing to do. He didn't resist, but I could tell he felt a bit awkward.

"I want to meet my niece," I said.

"Okay. Anytime you want to come over to the ranch, you're welcome."

He dried his eyes on his T-shirt and looked around to see that we were still alone.

"Today would be good for me. Whenever you're done jumping, I'll follow you home... unless there's someone there who wouldn't appreciate you bringing a girl home," I said, realizing that he may have remarried.

"My mom may have a heart attack, but once she finds out who you are, she'll be happy to meet you. I'm done jumping for the day and was just leaving when we ran into each other."

A few minutes later, I was on the road, following him home. I felt more excited than I could remember being in years—and apprehensive, because of some lingering pent-up anger. I had been deprived of having a real family for so long, the idea of gaining one made me a little nervous. One thing I knew for sure though. I wanted this first meet and greet to go well.

The drive took about forty- five minutes, about the same distance as McKinney, except in the opposite direction. He turned onto a tree-lined, paved road that led to the house. It was white and had an old colonial-plantation style about it. The front had a covered porch with huge pillars soaring to the second floor. I'm not sure what I expected, but I didn't expect something so old-fashioned. We pulled around to the back of the house and parked. Peter led me in through the back door, which opened into the kitchen. His mom was there, busy cooking something that smelled divine. My stomach rumbled, reminding me that I hadn't eaten since gobbling down some yogurt for breakfast. As his mother turned toward us, her eyes went wide. She just looked at me, speechless, for an uncomfortable length of time.

She regained her composure and smiled in a friendly sort of way. "Who's your friend? I didn't know you were bringing someone home. I'm Margaret," she said, offering her hand.

I shook her hand. "I'm very pleased to meet you. I'm Amy's sister... Kelly."

If she looked surprised before, her jaw dropped at this news.

"Peter... I don't believe you've ever mentioned that Amy had a sister." I could tell she considered saying more, and she was clearly annoyed.

He picked up on her tone and began to fess up. "I messed up, Mom. It never occurred to me to contact Kelly. I was too busy feeling sorry for myself and trying to be someone else. She came out to Skydive Dallas today to make a tandem and recognized me. She wants to meet Kelly Ann."

"Well of course she does, and thank goodness she recognized you, with that long hair and scruffy old beard," Margaret said.

The kitchen door opened, and an older man, whom I presumed to be Peter's father, stepped inside. He wore blue jeans, a short-sleeve khaki shirt, and a beat-up wide-brimmed straw hat. He, too, looked shocked at seeing Peter with a female, but Margaret caught him up to speed in short order.

"John, this is Amy's sister… Kelly. Peter was just explaining to us why we've never met."

John recovered from the surprise and stepped up and gave me a big hug. "I read about your mom. I'm very sorry for your loss, and I have to confess that her obituary listed you, but you disappeared soon after. I presumed you moved to live with family."

"John… you knew too?" Margaret said. "Why, I ought to take a frying pan and whop both of you in the head. This girl is family."

"I meant to tell you, and, well, life got in the way and then it was out of sight, out of mind and I forgot," John said. "I hope you're willing to forgive all for us shutting you out of our lives. Just like you, we suffered a great loss and have done the best we could to move forward."

"I know this is all kind of weird, just meeting me and all. I have to admit I was bitter about not knowing where you guys went. I ended up in Austin with an aunt and uncle. We stay in touch some, but as I told Peter, I don't have much in the way of family. I'd like to be included in yours," I said. I felt close to tears and tried to sniff them back.

Margaret came closer and gave me a long, affectionate hug—the kind that I always wanted and never got. The floodgates opened, and I couldn't hold it back any longer. I guess I had a stockpile of latent emotions bottled up inside. I sobbed for quite some time. She patted my head and just let me cry.

I finally got some semblance of a grip. "I'm sorry. I feel like a dope," I said.

"Honey, it's okay," Margaret said. "We've all got some baggage to sort through. You and I will have some girl time when you're in the mood to work through it."

"I'd like that," I said.

Peter had been silent since his dad came in. "Where's Kelly Ann? She's usually attached to your hip," Peter said.

"She said she wanted to go talk to her mom," Margaret said.

"You let her go down there by herself?" Peter asked.

"Son... if you haven't noticed, she's eleven years old and plenty old enough to walk down to the lake," Margaret said.

The confusion must have been apparent on my face as I tried to understand. Margaret picked up on it and said, "Peter had your sister cremated. He built a memorial for her on the property down by the lake. I think it would be the perfect place and time to meet your niece."

"Sound good?" Peter asked.

"Yes... please," I said.

The sun hung low in the sky as Peter walked me down to the lake. A sudden spring had followed the freakish snowstorm from weeks earlier, the vegetation was exploding with life. Every few feet, a different color of azaleas bordered a well-used dirt path.

"This is beautiful," I said.

"Thanks. I wish I could say I had something to do with the landscaping, but Mom designed it and was the overseer of the entire project. Plants are her thing, she loves it."

"What's your thing now?" I asked. Since it looked like I had some sort of acceptance going for me, I figured it was time for some answers.

"I'm a day trader of sorts. For the most part, I do my own thing, but I've accumulated a few clients that I do some consulting for."

"What about music?" I asked.

He regarded me with an odd expression, remained silent for a while, searching or groping for the words, then replied, "Music ruined my life. My musical ambitions set the stage for Amy's death, and I blame myself. I have regretted it ever since."

I stopped dead in my tracks. "You're telling me that you think your musical ambitions are responsible for my sister's accident?" I asked.

"Yes. I figured you knew. That's part of the reason I didn't look you up. I really didn't think you would want to have anything to do with me."

The serious look on his face told me he meant what he said. I just couldn't believe it came out of his mouth.

"Look, Peter... I may have only been thirteen at the time, but my memory is excellent. Amy wanted you to pursue a musical career—heck, it's all she talked about. I know. I heard it every day. She was so proud of you and what you might achieve, and so was I." I added myself into the equation without thinking about it until it was too late. I could see the wheels turning in that magnificent brain of his, but I had no clue if I was getting my point across.

He let out a big sigh. "In the big scheme of things, I spent very little time with Amy. Eleven years later, and all I remember are a few short moments of heaven and a very long time in hell," he said.

I started walking again, hoping he would take the hint and follow. We walked in solitude for a while, each within our own thoughts. I knew what I wanted to say, but I had no idea how it would be received. I had a vague remembrance that Peter didn't do irony very well, so I knew it had to be worded right to get my point through.

"I'm going to say something that I would like you to sit with," I said. "I don't want a reply today, not until you've had time to think it through. Okay?"

"Sure, I guess so."

"Just remember that I'm not being derogatory, but I am going to be blunt. You said it yourself, that you didn't get to spend a lot of time with Amy. Well, I did. If she could speak to you right now. She would be very angry with you. She loved you, and to her, that meant loving everything about you. Oh... you could have been a day trader and it wouldn't have mattered to her. But one of the things she loved the most was your music. Every time she talked about that trip to Chicago, her eyes lit up and she became animated. She said every time you played, it was like a personal concert meant just for her. To blame yourself or music for her death couldn't be further from the truth. The truth—and it's painful for me to say it—is that our mother was to blame. I talked to my sister several times after her Canadian adventure. At the end, when the snowmobile accident happened and Felix was injured, she faced a wolf and certain death. I still remember her words verbatim. *I'll never hear Peter play music again or see my baby.* What upset her most, more than anything else, was not seeing what you and her daughter would achieve in life. You and Kelly Ann meant everything to her. Our mother caused a lot of grief in all of our lives. You should be doing what you love, not what you think you should do out of guilt."

As if on cue, we came to a clearing and I could see the lake. I wasn't prepared for the size and the manicured shrubs and lawn around it. Just past the dam on the other side of the lake was a large marble mausoleum. I noticed a stone bench in front of it—and a little girl sitting on the bench, swinging her feet. As we got closer, I could hear her having a one-sided conversation. Then she sensed, or heard our presence and looked around.

"Daddy!" she said.

The one word expressed love, excitement, and pride, all combined. She ran up and almost bowled Peter over when she jumped into his embrace and then giggled while he spun her around. He put her down, and her bright curious eyes were on me.

"Who are you?" she asked.

I looked at Peter, not certain how to start off the introductions. He nodded his head to proceed.

"I'm your mother's sister," I said. It seemed easy enough to say, but the words felt awkward.

She gave me that curious look again but this time with a hint of bewilderment. "I don't think my mother had a sister," she said, looking back at Peter for confirmation.

"She's the real deal, sweet pea, and her name is Kelly too," Peter said.

That was good enough for her. She took my hand and led me over to the bench where she had been sitting and started filling me in on everything she knew and what she didn't. "I never got to meet my mom. She died the same day I was born, but it wasn't my fault. She was in an accident."

"Yeah... I know. I'm sorry it's taken me so long to meet you," I said.

"Where have you been? We've been here all of my life."

Kids are so honest; I liked her already, and I decided to be as truthful as I could. "I think your daddy thought I was mad at him," I said.

"Why?" she asked.

"Well... your dad blames himself for what happened, but I finally got to tell him that it wasn't his fault."

I looked up at Peter, wondering if there were going to be repercussions for being blunt in front of his daughter. He remained expressionless.

"Daddy thinks that music was to blame too, but I think his music is beautiful."

"Does he play for you?" I asked. It shocked me that she knew anything on the subject.

"Almost never," she said.

"Are you a musician too?" I asked.

"Yes... but I'm not as good as Dad."

"I don't think anyone's as good as your father," I said.

She smiled and nodded her head. "I don't think so, either."

Now that we were close to Amy's memorial, I could see that something had been carved in the stone. I stepped closer so I could read it and immediately recognized the words. I started crying.

"It's the song she wrote," I said.

Kelly Ann took my hand, tugging on it to get my attention. "It's okay, you don't have to cry. Mommy's fine."

I bent down and hugged her. "Oh... sweetie, I know, but I've never said good-bye. I loved her so much, and I still miss her."

"Will you tell me about her?" she asked.

"Until you're tired of hearing me talk," I said.

Chapter 24
Peter

After running into Kelly that Saturday afternoon, we saw her on a regular basis. It proved to be a much needed breath of fresh air for my daughter and me. At first, I tried to tell myself that the reunion was just good for Kelly Ann, but as the encounters became more and more frequent, I started to realize that I looked forward to seeing her as well. She came out to the Drop zone and went through the AFF program. She loved it, and I had no doubt that she was more of a natural than I was. Luke's suggestion that I go to the wind tunnel, is the only reason I made it through the program. Not the case for Kelly. She took to skydiving like a duck to water, and being a beautiful young woman gets you plenty of attention at any jump school.

I didn't really think of us as anything but friends, but as time went on, our mutual friends thought we were much more. Luke was a long-time friend that I hung out with most of the time. He was one of the best freeflyers around— freeflyers skydive in a head down or a seated position instead of the traditional belly-to-earth style—he had taken me under his wing early on. He was the sort of guy who either liked you or didn't but was gregarious either way. He accepted me and my occasional quirks without judgment and ended up being the only real male friend I'd ever had except for Big Tony, whom I hadn't seen in years. So it was only natural that Luke was the first one to ask me about her.

"So… what's up with you and Kelly?" Luke asked.

"We're just friends."

"Looks like it could be more than that, the way she looks at you. I'm telling you, she likes you a lot."

"Really? No… we're just friends."

"Oh… then you wouldn't mind if I asked her out?"

I guess either the look on my face or my nonverbal response was all the answer he needed. He laughed.

"Dude, I wish I had a picture of your face just now. You like her! No worries, I'm not going to ask her out. Pretty much everyone has figured out that you guys are an item, except you."

I didn't respond yea or nay, but it was something else for me to sit with. I filed it away with the conversation Kelly and I had about music, blame, and guilt, which had never been broached again since we'd met almost three of months before. Summer and the hundred-degree days were in full swing in Texas. I liked it better than the cold weather, so it suited me just fine. Even with all the time I spent skydiving, I never stayed around for the evening life. No reason, really. I hadn't had a drink in over nine years and had no interest. I guess it was the whole loner thing. That had changed, and all of a sudden, I didn't feel so eager to be alone all of the time.

It was about sunset, and I was done jumping for the day. The Drop zone's de Havilland twin-engine Otter was taking on the last load of jumpers for a ride to thirteen thousand feet. Kelly walked up, and we watched the plane take off. Talking over the noise of the spinning props is difficult, so we waited until it lifted off about halfway down the runway.

"Want to take a walk?" Kelly asked.

"Okay," I said.

It wasn't new for us to take a walk and talk, but most of the time; we did it with my daughter at the ranch, which was great because the girls did most of the talking. I just walked and listened and answered an occasional question. Private conversations were rare.

An open field that served as an alternate landing area lay just south of the hangar and deck. Everyone not on the last load of the day was congregating on or near the wooden deck to swap stories and have a beer. Kelly guided me in the opposite direction until we were out of earshot.

"Do you remember the conversation that I asked you to sit with?" she asked.

"Yeah… I'm surprised it took you so long to bring it back up," I said.

"There are a couple of reasons for that. I wanted you to have plenty of time to sort it all out… and I wanted to get to know you better."

"I have thought our conversation through, and I guess you're right. I shouldn't blame myself for Amy's accident."

It seemed that my answer pleased her, because she stopped to hug me.

"That is good news… and it makes me very happy," she said.

"Kelly Ann talks about you all the time. She really likes you. Every day, she asks. 'When's Aunt K coming over?'"

Her response took long enough to make me feel as if I had said something wrong.

"What about you?" she asked.

Confused, I said, "I don't understand."

Another pause came accompanied with an almost inaudible sigh.

"Do you… like it when I come over?" she asked.

I got it… and Luke had hit the nail on the head. I was the last one to know. One step ahead of most people on an intellectual scale and three down on social aptitude, it is who I am. I wanted to choose my response with care, but the more I dwelt on the verbiage, the more time that passed.

"Either 'Yes' or 'No' would be a good place to start," she said, interrupting my dilemma.

"Yes... Sorry... Well, I'm not sorry the answer is 'Yes,' but..."

I hadn't been this flustered since my first date with Amy. Kelly put her forefinger on my lips to shut me up. A vague memory of that happening a long time ago surfaced then flitted away.

"Look, I know this is a little weird, but I like you. I've had a crush on you since I was twelve. Amy said she would smash me into little pieces if ever told you. But I think things have changed, I would like to think she would be pleased."

Her eyes were wide open with intent and pierced me like an arrow through my heart.

"Of all the guys out there, why would you want a project like me?" I asked.

"Runs in the family, I guess. Always looking for a challenge," she smiled, paused for a moment, and then asked. "Are you happy... today... right now?"

"Happy enough, I suppose. Since you've been around, I've realized some things are missing."

"Are you really happy being a day trader? It's okay if you are, but I'm curious. Do you wake up in the morning excited about going to work?"

"It's what I do. I'm good at it, and it pays the bills," I said, wondering where the conversation was going now.

"So then, your answer is no. You're not excited about your work; it's just a job that pays the bills. Correct?" She paused but not for an answer. Before I could respond, she continued. "I'll bet you dinner that you haven't looked forward to a new day at work since you quit the band. Tell me I'm wrong and I won't say another word about the subject."

I didn't see that one coming. Then again, it wasn't the first time and it would not be the last.

"At the time, I was working my way out of an alcohol-induced haze. I still blamed music and myself for Amy's death. I was broke and owed the IRS a ton of money and very close to losing everything. Day trading just plopped itself into my lap. I made a lot of money and saved the farm... so to speak."

"Finally!" she said and then hugged me.

"What was that for?"

"Think about what you just said. You were talking in past tense. That means... if you choose to believe it, you did what you did as a result of what you needed to do at the time. The point of this conversation Peter, is. What do you want and need today?"

Facts as a rule were easy for me. If black meant bad and white meant good, then it made sense. Gray, on the other hand, often times messed me up. Over the last few months, that gray area had been thriving, and I felt hesitant. The tide that dragged me out to sea so long ago now began to push back. All the years I stayed drunk. My life remained in the black part of reality. I now started to realize that even though I was sober, my life had not changed. The gray area was the middle, and I needed to pass through it to get to the white.

"I do like you a lot," I said. "It's got to be obvious that the rest of the family adores you. Are you sure you want me in your life as more than just friends?"

"Not like you are now."

Just about the time I thought I understood Kelly, she threw me a curve. "I guess I've missed something." She smiled, and that softened the sting of what I perceived to be rejection. A little bit.

"I won't spend my life with a man who won't follow his dreams. You were that man, and you can be again. You just admitted that your current job just pays the bills."

"So you want me to jump back into the music business? For one thing, nobody would even know who I am, and I'm twenty-nine years old."

"I don't care if you play music or not, but I know it's a part of you, just like your daughter. What I want you to consider, is. What makes you happy? If you can't make yourself happy, how are you going to make me or your daughter happy? Twenty-nine is not old, and you have to know they still play your music on the radio."

"I wouldn't know where to start. I just walked out on Big Tony, the band, everyone. I doubt they would even care to see me."

"Will you just trust me one time? If I'm wrong, we'll find something else that makes you happy."

"Why does my being happy matter?" I asked.

"Because... I... I love you, but for us to work... you have to start loving yourself."

It was a word I had not heard in too long, and I have to admit, it felt good to hear it. Caution abounded, and the red flags of doubt reared their ugly heads. It's hard to ponder a subject when you know a quick answer is needed, so I stalled. "What do you want me to do?"

"The first thing is to give up the figment of your imagination of being someone you're not. It's rude to your friends and your family."

"Okay..." I guess I knew that being dishonest to friends or family was wrong, but it served as my protection from the pain of the past.

"The Fourth of July is in two weeks. The Drop zone is planning a big weekend, and people will be traveling long distances to be here."

"Yeah, it's a big deal. They're bringing in extra aircraft to handle the additional business. I usually skip the boogie weekends; it's a zoo out here."

"I want you to play on the Saturday night of that weekend."

"Oh... I don't know. It's been a long time since I've been in front of a crowd, and I don't even know if I can still see the colors."

"Colors? I don't understand."

"It takes time to prepare—"

"No... what do you mean about seeing the colors?"

"I guess Amy's the only one I've ever told about that. When I played and it was right, I could see colors for every note, every chord. It's hard to describe, but the closest thing I can relate it to is pure joy." I realized at that moment, Kelly was right and somehow had made me see the truth. I guess it means more when revelation comes from within.

"I think there's a band booked for Saturday night," I said.

"Stop making excuses. Doc Mike's Band is supposed to play, and he plays for the fun of it, not for the money. You won't be stepping on anyone's livelihood, and it's the perfect setting—full of friends who won't judge."

"You must not be talking about the same people I know out here. They're all judgmental to some degree. It's an eclectic bunch to say the least."

"Horse crap, Peter! Yes or no? All you have to do is show up. I'll take care of the details. If the night goes to hell in a hand basket, you'll have my appreciation for at least trying and my apologies for any ego bruising you may incur."

Her feet were planted apart with her hands on her hips—body language that I had seen before. And although I had already figured out that Kelly was nothing like her sister, they did share some similarities. I liked that on both counts.

"Let me think about it," I said.

"That's it? You're going to think about it?"

"Be careful what you wish for. Worse things could happen than a bruised ego," I said.

She was short and small, like a stick of dynamite. I figured it was no stretch of the imagination that she could be just as explosive, even though she came across as demure. This was not the same girl I'd met three months earlier. Even so, my attraction grew on a daily basis, along with a measured amount of confusion. A desire for us to be more than friends had grown over the short months since we'd met again. I'm not usually one to run on impulse, but call it nature taking its course. I bent down and kissed her. It was long and unhurried, and she pressed forward rather than pulling away. It was a kiss that could have lasted much longer if not for the whistles and cheers coming from the deck.

We parted, she observed me without comment for a moment, and then asked, "Will you at least promise that you'll show up? No expectations, no promises. Just that you'll be here?

I couldn't see the harm in agreeing since the worst that could happen would be to spend a Saturday night with friends that were usually daytime friends.

"Yes, I promise to be here."

Chapter 25
Kelly

It was like pulling teeth, but Peter agreed to at least show up. I was ecstatic, and for the first time in a very long time. I had a plan or at least, a method to my madness. As we walked back from the landing area, I could tell that he seemed somewhat embarrassed by the attention from his Drop zone buddies, who had noticed our first kiss. Although I didn't sense any remorse or regret on his part, I had little doubt as to his discomfort.

We hung out for a while, and Peter, I thought, dealt with the teasing from his friends quite well. I stayed just long enough not to appear to be in a hurry, said my good-byes, and headed for my car. Peter followed.

"Are you going to come out to the ranch?" he asked.

"No… I have some stuff to do at home. I'll come over next weekend, if that's okay?"

It was a white lie. I didn't really have anything to do at home per se, but my wheels were running at maximum. Even though I didn't get the exact answer I had been hoping for, I was going to run with my idea full steam ahead. I could tell he looked a little disappointed, and that fact, kind of felt good, and made it hard to go home.

"Sure, you can come over anytime," he said.

It was getting dark, and my parking spot offered a little more privacy than out in the wide open field. He kissed me again, it was definitely better than the first one. Any inhibition between us started to melt down like a nuclear reactor on its way to China. I knew if I didn't go soon. I would be following him home.

"I've got to go," I said, "but I will see you next weekend. Let's do something with Kelly Ann."

"Okay. I have a sailboat on Lake Texoma. We could all go spend the weekend at the lake."

"That sounds like fun. I've never been sailing before."

"I'll call you midweek," he said.

"Perfect."

On the drive home, my brain ran on overdrive. It was a risk to follow through, but I'd made up my mind. In the big scheme of things, I didn't know Peter well enough to know how he would react. What I planned to throw at him could be disconcerting even for the average person, and Peter was by no means common. This would be one of those times where you beg for forgiveness rather than ask permission. It was risky and I knew it.

The door to my apartment had barely closed behind me before I dialed the first number. Why I had saved Big Tony's contact information, I didn't know, but I was glad I had. Of course, the chances that the info was still good after eleven years were iffy at best.

"Hello," he said. Even though we had talked very little, the voice sounded just as I remembered.

"Big Tony?" I asked, more for validation than conformation.

"Depends on who wants to know."

A Chicago wise-guy tone permeated the receiver. Any other time, it would have been fun to mess with him, but too much water had passed under the proverbial bridge. There was a chance that Peter was right and that no one from the music days would be interested on any level to reunite.

"Hi… this is Kelly Stevens—Amy Shaw's sister. Do you remember me?" I asked.

"Sure, I remember you. How are you doing?"

"I'm fine—out of college and working." As much as I wanted to gossip, I was bursting with questions and didn't give him a chance to pursue any more niceties. "I ran into Peter a few months ago." I waited for an answer uncertain as to how the news would be viewed.

After a very long pause, he asked "Really? How's he doing?"

"He's done well. He got into day trading a few years back and seems to have a knack for it."

"Yeah, I did hear through the grapevine he had. I'm happy he was able to piece his life back together. I thought losing Amy would push him over the edge. How's his daughter?"

"Growing like a weed, she just turned eleven."

"Wow… it's hard to believe it's been that long." There was a certain amount of remorse in his voice, and I knew the moment of truth was at hand.

"I'm sure you know that Peter blamed himself for Amy's death," I said, changing the subject to the direction I wanted it to go.

"Yeah, I kind of figured he would. I tried to tell him that wasn't the case, but… well, you know…"

"Yeah, I do. I ran into Peter by accident about three months ago at Skydive Dallas."

"You ran into Peter skydiving?"

"Go figure. I went out to make a tandem jump and saw him there. He had assumed an alias, and no one there knows who he is. I confronted him in private and got him to admit his charade. All these years and I didn't know my niece. Since then, I've met her, and we're all good friends."

"That's great. I'm happy you guys connected. Peter had an unbelievable future in the music business. It's tragic on so many levels."

He paused. Either he was searching for the right words or curious as to the purpose of my call.

"I'm sure you're wondering why I called," I said.

"Well... to be honest, the thought did cross my mind. Don't get me wrong; I'm glad to hear from you. I miss Peter. I wish he had stayed in touch."

I took the comment as the first inkling that Tony might not have ill feelings. "I had a conversation with Peter today about playing again."

Our connection became so quiet I thought the call had dropped.

"Hello?" I said.

"Yeah, I'm still here. I guess I'm without words—and that doesn't happen often."

"He told me he would think about it. Here's the deal, he believes his friends in the music industry won't forgive him for just leaving."

I didn't have to wait long this time for an answer: "Well, that's just crazy. Are you kidding me?" he asked, not waiting for an answer. "I just had a reunion a few months ago with his old band. They were all reminiscing about the good old days, so to speak. They all still play, but none of them at the same level. Trust me; they would jump at the opportunity."

"I was hoping you were going to say that." I threw my plan on the table and waited for a response.

"I'm in, for better or for worse," he said. "If there's a chance to get him writing and playing music again, it's worth it."

It seemed as though I spent the next two weeks on the phone. The arrangements on my end seemed endless, and I could only imagine what Big Tony was going through. We talked or emailed several times a day. He never complained but became more and more excited as the event date grew closer. The hardest part was not being able to share my brainstorm with anyone. The only people in Texas who knew were the owners of Skydive Dallas, and they were very supportive. Even though it would be unadvertised and over before any previous fans would know about it, Tony wanted to set up a professional stage with all the bells and whistles. I'd had no idea what went into the behind-the-scenes infrastructure: carpenters, electricians, lighting technicians, sound system, power generators, caterers, motor homes for the performers, and the list went on and on.

But drop zones are like small towns. Nothing happens without everybody knowing about it—whether it's who's dating whom, or in this particular case, what's with the portable stage set being set up? It's a community of people like most folks, who love a little gossip, and the stories ran rampant. By the time the big night arrived, nothing could hide the fact that something big was afoot, and the rumor mill was out of control. Around four o'clock, four Greyhound-sized motor homes came up the drive in a caravan, and that's when the excitement hit a new level. Everyone had their cell phones out, gabbing to the world via cyberspace. I pretended to be as clueless as everyone else and played the devil's advocate at every opportunity.

Peter and I had spoken several times over the two-week span, and keeping my dark little secret from him proved daunting. I almost caved in a couple of times just because I felt a little guilty for not giving him a heads-up. I justified my actions by telling myself, it would either scare him away or add to his apprehension.

As I watched the huge motor coaches jockey for parking spots, I thought back to the previous Saturday. I had been helping Margaret clean up after a family dinner. Peter, Kelly Ann, and his dad went out to check on a new colt born the night before. We had gotten pretty close over the past few months, so when I wasn't the usual jabber box she had become used to, she started digging for answers—and Margaret was good at getting to the truth.

"I'm really glad to have you in all of our lives," she said.

"Thanks. It's nice to have a family again." I knew that the conversation was just getting started.

"I haven't seen Peter smile and have a little spring in his step since your sister passed away... and Kelly Ann adores you." She paused, her eyes piercing through me. I felt exposed, like a bug under a microscope. "And you, my dear, have a secret. What's going on?"

"Is it that obvious?"

"I don't think anyone else is as perceptive as I am, but yes, it is."

She smiled, and that put me somewhat at ease. I made the decision to spill my guts.

"Peter and I have had some pretty serious conversations about the guilt he's been harboring over Amy's death. I've been trying to convince him he should give music another try."

I looked back at her with a questioning look, hoping for a response before I continued.

"There's more to it than that," she said with the look of someone who already knows the truth but wants to pry it out of you anyway.

"The Dropzone is having a big celebration on the Fourth of July. I asked Peter to quit his pretenses of being someone he's not, tell his friends who he is, play some music, and see how it goes."

"And what did he say to that?"

"He said he would show up and that he would think about playing. He thinks that no one from the past still likes him, but I know that's not the case." I realized that I had dug a hole and stepped in with both feet, so rather than waiting for Margaret ask the next obvious question, I continued. "Well, crap, I guess I learned a lesson about trying to keep anything from you. I talked to Big Tony. He misses Peter and said that so does his old band. So… we're setting the stage for him to see some old friends and hopefully realize they still care about him."

"I like Big Tony. He was always a real sweet guy, and I believe it when he says he misses Peter. You have to know that everyone involved was making a lot of money."

"Yes, I know, but I think there is more to it than that— and I'm convinced Peter is unhappy without music in his life." As I said it, I knew there was some doubt, even in my own mind.

"You may be right, and just so you know, I agree, but we are talking about a unique individual who may or may not respond the way you or I think he should. There is some risk that he will pull away again. If that happens, you may lose what has been growing between you."

"I'm not sure if I follow you."

"Kelly, he's falling in love with you. Surely you can see it."

Her smile told me she approved. In the big scheme of things, I had missed the signs, despite the kisses we'd shared that day at the Dropzone. I mean, I knew I loved him, and I knew he *liked* me, yes… but love?

"You really think so?" I asked.

"There is no doubt in my mind."

A week later, that conversation played over in my mind, ending with the same uneasy feeling I had the day she spoke the words. It made me feel good and scared all at the same time. I knew my feelings for him had grown, and if my plan went to hell. There was more to lose than I first thought.

The sun was getting close to the horizon... and Peter had not shown up yet. The sinking feeling in my stomach grew worse by the minute.

Chapter 26
Peter

It's amazing how fast two weeks can slip by. I had good intentions of actually playing some, just in case I got up the nerve to get on stage again, but every time I walked into my studio. I would look at the piano and walk back out. It was five o'clock on Saturday, and somehow I had gravitated back and was once again gazing at my Steinway as if waiting for it to tell me what to do. I took a deep breath and started to walk out and found the doorway blocked by my mom and my daughter. Neither of them spoke. Kelly Ann had a look of curiosity, but Mom's was more of one hinging on anticipation.

"How are my two favorite girls?" I asked, hoping to quell my uneasiness.

"They were hoping you would play something for them," Mom said.

I never could tell Mom no. She rarely asked me for anything. Kelly Ann remained quiet, which was unusual for her.

"Okay," I said. "It's been awhile. I may hurt your ears."

I slid my hand down the cool slick surface, as I worked my way down to the business end of the black grand piano. I had only played a few times in the past several years—when Kelly Ann begged to hear me. Now the piano had a foreign feeling, one of unfamiliarity, and an excuse began its way to the surface. I started to turn away, but my daughter had followed me and taken me by the hand—and without a word led me to the bench. The ebony and ivory keys glistened, and I knew that was because, for the past eleven years, Mom had cleaned it every day. We sat.

"Daddy, play me Mommy's song," Kelly Ann said.

Her statement could have been looked at as a question. I could see that she was uncertain of her request.

"I don't know if I can, baby girl."

My eyes were already tearing up, and my emotions were welling up with them. She patted me on the hand with unquestionable understanding.

"It's okay Daddy, let me play it and you sing the words."

She started to play, and it only took a few notes before an avalanche of insight cascaded into my mind. She was really good. The sad part was that I didn't really know it until now. I looked up at Mom, who was smiling from ear to ear. Kelly Ann played the song all the way through with just a few mistakes that only I would notice. I waited until she stopped.

"I knew you were taking lessons, but I've never heard you practice. You are very good. When did you start taking lessons?" I asked.

She looked at my mom, who nodded yes. "Since I was five," she said. "Grandma said music made you think about Mommy and that it made you sad. So I practiced when you were at work. Daddy, is it okay that it makes me happy when I play?"

"Sure, honey. As a matter of fact, maybe it's time for it to help me be happy again. Play it again and let's see if I can still sing it," I said.

When we finished, Mom was crying and then hugged us both.

"That was beautiful. If there was ever any doubt that you could still sing, trust me, son, you've still got it," she said.

My eyes glanced at the clock. It was five thirty.

"Don't you have someplace to be in a couple of hours?" Mom said.

"You know?" I asked.

"You may be a grown man, but I still know everything and don't you ever forget it. As I see it, you have an engagement to play some music, and there's a girl who loves you and is counting on you to show up."

I blinked a tear, and said, "I need to go."

"Yes… yes, you do," Mom said. "And we'll be along to see you tonight, son."

I nodded, then bolted for the door and grabbed a quick shower. When I turned down the driveway that led to Skydive Dallas, I couldn't believe my eyes. I stopped in the middle of the road.

"I've been set up," I said to myself.

I eased the car forward and found a place to park, which wasn't easy. The parking lot overflowed due to the mammoth outdoor stage and motor homes. I had never seen so many people milling around at the Drop zone before.

Luke and another friend walked up and greeted me.

"Hey, Allen, any idea what's going on?" Luke asked.

Before I could answer him, I saw Kelly running up to join our conversation. "You came!" she said.

"Looks like you've been really busy," I said.

"I've had a lot of help from some old friends who can't wait to see you," she said.

"Would someone please tell me what is going on?" Luke asked.

I looked at my friend and decided to start the evening by coming clean. "Luke… I owe you an apology."

"Why?" he asked.

"My name is actually Peter Allen Shaw. I used to play music a long time ago. You're my friend, and I haven't been honest with you."

I don't think he really got the gist of what I was saying, and then Kelly interrupted.

"You guys can catch up later," she said. "Right now, Mr. Shaw, you have some old friends who have come a long way to see you tonight."

Then she began herding me to the motor home closest to the stage. A big hulking figure stood at the door, acting as security. He looked a few years older, but I recognized him immediately.

"Eddie... how are you doing?" I said.

He squinted at me for an instant and smiled. "Peter... I'm doing very well thank you. It's very nice to see you."

He gave me a hug that nearly crushed my rib cage before letting go, and then he stepped back and opened the door.

A head popped out the instant it opened. I almost didn't know who it was at first.

"Tony?" I said.

In a different setting I wouldn't have recognized him. He was much thinner with short gray hair, and a clean-shaven face.

"Peter!"

He bounded down the stairs and greeted me with another Chicago-style hug.

"You've lost a bunch of weight. You look great!" I said.

"The doctor said I needed to lose some baggage or die. It was a great motivator. I lost 220 pounds. Come on in! There's a bunch of folks anxious to see you."

He grabbed my arm and literally dragged me up the stairs. The coach was full of friendly and familiar faces. The entire band was there, including some new faces that I didn't know. Everyone tried to talk at once, and no one was being heard.

"Alright, everybody, hold it down for a minute!" Big Tony might have lost a bunch of weight, but he still possessed the same deep booming voice. "We all want to catch up with Peter, but we have a concert that starts in thirty minutes and you kids haven't played together for a very long time."

It felt like old times as Tony did the same pep talk from years earlier. He laid out a list of songs so we could decide which ones to play. It all felt a little awkward at first, and the butterflies were starting their journey up and down my stomach. Once we got down to the small talk to quiet our nerves, Kelly appeared in the doorway and glanced in my direction. I realized that she had been left outside and had not come in with me.

"Hey... have you met everyone?" I asked.

"Not yet," she said.

"Well, let's fix that. Hey, everyone, this is Kelly. If you want to blame anyone, it's all her fault," I said.

Everyone said hello, and then one of the people I had not recognized stood up and stepped closer. He was bigger than Tony but lean.

"I hope you don't mind that I came along to see you? Do you remember me?" he asked.

It took me a minute. "Felix?" I asked.

"That's right. I wanted the chance to thank you in person for helping me out with my little problem," Felix said.

"You are very welcome. Amy was quite insistent, and it was the right thing to do. This is Amy's sister, Kelly," I said.

Kelly stepped up and gave Felix a big hug. "Amy told me a lot about you. I'll be looking forward to hearing your part of the story."

"It will be my pleasure," Felix said. "Your sister saved my life."

"I hate to break up the reunion, but we have a show to do," Big Tony said.

When we stepped out into the night, it was just dark enough that no one could see us. The stage was set up like it always had been, and I felt a bit surprised that we all found our places without too much trouble. The band had chosen to play *Amy's Song,* as the opener. I guess the only thing different was how scared I felt, being on stage always started off with a certain amount of trepidation. It had been years since I played in front of an audience, and that made it worse. I took a deep breath and started to play. Any inhibition I'd had minutes earlier passed. I got through the introduction and began to sing *Amy's Song.*

For the first time in eleven years, I saw the colors again.

Also by Allen Hively

At her chateau in 1865 France, Kelly Jacobs spends a day with the young and yet unknown Claude Monet, who is finishing her portrait. The following morning, Kelly leaves through a time portal to the present day...

CPSIA information can be obtained at www.ICGtesting.com
Printed in the USA
LVOW06s1340270714

396209LV00001B/56/P